TH_
VEILED
EDGE
OF
CONTACT

JAMES BRAYKEN

The Veiled Edge of Contact

0: The Front-Runner

Gyamma grumbles as she carries the human brain from her boss's office and down the hallway. She's a senior neuroengineer, not a laborbot, and the brain along with its display box is heavy.

Two days ago, the director of Digital Cognitives Incorporated placed a request for this inactive, gray lump to be displayed in his office. This evening, the request for it to be removed came through. Apparently the brain has been "unpleasing to the eye" for his visitors, so Gyamma is to take the former test subject back to the lab, where it will be hardened and sent to a workshop to be plated in gold—the director's idea. Only then will the cosmetically enhanced brain be welcomed back into his office.

Gyamma reaches the lab doors and leans into the face scanner. With her hands full, she blows loose strands of coily hair away from her eyes. The scanner pings, and the senior neuroengineer pushes her way through before the doors have a chance to open. Ceiling lights brighten as she marches through the maze of equipment and slams the display box onto the edge of her busy workbench. The room hums with computers and machinery, a sound too familiar for Gyamma to notice. What *is* noticeable is the lack of people. "It's only 21:04," she mutters as she checks the Personal Assistant Band on her forearm.

The PAB's screen blinks with an unread message from the

systems analyst: "Told my team to go home and take the morning off. They were tired and making mistakes. Like I've said before, the pace of the project is too fast. The deadlines are unreasonable. Could you speak with the director about this?" Gyamma looks across to the free stimulants Digital Cognitives provides to be sure they did not run out. *They didn't.*

Scowling, she dictates her reply: "I will demote you and fine the rest of the team if you're not all back by 07:00. There are no excuses for leaving early when we're in the middle of critical procedures. Anyone concerned about the pace is free to find something less important to work on."

Gyamma sends the message, and as she turns to check the project metrics, her arm connects with something solid. She flinches at the sound of a crash, then sighs as she looks down at the brain on the floor, covered in glass.

A cleanerbot rolls from its nook and sucks up the shards. Gyamma picks up the plaque from the now-broken display box. She smirks as she reads its engraving: THE RECIPIENT OF THE FIRST EVER ARTIFICIAL EDIT OF A NEURAL PATHWAY IN A HUMAN BRAIN. A KEY MILESTONE IN THE HISTORY OF HUMAN INGENUITY, AND A BOLD STEP TOWARD THE END OF NEUROLOGICAL DISEASE. *DIGITAL COGNITIVES CENTRAL AFRICA, MAGAWI CITY, THE PEOPLE'S RIGHTFUL REPUBLIC OF MBAPAZU.*

The plaque makes their endeavor seem so noble, and curing disease is all well and good, but Gyamma knows Digital Cognitives is aiming for something more than this: the enhancement of the human mind beyond its biological limitations—unimaginable ability that may no longer be considered human. That's the long term, however. For now, her company's focus is on getting the world's first mass-market brain implant on the shelves ahead of the competition—a race that many in the industry believe is being led by Digital Cognitives.

In yesterday's project board meeting, Gyamma was shown

the latest sketches of the product they're aiming to create. Its working name is The Spider due to its spindly appendages, which protrude from either side of a teardrop-shaped control center the size of a fingernail—small and flat enough to be fitted beneath the skull with its "legs" wrapped around the brain.

Gyamma was informed that in addition to its neurological health functions, the implant is to provide users with web access and a groundbreaking type of communication that will make The Spider more appealing to a broader demographic. Brain implants have been around for decades, but their function limited to treating a small number of medical conditions. Digital Cognitives wants to create the first implant that's for everyone— that's convenient, useful, and fun. Management wants the product on sale within five years.

Looking back at the metrics, Gyamma is reminded that her project is behind schedule. She cannot afford for her or one of her team to spend time removing glass fragments from this test subject's membrane, then spend more time touching up the damage. They have dozens of inactive brains in cold storage that can be gold-plated instead. It makes no difference which one goes on display, and the director won't even notice. He just wants something shiny to impress clients and shareholders.

Gyamma grabs a pair of gloves, picks up the test subject, and turns it in her hand. The ceiling lights reflect on the fragments of glass, giving the inactive brain a shimmer that would appeal to the director. She imagines their future product wrapped around the cold lump. "PAB," she says, "remind me to suggest they quit calling it 'The Spider' before the name sticks. Nobody likes spiders. The implant will need a bullshit fancy name."

Gyamma opens a biohazard bin, tosses the brain onto the pile, and gets back to her business of keeping Digital Cognitives in the lead.

Part 1

1: The Fly

In front of me stand the trees that mark the edge of the Nsanba—the largest rainforest in Africa. Behind me, a chain-link fence topped with barbed wire runs as far as I can see from east to west. I've just dragged my gear through a gash in this fence, cut previously by my wife, Efawi. And I'm late. Thirty-three days late, to be precise. Too late, quite possibly.

Beneath a broken surveillance camera, a bent sign hanging from one bolt knocks against the fence in time with the breeze. NO ENTRY. TRESPASS PUNISHABLE BY— The last word is too faded by sunlight to read, but I know the consequences should I be caught.

Along the outside of the fence runs a pothole-ravaged gravel road. Beyond the road lies mostly flat scrubland in which I found a ditch to hide one of Efawi's bogus-registered cars. Dots of light toward the horizon indicate the nearest human beings, and the distance between civilization and I will only grow as I progress through the jungle. I won't see another person until I reach my destination, a twenty-day trek away, where my wife will be waiting for me—if I'm not too late.

I inhale a lungful of hot and humid air that has a sickly-sweet fragrance. The trees ahead sway as if ushering me toward them, then away, then toward them. I'll need to get among these trees before the evening light fades, or I'll risk my lights being seen

7

from a distance. "PAB, what's next on Efawi's instructions?" I ask my Personal Assistant Band.

"Once in armored trekking suit," the PAB replies, "wheel its case into nearby shrubbery—"

"Done."

"—so it cannot be seen from the road."

"I said *done*."

"Remember to always keep the suit and helmet sealed until just before putting them on."

The helmet lies on the ground beside me, its fabric seal unzipped. I go to pick it up and am stopped by the armored suit digging into my stomach. According to my wife's instructions, I will lose seventy percent of my body fat over the coming days. The suit will provide a better fit as I thin.

I suck in my stomach and try again. Sweat runs from my tangled afro and drips onto the grass. This time my gloved hand reaches the helmet, which I place over my head, and I lock the clasps around its rim to form a tight seal with the body suit. With the headgear on, the air is cooled and filtered. No allergens or smells.

The helmet is spherical and transparent at the front, allowing a good range of vision. Its weight is supported by the suit, which in turn acts as an exoskeleton that supports its own weight. Patchy brown, with two stripes of yellow running down each side, the armored outfit has an aggressive cut about it, giving me the look of a dirty ground-astronaut looking for trouble.

I lift the rucksack from the grass (which feels as light as a pillow thanks to the motors in the suit that give my movements a little boost) and swing it around my shoulders. "PAB, what's next on the list?" I ask.

"Enter the Nsanba," the PAB replies.

"Great," I mumble. I turn back to those distant twinkling lights—other people. "Well, this is it," I tell myself. "Time to become a part of history, like Efawi said." What that means exactly, my wife didn't divulge. All I know is I'm to head to an area in the Nsanba that she's calling the "Anomalous Zone." Apparently, she's discovered something important there—something she can use to pressure the People's Popular Alliance into lifting our arrest warrants. Unfortunately, she has no idea how long that will take.

I remain on the spot, shifting from foot to foot. The trees stand tall in front of me. If you'd told me a month ago that my wife and I would soon be trekking through a jungle, a strictly-prohibited-by-international-law jungle at that, both on the run from the PPA government, both wanted for sedition, disloyalty to the state, and a host of other felonies, I'd have thought you were crazy. I'm an easygoing househusband, not some mastermind criminal activist. And Efawi is an engineer-entrepreneur who may be passionate about politics—and she may sometimes take her passions too far—but she surely isn't guilty of what she's been accused of. She can't be.

With the light quickly fading, I will myself toward the jungle, and a black dot darts from left to right, then back again. *A fly.* Instinctively, I go to swipe the insect away, and my hand hits the outside of the helmet. The fly then makes an upward dive into my left nostril. I snort, and the winged insect exits my nose along with a splatter of mucus that stains the inside of my visor. "Damn it."

The fly continues to dart back and forth before coming to land on my right cheek. I reach for the clasps at the base of my helmet, but I'm unable to work the release mechanism. "PAB, read me the helmet instructions."

"Helmet instructions cannot be found."

I check the PAB's content manually. Many of Efawi's files appear to be missing. Did I delete them by accident when I put music on this thing last night? *Shit.* I need those instructions; I don't know how to use half of the equipment Efawi packed for me. To think she spent months secretly planning this trek (even

I didn't know about it) and now I've gone and messed it up.

My hand fumbles as I continue to scroll through the PAB's content. I had thought having songs to listen to might help me through this mess. The noise from ahead intensifies: howling, clicking, squawking, bellowing, screeching. It seems the jungle comes alive at dusk. A living thing made from many living things.

The LEDs on my suit automatically brighten. I can't hang about here; I'll have to work this out as I go. I pull my nanoalloy machete from its sheath and march forward, fly on cheek. Efawi always says, "If you're not going forward, you're going backward." I'm not sure I agree.

The jungle is quick to thicken. Giant leaves on lean branches block much of the evening sky. The suit's lights illuminate my surroundings, beyond which intricate shadows are formed by the weave of plant life. I keep my head down as much as possible, my eyes focused on my forearm where the PAB displays my progress as a pink line on a digital map. The location data is being sent to my PAB by the navicube in my bag's side pocket. As per its label, the navicube is a "quantum accelerometer" (whatever that means) and doesn't require a signal of any kind to know where it is.

A couple hundred meters in, and the jungle floor remains reasonably flat and not too dense. Apart from the fly and the missing instructions, this isn't as bad as I thought.

Fifteen minutes later, there's a dead body in front of me.

Heavily decomposed bone, sunk in dirt and overrun by vegetation. The skeleton is wrapped in a torn military uniform, the skull hidden behind a gas mask, the upper torso broken and ripped apart. My chest pounds as I stare.

This soldier will have died in The War. It seems soldiers who fought back then—around seventy years ago—didn't have suits like mine, but despite my protective layer, my time in the Nsanba will still be dangerous. There are no people to be concerned about (I'm told the jungle was cleared of all residents decades ago), but landmines used during The War may still be live. There are dangerous animals too: leopards, snakes, and hippos included. For all these reasons, my trekking suit is armored. Although, how much it would protect me from the direct blast of a mine, I don't know. And would my suit's integrity hold beneath a charging elephant's foot? Efawi thinks I'll be fine, but what if I slip and fall from a cliff or into a river? What if I get sick? Never in my life have I been so far from medical help or help of any kind should I need it. Nobody even knows we're here.

With my machete still in hand, I reach behind me for the emag rifle—the only thing I brought not on Efawi's list. I took it from beneath her side of the bed at our villa. It's legal. Registered. She's not a violent person; she's just paranoid about security. She's also vegan and expects me to sustain myself on this trek through packaged nutrients and plant life. I will use the rifle for hunting if I can, but I've never hunted before or even fired a weapon. Nor have I had a chance to learn how to use it yet (emags have lots of complicated-looking buttons and switches).

I turn from the dead soldier, grip the rifle against my chest, and recommence walking—a swift march in an attempt to negate a panic that could lead me back to the car. I try to distract myself by attempting to recall trivia such as what the Nsanba used to be called before The War (my grandfather told me everywhere in Central Africa was renamed when the new nations emerged) and what the difference is between a jungle and a rainforest (I have no idea), but I remain troubled by my terrible situation, made worse by the first dead body I've ever seen.

I keep marching, my legs trembling. The Nsanba grows thicker. Reflective eyes, yellow and orange, emerge from the darkness to stare before returning to the shadows. On a normal day, I'd be on the couch eating my pre-dinner dinner around now.

My anxiety peaks when my PAB says a combination of words I've never heard before: "You are out of range of all networks."

I gasp, childlike, despite knowing this would happen. And just when I'm about to decide for sure that heading back to the car would be a sensible decision, my panic is interrupted by the implant in my head: ~ *You have a new message,* ~ says my nôvono pro.

I stop marching.

A bird high above screeches like it's being murdered.

~ *But I'm out of range of all networks,* ~ I reply internally to my spider-shaped implant.

~ *You have a new message,* ~ my nôvono pro repeats inside my skull.

There's only one person I ever get nôvo-messages from. I instruct my brain implant to hit play, and my heart leaps at the arrival of my wife's thought-words: ~ *You want to turn around, don't you, Okon?* ~ she says. As usual, the clarity and intimacy of the nôvo-message is intense, as though Efawi is nestled in my brain, breathing warm, moist words along my neural pathways.

~ *I know being out of range of the web will disturb you, my dear,* ~ she continues. ~ *So, I'm leaving this message to remind you that you can't go home. As scary as the Nsanba might be, going back will be worse. We may disagree on politics, but the People's Popular Alliance cannot be trusted. You must realize this by now.* ~

The warrant for my wife's arrest was issued over a month ago. Only a handful of PPA officers were informed. They'd intended to take her by surprise, but lost track of her while she made a trip to our unregistered country villa. My wife worked out what was happening when she found her accounts being blocked one by one. All the while, I was at our primary residence in Magawi City, most likely puttering about in my underwear, entirely unaware of the unfolding drama.

My wife spent days isolated at the villa, unable to return

home without being arrested. Nobody knew where she was, and I assumed she was on another work trip. She desperately tried to reach me via the only means that hadn't been blocked: our nôvo-communications. But for reasons I prefer not to think about, I didn't receive her nôvo-calls or nôvo-messages. Not right away. Not until after she had no choice but to leave the villa and begin her mysterious Nsanba trek alone. This is why I'm late.

~If you look around,~ the message continues, ~you'll see a wireless memory drive, smaller than your thumb, tied to a branch with red string. I saved this nôvo-message onto this drive, and if you're receiving these words, you must have stepped within twenty meters of it.~

I spot Efawi's memory drive hanging from a nearby branch and walk toward it. She must have left it here when she entered the jungle thirty-three days ago.

~And if you're within twenty meters of the drive, then you must have received my previous instructions and picked up the trekking equipment I left you. So I can take comfort from knowing you have everything you need for the journey ahead.~

Her thought-words are laced with her feelings at the time of recording, which, as usual, form part of the nôvo-message. And so, thanks to my brain implant, I have two sets of emotions to deal with as I listen: Efawi's and mine.

~Oh, Okon. I had everything prepared for us to make this trip together. I was going to bring you out here and tell you all about my discovery, despite our agreement. I was leaving it to the last moment so you wouldn't have much time to think and say no. Then those bastards issued the arrest warrant, and all my plans were ruined. Has the PPA gotten to you? Is that why you haven't responded to my nôvo-calls?~

Efawi falls silent, but the message doesn't end, and her sentiment continues to seep through. She was feeling many things when she recorded this. Guilt. Frustration. A special blend of vulnerability and tenacity that I've felt in Efawi many times before. We had our nôvono implants installed the day they hit the shelves about a year ago, and since then, I've been uncomfortable with how intrusive their communications are. But with Efawi now being so out of reach, I appreciate being able to hear her so intimately.

~*I know things have been difficult between us lately, and that just makes this situation all the more heartbreaking,*~ she says while I untie the red string from the branch. ~*I guess all I can do now is hope you're okay. The thought that you might be just a day or two behind will be what keeps me going. But I wish I knew for sure you received my messages and are indeed coming. If I did know, I'd wait right here for you.*~

Efawi pauses again, and I can feel her trying to lift her mood. I pull the memory drive from the branch and stare at the little plastic thing. I picture my wife handling the drive before she left it here, and I grip it tightly, hold it to my armored chest. ~*I am sure, my love, that you'll soon be with me,*~ she says. ~*I'll see you when you reach the Anomalous Zone.*~

The fly buzzes within its realm before landing on my forehead. Efawi's message clicks to an end.

2: The Anomalous Zone

My trek to the boundary of the AZ took precisely thirty-one days. According to the PAB's navigation software, Efawi expected me to do it in twenty.

I arrived here about ten minutes ago and am taking a brief moment to rest and reflect while I stare into the zone—which looks no different from the rest of the damn jungle. So far, my trek has been a procession of screwups: I've had biting ants in intimate places after leaving my suit unsealed overnight. I've lost equipment—I still don't know how. Thieving monkeys? There have been food issues. Stomach issues. Followed by more food and stomach issues. I fell into rivers. Got my head stuck between two trees. Have been in a constant state of soreness despite my padded, movement-assisting suit. I was even attacked by a leopard, which thankfully couldn't penetrate my suit. The terror of a giant cat trying its best to rip my leg off is something I'll struggle to forget. And throughout all of this, I couldn't get my music to play. Not even a single track.

An agitation stirs in my chest as I consider that my trek isn't over: there's still the AZ to contend with, plus there'll be the journey back.

I suck on the straw that runs from the water purifier into my suit, and I try to consider the positives: I'm alive. I was able to restore *most* of the deleted instructions, learn about the helmet's release mechanism, and let out that fly. Efawi's weight-loss prediction came true (I haven't been so slim since my early twenties). And I'm here. *I did it.* I made it to the edge of the damn Anomalous Zone! A long time has passed since I last achieved anything. Efawi thinks I lost my ambition when she sold her previous company. She says becoming wealthy was the worst thing she ever did to me, that since then I don't really do anything. She even wants me to get my old chef job back, thinks it'll do me good. I think that's madness.

I continue sipping purified water as I stand just inside the circumference of the AZ. As per Efawi's instructions, the Anomalous Zone is a circle with a diameter of 8.9 kilometers. While struggling through the jungle, I had plenty of time to consider what could have inspired Efawi to come here. Like me, my wife has never been trekking before, and certainly has never been to the Nsanba, so I'm guessing she made her discovery via one of her company's satellites. If I knew more about Sabano's technology, the sorts of things they're looking out for and can scan and detect, I might have an idea of what she could have found. But I don't.

My wife's frantic final messages gave me the impression that although the zone itself is an important discovery, it's something *within* the zone that's really of interest. And that's about the extent of my knowledge. Even though nôvo-messages are as hack-proof as they come, Efawi said she wouldn't disclose more than she needed to in case the PPA interrogates me.

A cloud passes overhead, and the undergrowth darkens. The inside of my conditioned suit becomes a little too cool, which brings a prickle to the back of my neck. Should I be happy to have made it here or afraid of what's ahead? My chest tightens further. I think I've been standing and staring for too long. If whatever's in the AZ were dangerous, Efawi would have included the rifle among the gear she packed for me, wouldn't she? Or wouldn't she have told me not to come at all? She could have instructed me to hide out somewhere else, a place where she could eventually meet up with me. So what's here must be a good thing. After all, her original plan was for us to experience the Anomalous Zone together. In any case, I need to keep my focus on finding Efawi. The AZ and its contents are her thing, not mine. This whole situation is her thing, not mine. I just want us to reunite and go home without being arrested. To think we are fugitives. How on Earth did it come to this?

Every couple of days or so on my way here, I would step within the twenty-meter range of a memory drive left behind by Efawi. Her nôvo-messages were usually brief, giving me tips on what lay ahead. *Aggressive green mamba burrow coming up, so be sure to keep your suit fully on, my dear*–for example. Often she had to retread through difficulty just to give me warning. Sometimes she sounded hopeful that I was right behind her, and at other times she feared I might not be coming at all, but the overall sentiment carried by her nôvo-messages was one of increasing exhaustion. It seems the trek through the Nsanba was as taxing for her as it was for me. I had expected her to cope better and make fewer mistakes, but then lately she hasn't been her usual self.

‑*nôvono, replay Efawi's last message,*‑ I instruct, still holding the latest memory drive she left me just outside the AZ.

‑*Brumphh . . . eea . . . pheep . . . aephh . . .*‑

The scrambled noise continues in my head, which is strange because I listened to this message about ten minutes ago, and it played just fine. Could the drive be out of juice? If so, this is the first one to die. They only need a tiny amount of energy, and Efawi said their casing is made from "photovoltaic cells," so they shouldn't run out.

I check my location on the PAB. The icon that represents me flickers and jumps around the digital map. *Hmm.* I step back ten paces, and my location on the map corrects itself, placing me just outside the AZ. Once again, I ask my nôvono pro to replay Efawi's message, and this time her thought-words play in my head unscrambled.

~*I made it, Okon. The Anomalous Zone! I can hardly believe it. And if you're receiving this, you must have made it too. Well done, my love. I'm so proud of you. Have you lost the belly yet? I bet you're looking very sexy.*~ Efawi laughs, and a fragile joy flows through the nôvo-message. ~*If only we could have experienced this together,*~ she continues. ~*But there's nothing we can do about that now, and I need to communicate some practicalities, so pay attention. Within the Anomalous Zone exists a peculiar electromagnetic interference. In fact, it is this interference that demarcates the zone, and once inside, some of our equipment will be impacted by it.*

~*As per my tests just now, devices that rely primarily on transmitting and receiving electromagnetic waves, particularly those in the infrared spectrum, such as the landmine detector, will be unreliable. But this region of the Nsanba saw fewer landmines laid, and on the long journey here I didn't encounter any that were live, so the odds that we'll encounter an unexpired mine in this relatively small zone are tiny. Besides, as I'm ahead of you, it'll be me who triggers it. So if you see human splatter up ahead, you'll know what happened.*~ She gives a half-hearted laugh, which I don't appreciate.

~*My nôvono,*~ she continues, ~*seems to work just fine in the AZ except for receiving and transmitting comms, which we can't do without a network in any case. Same goes for the PAB. The navicube, however, is majorly impacted by the interference. And so, from here on, we'll need to use the backup navigation tools I packed for us.*~

Efawi pauses. She's sad I'm not with her, I can feel it.

~*Well, I think that's all the additional information I have for you. I'm going all the way into the zone now. I remain hopeful you're not too far behind. Remember to keep your suit on at all times. Once in the zone, if there's nothing obvious to head toward, then head as best you can for the center, and remember when you walked in on me crying on my last day at home. I love you. I miss you so much. And I'll see you soon—in the flesh.* ~ The nôvo-message clicks to an end.

I do remember walking in on her: she was taking a bath, and I heard crying—something Efawi never does. When I asked what was wrong, she muttered something about how beautiful the iridescence on the soapy bubbles was—how the play of color had moved her to tears. Of course, she wouldn't tell me the real reason she was upset, no matter how much I asked (there was a time when we would tell each other everything). I don't understand what her crying in the bath has to do with the AZ. Perhaps she's just having a subtle dig about our arguing that morning, which I suspect is what upset her. I'm not sure.

I hold the memory drive to my helmet and blow a kiss before I place it in my bag and pull out a small pack labeled "Backup Navigation." Inside is a pencil, a paper map, and a plastic triangle marked with lines and symbols, none of which mean anything to me. I search the PAB for related instructions, but I cannot find any. A deleted file I couldn't restore? I take another look at the map and the triangle's markings but remain clueless. "She said aim for the center," I sigh. "I guess all I can do is keep walking straight and hope that gets me there."

I put the archaic equipment back into my rucksack and march forward into the AZ. I don't get far before the pencil, map, and triangle are out again. Turns out walking in a straight line in the jungle is very difficult without a location and route laid out for me on the PAB's screen. While turning on the spot, attempting to establish north, I sight a pair of stripy buttocks. Okapi (or "the poor man's giraffe," as my grandfather used to call them) are usually skittish beasts. I know this from the handful of sightings during my trek. But this one standing ten meters away either doesn't know I'm here or doesn't care.

"You going to show me the way, big fella?" I whisper. The okapi's ears twitch before it proceeds to lick its left eyeball with a long, white tongue. "You seen a woman come this way? Short. Skinny. Dark complexion; almost as black as me. Has a walk like someone's following her." The okapi turns its tongue toward the stripping of leaves from a bush. "Well, if you see her, tell her . . . tell her I'm sorry she couldn't get through to me. It wasn't completely my fault."

I shake my head, having been reduced to conversing with a poor man's giraffe, and I hold the map up once more, a movement that catches the okapi's eye. The creature turns, doe-eyed and alert, and I flinch at the sight of a long, thin object hurtling toward it. A soft thud follows.

The okapi whines and keels over with a wooden stick in its side. A man and woman approach. I gasp, and they see me. They freeze, with the okapi between us. Their eyes are bulging, their dark skin glistening, their sinewy frames naked but for strips of material hanging about their waists, chests, and arms. My mind rushes to classify them: *Hunter-gatherers. Museum exhibits. Jungle people.*

I mouth a few syllables before abandoning them, too shocked by the sight of other people. Too unsure of what to say or whether to say anything at all. They decide to greet me by each hurling a short wooden arrow that swishes in flight. One of the pointy sticks thumps against my helmet and bounces to the ground. The other hits my arm, giving a sensation akin to a nudge from a finger. It hangs from the inside of my elbow, its stone tip caught in the armored suit's outer covering. I pull the arrow free and look back at the man and woman. They gasp, touch their heads, point to the sky, point to the jungle. They bend their knees while making drawn out *ohhh* sounds.

"Hello there. My name is Okon," I try, and I lift a hand to my chest to indicate I'm talking about myself. The woman swings her arm again. A rock this time, which smacks into my abdomen. With the suit on, the impact is minor. Painless. These people cannot hurt me.

I loosen my shoulders. The man and woman remain animated. Efawi didn't mention any tribal people in her instructions—unless she did so in a file I accidentally deleted. Could they be her big discovery? *No.* They can't be. Efawi said her discovery will bring "a wave of change across the globe." I don't see how these two could do that.

"I thought there wasn't supposed to be anyone living in the Nsanba," I say. "Not that it matters to me. I'm looking for my wife: Efawi. Do you know her?"

The peculiarities whisper between themselves while keeping their eyes fixed on me. I've heard of hunter-gatherer types that used to live in the jungle with little to no contact with the modern world, but they were supposed to have been documented and moved to townships decades ago for some political reason I never quite understood. Something to do with land claims.

I instruct my nôvono implant to turn on my translator implant, and I edge forward. The two stop whispering. "I assume you don't understand me," I say, "but you need to talk so my translator can hear what language you speak." The two remain silent while scanning the ground, presumably for something else to throw. "Please say something—anything," I add, and step closer still. The two glance at each other, look back at me, and dash out of sight.

Before I have the chance to mentally process the surreal encounter, my PAB's alarm rings. It's eight-thirty in the morning, which means time to set up camp and raise my fabric solar panel. (Nights are for trekking; days are for sleeping and charging equipment.) I flip open the suit's control panel and learn that my armored outfit has ninety minutes of battery left. According to Efawi's instructions, the walk from the edge of the zone to its center should take just over an hour. So I should be fine to get there without recharging. I might not know which direction the center is in, but Efawi must be close. There's no way I'm setting up camp now.

A smattering of drops on my helmet declares the arrival of a shower. I pick a direction and continue walking. The rain's intensity builds as I make my way through the AZ. The suit keeps me dry, but I can't see too well due to the splashing on my helmet and a forming mist in the understory. Since I arrived in the Nsanba, there's been at least one downpour every day, usually while I'm trying to sleep.

I keep an eye on the jumping navicube readings displayed by my PAB. Jumping is good; it means the navicube isn't working, which means I haven't accidentally veered out of the Anomalous Zone. After a further thirty minutes of trudging, I start to notice oddities: Markings in bark that don't appear to be the work of animals. Trees that seem felled rather than fallen. Fragments of what looks like woven palm discarded among foliage.

Something moves to my left. I jerk my head around to find leaves bouncing in the rain. Unnerved, I up my pace. A few minutes later, I think I hear shouting, barely discernible above the crashing downpour. I continue marching, unsure if I should head toward the voices or away from them, my gut telling me the latter.

I slip on mud and leaves as I go. The mist thickens, reducing visibility to a few meters. The shouting returns, still distant, but certainly not imagined, and there are further flashes of suspicious movements through the downpour. Swaying branches? Animals? Tribal people? "They cannot hurt me," I remind myself.

I quicken to a moderately paced jog, which is about as fast as I can go while I duck under branches, sidestep tree trunks, and clamber through foliage. My legs, shoulders, and backpack slap and bounce off surfaces. What was a distant shouting becomes full-blown hollering: multiple voices, clear and close. *Tribal-people sounds.* If there are enough of them, could they trap me, remove my suit? Was that Efawi's fate? Is that why she left me no warning about them? *No.* She'd be too smart to get caught. I'm almost running now, slipping all over the place, when my boot hits something hard. I fall forward, arms grinding against vegetation. My right shoulder hits the ground, my nose bashes against my helmet, and my backpack comes loose and falls away. I skid across mud until I'm brought to a swift halt by a pile of something.

A few seconds pass in a daze. Where am I again?

Oh, I'm in a jungle of course, upside down on a heap of chopped logs. Red stains my view, dripping up the inside of my visor, and there's a . . . *child?*

I flip onto all fours, shaken and bloody nosed but otherwise intact, the suit once again providing value for Efawi's money. In front of me stands a hut made from sticks and leaves, in front of which stands a boy, about eight or nine, smirking, soaked, and butt naked.

"You people leave firewood lying around uncovered?" I grumble as I gather myself. "Even I know not to do that."

The boy's smirk remains. I pull myself to my feet. The precipitation continues to limit visibility, but I appear to be standing within a small clearing, the rain hitting us hard without the buffer of the canopy.

Something presses against my shin: the boy prodding my suit with his foot. He's tinted red through the splash of nose blood on my visor. "Eketowa mahame daki. Halatowe de pwa," he chirps.

The translator implant in my neck gets to work, informing me that the boy's language has been detected. *~Auto-translation commencing,~* it says, speaking to me internally via my nôvono pro interface. With a synthetic approximation of the tone and inflection of the boy, his translated words are communicated to me: *~You look strange. What is that on your body?~*

I think my response, which goes from my brain implant to my translator implant, where my words are translated, synthesized, and sounded with slight delay from two small speakers installed beneath the skin in my throat: "It's an armored body suit; the AK-Trekker 500 Series."

The boy points at my mouth and screams. He was amused by the sight of a stranger running into logs, but hearing a man talk without opening his mouth must be too much for him. "Shush, it's okay. I might look strange to you, but I'm not dangerous." Once again my words are translated and emitted from my throat speakers. The boy continues to cry. Within seconds, a dozen tribal people emerge from the mist and surround me. The majority have come armed: spears, bows, arrows, rocks, hatchets. I reach behind me for my backpack, despite knowing it isn't there—that it has fallen somewhere out of sight, along with my machete and rifle.

3: The Death-Stick

The tribal people continue to encircle me, around thirty of them now, possibly more obscured by mist. Many of them hold round wooden masks to their faces, and those without masks peer at me from between fingers. Their slender bodies are mostly bare except for woven coverings held loosely together with vine. Their skin, ranging from black to dark brown, twinkles with splashes of rain.

They stand a couple of meters away and hold their weapons tightly. They won't be violent—will they? There's just no need. They'll realize that—won't they?—once they understand I'm not a threat, that I'm simply looking for my wife. A woman steps forward and whips the wailing boy from the ground. She gives me a look that transcends language.

"I didn't touch him," I tell her, again my words translated. The boy smiles at me over the woman's shoulder as they disappear into the crowd.

A man yells from behind a mask. His spoken words are foreign, but my translator implant sends a feed to my nôvono pro implant, which plays a near-live translation in my brain: ~It speaks Wuchumbu!~

The hunter-gatherers proceed to shout back and forth over the heavy rain:

~Someone should poke it!~

~My husband and I already threw poisoned arrows, which did

not hurt it.~

~Can we say stop saying "it"; he is an unassociated man.~

~If it is an unassociated man, then what is that around his body?~

~That is his magic.~

~Or his evil spirits.~

~Perhaps it is an evil spirit that has swallowed an unassociated man?~

~Tell us why your arrows did not work.~

~The arrows did not penetrate it—him.~

~Then we need more force, and we need to focus on its weakest point.~

~Big Man is the strongest. He should try poking it in the neck with a spear.~

~It does not have a neck.~

~Yes, it does.~

A man points his spear to where my helmet connects with my body suit. I raise a hand. "There is no need for any poking, thank you." A translation of my words is broadcast through my throat's speakers. The crowd collectively flinches.

~It speaks again!~

~His mouth did not move in time with his words.~

~He must be using magic to speak.~

~Finally! Here comes Mhaawu. Step back, everyone.~

Those to the right of me shuffle aside to form a path. I turn my suit's temperature control to its coolest setting.

~Why did you call me?~ comes a croaky female voice from behind the mist. *~Why do you always need me for every little thing?~*

~Mhaawu, without your mask, you are vulnerable to the unassociated man's evil spirits,~ pipes a concerned onlooker.

~What unassociated man?~ Mhaawu snaps. She hobbles from the white haze and into sight. An older woman, in appearance at least. She holds a panel of woven twigs above her head that

provides some protection from the rain as she makes her way toward the front of the gathering.

~*Mhaawu, there is a monster here,*~ a young girl shrieks. ~*Are we all going to die?*~

Mhaawu dismisses the girl with a grunt.

~*Mhaawu, your mask,*~ the concerned onlooker pipes again.

~*Only fools and children wear masks,*~ says Mhaawu, prompting some to lower theirs. The short, stooped Mhaawu steps into the gap between the crowd and I. She looks up, jerking in surprise, as though she hadn't believed their claim that a "monster" had arrived. Her eyes narrow as she assesses me. Blurred raindrops fall between us. To think that on a normal day at home, I wouldn't even be out of bed yet.

Mhaawu then steps forward and onto a log. Now level with me, she leans in with her "umbrella" held above us. Her breath fogs my visor as she stares. Her brown eyes contain flecks of gray that match the gray in her hair. "My name is Okon," I gulp, my translated voice mimicking my wavering tone. "I'm looking for my wife."

Mhaawu drops her shoulders, as if put at ease. She steps from the log and shuffles back toward where she came.

~*Typical!*~ proclaims a tall, slender man with piercing eyes. He steps in front of Mhaawu, says, ~*I thought you were supposed to be in charge?*~

~*Out of my way, Gommonogo, before I smack you in the head,*~ Mhaawu replies.

An even taller man with broad shoulders pulls Gommonogo to the side. Gommonogo slips on the wet mud and falls to one knee, and Mhaawu steps around him.

~*What do we do about the unassociated man-thing, Mhaawu?*~ yells a stocky woman clutching a stone hatchet.

Mhaawu doesn't respond and continues to snake through the crowd.

~*We need to kill him, then find somewhere else to live because*

27

the unassociated have found out about us!~ someone yells, their words pulling Mhaawu from her silence.

~Do what you think is best,~ she says, *~but we stay where we are.~*

This woman they call Mhaawu returns to the mist, and all eyes turn back to me. Only a few still hold masks to their faces, but everyone continues to grip their weapons tightly. I clear my throat and force a smile. "My wife's name is Efawi. She came this way about a month ago. Do you know anything about that? She's *this* high, would have been in an armored suit like mine. We aren't looking for any trouble. She just—"

My helmet reverberates like a gong.

I stumble forward, plant a boot in a puddle with a splash. I reach to the back of my head, am relieved to find my headgear is undamaged from whatever struck it. "Please. There's no need for—"

A spear is thrust into my chest. I stumble backward. The sharp stick is rendered nondeadly by my suit, but its diminished impact is still felt—something like a punch to the sternum by an eight-year-old trying their hardest. The tribal people chorus a gasp, presumably because I remain unharmed. With the rain easing, they spread out and stand with their feet apart and knees bent, arms ready to throw or "poke." A brown lizard waddles into the open, detects the impending violence, and scurries back into hiding. I need to find my backpack.

I make a run for it.

The tribal people unleash their fury.

They scream and shout as a flurry of hard and sharp objects hit me in an instant, knocking me in all directions. I try my best to get to where I initially fell—where my backpack unbuckled and went its own way. Anyone in my path is quick to remove themselves, seemingly afraid to make contact. The sludgy ground slows my progress, and I trip once more on chopped logs. *Stack your damn logs under cover, people!*

The barrage continues through the red tint of nose blood. I yell for them to stop. An arrow embeds itself in the PAB on my forearm, bringing a web of fractures to its screen. A thud ripples from an epicenter at my spine—a stone hatchet failing to get through to flesh. The larger objects swung or thrown with force do hurt and will likely cause some bruising, but the suit's integrity holds.

On all fours now, sweat dripping despite the cooling suit, I grope through mud and leaves searching for my gear, barely able to see beyond my reach for all the undergrowth and splashing. Arrows stick from me, neck to boot, caught in the body armor's outer fabric. I've become a human pincushion.

My bag should be here. *Why isn't it here?*

Finally, with the rainfall diminishing, I spot something that doesn't belong to the jungle: the emag rifle case, which is usually clipped to the side of the backpack. I reach for it, and a heavy blow lands, knocking me facedown into the mud. A log slides to the ground beside me. A chorus of cheers fills the air as if this monster has been slain.

I turn and lie on my back, helmet smeared in wet dirt, a centipede making its way across the visor. I wipe my helmet with my arm (only a minor improvement) and lift my head. The man referred to as "Big Man" and a shorter man are heaving a large log onto their shoulders. They make their way toward me.

I reach for the case, pull out the emag, unfold it, and jump to my feet. Everybody stops what they're doing. Jaws drop. People point and mutter. They know what a gun is. *Good.* What they don't know is . . . I've no idea how to use it. I wave the gun around while making "grrr" sounds. The tribal people jump and cower.

Upon realizing the emag is switched off, I flick open its base and turn on the power. The rifle's display lights up with confusing metrics, and a satisfying electrical charge builds in my hands. I point the rifle to the ground and press the trigger as a test. Nothing happens, as expected. Countless times I've tried to get this damn thing to fire.

With the hunter-gatherers no longer trying to kill me, I take a moment to catch my breath. The rain is now just a trickle, and the mist has thinned. Even more tribal people are present than I realized. Perhaps seventy or eighty quivering, sinewy bodies, all wide-eyed and focused on me. Adults have taken cover behind trees. Children peer through the undergrowth or look down at me from branches. Everyone and everything is soaked.

I instruct my translator to amplify the translation from my throat speakers, then I tell the onlookers, "If you continue to attack me, I will shoot you." Many of them stoop, touch their heads, and make sounds of distress that do not require translation. Perhaps Efawi did leave a warning about these people, and a bird or monkey stole the memory drive?

~It will kill us with his death-stick,~ cries a man with a child in each arm.

~Now that one unassociated has come, they will all come and enslave us,~ declares a woman who grips a large rock.

~It will be like our grandparents told us,~ yells a boy from high up in a tree.

The air fills with the sound of crying children. I move my hand from the trigger. "If you stop attacking me, I won't hurt you," I say. The tribal people look to and fro. Their children continue to wail.

They cannot be what my wife came here for. She's a future-focused technophile, and as fascinating as it may be to encounter these people, she certainly wouldn't describe the discovery of a hunter-gatherer tribe as "history-making" and "world-changing." They clearly aren't the cause of the electromagnetic interference within the Anomalous Zone, so there must be something else here, another reason why she came.

"Are there any others around here, people not like you?" I ask.

No response.

"Are you aware of anything unusual in the area?"

No response.

"You have the entire jungle to live in, yet you are here, inside this relatively tiny zone that my wife came to. Why?" They remain unwilling to talk with me. I need a different approach.

~nôvono, play a saved message from Efawi, and play it through my speakers.~

~Which message from Efawi would you like to hear?~

~Any message will do.~

"Are you playing VR games again?" comes my wife's voice, broadcast from my throat. "Is that why you're not answering my calls? I can't believe you forgot to take the pill, Okon. I only hope you didn't do this on purpose. You know I can't take it myself. And you know I don't ever want to bring a child into this world."

~nôvono, that's enough,~ I instruct, my cheeks burning.

"Tomorrow, I'll have to contact the doctor to fix this," the message continues. "How can you be so unreliable?"

~nôvono, stop playing!~ I command, and the message finally stops. How can the nôvono pro contain some of the most advanced tech in the world and not understand what I'm saying half the time?

~Why does he sound like a woman?~ someone asks.

"That was my wife," I say, thankful her words had not been translated for these people. "Do you recognize her voice?" I ask, but they continue to refuse to answer me and proceed to mutter among themselves. I take a long, deep breath. ~nôvono, what language is being translated?~

~Your words are being translated into Edowomu, with an accuracy rate of ninety-three point two percent.~

I've heard of Edowomu: a regional language used in some of the townships close to the Nsanba. Impoverished communities populated by descendants of those cleared from the jungle

31

decades ago. The Nsanba was once home to many tribes.

"Critical battery," says . . . something.

A red light flashes on my chest, causing a further stir. With all the craziness, I forgot the suit is due its charge. I open its control panel. *Two percent remaining!* I should be asleep with the solar panel up already. On my fourth night of trekking, I learned the hard way that when the battery dies, the suit becomes stiff— something to do with its protective layer of fluid turning solid without an electric charge. I had to wrestle my way out and charge the damn thing before I could wear it again.

"Where's my bag?" I yell. I fumble around in the undergrowth some more, the emag hanging at my waist by its shoulder strap. "It's not here. It's not fucking here. Efawi! Effawiii!" I shout her name until my lungs run out of air and desperately await her response. The jungle gives me nothing but squawking birds. The tribal people goggle at me as if I'm crazy.

"I want my bag, right now," I demand. I grab hold of my rifle, the hunter-gatherers return to cover, and their children recommence their wailing. They are all terrified. From their perspective, I must be the aggressor. A magical man-monster who's come to rob them of everything they have, to steal their children, to enslave them like conquerors of the past. No wonder they won't talk to me.

"Critical battery," I'm warned once more. I don't think the suit gives a third warning, and I simply can't let myself be frozen in this thing and at the mercy of these people. They'll find a way to pry it open and "poke" me, or they might build a fire around me, burn me alive inside my suit. My heart races at the thought. *No.* I can't let that happen. There must be a way to quickly win their trust; that's my only option now.

I lift the rifle's strap over my head, hold the gun out flat, and place it on the ground, pausing with my fingertips on the barrel before standing back up empty-handed. Big Man fidgets with the rock in his hand. Others dig their heels into the ground. "I've put my gun down because I don't believe you want to hurt me. Perhaps your people have had bad experiences with strangers coming here. Maybe that's why you attacked me? But I'm just a normal person, just like you, who doesn't want to harm anyone."

Twitchings and murmurings ripple through the gathering. I reach for the helmet's release mechanism. "My name is Okon. I'm thirty-six years old. I'm an only child. Both my parents have passed away. I don't really have any extended family, not that I speak to. I have a wife, Efawi, whom I mentioned. We don't have children, but I hope to someday. I wear this suit, which isn't magic, to protect me, and I don't need it now because I think we can be friends."

With shaking hands, I lift my helmet a few centimeters, and warm, jungle-scented air rushes in. The tribal people remain on edge but appear to be growing more curious than afraid. I check the suit's panel. *One percent!* "This is called a helmet," I hurriedly tell them. "Underneath it is my head, which is just a normal head of a man. I am not a monster, see." I lift the helmet further so its rim is above my eyes.

They chorus a gasp. *-It is shedding its skin,-* someone mutters.

Bolstered by their relatively passive reaction, I lift and hold the helmet above me. Direct sunlight, UV rays included, touches my cheeks and enters my eyes. I smile, and the tribal people step a little further from their hiding positions, gripping their weapons a little less tightly as they scrutinize my face. These people didn't want to hurt me; they were simply afraid. And all it took to turn them around was a little faith from me.

"I really hope we can cooperate and that you give my bag back, because it's very important to me."

The red light on my chest stops flashing. *Shit.* I try to move, but the suit holds its position with my hands stuck above me, the helmet held between them, and my head exposed.

The tribal people tread closer.

I use what little movement I have in my fingers to try to wriggle the helmet free so it drops back over my head, but the suit, including gloves, is too stiff. When this happened previously, I managed, with great effort, to open the thing up and wriggle out. Perhaps I'm weaker now, more exhausted and malnourished than when I started. Perhaps I could get out if my arms weren't caught in this awkward position. To think someone was paid a lot of money to design this suit!

The tribal people talk among themselves as they creep closer still. *~His magic has broken?~*

My head sweats. I force another smile. "If you help me, I will help you. Together, we can be good for each other."

~Can we trust him?~

~Of course not. He is unassociated.~

~This is our chance; we must kill him.~

"Wait!"

My head whips forward while my torso remains static, held in place by the frozen suit. The back of my skull burns, hot and wet. The jungle blurs. *~You are experiencing neurological trauma,~* says my nôvono pro. *~Seek medical attention immediately.~*

Two men joust with their spears at chest height. I'm knocked over, a solid lump as I crash through plants and hit the ground. The loose helmet bounces away. My head is struck again, and there is further movement and sound, further sensations across my body. I see feet and ankles, but everything is distant, like I'm no longer quite there, like this isn't quite happening to me. I think of my wife standing in the bedroom doorway, her last morning at home before the arrest warrant. I'm looking up at her from the bed. Her eyebrows are sloped. She'd just reiterated the reasons she doesn't want children. A young tribal man with a stump for an arm jumps on top of me, yelling. Then nothing.

4: The Caregiver

"I don't just blame the government. I blame people. Homo sapiens. We are all messed up. It's in our DNA. Thousands of millennia of coping with the demands of a cruel world has screwed up our minds. Harshness has shaped our psychology. We are the descendants of scarred animals, and all that struggle and disturbance is still in there—in you, in me, in everyone. We do irrational things because of it—are capable of awful, terrible things given the right circumstances. You know this about people, and that's why you stay at home."

I awake with words from Efawi fresh in my mind. Words from the last time we were together—the last time she saw or heard anything from me.

With my eyes still closed, I try to focus on the present. Birds are chirping, insects are buzzing, monkeys are screaming, and humans are chanting. I focus on the chanting. Repetitive tones. A deep, male voice, and the quieter squeaks of a woman.

I open my eyes and find myself in the same place I've been for I don't know how long: the inside of a small, circular hut, made from dried leaves tied with vine to a wooden frame. Sunbeams crisscross above me, originating at a dozen or so holes. A torn, woven drape hangs at the hut's opening near my feet. I remember being attacked, then nothing after that other than lying here on my back, naked on dirt. Alone. Barely conscious.

"My bag. I need my bag," I whisper to myself, dry throat rasping. This is the most awake I've felt for a while. I try to sit up. Everything spins. I lie back down and reach for my head, find it coated in a white paste that's all smooched in my hair. I take a deep breath, and using my elbows for support, I try sitting up again, slower this time.

My body is a patchwork of bruises. Someone has coated me in oil, and my right knee's been wrapped in leaves. I sit up further, head aching, and reach for the wrap, not really wanting to see what's underneath. I lift it and find more white paste spread messily over a round, black swelling where my knee should be. "Oh, god."

I lie back down, heart pounding. I try to recall the details of our home: the diamond-shaped elevator buttons, the worn leather of the toilet seat, the blue anti-inflammatory cream for the bridge of my nose that I keep beside my VR headset. My torso bounces with shallow breaths. They must have taken my suit off and beaten me, but aside from the headache, there's no pain in my body, only a degree of numbness. Am I numb from fear, or have they drugged me? The chanting from outside grows nauseating, and the hot, dusty inside of the hut begins to suffocate. "It's going to be fine," I croak. "It's going to be fine."

I stiffen at the sound of footsteps. A group of them are approaching. ~You must stop that awful singing,~ someone says, my translator and nôvono pro continuing to work despite the beating. ~Even the bonobos are leaping to their death to avoid hearing your noise,~ they add.

The chanting stops. ~If I do not sing, the unassociated one's evil spirits will enter our settlement and infect the Wuchumbu people. He should not be allowed to stay.~

~None of us want him here, but Mhaawu has allowed Ratu to keep him.~

~And so, I sing to protect us.~

The chanting recommences, louder than before. Other agitated voices enter the fray. ~ *The unassociated man's evil spirits can't be worse than your chanting!* ~

A hand appears on the drape at the hut's opening. Despite there being more serious concerns, my first thought is to cover my genitals. I grab a bowl of what I hope is water and place it over my groin. There's nothing else in the hut except for thirty or so stones stacked in a cone-like formation. I grab one, knocking the stack as I do, which reveals something shiny placed within it. I pull the thing free: my navicube. Smashed. Broken. Useless.

~ *What do you do in there, Ratu?* ~ someone asks.

The hand at the drape hesitates.

~ *Ratu wants to make friends with the unassociated because Ratu has no friends among the Wuchumbu.* ~

The drape is pulled back. The chanting grows louder still. I drop the navicube, close my eyes, and pretend to be asleep (keeping a stone in hand in case I need it). I hear this person, who I assume is Ratu, shuffle toward me.

~ *Ratu, is the unassociated man still alive? If he is dead, you must tell us so the shaman stops singing.* ~

My visitor says nothing as they edge closer, brushing against my side. It takes all my strength not to flinch or open my eyes, but when this Ratu slaps my left thigh, I yelp and look up. Beside me sits a young man, perhaps a teenager, smiling from ear to ear. His head is small, shaped like a pea. His hair big, not braided like the others, and his left arm is a stump that ends between his shoulder and elbow.

~ *My name is Ratu. What about you?* ~

He stares at me, wide-eyed, his grin persistent as he awaits an answer.

"What about me?" I ask, throat still rasping.

~ *Why is your hair like mine?* ~ he asks.

"Is it?"

~*How do you make the words come out like that? It looks funny.*~ The young man shuffles closer to my head. ~*Where are you from? Where did you get all your objects? What is it like outside the jungle?*~

"I—"

~*Our elders have told us stories of things the unassociated have made that look like people, and can walk and talk like people, but are not real because they have no eaduao.*~

"I—"

~*What about gigantic things, as large as the Nsanba, that float on water and carry people wherever they want to go—is it true these things exist outside the jungle?*~

"I am Efawi's husband. Is she here?"

~*Eff-aar-wee? This is the woman you are looking for?*~

"You've seen her?"

~*No. None of us have. You are the first person from outside the tribe I have ever seen.*~

His answer hits me like a punch to the stomach. Ratu continues to smile.

"So, you don't know anything about my wife? About where she is?"

~*No. I just told you that.*~

"But you all knew to be afraid of my rifle, so you must have seen others before."

~*Many years ago, a few of the tribe were attacked by men from outside the jungle who carried death-sticks. Since then, the Wuchumbu have had no more encounters, but we have all known about death-sticks for a long time, from stories passed down through generations. Is it true that people from outside the jungle eat their babies and can shoot fire from their eyes?*~

"I need to find Efawi."

~*If Eff-aar-wee is your wife, why did you not come here together?*~

"You wouldn't understand."

~Yes, I would. I am very clever.~

I take a deep breath and surprise myself by deciding to give him an answer. "We didn't come here together because she wasn't able to contact me."

~Your wife could not speak to you?~

"Because of her arrest warrant, the only way she could get in touch was via our nôvono pros."

~You are not making any sense.~

"I told you you wouldn't understand."

~So, why did you not come here together?~

"You already asked me that. The bottom line is, it's my fault we didn't come here together because I forgot I switched my nôvo-comms off. I simply forgot."

I know Ratu won't understand what that means, but getting it off my chest brings some relief. This has been my first opportunity to off-load and confess my mistake—my stupid mistake, which meant my wife couldn't contact me at a time of need. Thinking about that makes breathing a little harder. I switched my nôvo-comms off on the morning of her last day at home, and I forgot to turn them back on. My nôvono didn't notify me that my comms remained off, so for days I assumed they were on, and that Efawi hadn't sent anything—that she was just on one of her usual work trips. Eventually I realized my nôvo-comms were off, and I received the desperate messages she'd left that gave me instructions on what to do next. But by then, the PPA was already monitoring me and preventing me from leaving our home. Finally, an arrest warrant came through for me too, and I managed to escape using Efawi's instructions.

~What?~ says Ratu.

I shake my head and sigh.

~Are you capable of explaining why your wife came here?~

"Yes, I am capable. She came here because she couldn't return home and she'd received no response from me, so she had no choice but to come to this place to investigate a discovery

39

she'd made—a discovery that she thinks will help us negotiate with the PPA. Are you capable of understanding that?"

He probably doesn't even know what the PPA is, but the young man's lips quiver as he seems to try to make sense of things. ~*What is the discovery your wife came here for?*~ he eventually asks.

"I don't know."

~*How can you not know? Husbands and wives know everything about what their partner does.*~

"Efawi doesn't tell me about her more controversial activities because we agreed she'd stop involving me, and as much as I'm enjoying this conversation about my relationship with my wife, I need to find her." I go to sit up, and Ratu waves his hand in my face.

~*No, you cannot go anywhere; your body is broken. I have looked after you, but you need more time to heal.*~ He points at my right knee. ~*Gommonogo did that.*~

I try not to think about the damage this Gommonogo person and others have done to me. "How long have I been asleep for?" I ask.

The young man looks away. ~*I think you do not want the answer to that.*~

"Tell me," I insist.

He turns back to me, the smile no longer on his face. ~*You have been asleep for six years.*~

"Six years!"

Ratu laughs. ~*I am joking. Of course not six years. How can you still have bruises after six years? I thought unassociated people would be clever. Only three days have passed since you arrived. The others wanted to kill you, but I stopped them. I had to argue so hard and for so long, but I got my way. I saved your life.*~

Three days is long enough. "What is this white paste and oil on my body? And where's my suit and bag? I have medical stuff I can use."

~They put all your things on wood and floated them down the river. They believe it is bad to keep unassociated objects around.~

"My equipment is no longer here? Everything is gone?"

~Yes, apart from that.~ Ratu points at the navicube. *~These piled-up stones and the shiny thing are meant to absorb your evil spirits. I didn't put them there. The stupid shaman did.~*

All my equipment gone? I don't think I can handle that thought. I push myself onto my elbows and try to move my right knee, which refuses to bend. I wince in expectation of a pain that doesn't come. "Have you drugged me?"

~I used Nsanba medicine to make your body feel nice. Good stuff made by Feplao; not the shaman's rubbish.~

I close my eyes. This can't be happening. I never entered the Nsanba. I never even left our home. I'm just daydreaming, floating in our float room, supported by saline water, a projection of the cosmos on the low-domed ceiling, gentle music rippling across the pool.

Ratu presses a clammy palm against my chest. I open my eyes. His grin is psychotic.

"Why did you attack me? Why did you float all my gear away? *Why?* I told you I wasn't a threat. I told you I was just looking for my wife. I fucking told you."

The young man tilts his head. *~I do not know why you are asking me these questions. The others attacked you. I saved your life, remember?~*

The hut shakes. Someone outside is banging on the frame. *~Ratu, your mother wants you!~* they yell.

~I am busy!~ Ratu yells back.

~She said you must go to her immediately.~

~I do not care what she wants,~ Ratu replies.

He sighs, then shuffles toward the opening. *~You need more rest,~* he says. *~It will be a long time before you walk again, but do not worry. Ratu is taking care of you.~*

"You're leaving? Am I safe? I think some of the people

outside still want to kill me."

The young man laughs. *~Not some of them; all of them. So, do not leave this hut.~* He pulls back the drape. The sunlight blinds me. *~Before I go, I have an important question for you,~* he says. "Yes?"

~Are there beautiful women outside the jungle?~

I don't respond. My apparent lifesaver and caregiver bounds into the open, and the drape falls back into place, returning me to semidarkness. The shaman's chanting continues, quieter now. His words aren't translatable, but no doubt he's praying for my death. I lie back, close my eyes, and cover my face with my hands.

~I can hear the unassociated man crying,~ comes a voice from outside, not Ratu's.

~I told you he was not dangerous,~ says another, again not Ratu. *~It was clear he was only looking for his wife. We should have talked to him once he put down his death-stick.~*

~No. When there is an invader in our home, an invader with a weapon, an invader whose people have committed brutal acts against our ancestors, we have to defend ourselves without hesitation.~

~Well, at least we now know this unassociated man is not a threat. We have floated away his things. He is injured. He is alone. So, we can help him.~

~If his wife is nearby like he says, he is not alone.~

~And we do not know he is no longer a threat.~

~We have no idea what this man is capable of.~

Part 2

5: The Hill

"Two hundred and sixty-four. Two hundred and sixty-five. Two hundred and sixty-six." My right steps and left steps aren't equal due to my lopsided gait, but as long as I keep each side consistent, I can measure distances quite well.

At two hundred and ninety, I stop and look around. "Hmm, I messed up . . . Nope, there it is." I approach the markings I previously carved on a tree using a sharpened stone Beejalee gave me. Leaning against the tree, I adjust my grass loincloth and loosen my boots. Without socks, antique military-grade footwear rubs on the feet but is infinitely better than going barefoot in the jungle.

My carving is of an arrow and the number sixty. I take care to turn so I'm facing exactly where the arrow is pointing. "One. Two. Three . . ."

Before I get to sixty, I see what I came here for: a hill (not something I'd normally be excited about). Upon spotting a good sitting-branch near the base of the hill, I rest for a moment while taking care to keep my right knee straight. As always, I don't want to see my injury, so I look up. The hill is like a pointy paper hat with one vertical side that rises to about fifty meters. It's a little strange looking, but the Nsanba landscape is full of odd natural quirks. I think I called Efawi an "odd natural quirk" once.

A warm, soft thing settles on my shoulder. I freeze. *A giant millipede? A hairy spider?* I quickly twist my torso and raise a hand to flick whatever it is off—and I find Ratu standing behind me, laughing.

"Motherfucker," I growl. The word *motherfucker* is never translated, but I've explained it to Ratu before. "What the hell did you put on my shoulder?"

Ratu laughs harder and holds up some animal's bushy tail tied to a piece of vine.

"I told you to stop following me around, and now you've made me hurt my knee," I complain. He hadn't, but I look at the injury while pretending to be in pain. The skinniness of my legs accentuates the deformity: a couple of bulges to the side of my right kneecap, where broken bone has healed but not healed in correct alignment.

"How are those *boo-ootz* I gave you?" Ratu asks. "Do they make your baby feet feel better?" I'm so used to the translator implant in my neck working its magic, I no longer notice there's been any translation at all.

"They're good," I reply. "Would be better if you told me where the dead soldier was so I can have his socks too."

"I told you I found them far from here. I tried going back, but could not remember the exact location. You should be grateful for the boo-ootz, and that I saved your life on the day you arrived."

"You saved my life? You haven't told me that before." (Sarcasm has been my sole gift to the tribe. Possibly an unwanted one.)

"I have told you many times," Ratu replies. "Every day for the three months you have been with us." (Sometimes my sarcasm fails to get through.)

Ratu walks around to stand in front of me. "Why have you come to this place?" he asks.

"Because today's the day I begin." I struggle to my feet and

THE VEILED EDGE OF CONTACT

limp to the bottom of the hill. Ratu follows.

"Begin what?" he asks. "Will you try to get up there again? With your inadequate leg, you can barely walk on flat ground." I glance at Ratu's stump of an arm and bite my tongue. Truth be told, Ratu doesn't let the absence of his left arm hold him back in any way; I've seen him climb trees most of the tribe would struggle with.

I make my way up the hill, grabbing and pulling on trunks and branches, anything I can get a hold of to assist my ascent. The incline combined with my inability to bend my injured knee means I have to swing my right leg in circular motions. Ratu ascends behind me. With his one arm and my "inadequate" leg, we make an interesting demonstration of human movement.

Toward the top, the hill becomes rockier, and the trees thin, so I have less to hold on to. I struggle and eventually lose balance. Thankfully, Ratu—who already reached the top and came back to annoy me—grabs my arm and stops me from tumbling.

"Saved your life again."

"Again?"

I continue on all fours, dragging my right leg behind me, taking care not to press my hands onto anything unpleasant, like needle grass or scorpions. After a few minutes of crawling, I make it to the top, and once I've caught my breath, I head to the other side of the hill's peak. Beneath this side is a sheer drop to a forty-meter-wide area of open, rocky ground below. Ratu joins me near the edge.

The hill is higher than most of the immediate area, and I shade my eyes to take in the view. Beneath the pale blue sky, there is only jungle. A messy conglomerate of mounds, ridges, and depressions, on top of which sits a dense competition of trees, some of them round and lush, some nothing more than a lanky stalk with a leafy head. Green dominates, broken by yellow-tinted leaves and the brown gray of exposed bark. Misty patches cling to the canopy here and there. A dark line meanders from east to west, where a narrow gap in the trees follows the curved path of a river. A jagged mountain range sits three-quarters of the way to the horizon (my route to the AZ had to circumvent the worst of it). I take half a step back from the edge. "This is a wilderness," I mutter to myself, as if I didn't already know. "To think I walked all this way."

Ratu flings stones into the opening below, and the cliff and surrounding rock throw back echoes of each tiny impact. I turn my focus to where the Anomalous Zone begins and ends. The trouble is, I didn't navigate my way to the AZ; the navicube in my bag and the PAB on my forearm did. I merely followed a pink line on a screen, a route that had been mapped out for me by Efawi, so I had no need to pay much attention to the geography of the place. Despite this, I'm confident I reached the Anomalous Zone well before I arrived at the pronounced S curve in the river, which I can see from here. So, the AZ must extend to beyond that point.

Remembering that the zone is 8.9 kilometers in diameter, I visualize its area as a circle stretching out all around me, large enough to go beyond the S curve, and the enormity of the challenge hits me like a knee in the guts: it will take months to search the Anomalous Zone.

I gather a handful of stones and join Ratu in hurling them from the edge.

"You seem angry," he says.

I don't respond.

"What did you mean when you said, 'today's the day I begin'?" he asks.

"I thought if I could make it up the hill and survey the area, then I could plan a search for my wife."

"But you already started searching for Efawi. That is all you do. It is so boring."

"I've hobbled around near the settlement, which was the best

I could do while my leg was healing, but I need to cover greater distances in a more structured way."

"So, what will you do now?"

I pause my stone throwing. What will I do now? is a good question. "I'll find her, or she'll find me" is the best answer I have.

"But you said she came here a month before you, which means she arrived four months ago. Maybe she has since gone back to the place you are from."

"Possibly. But she can't go back until she's investigated her discovery and done whatever she needs to do to get our arrest warrants lifted, which may take a while, according to Efawi."

"I don't understand. Why is she not able to go back now?"

"Ratu, this is stuff to do with the outside world, which you have no knowledge or comprehension of."

"Well, you do not even know why your wife came here or what this 'discovery' of hers is. I think she is not here anymore."

"If Efawi has moved on, she would have left another memory drive with a nôvo-message telling me what to do next—so I'd need to find that memory drive."

"Your words make no sense," Ratu snorts. He rounds up some more stones before adding, "Maybe she never came here at all. There is no reason for her to come. There is only the jungle and the Wuchumbu, nothing else."

No matter whom I ask, the tribe continues to refuse knowledge of anything unusual in the area, but there must be a reason why they reside in the relatively tiny Anomalous Zone. With the whole Nsanba to live in, it's too unlikely to be a coincidence.

"Even if my wife is now somewhere else, I know she was here at least at one point because she left me a memory drive at the edge of the AZ. That is a fact, Ratu. Accept it."

"If she were here, someone in the tribe would have seen her."

"Maybe. Maybe not. It's not like the Wuchumbu are

consistent with their patrols."

"Well, if she is here, she does not want to see you—otherwise, she would have made herself known."

"Nonsense." The idea that Efawi doesn't want to see me *is* nonsense, but I can't help but recall that she wasn't thrilled with me when she last left the house. Our last morning together was spent arguing, and I sometimes panic that our stressful, angry exchange will be our last ever interaction. She hasn't heard a peep from me since, and although I've heard from her, it's only been in messages.

One of her nôvo-messages tied to a branch referred to our argument that morning and was a little cryptic: *~Our last conversation, our disagreement, has been on my mind. You were right; we need something new in our lives. Something positive. But we don't have to want the same things in order to be good for each other. With time, Okon, I believe we can give each other what we need.~* I have some ideas regarding what that's supposed to mean, but I wish Efawi had been as clear and to the point as she usually is.

"Maybe your wife does not know you are here, because you spent so much time sleeping in your hut," says Ratu.

I glare at him. "Not sleeping. Healing."

Ratu laughs; I'm not sure why. He throws another stone, then asks me to point to where I'm from. "That's the direction," I say, pointing south. "My home is in Magawi City, which is the capital of the People's Rightful Republic of Mbapazu. It's so far away you can't see it."

"*Emm-bapp-azuu* is the name of your tribe, yes?" says Ratu.

"Mbapazu is the name of my country, which is an independent state that emerged after The War. All the nations in Central Africa were redefined and renamed after The War. I guess you wouldn't know anything about that. You could consider Mbapazu to be like a very big tribe, I suppose."

"Is your tribe all around?" asks Ratu as he turns on the spot.

"No, no. There are other countries—very big tribes—that border the jungle. Somewhere over there, for example, is the Nation of Loalla, which is another state that formed about seventy years ago. My tribe and their tribe don't get along very well."

"If your tribe has tension with another tribe, I hope you have a good leader. You do have a leader?"

"There's a political party called the PPA who are in charge. Efawi doesn't like them. She thinks they're corrupt thugs."

"Do you dislike them too?"

"Until recently, I never had reason to think about them."

"Well, they cannot be that bad, because you are always talking about how much you want to go back there."

I release a heavy sigh and rub the bridge of my nose. "I do miss being home," I say.

The Wuchumbu tribe fears that other people will learn of their existence if I return home, but this isn't a problem they have to worry about, because it's impossible for me to leave the jungle, given my damaged leg, my lack of equipment, and my failure to develop the necessary navigational and survival skills while living with a tribe of hunter-gatherers the past three months. So, with confidence, they let this idiot from outside the jungle roam freely.

The Wuchumbu settlement is somewhere down and to the right of me, about a kilometer or so from the hill. It's difficult to spot from above, by design. With minimal clearing for their habitat—huts squeezed between trees—their settlement has no large unbroken sections of canopy except for the center, which is a communal area with a handful of larger huts. The shape of the communal area is intentionally irregular, giving the impression of a naturally formed bare patch in the jungle. And motivated by their fear of being found, the Wuchumbu add fresh green foliage to the tops of the larger huts on a daily basis.

According to Ratu, there are exactly three hundred and

eighty-two people in the tribe. (Why on earth he went to the trouble of counting everyone, I've no idea.) Ratu also told me past generations of theirs used to live over a broader area in smaller groups that would move around more frequently, but when The War ended several decades ago, they learned of other tribes in the jungle being rounded up, and so the Wuchumbu came together and went deeper into the Nsanba. Hiding is in their blood, apparently.

"Hey, is my navicube still here?" I ask. "The small shiny thing that was in my first hut, beneath a stack of stones."

"No. Someone floated it down the river. I thought you said it was broken and useless."

"It was, but it was still mine. Whoever did that should have asked my permission."

This means my nôvono pro and my translator implants are the only things from the modern world still within my possession. The Wuchumbu can't float them down the river without cutting me open. Thankfully, neither of my implants has battery requirements. Instead, they utilize energy produced by my body. The translator is invaluable in my relationship with the tribe and can work on its own, without the nôvono, if need be. And although the nôvono monitors and helps prevent neurodegenerative disease (exactly how it does this I don't recall), that's more of a long-term thing, and presently the brain implant isn't so useful in my day-to-day life with the tribe, given the lack of a network to connect to.

I didn't use it much when I was outside the jungle either. I never really liked the idea of having a brain implant, but Efawi, being the early adopter that she is, was keen for us to get them. She would lecture me on the nôvono pro's full range of benefits: health preservation, diagnostics, web connectivity, communications, and more functionality being added all the time. I was assured that major surgery wouldn't be needed for the install because the implant is folded and inserted through the nasal cavity, then lifted into position with magnets. But I was worried that other people, Efawi included, would be able to read or manipulate my mind. The Digital Cognitives rep convinced me this wasn't possible. They said nôvo-comms are hack-proof, and that communication can only happen when the user allows it. And even though the device itself has access to our thoughts and emotions for processing comms, it can't actually change my thoughts and emotions. "Devices like these are the future," my wife told me. A richer form of connection that will help us and everyone become closer again, that will remove our barriers, that will help Efawi and I understand each other like we used to.

It hasn't, and I never fully got on board with it. I throw my last stone into the rocky opening below.

"Aaargh!"

Ratu and I exchange wide-eyed glances before peering over the edge. The shaman is standing at the bottom of the cliff, holding his head with one hand and a bloody stone knife with the other. Ratu laughs. "Just raped and slaughtered another animal?" he shouts to the witch doctor below. "What was it this time? A mongoose? A duiker? The duikers are your favorite, yes?"

"You are not allowed up there, you *etowauda*!"

"You are a maa-ta-fa-karr!" yells Ratu.

"I told you it's pronounced *motherfucker*," I mutter.

Ratu throws another stone, just missing the shaman. The elder shouts again, words that go untranslated, and he staggers from the rocky opening and into the thickness of trees.

"We aren't allowed up here?" I ask.

"Ignore him. He has many pointless rules. How have you been able to live with the stupid Wuchumbu for so long? Even I had to move away from them, and I was born here."

Ratu's hut is a hundred meters from the settlement. He moved there before I arrived, after a big argument with his mother, Mhaawu (who I initially thought was his grandmother, but she must be younger than she looks). Ratu is the only tribe member who doesn't live in the settlement.

"You think everyone apart from you is stupid, Ratu. And I don't know what your problem with the tribe is, but it's not nice to insult them. Besides, you are Wuchumbu too, so if you call the Wuchumbu stupid, that means you're stupid as well."

"You called everyone an inbred idiot every single day for the first two months you were here."

"Yes, but I was angry with you all back then. I was in shock. Depressed."

"Well, the Wuchumbu are certainly not inbred," he huffs. "There are rules about who marries whom within the tribe, and the Wuchumbu used to travel far to mix with other tribes for marriage—until the Wuchumbu became the only ones left in the jungle. Also, it is not true that I think everyone apart from myself is stupid. Until I met you, I used to think all those from outside the jungle would be much cleverer."

I shake my head. "You are very arrogant, Ratu. Has anyone ever told you that?"

"Yes, but I do not care about their opinion."

"Well, there you go. And just so you know, those outside the jungle are neither cleverer nor stupider than the Wuchumbu. Although, your people do have some incorrect ideas about the world because you lack the benefit of science. You lack information that is obvious to a person from the modern world, such as . . . um, the fact that plants turn sunlight into energy through a process called *photo sinuses*."

Ratu looks confused. "I do not have incorrect ideas about the world," he says. "I do not believe in spirits and magic—not in the way the shaman and many of the Wuchumbu believe. I have never even drunk the Massas fruit."

"That's a fruit from the Massas tree that the tribe drinks to get high, right? I've heard Beejalee and Adienatta talk about it."

"They believe the fruit allows us to see spirits. Everyone stopped drinking it two years ago, apart from the shaman."

"I could do with talking to a spirit who can tell me where Efawi is."

"The Massas fruit does not work. It just makes you see and hear things like a crazy person."

"How do you know if you've never tried it?"

Ratu puffs his cheeks and picks up another stone to throw. "You will never find your wife, Okon. You are an incompetent person."

"Efawi and I *will* find each other, Ratu." I adjust my boots and head toward the side of the hill that we climbed. "And I am not an incompetent person, thank you." I take another step, slip, and roll several meters down the hill before a dried-out bush brings me to a halt.

I wince in pain. Ratu looks down at me.

"I'm okay!" I call out.

Ratu raises his arm as if to throw a stone, and I shield myself. He then opens his hand to reveal he isn't holding anything, and he bursts out laughing.

"You *etowoudo!*" I shout.

"You do not even know what that means," says Ratu, "and you pronounced it incorrectly."

I decide to shuffle the rest of the way. A minute later, Ratu yells at me from above: "Hold on, Okon! I have something important to tell you!"

"Why wait until I'm halfway down the hill to tell me something important?" I yell back.

I continue shuffling. Ratu continues to shout. "I am really impressed that you climbed this hill today! I never thought you would be able to do such a thing! Your achievement has given me an idea you will like very much!"

"And?"

"I will need to think some more before I tell you what my idea is!"

"Great! Thanks for sharing! I was about to speak with Habee

because he's good at finding honey and might have some tips on how to find Efawi! But I'm so excited about your idea, I don't think I'll be able to do anything until I hear it!"

"You are being saar-kaz-tick, yes?" yells Ratu.

I smile. He is learning.

6: The Unassociated

"Okon, what you are doing is very . . . strange," says Petonba. Her brow is furrowed as if she's concerned, but her lips curve upward as though she wants to laugh.

"Now, where's the stool?" I mumble.

I spot Babba hitting his brother with it. "Babba! That is not a plaything." Babba gives me a confused look, his little round face all cherub-like. He reluctantly hands back the crudely cut wooden block, and I place it beneath my right leg to keep my knee straight as I sit on my handcrafted chair. I try to ignore the murmurs of disapproval. Everyone else in the communal area sits on mats of fur and woven grass.

"This is more comfortable for you?" asks Adienatta without looking up, weaving as always with her slender fingers.

"He does not look comfortable," says Petonba.

"He looks like an idiot," says Gommonogo, voice rough like a lawnmower.

I release a heavy sigh. After getting advice from Habee yesterday afternoon, I began my more structured search for Efawi this morning, and right now, all I want to do is relax.

I adjust my position, and the chair rocks heavily despite my best efforts to make the legs even. The chair's seat is hard and square, and the backrest too upright. I haven't yet worked out how to make armrests or cushions, but despite its shortcomings,

I'm proud of my handiwork. It's the first time I've ever constructed anything.

"I do not know what this is," says Gommonogo, "but it appears to be the work of a crazy person."

I shift my position again, trying to get comfortable.

"It is not acceptable for this to be here," Gommonogo's twin sister declares. She stands for attention and points. Her frame is lean and her eyes piercing like her brother's. I can never pronounce her name right: *Gommonaadogo*, or something like that. Learning the names of the Wuchumbu hasn't been easy, and there are more I know by face than name.

"What is not acceptable?" I ask and pretend to look around, despite knowing she's referring to my chair.

"It is unassociated," she adds. Others mutter in agreement. *Unassociated* means no association with the Wuchumbu. Given the tribe has managed to isolate themselves for decades, the term essentially applies to everyone who is not Wuchumbu, along with everything that was made or designed by people who are not Wuchumbu.

"If you're referring to my chair, I need it to support my back."

"Your back is pathetic," says Gommonogo. "None of the Wuchumbu need support when we sit."

"Yes, well, I haven't spent my life lounging on the floor," I say. "I lounge in chairs."

"Is there any part of your body that is not weak?" asks Babba, his tone sincere, not intending to mock. I knew they'd take issue with the chair, but in time they'll begrudgingly accept it, like they have my boots.

"I'm still not happy about those things on your feet either," snaps Gommonaadogo.

I roll my eyes and reach for the food on the ground beside me.

"Okon, that is not your *uddu*," says Gommonogo.

"Habee gave it to me this morning," I reply. I lift the gray-white, boiled African-yam paste mixed with honey onto my lap, taking care none drops from the leaf on which it sits.

"Habee gave you the honey only," says Gommonogo.

"No. He gave me the honey and the uddu," I reply.

"But he did not gather the yam or sap for the uddu. He got that from someone else."

"Did you contribute to the making of this uddu, Gommonogo?"

"No."

"Well then, what are you complaining about?" They all know how to get any amount of food from the jungle, uddu included. Sure, the honey is a bit harder to come by, but as usual, Gommonogo just wants to harass me for the sake of harassing me. He steps closer.

"Leave Okon alone," says Adienatta.

"But we always share food," Gommonogo replies. "It is the Wuchumbu way."

"I've been here long enough to know you people don't share food unless you want to, which isn't often. Hey, hands off!" I swipe air as Gommonogo digs his mitts into my uddu, takes a large scoop, and knocks the rest from my lap in the process. He sucks up the paste and licks his fingers.

"Are you going to eat that?" he asks, pointing at the remainder.

"No," I huff, worried my chair might tip over if I try to reach it.

Gommonogo scoops up the uddu and gives some to his sister. "See, we share," he says.

I sit back as much as the chair allows, close my eyes, and imagine there are no annoying people taking my food, no insects buzzing in my face, no constant squawking or bellowing or howling all around, no sun beating down on me. Instead, I'm in my entertainment room. The air con is humming. I'm eating frozen moabi cream. My Raizer game system is jingling as it starts up. My beautifully cushioned, custom-made, haptic chair is perfectly aligning with the contours of my buttocks.

"Instead of making stupid things to sit on," says Gommonaadogo, "why do you not do something useful?" I open my eyes to find her standing over me. The Gommo twins are particularly keen to harass me today. I adjust my position again while keeping my leg straight on the stool. This thing really needs cushions. Many cushions. And armrests.

"For once you might help to sweep leaves?" she continues. "Repair huts? Forage? Cook? Tidy?"

"When will *you* do any of those things, Gommonaadogo?" says Beejalee as she approaches with a heavy clay pot in her powerful arms.

"I do as much as everyone else," Gommonaadogo claims.

"Which is not much," Beejalee huffs. She straightens out the furs on the ground with her short legs and puts down the pot. "We have become disorganized. We have become dysfunctional. We have become lazy."

Ratu told me the tribe has been this way for as long as he can remember and that they became worse about two years ago. When I asked him why they became worse, he backtracked and said I misunderstood him.

"If we are lazy," says Gommonogo, "then what about Okon? He did not even make his own hut."

"I did, but it collapsed with me in it, and Adienatta, Beejalee, Petonba, and others were kind enough to make me another. There's nothing wrong with having helpful friends."

Adienatta smiles and gracefully bows her head. Her woven leaf creation appears to be taking the form of a fan. Something for me, I hope.

"You have not answered my question, Okon," snaps Gommonaadogo. "When will you do some work?"

"He is not capable of work," says Gommonogo. "His body is

feeble and uncoordinated, his feet are soft like a baby, and his mind is dull. How many times have Ratu or Beejalee or Babba or Habee shown him how to find food, how to grow *mfumbwa*, how to hunt duiker? And yet he remains useless. He does not even make his own uddu."

"Where I'm from, we have machines—*devices, things* that make our food for us," I retort.

A handful of those listening groan disapprovingly. They don't like it when I talk about the unassociated world.

"Well," says Gommonogo, "instead of making things to sit on, why do you not build one of these things that make food?"

"Because they are complicated and I don't know how. I would imagine few people do."

"Then you cannot feel superior if you do not know how to build them. It seems you are reliant on others for your survival both here and where you come from."

"Gommonogo and Gommonaadogo, that is enough!" says Beejalee. "You must stop being mean to Okon. He is already sad today."

"Why is Okon sad?" asks Babba as he sits next to me.

"He is sad because he spent all morning looking for his wife and could not find her," says Adienatta.

"But I saw him lying in the rock pools doing nothing, as usual," says Gommonogo.

"I briefly went to the rock pools *after* I spent the morning searching for my wife."

Gommonaadogo groans. "Please, can we have one day without Okon talking about his wife?"

"I heard you climbed a hill yesterday for a better view of where to look," says Beejalee as she commences stirring what I hope is more uddu in the pot.

"Yes, I did, and although it's going to be difficult, I now have a proper plan for my search. Today was my first day of that plan. I started at the little waterfall near the settlement, from where I'll continue to work my way outwards in increasingly wider circles—Habee's idea. I'll walk counterclockwise so I turn on my good leg, and I'm marking trees as I go so that—"

"Please stop talking," says Gommonaadogo.

"Your wife must be very special," says Babba.

"There must be something wrong with her," says Gommonogo, "otherwise she would be with a better man."

"There is nothing wrong with my wife. She's the most incredible person I've ever met."

"How so?" asks Babba.

"Well, for example, unlike most people, who just like to moan about problems"—I take an exaggerated glance at the Gommo twins—"Efawi actually takes action to fix them. She's driven like no other to make the world a better place."

Babba scratches his head. "What does she do to make the world better?" he asks.

"Many things. For instance, a few days before I last saw her, Efawi and I were in District 5, Magawi City, which is where we're from. We were out in the open, around lots of people, when Efawi noticed a woman being abused by a man. My wife was the only person to rush over and defend her. The man punched Efawi in the face, but that didn't stop my wife from rescuing the woman."

"Why did you not protect the other woman instead of allowing your wife to be hit by a man?" asks Gommonaadogo.

"Because Efawi was—she was just too quick for me. It was all over before I could do anything."

Gommonogo yawns. "What does this boring story have to do with anything?"

"You insulted my wife, so I'm defending her."

"I think his wife does not exist," says Gommonogo. "Okon looks too much like the back end of a *tawatu* to get a woman, even an unassociated one."

"Right, that's it; I've had enough," I say as I wave a finger in

62

the air. "I simply wanted to sit and relax and eat my honey uddu, but clearly that won't be possible."

I press against the chair to get up, but the backrest comes loose and I fall backward. For a moment, I'm stuck with my buttocks on the seat, my head on the ground, and my back arched between the two. I try to move, and the seat itself collapses. I yelp as the stool tips over.

Gasps of surprise are followed by some chuckles. I swivel my head for a worm's-eye view of the amused and concerned Wuchumbu. "If you had helped me build the chair . . ." I grumble. As helpful as many of the tribe have been, they refused to help me build something so unassociated. I hold out an arm, and Beejalee picks me up. I dust myself off and limp toward my hut. The Gommo twins continue to laugh.

"And Gommonogo," I say as I look behind me, "where I come from, I'm told I'm very handsome. That's just one of the many reasons Efawi fell for me." I turn back to where I'm heading, and my face slams into a piece of wood that juts from a dilapidated hut.

"Damn it!" I cry. "Will anyone ever cut down this piece of wood? Every single day someone walks into it, but nobody does anything. I mean, look around. This place is so disorganized."

My head throbs. The Gommo twins are in stitches. I take a deep breath. "Before I came here, I had an idea in my head, a stereotype if you will, that hunter-gatherers were these slick, efficient operators who knew how to be at one with nature—who were uncorrupted, who had wisdom, who would sit around a crackling fire every night exchanging insights—insights about the circle of life or something like that. Insights I could learn from. Insights I need! Well, having lived here all this time, I want you to know I'm deeply disappointed. Not with all of you—just some of you."

I glare at the Gommo twins. Although I try not to think about it, I still hold some resentment for the tribe's attack on me.

Many of them were involved, and most of them have since apologized. They explained to me their mistrust of people from outside the jungle and shared with me the horror stories that were passed down to them. Gommonogo's great-grandfather, for instance, was whipped and his legs cut off because he refused to gather materials from the Nsanba for unassociated people. This might be why Gommonogo broke my leg. A revenge of sorts, but generations too late. What happened to his great-grandfather took place long before Gommonogo or I were even born. Had nothing to do with me.

I open my mouth to continue my rant but spot Mhaawu watching me, her face the usual picture of discontent. She's in her customary spot just to the side of the settlement's central area, where she can sit alone and still see what's happening, her eyes on me more often than the others. Something tells me I should keep my mouth shut.

I look away, rub my head, then risk another glance at Mhaawu, who is now gazing at the sky. Nobody embodies the malaise of the tribe better than her. Many consider Mhaawu to be in charge, but she provides no leadership whatsoever. Her husband, who was Ratu's father, died not long before Ratu was born, murdered by a group of unassociated in the jungle (the last unassociated anyone in the tribe had seen until I showed up).

Most Wuchumbu adults have at least four children, whereas Mhaawu has only one. I don't know if the loss of her husband, along with the difficulties she has with Ratu, have anything to do with her moodiness. On the few occasions I've worked up the courage to speak with her, she's dismissed me with a grunt.

"Okon, please stay and rest," says Beejalee. "I will serve you more uddu. Gommonogo and Gommonaadogo, you are not allowed to talk to Okon for the rest of the day."

I apologize for criticizing the tribe and the settlement, and I'm about to thank Beejalee for being so gracious when I spot two things: Babba ambling past me, and a snake approaching his side from around the corner of the hut.

With no time to think or hesitate, I leap at the boy using my good leg, shove him out of harm's way, and kick at the snake as I fall backward. "Snake!" I yell, pointing at the creature. "There's blood on my shin. I've been bitten!"

Everyone stays where they are. My leg starts to burn.

"Why aren't you helping me?"

"Okon," says Beejalee, "this snake is not dangerous. It is just an egg eater. No venom."

"And no fangs," adds Gommonogo.

The snake disappears beneath the hut. I take a closer look at my shin. The blood is just a scratch, probably from when my chair collapsed. "Not dangerous?" I mutter. "But I didn't know. How was I supposed to know?"

Adienatta and Petonba help me to my feet. "Thank you, Okon," says Babba's mother.

"Yes, thank you," says Babba, who gives me a hug. I'm grateful when the group's attention moves from me to an approaching disturbance: Beejalee's youngest daughter, Hattee.

If Efawi and I ever have a girl, I want her to be as sweet as Hattee. Although at this moment she's screaming her lungs out as she sprints into the communal area and toward her mother. "Obee and Naee saw an unassociated! Obee and Naee saw an unassociated!"

Beejalee lifts her child into her arms. "Where?"

"Where the river curves like a *gowetu*."

"And where are your brother and sister?"

"They said they will hide and watch the unassociated. They told me to get help."

"Is the unassociated person a woman?" I ask.

"I do not know. I did not see," gulps Hattee before she bursts into tears.

"Okon," snarls Gommonogo, "who is this unassociated you have brought here?"

"I haven't brought anyone, but it could be my wife! You mustn't attack them until I—"

"Unassociated are coming! Unassociated are coming!" shouts Babba as he runs around in circles. The communal area fills with Wuchumbu. Big Man and others charge across the opening, handing out bows, arrows, spears, and instructions.

"The strong must go to the river!"

"The children and the weak must stay here!"

"We must kill the unassociated before they find our settlement!"

"Can someone decide if we need masks or not?"

"Wait!" I cry, but nobody's listening as they run back and forth. This must be like the day I arrived, only this time I'm witnessing events from the Wuchumbu perspective.

A hand grabs my arm, pulls me along. "You are coming to the river," says Gommonogo. My right knee catches midstep but refuses to bend. I almost fall over.

"Gommonogo, stop," says Beejalee. She pulls me free from his grip. "Okon cannot walk properly, so he should stay here with those who cannot defend themselves."

I don't know whether to thank her or be offended.

"It's okay, I want to go," I say, "but I can't get there as quickly as the others, and they need to wait for me before they attack the unassociated person."

Before Beejalee can respond, a young boy falls to the ground and is almost trampled on amid the commotion. Beejalee rushes to help him. I spin around looking for Big Man, but it seems a group led by him has already left for the river. The vulnerable are being huddled into the center of the communal area, which is where I already am. Around us, fifty Wuchumbu stand guard, fidgeting with their weapons. Others are forming groups to patrol the settlement. The Wuchumbu's defensive strategy is well rehearsed, and I barely recognize them in such an organized state.

Gommonogo shoves a spear into my hand. "Do not hide

here, coward," he huffs, then storms off with a bow across his shoulder. I scramble after him, but he's quick to disappear among the trees. Big Man's group will already be much further ahead. What if Efawi isn't wearing her armored suit? What if she falls into the river while trying to get away and drowns? I hobble as fast as I can through the settlement, snake my way around the jumbled huts, and enter the naked jungle.

Twenty minutes of struggle later, having traced my way along the riverbank, I arrive at the narrow, shallow section of river that curves like a snake reaching for its tail. The flow is fast here, and the trees grow all the way to the edge, their branches overhanging the water.

A group of armed Wuchumbu, the vanguard, stand and chatter while pointing at something further ahead. As I get closer, the focus of their attention comes into view: an unassociated person in the water—not my wife, not even female, and from the look of him, long dead.

His backpack has been snagged by a low branch, which holds the man's torso partially upright. With the flow dragging his legs forward, his body bobs. Given how he's being held, I can understand why Beejalee's children thought he was alive.

"Who is this unassociated man?" asks Petonba. She's generally friendly with me, and her question is asked nonaccusingly, with the assumption I have the answer. (Everyone knows everyone in the tribe. They find it difficult to appreciate that's not the case outside the jungle.)

"I have no idea," I reply.

Big Man steps into the river, stone hatchet between gritted teeth. He carefully wades toward the dead man through rushing water, and while the Wuchumbu chatter behind me, I step to the edge for a closer look.

The deceased man's face and arms are bloated, and his black skin tinted gray. He looks about thirtysomething. There's no tech about him that I can see, just the backpack and cheap clothing. His hair is a mini-fro, similar to mine when I entered the Nsanba (my hair is now braided courtesy of Adienatta's children). His cheeks carry tribal markings. Could he be from the townships close to the Nsanba that house descendants of people from the jungle? Ceremonial scarring is not practiced by the Wuchumbu, so he must be descended from another tribe. I'm surprised they keep such traditions after being booted from the jungle generations ago. What reason would this man have to enter the Nsanba? I have no answer. And since he has no visible wounds or injuries, the cause of his death is also a mystery. For all I know, he may have died many days ago, hundreds of kilometers upriver, his backpack eventually snagged by this branch as his body passed through.

"Even the crocodiles know not to touch the unassociated," someone whispers.

Gommonogo pokes me in the back. "How many more will come?"

I don't respond. My eyes remain fixed on the unassociated man. If I were to die here, nobody outside the jungle would know what happened. My body could be caught on the river like this and slowly decompose, or be ripped to shreds by crocodiles. Did this man achieve what he wanted in life? Did he say goodbye to his loved ones before he left?

"The shaman has arrived!" Ratu declares. "I am so happy we are all now safe," he adds. The teenager's sarcasm stirs my pride.

The witch doctor totters toward the group with effortful grandeur, his scant weight carried in part by a wooden staff. Today the shaman has gone for his furry headdress: a conglomeration of animal faces stitched together, the load of which his neck struggles to support. Feathers, beads, and bone tied together with vine decorate his neck and wrists. Tattoos made from black fungus cover his arms and chest. His eyes, as always, are red, presumably because he's once again as high as a kite. I wish I had more respect for the tribe's shaman. Most of the Wuchumbu don't have much respect for him either.

Behind the man, his senior apprentice struggles with a bundle of objects (pots, amulets, and whatnots) from which the shaman grabs a wooden carving of the head of a forest antelope with multiple humanlike eyes. The other objects fall to the ground. The assistant waves her hands in despair.

"Step aside, everyone," the shaman commands. He holds the blue-painted carving in front of him like it's a shield. "I will use the power of the great Massas to purge the unassociated spirits from the dead body and banish them from the mighty Nsanba. This may take some time and will require much of my strength, but for the sake of all Wuchumbu I will persist until—"

The sound of a hatchet striking wood, followed by a branch snapping and a splash, interrupts the shaman's moment in the spotlight. We all turn to see the corpse floating away from Big Man and down the river before disappearing out of sight.

Such a shame. I had my eye on the poor man's socks.

The wrinkles on the shaman's forehead extend and deepen. He lowers the carving of their sky god—their "Massas."

"I guess your work here is done," says Ratu. "Once again, you are about as useful as a broken toenail."

I cannot help but smirk, and the witch doctor notices. "Do not be fooled," he cries to the group. "The body in the river may have been cut free, but its spirits linger and will now be more dispersed. My work has been made harder, but I will do what it takes to ensure our people's safety. Take my items to the river. Hurry, you dolt!"

The witch doctor's assistant takes her time to pick up their things from the ground. Half the group mumble a few words of gratitude to the shaman. The rest don't seem to be paying him much attention. Big Man makes his way out of the river, hatchet in mouth, seemingly unaware that he'd spoiled the drama queen's performance.

"Even when I finish my work, we will not be safe from other

dangers," the shaman declares to the group, fixing his gaze on me. "Evil remains among us. Conversing with us. Eating with us. Playing with our children. Involving itself in every facet of our lives." My pulse quickens, and my cheeks warm, but when I look around, I'm relieved to find mostly sympathetic faces. The shaman steps toward me. There's a long gash above his hip, partially covered by his embellishments. The wound looks recent. Caused by the claws or horns of another animal he has slaughtered? I'm not fooled by the witch doctor's feeble appearance. *This is a violent man.*

I grip my spear and hold my breath while he whispers in my ear: "I have seen the evil inside you, Okon. *You*, however, are just a shell. A weak, pathetic creature. This is why you have no children of your own." The shaman draws a few wheezy breaths before he adds, "The weak often find their way to the river."

He steps away from me. My spear is shaking.

"And you, Ratu, are just as unwanted!" the shaman shouts from over his shoulder as he saunters away. "Both you and your friend will die alone, your worthless spirits condemned to the riverbed."

My eyes flick to Ratu, who turns away. The shaman's assistant offers me an apologetic nod, then scrambles after her master. I want to run after him and hurt him. I want him to know he can't talk to me like that. But I stay where I am. Weak and pathetic.

"Are there more unassociated coming?" Gommonogo snarls, spittle flying from his lips. I hesitate with my response; the question doesn't deserve an answer. A hog on the other side of the river commences a vigorous round of grunting.

"Gommonogo, your sister is calling you," says Ratu as he points to the hog.

The group laughs. Gommonogo goes to speak, pauses, then storms off. Ratu talks to the hog, addressing it as Gommonaadogo, but the joke has passed. I struggle to shake the image of the stranger's corpse in the river. I imagine I'm the one snagged by a branch, my lifeless body bopping up and down. I shiver and rub my bad knee.

With nothing left to see or do, the group heads back to the settlement. Although the shaman vowed to stay and complete his "work," I do not see him or his assistant anywhere. Ratu is kneeling beside the river by himself. I hobble toward him.

"You okay?" I ask.

Ratu spins around. I glimpse what appears to be a metal flask, which he now holds behind his back. He must have just found it. Probably fell from the dead man's backpack.

"Yes. Why wouldn't I be?" he replies, his words shaky. He's upset. It's obvious.

I look past him to where the dead body was, and Ratu looks to the same place. "Are you worried you will end up like him?" he asks. "That one day you might fall in and die, or be pushed in by one of the Wuchumbu?"

"Are you?" I reply.

Ratu sighs, then turns to face me, his usual grin replaced by a pout. "On the hill yesterday, I mentioned an idea that you will like very much," he says. "Well, part of the idea involves helping you out of the Nsanba. Okon, meet me tonight when everyone is asleep and the civet makes its first call."

My mind races at the thought of leaving the jungle.

"What does a civet sound like?" I ask.

7: The Close Encounter

A woman crying? Maybe a child? Unless Ratu's demonstration of a civet crying was way off this afternoon, what I'm hearing right now is definitely not a civet, and it's too humanlike for comfort.

I don't like this walking-in-the-jungle-after-dark business. It's dangerous, and the Wuchumbu avoid it for good reason. Animals can be a threat. Nocturnal antelopes have been known to kill people. Leopards mostly hunt in the shadows. The main concern, though, is getting injured or lost, and without the light from tonight's full moon, I would already be the latter, at least.

I keep on limping. I'm still unable to identify the sound of a civet, and therefore I don't know if I'm early or late. I'm skeptical about Ratu's "idea." He's had big ideas before and not followed through. Besides, what if he helps me return to Mbapazu only for me to discover that Efawi isn't there? How would I find my way back to the AZ? Under normal circumstances, I could have my leg fixed, reequip, and return, but I can't if the PPA is still after us and our funds remain frozen. Regardless, I've decided to at least hear Ratu's idea in full before I make any decisions.

I'm now about midway between the settlement and our rendezvous point, and the humanlike whimpering and wailing continue to grow louder. Am I moving toward it or it toward me? I would swear this sound is being made by a person, but I've made that mistake before in the Nsanba. Strange noises and the jungle go hand in hand, especially at night. I stop limping and turn my head to gauge its direction—the wailing is coming from the left.

Although Mhaawu frequently tells the tribe not to venture too far from the settlement, especially when alone (which is about the only instruction she ever gives), what if someone did so and needs help? What if little Babba or Hattee or Buchee woke up in the night and went for a walk and hurt themselves? If I could have helped them, but didn't, I don't think I could live with myself.

I use my stone knife to mark the trees and limp-march to the left. Ratu will have to wait. He's got nothing better to do anyway.

Thirty paces later, I smell smoke.

Another thirty paces and I spot a bonfire. The tribe never lights large fires at night for fear of being seen. I approach with caution.

The silhouette of a short man standing in front of the flames comes into view. I crouch behind a tree and watch as he flounders and makes gurgling noises. The outline of the man's unusual outfit discloses his identity. He slumps to his knees and commences a peculiar falsetto warble. Mystery of the sound solved: the shaman is a nutcase.

He appears to be alone, and tonight he's donned his sexy leopard-fur poncho with the big blue eyes painted onto it. On the ground beside him is a clay bowl and a basket with a pelt draped over the top. The shaman takes a swig from the bowl—the hallucinogenic Massas fruit, I'm guessing—and recommences his rhythmic groaning interspersed with screams, whines, and chanting. He throws up something brown and foul before stumbling around the flames some more. Clearly, I've wasted my time.

I stand up to leave when the chanting reaches a crescendo. The shaman staggers to a stop above the basket and tosses its cover to one side. From the basket emanates a white light that melts into a kaleidoscope of red, gold, and violet.

"Iridescence?" I mutter to myself. In the message Efawi left just outside the Anomalous Zone, she told me to "head as best you can for the center, and remember when you walked in on me crying." I think I get it now.

I cannot see the contents of the shaman's basket, only the light emanating from it, which fluctuates in hue and intensity. Efawi had been in the bath, and when I asked her what was wrong, she said the play of color on the surface of the bubbles had moved her to tears. Was Efawi's instruction a coded way to direct me toward a play of color?

The shaman sweeps the basket from the floor and raises it above his head. "For twenty-four moons, every fiber in my body has told me to activate you, the light in the dark, the light from another place. But the great Massas tells me not to, so I do as the almighty says."

He tosses the basket's contents into the fire: not bubbles, but little cubes that shine with multicolored light and fall like confetti. Although I only catch a glimpse of them before they disappear among the flames, it's long enough to know that whatever they are, they are *not normal.* This must have something to do with why my wife came here—I'm sure of it.

The fire burns white. A wave of heat hits my cheeks and forehead. The shaman releases a spine-tingling howl, and he turns from the fire with flames licking the end of his poncho. The damn idiot got too close.

I remain hidden at a safe distance. The shaman waves his arms as the fire makes its way up his torso. He screams so loud I have to cover my ears. I'm scared, but if I stay where I am, I'll be fine. *No,* I can't just let him burn to death. Efawi certainly wouldn't. The fact that he's an asshole is irrelevant. My conscience forces me to move.

The fire has returned to its usual amber color. The shaman

thrashes back and forth, his entire upper body now engulfed in flames. I grab the pelt that had covered the basket and edge toward him. *Fur flammable? Risk catching fire to save shaman?*

While I hesitate, his wild and blind thrashing leads him toward me. I panic and step on something, possibly the tail of whatever animal this fur belonged to. My bad knee refuses to bend, and I fall forward into the shaman. Instinctively, I hold the pelt between us as my tumble takes us to the ground. I land on top of the witch doctor and roll away from him.

I'm not on fire, but the hairs on my arms and hands are curled and burned, and my face is hot. I touch my cheeks, fearing melted black toffee and exposed bone, but to great relief I find my skin intact. The shaman is lying on his back beneath the pelt, which covers him from the waist up. Smoke rises from underneath. Tiny flames are at his wrist; a set of bracelets burning.

And he isn't moving.

With my heart beating in my ears, I reach for the fur and drag it to smother his burning jewelry. I have to pull hard to free the parts that must have fused with his body. More smoke rises as I expose the shaman to air, but he's no longer on fire. The fumes make me cough. *I'm inhaling burned shaman.* I motion to vomit without following through.

"Are you . . . okay?" I croak.

No response.

Bracing for a gruesome sight, I pull the pelt to one side and shuffle closer to the shaman for a better look. Thank goodness it's nighttime. The bonfire brings a dance of shadows to the shaman's body, camouflaging much of the damage. Already present scars, blemishes, and sagging skin are difficult to distinguish from the fresh burns. On anyone else, the fire damage would look much worse. But he's still not moving, and he no longer seems to be breathing. Is this where I administer mouth-to-mouth? Not that I would know how, but surely I should try?

Still nauseous, I hesitantly lean in, mouth open.

I'm both startled and relieved when the shaman releases a groan before I make contact. His lips quiver as he mumbles something unintelligible. He's probably telling me he'd rather die than receive the kiss of life from an unassociated.

Footsteps thunder toward us. I sit up beside the smoking witch doctor just as Big Man bursts through the trees, followed by ten or so others who collide as they bring themselves to a halt. They don't know where to look: the bonfire, the shaman, or me.

"We heard the screams of a baby," says Big Man.

"He needs help," I reply, as if it weren't obvious. A number of them rush to the witch doctor and kneel by his side. I'm relieved to no longer be in charge.

"Who did this to the shaman?" Gommonogo snarls, his gaze directed at me.

Those tending to the shaman gasp as he musters the strength to raise a skinny, trembling arm in response to Gommonogo's question. Now, unlike the witch doctor, I don't pretend to have prophetic ability, but I know where that wrinkled arm is heading. As predicted, the shaman extends a blackened index finger and points directly at me. *Shit.*

Gommonogo stomps toward me with clenched fists. "You did this?"

I profess my innocence and shield myself as Gommonogo raises a hand to strike, but Big Man catches his wrist, and Etoole grabs the angry man by the waist. Together, they pull the Gommo twin away. "Okon must be punished!" Gommonogo cries as he struggles to free himself.

"Everyone, shut up!" yells Beejalee. "The shaman is trying to say something."

The witch doctor treats us to an extended clearing of his throat before speaking with a croaky voice that's barely audible over the crackling blaze. "I enraged the fire and was standing too close. Okon risked his life to save me."

"Tell me you all heard that," I say.

"Shush, he hasn't finished," says Beejalee.

"Okon is a degenerate, but not a complete degenerate," the shaman adds.

Great. Despite the insult, it seems the shaman's exoneration of me was heard, and Gommonogo's rage subsides enough for Big Man and Etoole to let him go. The group's focus turns to arguing about how best to help the witch doctor. My focus turns to what he threw from the basket. I crawl past everyone for a clearer view of the fire.

Between the flames I see only blackened wood. So I shuffle closer, the heat aggravating my already sore face, but there's no sign of anything multicolored. So I edge closer still, the temperature almost unbearable.

"Okon! Have you lost your mind?" yells Beejalee. She grabs me beneath the arms and pulls me back.

"He threw something in there!" I protest.

"The shaman's spirit has departed," comes a solemn announcement. A chorus of *ohhhs* fills the air. Beejalee lets me go, and I sit back, my eyes on the flames while the Wuchumbu go about doing whatever it is they need to do.

Not long passes before Big Man and others smother the fire with mud and pelts. Everything turns black aside from an optical imprint of the flickering flames. I wait for my eyes to adjust. The taste of burned shaman persists at the back of my throat.

Beejalee puts a hand on my shoulder. "We are returning to the settlement. If you hurt yourself while trying to save the shaman, Big Man can carry you." The towering man bends down to lift me. I wave him away and squint at the blackened remnants of the fire. A small procession of glum Wuchumbu passes by with the shaman's body on their shoulders.

"Tiny glowing squares," I say, "like pieces of light. Cubes, I think. Does anyone know what they are? Red, green, blue, orange. All the colors. All of them!"

"We do not understand what you are saying," says Beejalee, "but it is not safe for you to stay here on your own."

I shake my head. "Beejalee, I finally have evidence of something unusual in the Anomalous Zone. I'm sure what the shaman threw into the fire has something to do with why my wife came here. If I find out what it is, I might work out where she is. I can't let this opportunity slip away from me. I'm going to stay here until it's light enough for me to see what's left among the ashes."

I grab the end of a scorched piece of wood, use it to poke around the ashes, and burn myself in the process. I drop the stick and give my hand a shake. A warm body crouches beside me. "Big Man and I will stay with you," says Beejalee.

Behind me, Big Man stands alert. Everyone else has left. "Now, take some deep breaths," says Beejalee, "and tell me what happened."

8: The Remnants

"My offer still stands, but this is your last chance," says Ratu.

I kick around in the ash some more, my boots vanishing beneath a cloud of dust.

"Meet me tonight," he continues, "when you hear the first cries of the civet—"

"What is it with you and civets?"

"—and I will escort you to the outside of the jungle."

Ratu walks around the pile of burned wood to stand in front of me. He glares, waiting for a response. I stop kicking. "You're standing where he died."

"I do not care," Ratu snaps.

I give my knee a rub and step from the pile of wood and ash. "I don't understand why you're so offended. Yes, your offer is generous, but seeing what I saw last night changes the situation. I finally have a clue. A multicolored clue that could lead me to Efawi."

"Are you crazy? I can help you out of the jungle. You can go home. You and your wife can have sex and make a family like you always say you want."

"She might not be there."

"Well, she is not here."

"We don't know that, and we've been through this already. Besides, even with your help, it would take months for me to limp out of here."

"Nonsense. I saw you climb the rocky hill. You are strong and nimble like an agama."

"A what?"

"Your knee is better than ever."

We both look at my right knee, which is shaped like an old sock filled with marbles.

"Why are you so insistent about this, Ratu? You know if you help me leave, the tribe will hate you even more than they already do."

Ratu's body tightens.

"Sorry," I add. "Didn't mean for that to sound so harsh."

"I do not care if they hate me. I just want to help you reunite with your wife."

"Why?"

"Because I am Ratu, and I am your friend."

"Hmm."

I turn away from the annoying teenager. Clearly, this is a spot the shaman has used many times before. Creepy ornaments made from feathers and bone are dotted about the branches. I hobble over to a short wooden stand that's been wedged between two trees. A litter of objects crowd the surface. Potions, charms, masks, and other things I already rifled through this morning in search of another clue.

In front of the stand is a small carving of the Massas: the Wuchumbu's god of the sky, their most powerful god, who gifted the Earth a hallucinogenic fruit. I pick up the carving and examine its crudely whittled details. The Massas has the head of an antelope with ten almond-shaped eyes. A large mane frames its face, beneath which is a human torso with twice the usual number of arms, thick bird legs, and a pair of wings to boot. The wood has been painted with blue pigment, which is chipped and muddy. According to Wuchumbu mythology, it is the Massas's blueness that gives the color to the sky.

"Efawi would hate all this mythology stuff," I mumble, and an aching stirs in my chest—a need to be with my wife. I instruct my nôvono pro to send her a message.

~Hi there. I know these messages aren't going anywhere right now, but I'm looking at something that reminded me of the time you held an antireligion protest outside that high priest's house. She was the head of some church or other. Oh my, what a stressful day. That was the last time I attended any of your protests.

~Anyway, I saw some multicolored things. Little glowing cubes. I've no idea what they are, but I think they might have something to do with you. You were trying to direct me toward a play of colors, right? Hence your reference to you crying in the bath? Did you come all the way out here for this multicolored stuff? What is it? What does it do? How can it possibly help with our arrest warrants? How can it change the world? As you can see, I have a lot of questions. And I'm trying my hardest to find answers. Around thirty or forty of those cube things were thrown into a fire, but I'm hoping there are more somewhere. It's just that——~

I instruct my nôvono to hit pause. I'm getting angry, which will form a part of the message, and I don't want Efawi to know how I feel. But . . . it's only right for her to know, isn't it? After all, she's the reason I feel it. Why should I have to keep it to myself? I continue with the recording: ~I came all this way, followed your hundreds of instructions, and I'm right here, right where you guided me, so where the hell are you? Why haven't you left me any more instructions? I warned you again and again not to antagonize the PPA. Now look where your actions have gotten us.~

I pause the message once more and take a few breaths. The six months prior to our arrest warrants were difficult for our relationship, probably the most trying time we've ever had. We allowed ourselves to drift apart, and I'm not completely sure why. Despite this drifting, I never stopped feeling close to Efawi. This may sound like a contradiction, but it would be impossible not to feel close to her. We've been together too long, are too engrained in each other. I've known her since I was eight, and we've been married for sixteen years. We became husband and wife as soon as we legally could. Counted down the days until my twentieth birthday and got hitched one day later (as Efawi wanted to make sure my birthdays would remain about me). Even now, when I don't know where she is, she feels close because she's a part of me. If I were cut open, I think there'd be an Efawi-shaped impression on my insides.

I continue with the recording:

~*I'm sorry. I didn't mean to get upset. I know my frustration will be captured in the message, but I guess you should know how I'm feeling. Anyway, I have another question for you. That thing you said about how, with time, we can give each other what we need— well, I'm not quite sure what you mean. Are you saying that, with time, you might change your mind about having children?*~

I bring the message to an end and mouth along with the nôvono pro's standard response: ~*Unable to send message. There are no networks to connect to.*~ My brain implant adds the message to my long list of unsent comms.

"You believe the shaman's stories," Ratu hisses in my ear, jolting me from my internal activities. "You think the shaman threw magical things into the fire," he says. "This is a stupid reason to stay. Besides, you are too fat to find what you are looking for."

"Too fat to find what I'm looking for? What's that supposed to mean? And no, of course I don't believe in magical things."

"But you believe in the Massas?" He points at the carving I'm still holding. "Okon, I worry that you have been living with the Wuchumbu for too long."

I wave the Massas at him. "No, I don't believe in your sky god or any of the Wuchumbu gods of whatever. That would be ridiculous. Isn't there someone else you can go bother?"

I put the carving down and turn back to the burned-out fire. *Someone* in the tribe must know what's going on. I wasn't able to get much information out of Beejalee or Big Man last night. Neither knew anything about the cubes of light. According to Beejalee, the shaman did weird things all the time, and his behavior would often be ignored. I don't understand how he came to be the tribe's shaman, given that the Wuchumbu mostly disliked him and didn't care for his "work." Perhaps he bullied his way into the position a long time ago. Who knows? But Beejalee said he was quite troubled for the past couple of years, during which time his behavior became increasingly erratic.

I turn back to Ratu. "I know I've asked you before, but the date of two years ago keeps coming up. What happened back then?"

"Nothing important," the teenager replies.

"But you told me the Wuchumbu regularly drank the Massas fruit as part of some ceremony and that they stopped two years ago. Why?"

Ratu puffs out his cheeks. "Mhaawu went a bit crazy, that is all. And her craziness influenced everyone else."

Beejalee did suggest I talk with Ratu's mother, who is one of the few people in the tribe I haven't had some kind of dialogue with. If anyone knows anything about the goings-on in the Anomalous Zone, it's Mhaawu. I just don't know how to win her trust so that she'll speak with me.

A pitter-patter of approaching footsteps interrupts my thinking. Babba bursts into the open and skids to a halt between me and Ratu. (Should Efawi and I ever have a boy, I don't want him to be like Babba. Sure, he's warm, kind, and entertaining, but he's also completely uncontrollable.)

"The shaman"—gasp gasp—"has been calling for you, Okon"—gasp gasp—"all morning"—gasp.

Ratu and I exchange a look. We simultaneously grunt, "Huh?"

"Okon, you need to go to the shaman now!" cries Babba. "You are keeping everybody waiting!"

"I thought you said the shaman died last night?" Ratu asks me.

"You mosquito brain," says Babba. "The *new* shaman needs Okon. The shaman's apprentice is now the shaman."

"Okay. Well, why is the *new* shaman calling for me?" I ask.

Babba's eyes widen. "She needs you for the *Hundukkah*."

9: The Hundukkah

The Wuchumbu have filled the central clearing and are spilling out into the trees. Since returning to the settlement with Babba and Ratu, I've been whisked around, unable to get a word in, then plonked here, center stage, at the prior shaman's funeral. Every damn eye is on me. The midday sun beats down like a spotlight. And I still don't know what a Hundukkah is.

Beside me stands the new shaman, the master of today's ceremony. Behind me, the ex-shaman's body lies on a wooden platform that's been placed on a large carving of half the Massas (which is always on the ground in the center of the settlement— I've no idea where the other half is). A variety of smelly botanicals have been dashed about the place, including onto those sitting in the front row, much to their annoyance.

The new shaman smiles at her audience as though she can't quite believe she's finally getting some attention. Her impossibly creased face cuts an even older but much friendlier image than her former boss, and she's already wearing one of her predecessor's costumes, giant headdress included. Raising a feathered staff in the air, she declares, "the ceremony can begin!"

"Begin?" cries an agitated onlooker. "I thought we were almost finished!"

"If the shaman has to lie there any longer," another complains, "he might return and bring this funeral to a close himself."

The new shaman pulls me toward the prior shaman's body. She whips away the fur that was covering his torso and directs my gaze to where his ribcage has been cut apart, his heart ripped out and placed on top of the grisly mess. The restless crowd falls silent.

"Pretty sure he wasn't like this yesterday," I sputter.

"Go ahead," says the new shaman, still smiling. "I am offering you the honor."

I shake my head. "The honor of what?"

She waves me closer, whispers as though sparing me embarrassment, "This is the Hundukkah, and I grant you the honor of first bite." She gestures with a flat palm to the prior shaman's heart as though offering me a slice of cake.

I take a step back and give my throat a tap in case my translator implant is playing up. "Can you say that again?" I request.

The new shaman leans into me, quietly says, "Many powerful spirits live in that heart. My predecessor spent his lifetime drawing them to him so they might bless us all with good fortune. Now they can be passed to you."

"Speak up, we can't hear you!" someone yells.

"Is this a joke?" I ask. "Nobody ate anything at the other funerals."

The shaman frowns, her face a ball of wrinkles. She leans her staff against the wooden platform and scoops up the prior shaman's heart. The crowd gasps. "Now this was worth waiting for," someone remarks.

The witch doctor presents me with the pale pink organ, flies already swarming, blood dripping from her fingers. "I know the prior shaman was dear to you, Okon," she says. "You put your life in danger to try to save his, and he blessed you with his final words. This is why I have chosen you for the honor of first bite."

She edges toward me, and I back away. "I fear for you,

Okon," she says. "You are not from here, and there is corruption within you. One bite will purge you of your evil."

"Maybe you should have the first bite?" I stutter.

"My heart is already full of protective spirits," she replies.

"Well . . . I think someone else should have the honor then."

The new shaman continues to offer me the heart. Why does she even care that I'm the one who goes first? Perhaps she doesn't want to lose face now that she's made me the offer, especially at her first ceremony. Murmurs of unease ripple through the crowd, and I worry I'm offending everyone by not relishing in the "honor" of first bite.

I turn to those watching and catch sight of Mhaawu, who is staring right back. I focus on her puffy eyes, tightened lips, pained brow. This is a woman who's been carrying a weight, a secret, for too long. She knows something about the AZ, about the multicolored things, I'm sure of it. I should have focused my efforts on her sooner.

A soft, wet lump is pushed into my belly. I look down and recoil as the shaman presses the heart against me, the antlers on her headdress almost poking me in the eyes. "The Hundukkah is Wuchumbu tradition," she says.

I turn back to Mhaawu. The tribe's leader narrows her eyes and raises an eyebrow. What does that mean?—does she want me to accept the shaman's offer? Still, I refuse to take hold of the heart. A man near the front stands up and shouts, "This behavior is unacceptable!"

"Boring!" another complains.

I turn back to the shaman. "If I do this, will Mhaawu place more trust in me?"

"Oh, certainly," the shaman replies.

"So, she likes this sort of thing?" I ask.

"She loves it. They all love it. They can barely wait their turn." Her words are all breathy and excited. Not once before today has there been any hint of cannibalism within the tribe.

Perhaps they hid the practice from me, along with their other secrets.

I look back at Mhaawu. To have any chance of finding my wife, I have to find out what's going on in the Anomalous Zone. The prior shaman had the multicolored stuff, so surely the tribe's leader knows something about it too? I can't believe I'm even considering this.

I take hold of the organ, not quite believing there's a human heart in my hands. Heavier than expected, it squelches with the slightest movement. The shaman sighs with relief and rubs her forehead, leaving a smear of blood above her eyes.

I think about the word *cannibal* and how badly I don't want to be one. Does doing the act once mean you're always a cannibal, or is it a practice that must be maintained in order to keep the label? What about someone who bites but doesn't swallow? Blood drips onto my boots, covering the old crimson stains from their previous owner. The tension from the crowd blasts me like a heat from the side. *They want the heart for themselves.*

I bring the lump to my face and for a moment I think I see multicolored flecks twinkling in the organ's muscles. I bring the heart closer, and a waft of fresh meat fills my nose, makes me gag.

"Hurry or I will give the honor to another," snaps the newly appointed witch doctor.

Efawi, I'm doing this to find you. I turn to be sure Mhaawu can see, and I sink my teeth in. I go deeper than needed, but I want a good-sized chunk that can't be doubted. The attendees fall silent, freeze like a picture.

I yank my head away from the heart and check again to be sure Mhaawu has line of sight. A hunk of meat sits on my tongue, cool and tangy. I roll it around, pretending to chew. My stomach convulses. The shaman snatches the heart from me as if I were planning to keep it. She spins around to address the crowd, and I wait for my opportunity to spit the lump out without being noticed.

"Wuchumbu, listen to me," she cries, lifting the heart above her. "The Hundukkah has begun, and now you—"

"He has not swallowed!" yells an onlooker from deep in the crowd. I cannot see him, but I recognize his voice. I vow never to speak to Ratu again.

The shaman turns to me. "You have swallowed, yes?"

I nod and mumble, lips sealed tight. The shaman seems satisfied and turns back to her audience, but the teenager who saved my life isn't finished. "Tell him to open his mouth so we can see!"

I catch sight of him in the crowd, giggling. The shaman sighs. "Open your mouth, my child. Prove to them you have swallowed," she says.

This is all too much. I'm worried about my own heart. I turn to Mhaawu once more, hoping she's already left, but no such luck. She's still watching, assessing my worthiness of her secrets. The gathered tribe members struggle to contain themselves.

"His head is turning red!"

"I am so glad I stayed!"

The new shaman walks toward me. "Open your mouth, Okon."

I take one more look at Mhaawu before I tilt my head back and swallow. The piece of human heart slides down my throat with ease. My stomach hates me. I hate me. The witch puts her hand on my chin and pulls on my jaw, but I open my mouth willingly, stick my tongue out, and roar at the crowd until not a wisp of breath remains.

My frenzy passes to them like a contagion. They jump and scream as if celebrating a home-team score. I even hear a drum when the Wuchumbu have banned drumming for years for fear of being heard. But it's not a drum; it's my pulse thundering.

I did this for you, Efawi. Mhaawu will have to trust me now.

I'm struggling not to vomit. The shaman faces her audience

once more and holds the heart above her head, a piece missing from its side. "Silence, people. The time has come for you to take your turn. Do not all rush at once; step forward one by one."

I brace myself for further mayhem. The crowd exchanges looks among themselves, but nobody steps forward. Nobody says a thing. And after what seems like an age, the silence is broken:

"You want us to take a bite from that?"

"We are not going to eat the shaman's heart. Why would we?"

"That would be disgusting."

"Only an evil person would eat someone's heart."

Oh my; what have I done? The crowd stares at me, and I turn to the new shaman. "You said this was your tradition," I snap. "You told me I should do it."

"Silence," cries the shaman, the confidence in her voice wavering. She lowers the heart to her chest. "My great predecessor told me the Wuchumbu people have lost their way, and that we need to rekindle our traditions of the past. He wanted me to reintroduce the practice of the Hundukkah in the event of his death."

Her words are met with confused faces. I'm losing my sense of reality. Despite being surrounded by the tribe, I am alone. Isolated. A disgusting cannibal left to bake in the sun.

"Surely those of you who are old enough will have heard of the Hundukkah?" the shaman continues. "When someone special from among our people leaves this realm, we must keep within the tribe the good spirits they have garnered. This practice is called the Hundukkah—the eating of the heart."

More confused faces.

"Never heard of it," someone says.

"I am the oldest here, and we have never done anything like that."

"Was still worth waiting for."

"I did not realize Okon is so barbaric. Those from outside

the jungle must be savages."

"Okon is *not* barbaric. The shaman tricked him into doing it."

My blood boils. I march up to the shaman as she stomps over to the prior shaman and drops his heart back into his chest. "So I ate that for no good reason?" I complain. She doesn't respond. She won't even look at me as she gathers her things from around the wooden platform. I look for Mhaawu, but with the attendees jostling as they chatter, I can no longer see her through the bodies. After this debacle, there's no way she'll trust me with her secrets.

Gommonogo brushes past me. "Animal," he snarls. He grabs one end of the wooden platform. "Come, everyone. Let us finish this madness and show our deceased spiritual leader some respect. To the river!"

Long ago, the Wuchumbu stopped cremating their dead for fear of the fire being seen. They now feed their corpses to the crocodiles. A dozen rush forward to help. They lift the platform on which the body lies and rotate it to face the direction of the river. I catch one last glimpse of the prior shaman's face. His lips are tight and upturned—a final mocking smile. They carry him away, with a procession in tow. Finally, this feels like a funeral.

I stare at the ground, hands on hips, not quite believing what I've done. Many of the tribe rub my back as they pass, a Wuchumbu gesture of support.

"I am sorry, Okon."

"I did not understand what was happening until it was too late."

"I would have stopped you, but I could not hear what the shaman was instructing."

My stomach stirs. It wants to vomit, but I cannot bear the thought of more attention, so I resist until the long mourning party has left for the river. While I wait, I try to convince myself I can work out the connection between Efawi and the multicolored light without the need for Mhaawu or anyone to tell me what they know. Did the shaman's heart really contain flecks of the light, or did I imagine that?

The smell of the thing comes back to me. My gagging muscles contract, and my guts spill. The "first bite" flops onto the floor, along with this morning's uddu.

"Not there!" cries the shaman.

She pushes me aside. Thankfully, most of the tribe have left the area, and only the shaman seems to have noticed me puking. Although, thinking about it now, perhaps I should have made a show of it?

The shaman wipes a bundle of leaves that I had inadvertently vomited on. I go to speak but cannot, my throat desperately dry and agitated. I swallow and try again. "Great service today, shaman," I rasp. "You really won them over."

The shaman continues to wipe the leaves while huffing and complaining. "This is very special. I was going to unveil it at the end of the ceremony. You better not have spoiled it."

As she fusses with the thing, I realize it isn't just a bundle of leaves—the leaves are wrapped around something. One by one, the shaman pulls away the leafy layers, and as she does so, I can scarcely believe my eyes. Shining through the wrapping is an emerald light that turns to violet, then amber and red. My vomit led me to it! (In a way, the former shaman led me to it.)

"Put that away!" someone barks from behind us. Mhaawu marches up to the new shaman, snatches the thing from her, and hastily replaces the leaf wrapping until the light no longer shines through. "What is it?" I ask.

The tribe's leader glances left and right, the same way Efawi used to look around when she thought she was being watched. "Tell me where you got this," Mhaawu says to the shaman.

"It was among my predecessor's possessions," the shaman replies.

"What is it?" I ask again. "I've seen that light before. Last night, the shaman, the dead one, threw multicolored things into a fire. And it's connected to my wife somehow—she knows something about it. So, what is it? I have to know." The tribe's leader narrows her eyes. "Please, Mhaawu. This could be my only chance of finding my wife. And if you're concerned about the heart eating, look there—I puked it up. Technically, that means I'm not a cannibal."

"Do not give it to him," says the shaman.

"You do not even know what it is," snaps Mhaawu. "Now leave us."

The shaman huffs but does as she is told. Mhaawu continues to stare at me, assessing me, the wrapped-up thing held against her chest. Her thin body is so tightly wound, I worry it might snap.

"The only people to have seen this," she says, "are the prior shaman, myself, and now the new shaman. Yet somehow you keep stumbling upon the secret light. Tell me, Okon, do the unassociated torture their babies?"

"Excuse me?"

"Answer the question."

"Of course the unassociated don't torture their babies. What does that have to do with anything? Is that a glowing multicolored baby you're holding?"

"How can this be a baby? Do not be absurd. I had heard that the unassociated torture their babies. Now, tell me, how many people are there outside of the Nsanba?"

Apart from Ratu, the tribe doesn't ask me about the outside world. They picture it as a hellish place that superstition prevents them from talking about. "I don't know exactly how many," I reply. "We're talking billions." My last word goes untranslated, so I add, "*Billions* is a very high number. Let's just say there are more people out there than there are trees in the Nsanba." (I've actually no idea how many trees there are in the Nsanba.)

Mhaawu's jaw drops. "That is too many. How can this be

possible?"

"Well, I guess lots of people had lots of babies over many years."

"How many of those outside the Nsanba are good?"

"Mhaawu, can we please talk about the thing you're holding?"

She flicks my forehead with a finger. "*Ow!* It's not right for you to touch me," I complain.

"How many of those outside the Nsanba are good?" she repeats.

"I guess no one is perfect," I huff, "but most people are good. Most are just trying to live their lives as best as they can."

"Do the people outside the Nsanba care about each other?"

"Yes, people care about each other."

"And they have families?"

"Of course."

"Are the unassociated making something that will cause a lot of suffering?"

"Like what?"

"Like a god."

"No. Of course not. How can anyone make a god? Many of the unassociated don't believe in gods anyway. Please, Mhaawu, I have to know what it is you're holding." I lift my hand to protect my forehead.

"Then answer this final question," says Mhaawu. "I suspect Ratu will one day ask you to leave the Nsanba with him, if he has not already done so. If you do ever leave, will you promise not to let him live with you in the world outside the jungle? Doing so would only encourage his ambition to exit the Nsanba."

"I won't let Ratu live with me. I can certainly promise you that."

Mhaawu stands in silence for a moment, shoulders stooped, eyes alert. I glance at the bundle she's holding, excited I might be about to get my hands on it—finally see what this multicolored stuff is.

"I do not know how you came to be here," says Mhaawu, "or how you continue to find your way to the light of many colors, but the fact that you are here and have seen the things you have seen leads me to believe I was right in letting you live, and that you are meant to have what I am holding."

She extends her arms, and I go to take the thing from her, but she pulls it back to her chest. "I have one final question," she adds.

"You said that about the last question."

"Can you promise me you will never show this to anyone nor tell anyone about it, neither the Wuchumbu nor the unassociated?"

"I promise," I reply with confidence.

Mhaawu holds the thing out once more, and I finally take hold of it. Unnervingly, it's about the weight of a newborn baby. I go to lift the leaves, and Mhaawu threatens to flick me on the forehead again. "What did you just promise, Okon?"

"I was only going to take a peek!"

The tribe's leader turns to the witch doctor, who's been watching from a few meters away with a sulky pout. "Come, shaman. We need to talk," says Mhaawu.

"Before you go," I call out, "can you tell me how this is connected to my wife?"

"I know nothing about your wife," Mhaawu answers from over her shoulder.

"Well, is there anything I should know about this thing?"

"If you are meant to know, you will work it out," she says. "Consider this a test."

I look down at the bundle in my arms and feel one step closer to Efawi.

10: The Thing

Now, I'm not the obsessive type, but the multicolored thing has a hold on me. In private places, after making sure Ratu hasn't followed me, I stare at it for hours.

The leaf wrapping is entirely unrelated to the thing itself, which I assume is only kept covered to hide its glow. Once the multiple layers of leaves are removed, I'm left with an object about twenty centimeters long, less than half as high, and shaped like a sphere stretched at two ends. Comparable perhaps to a stubby submarine without the rudders. But irregular. More like a battered submarine. And there are little blunt horns dotted about its surface.

The most striking feature of the thing, what really sets it apart from everything else, is its multicolored glow. Fragments of pulsating light flow along its surface and form geometric patterns that morph and radiate and retreat in ever-changing ways. When it's held in my hand, I can feel tiny nodules rise and fall in time with the changing light. If I stare at the thing for long enough, the dancing light expands until it is all I see and my heart races.

After five days of looking at this thing, I've not been able to deduce what it is made of, but it is hard, is a little heavy for its size, and makes no sound when I shake it. The object does emit a fragrance, similar to the flowers sometimes gathered by the Wuchumbu, which I used to find unpleasant but I quite like now.

As fascinating as the multicolored thing is, and as much of my time and thinking as it has occupied, Mhaawu's gift hasn't gotten me any closer to my wife, because I still have no idea what it is or where it came from or how many of them there are or how this submarine-shaped thing relates to the shaman's little cubes or where the shaman got his cubes from or why he threw them in a fire or how any of this relates to Efawi.

I've fired questions at Mhaawu every day, but the only ones she ever answers are those about Efawi, and her response on that matter is always the same: "We know nothing of your wife. We have never seen her."

To make matters worse, yesterday afternoon I was alone by the river with my gift from Mhaawu, and I fell into a trancelike sleep while engrossed in the dancing light. When I woke up, the thing was gone.

11: The Metal Ant

This morning I awoke early again, having dreamed of patterns of light. I left the settlement at dawn, came to the river alone, and tracked the same route I've searched three times already. Twenty days have passed since I lost the multicolored thing, and I haven't dared tell Mhaawu.

My current working theory is I rolled over or swung an arm while napping by the river and knocked the thing down the sloping bank. I've been giving myself a harsh time ever since— criticizing myself for blowing this chance to find Efawi, which makes me want to curl up and disappear. I try to remind myself that all I did was fall asleep. The thing made me stare at it for so long that inevitably I would become drowsy. Could have happened to anyone—couldn't it?

Today I'm searching the furthest downstream I've been, well outside the Anomalous Zone. If the thing floats, who knows how far the river might have carried it. I try to get as close to the water as I can, hoping to spot the thing washed up and waiting for me, all pretty and wet. As I hobble along the edge of the bank, struggling to maintain my balance, I recall the deceased shaman's words: "You are a weak, pathetic creature . . . The weak often find their way to the river."

A man's voice interrupts my cheerful thoughts: "Nasty injury you have there."

A moment passes before I realize something unusual: this man's words didn't need translating from Wuchumbu. "Careful you don't make it worse by falling in," they add with concern, once again in my native Mbapaz. I spin around to find an ant-like humanoid leaning against a tree, the shock of which almost results in their words coming true. I ready myself to run, then remember that running isn't something I can do anymore.

I steady myself. The metal ant lifts a hand. "Good to see you again, Okon. Nice boots. Seems a lot has changed since we last met." A slight distortion in the sound indicates the voice is being run through a speaker.

I open my mouth, but don't know what to say.

"It's me," the metal ant chirps. "Efawi's friend, Thembe. Your wife and I used to work together. Aren't there crocodiles here?"

He steps toward me in what I assume is an armored body suit, headgear included, maroon and much thicker than mine, as though designed for battle rather than long-distance treks. Its intricate panels of shielding fit together in insect-like segments. Instead of a see-through visor, ten or so black dots, which I assume are cameras, must be feeding images to the wearer.

"We met many years ago," he adds. "Perhaps you don't remember?"

His name doesn't ring a bell. "Might help if I could see your face," I say.

"Good point. This is my first outing since I arrived, and I was told I need the armor in case any of your friends make an appearance. Seems like overkill to me." He stops a couple of meters from me. In my flimsy grass loincloth, I may as well be naked. "I'm an independent consultant to the PPA's Sensitive Interests Division," he continues, "and, as mentioned, I'm a longtime friend of Efawi. She and I don't see much of each other these days. Our schedules don't make it easy to maintain friendships, unfortunately. You are free to verify my ID."

He holds out his wrist, and I stare at him like an idiot. I flick a bug from my leg without glancing down. The metal ant keeps his arm out and looks around, revealing more cameras on the sides and back of his helmet. I'm lost for words, panicking at his mention of the PPA. I focus on unimportant details, such as why he needs to turn his head when he has cameras facing every direction.

"Of course," he says as he pulls his arm back. "You have nothing to scan with. Forgive me. I didn't get much sleep on my journey here."

I continue to stare at him, then ask if he knows where my wife is. "I'm afraid not," he says. "Do you?"

"No. So, are you here to arrest me?"

"Absolutely not."

"Well, in that case, it's been nice to meet you, but I have some things to do."

I take a couple of side steps in the settlement's direction, and this apparent longtime friend of Efawi's hops onto a boulder and looks into the river. His movement is surprisingly agile, given the robustness of his suit. "Okon, aren't you going to ask me how I found you or why I'm here?" He turns from the river to look down at me.

"Well, you said you're PPA. Efawi wouldn't want me talking with anyone from the PPA."

He huffs as if offended. "I certainly am not the People's Popular Alliance. I'm an independent consultant *to* the PPA. They are a client of mine; I am not one of them."

"So, are the PPA here?"

The metal ant nods. "They set you up, Okon. Pressured you into leaving your house in the hope you would lead them to your wife."

"I led them here?" I ask, my voice shrill.

"Apparently you were carrying a tracking-enabled device. They simply followed you as you traveled to a second location, an unregistered villa I'm told, then on to the jungle."

Efawi's instructions had been clear: take all steps necessary to ensure the PPA never find out about the Anomalous Zone. And I had followed her instructions for the most part. She did tell me to leave my tracking-enabled devices at home, and I left my tab in the car by mistake, but its battery was dead. Surely, they couldn't track a dead tab?

"Did you really think it would be so easy to get away from the PPA?" he adds.

I look up at the sky. "So, they've been here all this time, watching me?"

"Not from above. The entire Nsanba is a strict no-fly zone, of course. A team of agents followed you through the Nsanba on foot and have been observing you as best they can while keeping their distance, especially with your friends around. I've been told the area contains electromagnetic disturbances that have been hampering much of the team's equipment, making their observations of you difficult."

I led them here. Efawi will be furious. The Wuchumbu will be furious.

"Okon? You seem uncomfortable with my presence, but you should know I had nothing to do with the PPA pressuring you out of your home. This is a big case, with many teams involved, and the good news is that I've been placed in charge of operations in the Nsanba. This means you have someone on your side. Someone who doesn't want Efawi to come to any harm."

I take a few more steps in the settlement's direction. "All this effort just to find my wife? Doesn't the PPA have anything better to do?"

"Well, they're bound to take sedition seriously. Then the discovery of the unusual field here gave rise to an even more complex set of concerns."

"The charges against my wife are nonsense. They must be. And the charges against me—ridiculous. How can I be guilty of unlawful interference in democratic processes? I barely leave my home. I'm not interested in politics. I don't even watch the news."

The metal ant puts his hands on his hips. "We have a lot to talk about. Why don't we head back to base, where we can more comfortably go through everything?"

"You have a base here?" I ask, my shock evident by my squeal.

"Yes, outside the area of interference, about a two-hour walk from where you're living. A basic, temporary construction. Our presence in the Nsanba needs to be clandestine, so we're keeping our footprint small. But we have medical staff and a Valaddo." He points at my knee. "Could fix you up. I've seen the Valaddo repair a lot worse."

I've been fantasizing about using a Valaddo ever since my knee was damaged. "You're offering to fix my leg even though I'm a wanted man?"

"You don't have to worry about that for now. When we get to base, we can go through the details. I want us to put our heads together and see if we can work out where Efawi is. Make sure she's safe. We can use the asymm scooter and be there in no time."

"Asymm scooter?"

"They're not available to the public and apparently are beyond the considerable reach of Efawi too. Asymms are excellent for terrain like the jungle. I was brought here on one. Okon, I want you to know that you're not in any danger from the PPA. In fact, you're in a very important position, and the team here will go to great lengths to ensure your safety."

I consider this for a moment. "So, you're definitely not PPA?"

"Absolutely not. I accepted this contract for one reason only: to ensure the wellbeing of my friend, Efawi."

"What did you say your name is again?"

"Thembe."

I stare at him blankly. The name means nothing to me. The metal ant shakes his head. "This will not do," he says, and moves his gloved hands to his neck while mumbling something about the suit being a barrier to communication. A few swift hand movements later, and Thembe lifts his helmet over his head. "That's better," he says. He looks at me with a confident smile. His eyes are bright, his face strong featured, his skin as dark as mine. "We met at one of those Sabano annual dinners," he adds.

I don't usually pay attention to my wife's work friends, and I wouldn't normally remember my interactions with them, but as I study this man's face, a familiarity stirs. Years ago, at one of Efawi's dull business functions, he made an effort to talk to me. Just some small talk, but I remember it because usually at these events the attention is all on Efawi and I barely get noticed— except for some glances from some of the women. I remember thinking this guy seemed alright compared to Efawi's other business associates.

"I remember you now," I reply. "It was about five years ago."

"I believe you'd not long quit being a chef," says Thembe, "although I don't recall where you'd been working."

"It would have been at a, um, small, boutique sort of place."

Thembe nods enthusiastically. "Your wife has told me about the wonderful love story you two make. How you were poor kids from block housing. Neighbors with nothing good in your lives apart from each other, and that you've been together ever since. Efawi and I used to work together long before she became the success story she is today. She asked me if I wanted to join her at her first company."

"Her first company?" I ask.

"Yes. Riltolo."

"That wasn't her first company. Efawi and I started several business ventures together long before that, before she won her grant to study engineering."

"Oh right. I wasn't aware," says Thembe. "How lovely that

you used to work on ventures together before she qualified. Well, anyway, Efawi had even offered me a small stake in Riltolo, but I turned her down and went into consultancy. If only I'd known that two years later she'd sell the business for three hundred thousand Mbapazu standard."

He laughs, his teeth just the right shade of white. Now that he's reminding me, I do recall Efawi mentioning his name a while ago. Work stuff.

"Obviously, she'd then go on to found Sabano," Thembe continues, "and nowadays I'm occasionally involved in some of the international negotiations around Efawi's satellite technology. She's an incredible woman. A rebel. Very strong. Very determined. You're a lucky man, Okon."

We stare at each other in a moment of awkward silence before Thembe hops from the boulder. "Come," he says. "We have food that isn't made from boiled African yams, and I'm starving. I haven't eaten since I arrived this morning. But I won't force you to join me. The choice is yours."

I turn back to the river. The multicolored thing most likely went straight to the bottom of the murky water, and that's probably for the best. Wouldn't want the PPA to get a hold of it. But I do want to see those lights again. Hold the thing close so the light is everything. I've considered asking Mhaawu if she has another one, without mentioning that I lost the first. But if she works out I lost it, she'll never trust me again.

"Before I interrupted you," says Thembe, "you seemed to be searching for something in the river?"

"Er, yes . . . Efawi."

"Well, that's depressing." Thembe shakes his head. "Let's see if we can get your knee fixed up, then you'll have a better chance of finding her—not in the river, I can only hope."

Do I really have a choice, or is he just playing games? He does seem sincere in his concern for Efawi, and I'm pretty much stuck in my efforts to find her. With two functioning knees, I certainly would do a better job of searching.

"You said the team here will ensure my safety because I'm in an 'important position.' How so?"

"Okon, you are at the center of something much larger than you realize. I can explain all this at the base."

My heart quickens at the unpleasant thought of being at the center of something. Regardless, the PPA won't be leaving this place until they get what they came here for—and if they want to arrest me, they can do so whether or not I voluntarily visit their base. There's no need for them to lie about having Valaddo to entice me. So it would probably be best if I go with this "independent consultant" now, get my knee fixed, and hear what he has to say.

Before leaving with Thembe, I glance around to be sure we're alone. If the Wuchumbu were to see me with this man, they might get the wrong idea and think I'm colluding with the unassociated.

As we head south, away from the river, I catch sight of a figure following us, head to toe in armor with camouflage veneer and a rifle in hand. "Just an escort for security purposes," I nervously mumble. "Thembe said I'm important."

12: The Valaddo

When I awake, my head hurts more than my knee, which is strange after having knee surgery. Must be the anesthetic. In any case, I'm not sure what I had was technically *surgery*, not in the traditional sense, not with a machine like the Valaddo. The operator described the procedure as "the provision of salubrious stimuli optimized for rapid rejuvenation"—or something like that.

Whatever it did, I can't stop stroking my knee, which is a little red and a little swollen but otherwise beautifully normal. I'm not surprised by the result. I used a Valaddo a few years back after breaking my ankle. I'd fallen down the stairs wearing a VR headset.

The PPA's base is made from prefab panels. Like the Wuchumbu, they've topped their site with green foliage and appear to have minimized any clearing of trees. From what I've seen, the base is single story, not big, perhaps a dozen rooms. I am alone in one of these rooms, their air-conditioned recovery room, wrapped in a plush white gown and lying on a soft leather bench. The luxuries are whetting my craving for home.

A knock comes at the door. "Your food is ready, sir. Would you like me to bring it to you?" The service has been excellent. Could be fooled into thinking this is a retreat. I sit up and slide into a pair of cotton slippers. My head still aches, but my right knee bends with ease. I've been advised to wait ten days before undertaking any vigorous activity. Nevertheless, the joint is back to normal, bone and ligament aligned. No lumps where there shouldn't be any.

I request the food be brought to me, and a young soldier wheels in a generous spread and leaves me to it. Fried antelope, barthii rice, cheese, fruit, and plenty more. A perfect morning (aside from the Valaddo almost going to town on my left knee before the operator intervened and guided it to my right).

I'm so focused on putting food in my mouth, I don't look up to see who enters the room next. "Sorry to keep you waiting. Have been in a very frustrating meeting with head office."

Thembe takes a seat beside the bench as I bite into a juicy pickled shea. I'm unsure whether I should offer him anything. I choose not to.

"How's the knee?" he asks.

I nod and hold my leg out, mouth too full to speak.

"And the food? We mostly store synthesized meal packs, but I instructed them to serve you the best we have."

"The food's delicious," I say, and reach for a napkin to wipe the spatter from my lips. Thembe smiles, places his palms together in front of him. With his saturated brown eyes, dimpled jaw, and perfectly smooth skin, he's too handsome not to have been cosmetically enhanced. He looks like he's in his midforties, which probably means he's at least midfifties.

"How were you able to have a meeting with head office when there's no network out here?" I ask before stuffing my mouth with warm nutbread.

"The PPA has positioned short-range transmitter-receivers every fifty meters from this base to a facility just outside the Nsanba. This creates a narrow corridor through which encrypted communications can flow. A lot of effort, but necessary, as we're not permitted to send powerful long-range broadcasts to and from the Nsanba, since other states might detect them. You are aware of the political sensitivities regarding there being an Mbapazu presence—or any human presence—within the boundaries of the Nsanba jungle?"

"Yes, of course," I reply, although my knowledge of the subject is sketchy. I do know that each nation in the region has claims over the Nsanba that were not resolved by The War. For fear of further fighting, a treaty was signed by all parties, agreeing that none would take up a presence in the jungle until the dispute was resolved. The dispute was never resolved.

Thembe continues, "So you can imagine the reaction at the PPA's head office when the team who tracked you through the jungle discovered there are people living out here. Furthermore, that they live within an area where there appears to be technological activity: electromagnetic disturbances, problems with equipment, strange readings, and so forth."

"I imagine the PPA lost their shit when they found out about this place." I spot a pair of socks and underpants laid out in the corner. My day keeps getting better.

"That's right," says Thembe. A hint of gray at his temples, most likely by design, adds to his air of authority. "I'm pleased you already appreciate the broader political landscape," he continues. "Saves me time explaining the severity of the situation."

I nod enthusiastically, reach for the pancake topped with yogurt, and wonder whether Thembe and his team know anything about the multicolored stuff.

"So," I say, "what does all this have to do with Efawi?"

"I was going to ask you the same question."

"Well, I already told the officer who kindly broke into my house with a RAIDsquad that I know nothing about my wife's activities."

"And yet you knew to come here."

I choke on pancake, cough bits onto the floor. I only knew to go to the AZ because my wife's nôvo-messages guided me to where she'd left further instructions, and in those instructions she made it very clear I mustn't tell anyone about our nôvono pros. The PPA doesn't know about them because they're not registered in our names, courtesy of my wife's paranoia. If the government had known about our brain implants, they would have shut our nôvo-comms down like they did everything else when the arrest warrant for Efawi was issued.

I sip some juice while I make up a lie.

"Efawi left a set of instructions in the house for me in case of an emergency," I reply. "I guess she anticipated the PPA might suddenly isolate her. The PPA's RAIDsquad missed it, and I didn't spot the instructions for days. But she only gave me very limited information. She trusts me, obviously, but she was worried I might be vulnerable to interrogation. So she only told me just enough to get me here."

Thembe lifts his chin and peers down his nose at me. "And she had prepared trekking equipment for you in advance?"

"That's right. She prepared everything in secret at her villa and had purchased two of everything, one set of trekking gear for her, one set for me. I had no idea this was happening. Thought she was just busy working like usual. So, you and the PPA don't know why Efawi came to this place?"

"No. We do not."

I'm not sure if I should be relieved to hear that. I recommence picking at the food and intermittently glance up at Thembe while he seems lost in thought. Despite being in the jungle, the man has kept himself tidy. His skin is free from insect bites, his hair is groomed, and his nails are clean, trimmed, and polished. My fingernails remain lined with dirt despite the shower before my procedure.

"Do you miss her?" Thembe asks.

"Of course I miss her. She's my wife. She's all I can think about."

"The file says you were having relationship issues before she left."

How does the PPA know about that? My stomach groans. I will myself to stop eating and lean back from the food trolley.

"What was her state of mind the last time you saw her?" Thembe asks.

"On her last day at home she attempted to hit a man over the head with a spade outside our front gate," I reply, a little too flippant, and I immediately wish I'd said less.

"A PPA agent," Thembe replies. "Yes, I was made aware."

"So, that *was* an agent outside our house?"

Thembe nods. I didn't believe Efawi at the time. Thought she was being paranoid.

"Did you have any reason to be angry with your wife before she left?" Thembe asks, his expression blank. His tone flat.

"No, of course I didn't. What does that have to do with anything?"

"Had you been arguing much?"

"Define 'argue.'"

"When did you last have sex?"

"Are you kidding me?" We last had sex the morning of the day she left, VR headsets on and BangAtar app running as usual. I don't remember the last time we did it without headsets. And none of this is Thembe's business.

"Despite being gone for days, you weren't concerned about your wife's whereabouts?"

"I didn't know there was an issue until the RAIDsquad broke in and told me about the charges against her. A few days before she left, she mentioned going on a work trip, and she frequently goes on work trips, sometimes longish and abroad and offline. Often at short notice too. So, I thought nothing of it."

"And Efawi not saying goodbye before she left, not calling you from the airport at least, didn't raise your suspicion?"

"She was so busy all the time, and I've been absorbed in my own thing. We hadn't been as good at communicating as we normally would. I've been through this already with the officer at my house." I take a deep breath. Thembe nods, judging.

"Okon, you should know that some within the team have raised the possibility that you killed your wife, either intentionally or by accident, and that you came here on the run, perhaps looking to defect, and stumbled across this unusual place in the Nsanba."

"Ridiculous."

"I'm aware, but you have a right to know that this possibility has been raised, and some might find it hard to believe you knew so little about your wife's activities. It's as if you don't talk to each other."

"Of course we talk," I snap. "Tell me, do you have a partner? Someone you've been with for more of your life than not?"

Thembe silently stretches for the last slice of antelope.

"Because if you don't," I continue, "then you wouldn't understand. Efawi and I have been together for so long, and we are so damn close, we can afford to have periods of time where we're a bit distant with each other, because we know our relationship will outlast whatever phase we go through."

"I see," he says, his face unreadable. "Let's move on to something else," Thembe suggests. "Her interview with *The Unseen Prison Show* the day before she left. Efawi told the host that she had learned of 'something new at our door' and that she is going to 'let change in.' Any ideas?"

"No. None. Efawi and I have a deal: she doesn't involve me in her battles with the PPA, and I don't hassle her about them. I've never approved of her protests or agreed with her frustrations about the government. Until this mess happened, I didn't really have anything to do with the PPA, and they didn't seem so bad to me. I thought Efawi was making trouble where there was none. Anyway, our deal is why she doesn't tell me about this stuff. She is honoring our agreement."

Thembe nods, silently judging me again. Not knowing all

these things about my wife's life doesn't make me a bad husband, does it? Perhaps Efawi deserves better? These questions lead me down a familiar pattern of thought: If Efawi and I hadn't gotten together when we were young, made our commitment to each other long before she was so successful, would she ever even consider being with someone as unremarkable as me? Of course, Efawi has never said anything that should lead me to question this, but the thought sometimes troubles me nonetheless.

"This must all be very difficult for you," says Thembe. "Being abandoned by someone you love is a terrible thing."

"She hasn't abandoned me!" I push the trolley from between us, and it squeaks as it rolls away. "I'm sorry, but you're wrong about that. Efawi had no choice. Once the PPA shut her down, she had no means of contacting me or returning to the house. Do you know what our marriage's mission statement is?"

"Your marriage has a mission statement?"

"Our mission statement is 'Apotheosis through union.' This means that by being together, we make each other the best we can be. So, yes, we may have been going through a rough patch, but she would never abandon me, and I'll never stop looking for her. Without doubt, we will be reunited."

"And I sincerely hope you will. I assume the mission statement was her idea."

I fold my arms and shake my leg. Thembe sits still while keeping his gaze on me. "Okon, we should get to the point," he eventually says. "Efawi has made many enemies within the PPA. For the most part, the charges against her—and you by association—are bogus. Politically motivated. As such, there is a path open to Efawi where your arrest warrants are revoked, and you return home together as free citizens." He leans forward, his breath antelopy. "Your wife has something the PPA wants. If we can persuade her to stop being so stubborn and cooperate, they will drop the charges. So, it's in Efawi's interest to turn herself in."

Thembe sighs and rubs his forehead. "I fear for her, Okon. I really do. If at any point you make contact with your wife, you must convince her to swallow her pride and compromise with the PPA. If she remains on the run, then she remains a target, and that's a dangerous game to play. Do you understand?"

I nod, and Thembe leans back in his chair. Although I'm not convinced I can trust this man, the fact that the PPA is going to such great lengths to find Efawi is evidence enough that she's in significant trouble. What could she possibly have that they want so badly? What did she do to bother them so much? For years I've been telling her she takes her protesting too far.

"So, let's talk about the jungle people," says Thembe. He smiles, and his dimple deepens.

"You mean the Wuchumbu?" I ask.

"Is that their name? We didn't know. They aren't on any records."

"They refer to themselves as Wuchumbu a hundred times a day. I thought the PPA was observing us?"

"Well, the fact that we didn't know their name demonstrates the difficulty the team has been having. Observations on the ground have been hindered by the dense vegetation and the need to avoid being sighted by the jungle people. Plus, the team's been unable to use micro-drones or any monitoring equipment due to the interference in the AOI."

"AOI?"

"Area of Interest—the area with the unusual readings. The PPA can't even use satellites to make observations, given the current ban on government-controlled satellites above Central Africa."

"Efawi has already named the area the AZ, which stands for Anomalous Zone. I think AZ sounds better than AOI."

"Well, having lived with the tribe inside the 'AZ' for the past one hundred and ten days, you must have worked out a lot more than us about what's going on."

Thembe stares at me expectantly. I stand up and shuffle to the trolley in my robe and slippers, and I pick at the bush butter, despite being more than full. "I've learned some things," I say, "and I've been working on some theories, but I was attacked when I arrived. It took a month for me to recover enough just to stand, and most of the rest of my time has been spent hobbling around the settlement. The tribe insists they haven't seen Efawi and that I'm the first unassociated person—the first person with no association with the tribe—that they've seen in years."

"Do you believe them?"

"I believe they don't know anything about Efawi."

"What else have you learned?"

"Well, I guess most of what I've learned has been about living with the Wuchumbu. So, I'm afraid I have nothing further that might be useful to you. I'm sorry." I head to the other side of the room, grab the socks, and add another "sorry."

"Okon, you have nothing to apologize for. Most would not have made it this far, which is very far indeed. As to the information you have acquired regarding the tribe, this may well come in handy."

"In handy for what?" I ask.

"For finding Efawi, of course."

I don't see how. I pull the new, clean socks over my bruised, sore feet, the state of which reminds me that this morning's modern luxuries are only a distraction. It may be a while before I get to wear my own socks again.

"Does the tribe have a leader?" Thembe asks.

"They have a leader of sorts," I reply. "A woman called Mhaawu."

"And what is this *Mhaa-wuu* like?"

"She, um . . . let's just say she keeps herself to herself most the time."

"Does she have any relatives?"

"Her husband died a long time ago, but she has a son, Ratu."

"The name sounds familiar. You've been spending a lot of time with this boy, yes? The team has seen you together. They've heard you angrily shout his name. Tell me, is *Mhaa-wuu* close to her son?"

"They don't get along, but she cares about him. Shouldn't we be talking about how to find Efawi?"

"Ratu is the one with the missing arm, correct?"

"Yes."

"Well, that works out perfectly." Thembe stands up suddenly. I flinch and spill juice on my robe. "It's time to get things moving," he says. "Head office has grown impatient with the lack of progress. They want answers, Okon, and I need to deliver them or they'll replace me with someone from within the PPA. Someone who will be overly forceful and cause more harm than good."

Thembe marches toward the door. "We need you out of the robe and socks and back into the loincloth right away."

"But why?" I ask.

He stops with the door half open. "Because I'm going to pay the hunter-gatherers a visit, and I need you to help me win them over."

13: The Arrival

The short, slightly knock-kneed Wuchumbu fellow, whom I know by face but not by name, throws a wet fist in the air. "If an unassociated man comes here, I will poke his neck with a spear and nobody can convince me otherwise!"

I told Thembe this was a bad idea.

But he insisted and asked I go ahead of him to prepare the tribe for his arrival. "There mustn't be any poking!" I cry as I hurry through the settlement, looking for Mhaawu. I take care not to slip on the ground, which is wet from this afternoon's downpour—now a drizzle. My right knee remains sore but functional. The Wuchumbu were in disbelief when they first saw me running. ("No, I didn't use magic to fix my leg"; "No, I didn't strike a deal with an evil spirit"; "It was unassociated know-how that fixed it.")

Their interest in my knee was quickly displaced by my news that an unassociated man called Thembe is on his way. And as word of his imminent arrival spreads, the number of soaked Wuchumbu in the central clearing grows rapidly.

"Okon, an unassociated man is coming here?" asks Beejalee.

I stop running and spin around, spot Beejalee amid the bustling crowd, her face full of concern. "Yes, and he mustn't be attacked," I reply. "Where's Mhaawu?"

Before Beejalee can answer, I'm jostled back by a group

handing out spears. "We need to put the weapons away!" I cry.

Beejalee says something further, but it's becoming hard to hear as erratic shouting echoes through the central clearing. I catch sight of Big Man rushing past, and I chase after him as he issues instructions and the tribe goes about their defensive routine of ushering the vulnerable to the center, arranging guard, and forming groups to patrol and meet the threat. Finally, Big Man spots me amid the commotion.

"Okon, when will the unassociated man get here?" he asks with urgency.

"Soon," I reply.

A hand grabs my arm and spins me around. "You invited an unassociated man here?" snaps Etoole, his short, stocky frame all tight and ready for battle. "Why? What does he want?" he adds.

"I didn't invite him; he insisted. And I don't know exactly why he's coming. All he would say was that he wants to help the tribe." As unsure as I am about Thembe's trustworthiness, he did follow through with his promise of the Valaddo and the food and the PPA not arresting me. So, I can only hope he continues to stay true to his word.

"We do not need any help," spits Etoole. "Especially from an unassociated."

"Well, whatever he does, you must not attack him," I say. "There'll be severe consequences if you do. The people he represents are incredibly powerful."

"So we should allow him to stroll into our home without challenge?" asks an incredulous Etoole.

"Yes, that's exactly what you should do. He has body armor—the thing that was around my body when I first came here, except his is even better. You won't be able to stop him."

"The unassociated man is almost here!" Babba yells.

The throng grows even more agitated, and I'm unable to stand still for all the jostling. Gommonogo appears beside us, half bumping into me. "Maybe we can take Okon hostage and use him as leverage?" he proposes.

"No, I will not do that to Okon," says Big Man.

"Me neither," says Etoole. "Has Mhaawu given any instruction yet?"

"Of course not," says Gommonogo.

"Can we put the weapons away, at least?" I request for the umpteenth time.

"No," says Big Man. "If we cannot attack the unassociated man, we should at least demonstrate we are willing to fight if we have to."

"He's here! Over here!" someone yells.

Bodies push past me as they head toward the shouting. I step onto one of the randomly strewn logs. Spears, bows, arrows, clubs, hatchets, and rocks all bop and quiver amid a turbulent sea of Wuchumbu. "Calm down, everyone," I plead. "Calm down!" The unassociated man steps into the central clearing. "Oh no," I mutter. "Where is your metal ant suit?"

Composed of a burgundy satin shirt, white trousers, and brown shoes, Thembe's outfit is fitted, stylish, and useless. Soaked too. Despite this, he approaches with confidence. A tall, athletic figure who strides with his chest out, muddy water splashing his shoes, the crowd parting to give him space.

Moments later, two others emerge from the trees, flanking either side of him. Tip to toe in body armor, they carry rifles, massive ones that are surely too heavy to hold without the aid of an exoskeleton. They point their death-sticks to the ground. Had Thembe specified he would arrive alone, or had I assumed it?

The appearance of the three unassociated has caused the tribe to freeze with weapons tightly gripped. Despite Thembe's bulky security, he's not safe. Only one Wuchumbu has to panic and let fly an arrow or a spear for the independent consultant's life to be over. Efawi's friends are meant to be smart, but clearly she made an exception for this one.

Thembe spots me standing on the log and waves from across

the clearing—mistake number two. Big Man jumps toward him, spear raised, and the two guards lift their rifles.

"No, Big Man!" I cry. "They'll kill you!"

Big Man holds his position, a demonstration that he's willing to fight like he said. He raises his other hand, palm flat, a signal to the rest of the tribe, who jump and holler and wave their weapons in the air in what I assume is an attempt to intimidate the unwelcome visitors.

With their rifles aimed at the anxious tribe, the two guards edge together, squeezing Thembe between their backs. Somehow, the independent consultant appears undisturbed. His arms hang loose at his side, his chin held high while he observes the Wuchumbu dance around him in the spray. His confident defiance reminds me of Efawi.

After what feels like an age, Thembe speaks to the armored figures, who aim their rifles at the tops of the trees and unleash a round of bullets. The gunfire is surprisingly quiet, silenced to pops and hisses, but branches explode into pieces, birds scatter, leaves dance in the air.

I jump to the ground and cower. Some of the Wuchumbu do the same, while others remain standing but concede their threatening display. Not until everyone has lowered their sticks and rocks does Thembe instruct his armored associates to stop firing. He steps from between the two guards, straightens his shirt, and surveys the sea of Wuchumbu, many of whom remain crouched or sprawled on the ground.

"Let's start again, shall we?" he says, his words translated by what must be a translator implant of his own. "I have been authorized to come here, to location G7XY52.R32.771, to issue the following order: The Office of National Defense, as decreed by the Court of the Premier of the People's Popular Alliance, the ruling authority of the People's Rightful Republic of Mbapazu, has become aware of your presence in a restricted zone of category type SV1. You are in continuing violation of the

Dakada treaty, specifically article 7, clause 1.7. Thusly you, the *Wubumchu* people, are under arrest. Each one of you is to report to a PPA station within twenty-four hours for processing."

Thembe's order is met with fear, confusion, and the screams of children.

He nods, as if with sympathy, then adds, with a less severe tone, "People of the jungle, if you can refrain from returning to your posturing and instead behave like civilized human beings, then we may sit and talk about your options." He grabs a case from his security. "I brought tea. Now, which one of you is Mhaawu?"

*   *   *

The rain has stopped, and all that can be heard are the usual jungle suspects chirping, clicking, bellowing, buzzing, snorting, and squeaking, along with the sound of water in a container approaching boiling point.

Thembe has laid out a tea set, including a heat pad, kettle, and some elegant porcelain ware. Only two of the cups will be used, me being the only person to accept his offer. As peculiar as his behavior has been, Thembe has managed to conduct some initial negotiations with the tribe. All sharp sticks and rocks remain on the ground, and in return, Thembe has dismissed his security.

He and Mhaawu have taken center stage in the middle of the communal area. Both insisted I sit with them, and so I have placed myself between the two, a little closer to Mhaawu than to Thembe. The rest of the tribe surrounds us, listening to and watching his every move. Ratu stands at the front, closer to Thembe than anyone else.

"This unassociated man has nice skin and powerful arms," someone whispers.

"Maybe not everyone from outside the jungle is feeble like

Okon," says another.

I check my arms, give them a flex, then adjust the socks beneath my antique boots. Although Thembe insisted I get back into my jungle attire (because he doesn't want the tribe to see me differently), he let me keep the socks after I showed him my sores.

Turning from red to green, the heat pad gives a *ping* that reminds me of modernity. Thembe, who is sitting on a log that he covered with a cloth, pours the water into the teapot. "We'll let that steep for a few minutes," he says, turning from his tea set. "Ah, I see you people do art," he adds, his eye caught by the large wooden carving of the Massas that lies discarded where it always is. "What a delightful surprise, and a pleasant shade of blue. I like how you've only carved half the figure, as though the other half were bitten off by some gargantuan creature."

Nobody responds. A silent tension hangs in the humid air. Lots of fidgeting and whispering among the onlookers. Mhaawu already looks like she's about to snap, and they haven't even started talking yet. I'm still struggling to comprehend Thembe's decision not to wear body armor.

"Now, Mhaawu," says Thembe, "I don't expect you to have understood the official order I issued to your people, or even to know what an official order is, but I was following legal protocol—another concept I do not expect you to understand. So, allow me to simplify your predicament in a way you can grasp."

Mhaawu continually shifts her position on the mats. Her legs shake with—fear? rage? a combination thereof? Why she was much less troubled by my arrival than she is with Thembe's, I don't know.

"Outside of the Nsanba," Thembe continues, loud enough for all to hear, "there is a very large and powerful tribe called the P-P-A. I am a representative of that tribe, and this land you are on belongs to them. This land is also prohibited, which means that by being here you are breaking the law—the rules set by the

PPA. As punishment, you are all to spend a lifetime in incarceration. That means imprisonment. Detainment. You will be separated from each other and forced to live in a place that will make you miserable every single day. You will never be allowed back into the Nsanba."

Thembe pours the tea into the two cups and stirs. "Mhaawu, can you confirm you understand what I just told you?" He passes me a cup.

Mhaawu turns to me as if looking for advice. A lump forms in my throat. *I led the PPA to them.* The decades-long secret of their existence is out of the bag and can never be put back—and now they're going to prison! I break eye contact, look down at my tea. Gommonogo snarls, "I do not understand this unassociated man. His mind is as dull as Okon's."

"He is saying we should not be here," says Etoole, six of his seven young daughters clinging to his stout frame.

"He is saying we will be punished," adds Petonba.

"Okon is to blame for this," says Gommonaadogo. "He is the one who brought him here."

I brace myself for a backlash from the tribe, a backlash I deserve.

"Actually, that isn't true," Thembe interjects. "Okon didn't tell me or the PPA about you. We discovered your existence through other means and came here of our own volition. Okon has done nothing but try to protect you. You owe him your gratitude."

Gommonaadogo huffs.

Thembe gives me a subtle nod before turning his attention back to Mhaawu. "I'm sorry to be the bearer of bad news, but it's only right that you have the facts. Your tribe's circumstances are dire." He puts his tea down, swats away a fly, and places a saucer over the cup. "This is where I come to some good news. The PPA are not unreasonable people. They understand your situation is unique. Furthermore, you are in the fortunate position of having something to offer in exchange for a withdrawal of the charges against you. In return for your freedom, all the PPA wants is some information."

Mhaawu remains tense. I worry she might instruct the Wuchumbu to grab hold of the unassociated man and boot him from the settlement, and then his security might return with guns blazing.

"We know that people from outside the jungle have come here," Thembe continues, "and maybe they're still around. What can you tell me about them?"

I've no idea who Thembe is referring to. Mhaawu remains silent. She hasn't said anything for a concerning amount of time. "Do I need to remind you of the consequences of not cooperating?" Thembe adds.

"I can answer your question," Mhaawu finally replies, her voice strained. "A long time ago, five unassociated were in the Nsanba. We stumbled across them while hunting. They killed my husband and his brother, and we killed two of them."

"How long ago exactly?" Thembe asks.

"Seventeen years," says Mhaawu.

I glance at Ratu, who doesn't seem to react. His mother was pregnant with him at the time. His father, whom he never got to meet, was the previous leader of the tribe, a leadership that was passed to Mhaawu when he died.

"What happened to the three 'unassociated' who lived?" Thembe asks.

"They ran away. We never saw them again."

"Did they leave anything behind?"

"No."

Mhaawu rubs her wrists. For the first time, I notice they're scarred. Thembe finishes his tea. Everyone's on edge as they wait for his response. This ceasefire is a fragile one. I run my hand along the new contours of my knee in an effort to comfort myself. Ratu is gesturing to me; I think he wants me to pass him my cup.

"I am sorry for the loss of your husband," says Thembe. "However, what the PPA are interested in is likely more recent than that, probably involving many more people from outside the jungle. It may be these people are still nearby, but if not, they will have left things behind. Technology—does that word translate correctly for you? I am talking about advanced technological apparatus that clearly does not belong to your tribe. Artificial things. Items that are not natural."

"After the encounter seventeen years ago," Mhaawu replies, "the next time any of us saw an unassociated person was when Okon arrived almost four months ago."

"Let's not forget my wife came here too, about a month before me," I add, not meaning to involve myself in the discussion. I've switched my translator's settings so it doesn't run through my nôvono pro. This means I have to speak rather than think my words that are to be translated, which I often do anyway; otherwise, Thembe will realize I have a brain implant.

"As I have told you many times, Okon," says Mhaawu, "none of us have seen your wife." She turns to Thembe and adds, "There is nothing in or around our settlement but the jungle and the Wuchumbu."

"And how long has your tribe been living in this particular location?" Thembe asks.

"We came here before most of us were born," replies Mhaawu.

"There is nothing here, you stupid man. So, fuck off!" shouts Gommonaadogo. Her cussing jolts me. Not once have their words been translated in such a way (and I immediately want to know the Wuchumbu equivalent of "fuck off").

Thembe and Mhaawu commence a stare down, flies harassing the both of them. Thembe's face twitches as the insects buzz around his eyes. Mhaawu keeps her gaze steady. I told Thembe this "meeting" wouldn't work. The stare down ends when a disturbance arises from behind the surrounding crowd. "More unassociated people are coming!" cries Babba.

"Ah, they're early," says Thembe, rising to his feet. "There is no need for alarm. I assure you they're unarmed. In fact, what they bring will please you."

He heads toward the commotion, and the anxious crowd cuts a wide path for him, to avoid physical contact. Mhaawu stays where she is, her back stooped, her head low, her breathing heavy. She turns to me, says, "Keep an eye on him."

I pull myself to my feet.

The tribe has encircled Thembe at the edge of the central opening, half standing in the opening itself and half crammed between huts and trees. Two armored but unarmed figures are walking away, leaving Thembe with a large white crate. He waits for his audience to settle before speaking.

"In here"—Thembe slaps the side of the box—"is a gesture of goodwill from the PPA and me to you, the *Wugunchu* people."

The crowd jitters as he slides the lid from the crate and reaches inside. I suspect he keeps getting their name wrong on purpose. I don't know why he's doing it, but it bothers me. Thembe pulls from the crate a blue box wrapped with a pink bow. "Where are the children?" he asks and scans the crowd. Upon spotting two boys and a girl, he kneels in front of them and presents them with the box. Big Man places the tip of a spear just centimeters from Thembe's temple.

"Stab him in the neck!" shouts the knock-kneed man.

Thembe sighs. Despite the hovering spear, he opens the box and pulls out a piece of candy, which he holds up for all to see before putting it in his mouth. "*Mmm.* Delicious. You will never have tasted anything so good." He places the box on the ground and gestures for the children to help themselves before he steps back to the crate. Big Man lowers his spear. Sweat from my forehead stings my eyes.

"There are many gifts in here that will improve the quality of your lives," Thembe declares as he rummages through the crate, holding up item after item for all to see. "Clothing. Bedding. Diapers. Detergent. Crockery. Cutlery. Grains. Cakes. Protein. All food enhanced for more nutrition. Metal tools. Toys. Rope. The list goes on, and you can take your time to enjoy discovering everything for yourself. Each gift comes with a set of pictures that explain how to use them."

He's supposed to be searching for Efawi, not acting like a missionary. Why has the PPA gone to so much trouble to "help" the tribe? Thembe reaches deep into the crate and wrestles out a large case. "This, I specifically want to show you because it will save lives."

Thembe places the case on the floor and opens it to reveal a myriad of items organized into trays and compartments. "When you are sick or injured," he says, "you should use these to make yourselves better. Antibiotics, antivirals, dressings, painkillers, test kits, vaccinations, and so forth. We even have a mini-defibrillator in the back here. Again, everything comes with picture instructions, which you will need to familiarize yourselves with. Some, however, are too complicated for pictures, and have written instructions in Okon's native language so you can consult with him if need be."

"Um, Thembe," I interrupt. "The Wuchumbu do not have a writing system."

"And?"

"Well, I . . . I'm not sure it's a good idea to introduce them to the concept."

"Nonsense," he replies, dismissing me with a wave of the hand before he turns to address the crowd. "If you are willing, we can assign to you a full-time medical team who will cure your ailments, heal your loved ones, increase your life spans, make you healthier than you've ever been."

Most of the Wuchumbu remain distressed, but flickers of interest emerge on the faces of some. Ratu shifts from one foot to the other, itching to get his hand on these unassociated things. Is this my fault? Have I desensitized them to the unassociated?

Thembe pulls a disk from the case and unfolds it. "Should you need to apply treatment to yourself, we've included a mirror so you can see what you are doing." He opens the disk to reveal the reflective surface inside and slowly rotates it back and forth. The Wuchumbu jump and huddle together.

"He has trapped people inside the round thing?"

"They look like us!"

"What evil, unassociated magic is this?"

A haunting chorus arises from the gathering. "*Ohhh. Ohhh.*" Many lower themselves, touch their heads, point to the sky. Their anguish stabs me. Thembe seems confused.

"The mirror. You're scaring them!" I yell.

He looks at it front and back, unable to comprehend the problem, then finally closes the mirror and returns the disk to the case.

"I think the Wuchumbu have had enough for today," I add.

Thembe glares at me, a momentary flash of anger in his eyes before he returns to his usual calm demeanor. I need to remind myself that this man may know Efawi well, but to me he is almost a stranger. He reaches into the crate once more and pulls out a decorative yellow box. "There is a young man among you by the name of Ratu," he says. "Come forward. This last gift is for you."

Ratu stands up straight, his eyes wide, his mouth open.

"How does the unassociated man know your name?" asks Gommonogo.

"You should stay where you are," says Beejalee.

The teenager hesitates, then steps forward.

"Ratu, no!" screams Mhaawu. She pushes her way to the front of the gathering. I hadn't realized she was watching.

"But that is for me," her son complains. Thembe holds the box out to him, and Big Man edges forward with his spear.

Thembe looks at me.

127

I look at Mhaawu.

The naughty teenager snatches his gift, knocking the lid from the box. An item slides out and falls to the ground—a mechatronic prosthetic arm, beautifully sculpted with metallic-white finish and a strip of colorful artwork that curves its way from the fingers to the elbow.

"What is it?" Ratu asks.

The arm and a number of accessories lie scattered on the wet dirt. Mhaawu orders Big Man to grab her son. Her loyal follower leaps forward, but the slippery Ratu scoops up his gift and darts into the crowd. Big Man tries to push his way through, but the much smaller Ratu gets away. The tribe stands in shocked silence. Mhaawu's body trembles; this woman is about to explode.

"I did not mean to cause an argument between you and your son," says Thembe. "I only wanted to demonstrate how much your people have to gain by cooperating."

"Leave, and take everything with you," says Mhaawu, her voice low and strained.

Thembe nods thoughtfully but stands his ground. "You can deny knowledge as much as you like, but with the whole jungle to live in, there must be a reason why your people live in this peculiar place, this area of anomaly—a mere dot hidden within the vastness of the Nsanba. If I were to talk of a light that radiates in many colors, would that help jog your memory?"

My already racing pulse skyrockets. So they do know about the multicolored stuff. Could the PPA have seen me with the multicolored thing? Perhaps they even took it while I slept? The tribe's leader grits her teeth and says nothing. Thembe glares at me. "Make yourself useful, Okon. Help put Mhaawu at ease."

I want to help but can't find the words. I seem to know less about what's going on than anyone else; all I have are questions. Thembe continues to glare at me, and Mhaawu marches up to the unwanted visitor. "If you do not leave, we will kill all unassociated," she says.

The crowd stirs, encouraged by their leader's fighting words.

"And how will you do that?" Thembe asks, calm and seemingly sincere despite knowing Mhaawu's threats must be empty.

"The many colors is a weapon," she says, "more powerful than anything the unassociated can make."

"And where did you get this weapon?" Thembe asks.

Mhaawu points to the sky. The crowd cheers. To my dismay, they are brandishing their spears and rocks again.

"Show me," says Thembe, maintaining his cool despite the danger he's in.

"I will not warn you again," threatens Mhaawu. They stand centimeters apart, Mhaawu's head tilted up, Thembe looking down. I've stopped breathing. This meeting is going to end with a sharp stick in this independent consultant's neck, I'm sure of it. Doesn't he realize how vulnerable they feel around the unassociated? Where is his damn metal ant suit?

"I will respect your wishes, Mhaawu, but I expected better from you," says Thembe. He shifts his focus from the small, infuriated lady to those standing around him. "Listen carefully, people of the *Wichunga* tribe. For you, two paths exist. Along one of these paths, you are free to live wherever you choose, however you choose, interacting with those from outside the jungle only if you wish to. Then there is the *other* path—a path where you are dragged from the Nsanba, separated, confined, and forced into hard labor for the rest of your lives. I came here with the hope I might convince you to choose the right path, because I want you to be free, and I want you to flourish. But today your leader has let you down."

Thembe pauses. Mhaawu stands with her fists clenched at her sides. The yellow bow from Ratu's gift box lies muddy on the ground between them.

"However, all is not yet lost," Thembe continues. "I will give you a second and final chance to make the right decision. I will return at the same time tomorrow. You have until then to either convince your leader to see sense or to disregard her and provide me directly with the information the PPA tribe seeks. It's your choice: ruin or freedom."

Eyes widen. Shoulders tighten. Mutterings and whimperings emerge from the silence. Babba is crying. I hold his head and tell him everything is going to be okay. Mhaawu remains defiant. She stares Thembe down as he walks away. The crowd parts to allow his exit.

"Okon, a word," Thembe calls out.

I don't want to go. I look to Mhaawu in the hope that she tell me to stay, but she says nothing, her mind elsewhere, and so I reluctantly follow him, initially limping, then remembering I no longer need to. I pass the children whom Thembe offered candy to, who now hold his gift box and are chewing on the treats. A woman knocks the candy from their hands and orders them to empty their mouths. A handful of others, adults and children alike, gingerly approach the large crate and peer inside. They hesitantly look at each other before one of them reaches inside.

14: The Bridge

Thembe shakes his head as I walk behind him. "Okon, given that you want to find Efawi, and that you apparently care deeply for the tribe, why do you continue to be so fucking useless?"

"Excuse me?"

"Explain to me what just happened," he says.

"Well, I'm not quite sure. The whole thing was a bit odd: Your gifts for the tribe. Your legal speak. Your lack of body armor."

"Every action I took was a considered one. Body armor communicates weakness, and I need the tribe to understand the gulf in power between us—how untouchable I am. As for my legal speak, my strategy was to confuse and destabilize. Negotiating is my expertise, Okon. How did your first encounter with the tribe go?"

"I was unconscious for most of it. And what was with the tea? Was that part of your strategy too?"

"Not really. I like tea. It helps me think."

"But you didn't even ask them about Efawi, which I thought was the whole reason you're here."

"You already established they haven't seen her. So, to find Efawi, we need to work out what's going on in the Anomalous Zone."

"Well, I'm concerned about your antagonizing of the

Wuchumbu," I say. "They're stressed enough as it is."

Thembe waves a swarm of bugs from his face. "The tribe's welfare is at the center of my concerns. Do not doubt that. I ensured my team and I were health-checked and our equipment and gifts sterilized in case the tribe lacks immunity to viruses from outside the jungle. Did you or Efawi take such precautions?"

"I . . . I didn't know I'd be interacting with an uncontacted tribe."

"You were careless. Could have wiped them out with a sneeze."

With no comeback, I release a heavy sigh.

"And you're not here to question my strategy, Okon. You're here to explain *your* behavior."

I don't agree. It's Thembe who has the explaining to do. I want to ask if his team stole the multicolored thing, but I can't specifically mention the thing in case it wasn't them. I'd rather they know nothing about it. "Back at the settlement," I say, choosing my words carefully, "you mentioned a light that radiates in many colors. What were you referring to?"

I watch the back of Thembe's head, wishing I could see his reaction. "As always, I'm going to be honest with you," he says. "I have very limited knowledge about the light—hence my attempts to elicit information from the tribe. I do know there is a connection between the light and the Anomalous Zone, and what little else I know I may discuss with you at some point, dependent on how matters play out, but now is not the time."

"Well, you said I'm in an important position. I can't be that important, given you're keeping information from me."

"You *are* in an important position."

"No, I'm not."

Thembe stops and turns to face me. I don't like how his additional fifteen or so centimeters in height mean he's always looking down at me when we talk.

"I'm not sure if your reluctance to accept the critical role you've stumbled into is due to fear or ignorance or both," he says.

"I don't understand what you're talking about."

"You are the bridge, Okon—the bridge between the tribe and the rest of the world, between Efawi and her striking a deal with the PPA, between the sorry mess we find ourselves in and a peaceful outcome."

"Well, I don't want to be the bridge. I don't even like bridges. You seem to forget none of this has anything to do with me. I'm not supposed to be involved. I just want to go home with my wife and for us to be left alone."

I squat and flick some debris from my boots. I wish I could simply lift a headset from my nose and discover I'm not really here, that this whole Nsanba adventure has just been a shitty game.

Thembe sighs and looks across to our escorts. "Give us ten," he instructs. The two armored figures nod and disappear among the trees. Thembe waits for me to stand before he continues. His eyes have hardened, and I don't think I'll like what he's about to say.

"Okon, the information I'm about to tell you is classified to the utmost. You need to appreciate that what's happening in the Anomalous Zone is taking place within a broader political context. We live in tense times. Relations between the states that surround the Nsanba are at their worst since The War. Skirmishes at borders, violent exchanges, are becoming ever more frequent. After three generations of fragile peace in the region, the fear of war is wearing off, at least for those in power, while their ambitions have only grown and their eyes have returned to the jungle.

"You see, not only is the Nsanba invaluable due to its natural resources, but more importantly, the jungle remains a symbol of failure for each nation that holds a claim over it. The jungle is a reminder that the land dispute which arose during The War was never resolved, and therefore never won by anyone."

"You told the tribe the land they're on belongs to Mbapazu," I say. "But it doesn't, does it? The entire Nsanba is nobody's in particular because no one can agree who owns it."

"That is true, but you tell the PPA the Nsanba doesn't belong to Mbapazu and see what happens to you."

Obviously, I won't do that.

"Now," Thembe continues, "during this backdrop of heightening tension, your wife's technology company, Sabano, became embroiled in a dispute in which a satellite was used to garner information of a politically and militarily sensitive nature. You don't need to know the specifics of what the information included—I'm not senior enough to have been told myself—but I believe this was the work of a handful of corrupt engineers within Sabano and not the doing of your wife. That was her position, at least. Efawi told the PPA she intervened as soon as she realized what was happening, and she obtained the sole copy of this data—data with national security implications that several governments in the region would kill to get their hands on. And so, your wife suddenly found herself in the middle of a—"

"Shitstorm."

"Yes. A shitstorm," says Thembe.

My stomach tightens. The pressure Efawi must have been under. "When did this happen?" I ask.

Thembe slaps his arm, failing to swat a mosquito. "Efawi intercepted the illegal data about six months before she went missing."

Many times during the past six months, Efawi came home even later than usual, and even more flustered and distracted than usual. On one occasion, in the middle of the night, I found her in the kitchen microwaving a watermelon. The thing exploded before I could turn the microwave off. I complained, and she apologized. She said her mind was elsewhere, that she wasn't paying attention.

"What happened next?" I ask.

"Efawi tried to use the sole copy of the data for bargaining. Said she would release some of the information only if the PPA made sweeping reforms. Her aim, as always, was to create a fairer society."

"And did they agree?"

"Of course not. The PPA continued to apply pressure on Efawi. Interfered with her company's affairs, bribed colleagues to betray her, involved themselves in her private life, followed her, made threats, tried to push her until she'd give up the data. She's lucky she could afford the security she had, or I don't know what would have happened. How can you live with Efawi and know nothing about this?" Thembe narrows his eyes as he judges me.

I look to the trees. She must have kept quiet about it all because she wanted to protect me, and we had our deal she was honoring. She knows how stressed I get about her extracurricular activities, which we used to argue about constantly. So instead, we decided not to talk about the things she was up to, but I realize now that was a mistake. We should have continued to argue rather than go through months of being distant. At least we might have argued our way to some kind of solution.

"So," says Thembe, "after months of PPA pressure, Efawi remotely sabotaged her own satellite systems so that data such as this couldn't be acquired again. That was the final straw for the PPA, and an opportunity for them to issue a warrant for her arrest. The charges listed on the warrant were exaggerated or outright fiction, but with the PPA exercising influence over the courts, Efawi's outlook was—"

"Bad enough to prevent her from coming home," I say. I lean against a tree and slide to the ground, not caring that it scrapes my back. "I should have been there for her," I mutter. Thembe hears me and nods in agreement. I know what he's thinking. He's thinking, Why is someone like Efawi with someone like Okon? And I'm wondering the same. What's the point in being married if your husband doesn't support you during difficult times?

"Do you think she's still in the Anomalous Zone?" I ask.

"Efawi is the smartest, most obsessive person I know," says Thembe. "I can't imagine her walking away from this place until she got what she wanted, and if she got what she wanted, whatever that might be, I have a feeling we would know about it."

I nod, half lost in reverie. "The last thing she said to me before leaving the house was that she loved me. Can you guess what the last thing I said was?"

"That you love her too?" Thembe replies.

"Possibly. The trouble is I can't remember, and it's been bothering me ever since."

"Okay, that's enough." Thembe walks over to me, grabs me by the arms, and pulls me to my feet. "You won't find Efawi by wallowing. Now, let's get back to the purpose of this conversation: how useless you were just now."

"But—"

"Okon, listen to me," he says, accentuating syllables as if I'm a moron. "As I've told you already, to find Efawi, we need to figure out what's going on here. And for the hunter-gatherers to remain free, they need to cooperate and help us understand what's in the area. In conclusion, it's in the interest of Efawi and the hunter-gatherers for *you* to help *me* acquire the information I need. Understood?"

"Of course I understand."

"Well, keep listening, because that's only part of the picture. Up to this point, the PPA's head office has instructed their jungle team to exercise caution due to concern that another nation is active in the area. However, scientists on the ground have concluded that the electromagnetic disturbances are being produced by a technology more advanced than anything we are aware of."

"I probably could have told you that."

136

"I doubt it," says Thembe. "In any case, those in the upper echelons of the PPA have become extremely anxious, fearing not only that another nation is involved here, but that it is involved with a technology beyond what we can presently understand. You'd think that would give the PPA reason to be even more cautious. But no. After months of the team following you around and not making much progress, those in power have run out of patience, and they are instructing us to enter the AZ heavy-handed and seize whatever we find. They want evidence that another nation is active here, violating the Dakada treaty."

"When you say 'heavy-handed,' do you mean soldiers?"

"I'm talking about a military incursion," Thembe replies. My heart quickens at the thought of troops swarming the AZ.

"You don't need to look at me like that," says Thembe. "I agree; an incursion is a terrible idea. There is too much we don't know, too much that makes no sense. Why would another state come all the way out here to work on an advanced technology? And if there is another state active within the AZ, where the hell are they? We might not have been able to fully search the area, but surely we would have received some indication that a team of people other than the tribe is active here. And if not, if they have abandoned whatever it is they were working on, why?"

"To add to that list of questions: Why on Earth did Efawi come here? What was she expecting to find?"

"Exactly," says Thembe.

"And why do the Wuchumbu live in the very spot where all of this is taking place?"

"Yes. Although, having met them, it's clear they're not responsible for the electromagnetic disturbances and won't understand the technology involved. So I can only assume they've had the misfortune of being in the wrong place at the wrong time. That said, they should at least be able to point us to what is here, maybe even give us an indication as to who brought it. If what Mhaawu says is true, it seems we are looking at a weapon of some sort."

"So you believe Mhaawu when she says she can kill everyone?" I ask.

"Obviously not. If there is some type of advanced weapons system within the Anomalous Zone, Mhaawu and her jungle clan couldn't possibly know how to use it. Nevertheless, bursting into the AZ with soldiers before we understand what's going on, I fear, will be a grave mistake."

"How grave?" I ask nervously.

"Well, in addition to there being casualties among the tribe, given the current political tension, the historical rivalry between the Central African states, and the sensitivities regarding the Nsanba, I don't believe it would take much to ignite a violent clash here that could escalate into another war."

I struggle to catch my breath. "I'm sorry . . . did you say 'war'?"

"Yes."

"But . . . I just don't . . . Efawi worries about things like that, but who in this day and age would start a war? I can't imagine it. There's no need. I don't understand why Mbapazu, Loalla, and the other nations of Central Africa can't just cooperate, or at least not be hostile to one another. It shouldn't be that hard."

Thembe smirks as if I've said something stupid. "It is hard because we are in a race, Okon. From nation-states to individuals, we're all racing for our very existence. Several races at once, many of which never end. In some of these races, you don't have to be the winner to survive; you only need to make sure you aren't left too far behind. In other races, everyone but the winner is obliterated. The PPA and their counterparts in other nations know this, and so they perpetually push for the lead for the sake of their survival."

"Well, that's a very cynical view," I reply. "And I just don't agree. People are more cooperative than that. Sure, there's competition, and sometimes the competition might be necessary, but it doesn't have to be a race all the time. I haven't been in a race for years."

"Oh yes you have, Okon. Until very recently, you've been cradled in the arms of Efawi while she sprints along in first place. But she isn't here to carry you now, and you need to accept the reality of the catastrophic consequences should we fuck up."

"Well, I don't want that kind of pressure. I'm not responsible for any of this. I'm—"

"Trembling," says Thembe.

I hold my hands in front of me. They're shaking and I hadn't realized.

"I may be in charge of the team in the Nsanba," Thembe continues, "but I have to take orders from the PPA's head office, and as I've told you before, they'll replace me if I continue to argue for a more cautious approach without being able to demonstrate results."

I don't want to have to deal with someone other than Thembe, especially if that other person is less willing to exercise caution. At least I've met Thembe before, albeit briefly, which confirms he knows my wife. His replacement would be an unknown entity.

"Would you like to know how the PPA have profiled you?" he asks.

"No. I don't," I reply.

"Weak-minded and lazy," he says. "That was your four-word character summary. *Weak-minded and lazy.*"

"Great. Thanks for sharing."

"I'm telling you this because on my way to the Anomalous Zone, I was advised to have you extracted from the Nsanba. The PPA believed you had nothing to offer, and that you were a risk to operations due to your obligations to your wife and her anti-PPA stance. But I believed you could be the bridge between us, the tribe, and Efawi. So I convinced my superiors that you should stay—for now at least."

"*Extracted?* To where? Prison? No, I have to stay. I can't be extracted. I just can't. Efawi is probably still here. You said so yourself."

Thembe narrows his eyes. "Well, then, remember the tribe has accepted you, Okon, and whether you like it or not, you *are* involved. So the next time I'm in difficult negotiations with the hunter-gatherers and I look to you for assistance with smoothing relations, what will you do?"

"I'm going to be a bridge."

"That's right. I need your *full* cooperation. Do you know how useful half a bridge is? Or even three-quarters of a bridge?"

"I understand," I say. And I do understand, but my head is spinning. I'm struggling not to be overwhelmed.

Thembe gives me another stern look before glancing around. "Where are they?" he says, referring to our escorts.

We wait in silence while I stew. Words bounce around in my head and collide. *Efawi. Wuchumbu. PPA. War. Suffering. My fault.* I pace up and down in the awkward jungle terrain while Thembe patiently stands. I've always envied those who can maintain calm under pressure.

"Their language is surprisingly rich, don't you think?" he says in a conversational tone. "Unless, perhaps, our translators are adding a sophistication to their speech that isn't there. When I first heard about the tribe, I expected them to have only a limited number of words, but to communicate with them so fully has been a welcome surprise."

I try to bite my tongue, but in my heightened state I'm unable to resist responding. "I don't know why you thought they wouldn't have a rich language. You shouldn't confuse naivete about the modern world with stupidity. What do you know about their world? Nothing. Does that make you stupid?"

"I never said the *Wachumbu* were stupid. Clearly, they are not."

"But you expected them to be. And it's *Wuchumbu*. Not

Wachumbu or *Wukumbu* or whatever other made-up word you've been uttering. Wuchumbu. Get it right, *Thimba*."

He stares at me, mouth ajar. I fear he might have me extracted after all, but instead, he smiles. "Good to see you're finally growing some balls, Okon. Keep it up."

Leaves rustle to the side of us. His two armored escorts are returning in a hurry. "Sorry, sir. We got lost," says one.

"I told you to tell him a gorilla attacked us," says the other, who shoves his partner in the chest.

Thembe sighs and turns back to me. "I will return to the *Wuchumbu* in twenty-four hours. That's how long you have to convince Mhaawu or anyone who knows something to start talking. If you fail, I will have no choice but to order a full sweep of the area, and when that happens, the tribe will fight, and they will suffer, and who knows what other troubles will be stirred up—troubles that could escalate out of control."

My heart pounds. Thembe doesn't realize that the tribe seldom listens to me. But if I confess my lack of influence, he might well have me removed.

"Off you go, Okon. You're going to need all the time you can get."

I hurry back to the settlement as fast as an unfit man in a dense jungle can go, heart pumping, mind racing, no mental space to appreciate my beautifully functioning knee. I quickly reach the empty outskirts, drenched in sweat from the short run. Arguing echoes from the central clearing. A woman screams, "Get away from me! Get off me! You're killing my husband!"

15: The Mirror

Petonba is on her knees, face all wet from tears and snot. Her two sons, Babba included, cling to her. The medical case has just been pulled from her arms, and the tribe is split in three: some want to keep Thembe's gifts, especially the medicinal stuff; most want to take everything to the river; the rest don't know what the hell to do.

"Are all the unassociated items back in the vessel?" asks Mhaawu. "Big Man, there is another over there," she adds.

Big Man marches to a plastic bag on the ground, skewers it with his spear, and returns the bag to the crate without touching it.

"What about my husband?" cries Petonba. While I was with Thembe, Petonba tried to take the medical case to her hut, where her husband lies deathly sick with fever.

"It all has to go to the river," says Mhaawu. "Since when do we allow unassociated things in our home?"

"Since we let Okon wear those monstrosities on his feet," says Etoole.

We all turn to my boots.

"The unassociated fixed Okon's leg," says Adienatta. "So, perhaps the Wuchumbu should benefit from their medicine as well."

"I agree," says Beejalee. "We have to let Petonba take the

medicine to her husband, or he will die. Okon can show her how to use it. What do you think, Okon?"

All eyes turn to me. Time to be a bridge. But before I can think of a solution, Naee proposes one of her own. "We can let Petonba use the medicine just this once," she suggests, "then we can take everything, medicine included, to the river."

Damn it. Beejalee's fourteen-year-old daughter has more to offer than me. I hear Thembe's voice in my head: "Useless."

"That is a wonderful idea," says Petonba. She rises from her knees, looks to Mhaawu for approval.

"If Petonba can give the medicine to her husband," says Etoole, "then I should be allowed to give it to my youngest." Etoole has seven children, all girls. His youngest has been unwell for months.

"And I need the medicine for my brother because yesterday he fell from a tree," adds Habee.

"I want the medicine too," requests a tall, gray-haired lady whose name escapes me. (She once saved me from eating a poisonous nut—may have been a berry.) "The shaman's medicine is useless," she adds.

The shaman plays with her bead necklace, seemingly oblivious to the conversation. An outpouring of requests for Thembe's medicine follows, with "If Petonba can use it, why can't I?" being the gist of their argument.

Mhaawu looks on, her brow furrowed. "Are you all blind?" she yells.

"I am," says Didiwa (who has cataracts).

"If we use these unassociated things even once," says Mhaawu, "we will want to use them again. But we do not know how to make these things ourselves, so we will have to rely on the unassociated to give us more. Then one day, not too far from now, we will forget how to live without these things. When that happens, we will be dependent on the unassociated, and our way of life will be over. We will not be Wuchumbu anymore; the

Wuchumbu will have died."

Those who were demanding to keep the medical case exchange nervous glances.

"We are wasting time," says Gommonaadogo. "We should talk about how to stop the unassociated from killing us when they return tomorrow."

"The unassociated man did not say they will kill us," says Beejalee. "He said they will take us away."

"I believe that means the same thing," says Habee. He tightens his grip on his wife's hand.

"Tell us about this weapon you spoke of," demands Gommonaadogo.

All eyes turn to Mhaawu.

"The weapon is irrelevant because we cannot use it," says their leader.

"But you told the unassociated man that the *many colors* is a weapon," says Gommonaadogo. "So, there must be a connection between the weapon and the evil spirit inside the *Ban*—"

"Do not say it!" someone cries.

"*ooch*—" Gommonaadogo continues.

"Stop!"

"—*chee,*" Gommonaadogo finishes.

"She said it!"

"We are all cursed!"

"*Ban* what?" I ask.

"Okon, shush, for the sake of your spiritual integrity."

"If there is a weapon inside the *Banoochee,* then we must use it," says Gommonaadogo.

"She said it again!"

Is the multicolored thing I lost some kind of weapon? And is someone going to ask for it back?

Mhaawu grunts dismissively and turns to Big Man. "Is everything in the vessel now?" she asks.

"There is one item that has not been returned," he replies. I assume he's referring to Ratu's prosthetic arm. Mhaawu's son hasn't been seen since he ran off with his special gift.

The tribe's leader takes a deep breath. "We will have to deal with that later."

"Mhaawu, why can we not use the weapon you spoke of?" asks Habee.

"I do not want to talk about it," says Mhaawu. "Now help me put this thing on top of the unassociated vessel." She tries to pick up the crate's lid with a stick, and those closest to her help.

"What about my husband?" screams Petonba.

"What about my daughter?" complains Etoole.

"What about me?" protests the gray-haired lady.

Mhaawu ignores them all, and with the lid in place, her attention turns to taking the crate to the river. "We need to slide wood underneath so we can carry it."

"No, I will not allow it!" cries Petonba. She lunges at the crate and wraps her arms around it. Big Man tries to pry her off, and half a dozen others come to her defense. Pushing and shoving breaks out between those who want to keep Thembe's gifts and those who don't. The air fills with shrieks. I cover my ears. A flash of reflected light above us catches my attention. It loops down on a curve and crashes onto Beejalee's head.

The quarreling stops.

Beejalee wobbles and is gently lowered to the ground by those around her, a line of blood trickling down her forehead. The mirror from the medical kit lies scattered in pieces on the ground. We all look to Babba, his eyes bulging, his mouth wide open. He must have pulled the mirror from the medical kit before it was taken from his mother.

"I was aiming for the vessel. I did not mean to hit anyone," he blubbers, then bursts into tears. I mentally reaffirm my position that should I one day have a boy, I don't want him to be like Babba.

"Can we use the unassociated medicine to help her?" requests

Beejalee's eldest son, Obee.

"I am okay. Do not worry about me," says his mother, her voice unsteady. She tries to stand, loses balance, and is caught by those around her once again.

"We do not have time for this," snarls Gommonaadogo. "The unassociated man did not accept Mhaawu's answers to his questions. He wants to know about the many colors, so we need to go to the Banoochee and find the answers he is looking for. It seems Mhaawu has been lying to us about what is in there. The shaman too."

"I have not lied about anything," croaks the shaman.

"Not you," snaps Gommonaadogo. "The imbecile you replaced. He and Mhaawu are the only two to have entered the Banoochee since the many colors arrived."

A wave of mutterings rolls through the gathering. Apart from Ratu, I've found the tribe to be an honest people, but it's now evident they've all been keeping secrets from me.

Adienatta taps me on the shoulder. "You understand the unassociated better than any of us. What exactly is it they want?"

All eyes turn to me. I picture myself as a bridge, everyone merrily trampling across. "Okay, well, Thembe needs to know what's going on around here. For example, you need to tell him about the many colors. I want to know about it too."

"We must poke this *Thembe* in the neck," says the knock-kneed man. "All of their necks need a good poking!"

I wave my hands in the air. "How many times do I have to tell you that you mustn't try to fight them? And the situation here is even more dangerous than I realized. Thembe just told me that a war could be kicked off. And the people outside the jungle, including Thembe's tribe, are more powerful than you can imagine. They have weapons that can kill you from a great distance. They can eradicate every single Wuchumbu in an instant. To you it will seem like magic; to them it will be easy. So please, whatever you do, do not try to fight."

A chorus of *ohhhs* fills the air. Heads are patted. Knees are bent. Crying children are gathered in arms and held tightly.

"So, we could die at any moment?" someone asks.

"You can keep yourselves safe by cooperating with Thembe," I try, but I've lost their attention as they focus on how vulnerable they are.

"Enough crying!" yells Gommonaadogo. "If the unassociated can kill us at any moment, then I am going to the Banoochee right now."

"Me too," says Gommonogo.

The tribe's leader is a static knot of frustration as the Gommo twins march past her, spears in hand. Many fetch weapons of their own and follow the siblings. Mhaawu opens her mouth, and I expect her to order everyone to stay, but she appears to be torn, twitching as if to speak but ultimately restraining herself. The tribe continue to argue among themselves:

"If they enter the Ba—, the place we do not speak of, then the evil spirit will be released and invade the settlement."

"They have to try something. You heard Okon; the unassociated do not even have to be here to kill us."

"But Mhaawu has told us not to go into the Ba— ever since the many colors came. We should not disobey her."

"I do not want to disobey her, but the alternative is to be slaughtered."

I fire questions at them: "What is the many colors? What is this place called the Ba—something? Why am I only hearing about this now?" But nobody is listening, my bridge is a pile of rubble, a third of the tribe has left for the march led by the Gommo twins, and the rest loiter uncomfortably.

I recoil as I notice Mhaawu's eyes fixed on mine. Does she blame me for accidentally scaring the tribe into action? She stomps in my direction. I posture up, expecting a forehead flick or worse, but she grabs me by the arm and pulls me in the direction of the march.

It seems we are heading to the Ba—.

16: The Failure

The Wuchumbu squeeze through the jungle, every opening on the tribe's collective path weaved through by at least one person. We could spread out, which would make it easier to progress, but we stick together as we march.

Most of the Wuchumbu have joined the procession, some in front of me, some behind. Spotters have been dispatched to be sure we're not being watched by the PPA, something that would be hard for them to do this deep in the AZ anyway. I imagine Petonba and a handful of others will have stayed behind to take and hide the unassociated medicine, but Mhaawu's focus has shifted from Thembe's gifts to wherever it is we are heading.

"You told me there are many good unassociated people, more than there are trees in the Nsanba, yes?" says Mhaawu. Her arm remains locked around mine as she hurries me along, and we overtake others as she works us toward the front. Efawi hooks my arm in the same way when we walk, always in a rush to get to where she's heading.

"Yes, something like that," I reply as a branch slaps me in the face. "What is the Banoochee, Mhaawu?" I ask for the umpteenth time.

"When we get there, you need to tell them what you told me," she says. "You need to tell the Wuchumbu about the unassociated people—how many there are, that they have families, that many are good, that they do not torture their babies. This is the reason you are here. Today is the day, Okon."

"Today is what day for what? Please, Mhaawu, tell me where we're going."

"We are going to the place where the many colors I gave to you comes from."

"About that—there's something I've been meaning to ask. If I weren't to give it back, would that be a problem? You have more of them, don't you?"

"Yes, plenty more," says Mhaawu.

I breathe a sigh of relief.

"You must have worked out its secrets by now, yes?" she says. "I took a huge risk by allowing you to live with us. Today I need you to prove that I was right and that you are meant to be here."

"Haven't I proved myself already? I ate the prior shaman's Hundukkah for one thing. Now I know that's not actually your tradition, but still, I did go along with it."

"What you did was unnecessary and disgusting. Besides, you expelled it afterward."

"Well, if taking a bite from someone's heart isn't enough, I don't know what is!"

I duck to avoid colliding with another tree. The grooves in Mhaawu's forehead deepen. She squeezes my arm. "Okon, you have a very important role to play. I believe you can be the bridge between the Wuchumbu and the unassociated." (What is it with everyone and bridges!) "But I cannot allow you to come with us to the Banoochee unless you tell me the secrets of the light of many colors."

If the Banoochee is where the multicolored light comes from, then I'm sure that's where Efawi headed. Once again, I have the sinking feeling I'm about to blow an opportunity to find her, and to think I might never find Efawi is terrifying enough, but if not finding her is the result of my failure in some task, then the terror takes on additional, unbearable baggage.

"Please give me a moment to think," I request. My throat is dry, and swallowing has become difficult. Mhaawu continues to move us at speed. I try to dismiss unhelpful thoughts such as "Why should I have to prove myself?" and "Mhaawu doesn't have the right to stop me from finding my wife." Instead, I need to see this as an opportunity. A chance to show I'm not a weak-minded, useless man who spends his days playing VR games. *Come on, Okon. You can figure this out.*

"You have not worked out its secrets, have you?" says Mhaawu.

"I'm afraid not," I mumble.

She pulls me to a halt. The marching Wuchumbu cut around us, their excited, sinewy bodies slipping between trees, their tough feet untroubled by the unforgiving jungle floor.

"But the answer is obvious," says Mhaawu. "Why must you have the brain of a goliath beetle?" She shakes me with frustration. My heart sinks. I prefer the Mhaawu who used to silently scowl at me from a distance.

"If I had more time," I suggest.

"We don't have more time," she replies. "We need to get to the Banoochee before anyone does anything stupid." She seems devastated that I don't have the answer.

"I'm sorry, Mhaawu. I'm sorry I've failed your test. But the light is somehow connected to my wife, and I need to—"

A warm hand runs along my back.

"I am so happy you have come with us," says Beejalee as she gingerly passes with Habee and their four children.

"Yes, you deserve to be a part of this," her husband adds, also running his hand across my back.

Their children smile and wave at me. "Okon understands the unassociated, and he will help us defeat them!" declares their middle daughter, Buchee.

I smile back, too embarrassed to inform them I'm about to be sent back to the settlement. Mhaawu taps her feet and fidgets with her hands, seemingly deep in thought as she glances between me and those overtaking us, a few more of them rubbing my back as they pass. Then she looks up to the canopy. "During the last four months," she mutters, "anyone from the tribe could have pierced his flesh or cracked his skull. It would have been easy for them. A child could have done it."

"I assume you're talking about me?" I ask.

"Yet since the initial beating," she continues, as if thinking out loud, "he has managed to survive without a further scratch from the Wuchumbu. Not only has he survived, but most of them feel he belongs. Perhaps *that* was the test. Perhaps *that* is proof he has the right to enter the Banoochee."

"Yes, that should be more than enough proof!" I say. "Does this mean I passed?"

Mhaawu turns her gaze back to me. With her standing so close, I'm reminded of when we first met, her breath fogging my helmet as she assessed me. "Yes, you passed the test," she says.

"Thank you, Mhaawu! Thank you so much." I'm about to open my arms to suggest a hug, but don't quite dare. Mhaawu grabs my wrist and hurries us forward once again. "Perhaps I'm not so useless after all, Thembe," I mutter to myself.

"Your decision on this is final, isn't it?" I ask Mhaawu once we're back in our stride and overtaking others.

"My decision has been made, Okon."

"Well, given that I passed the test and that your decision to let me into the Banoochee is final, now is probably a good time to let you know I lost the multicolored thing."

"You lost it?" Her grip on my wrist tightens.

"I'm sorry, Mhaawu. Really sorry. I fell asleep. I think it may have rolled into the river, but I'm not sure."

Mhaawu huffs and mutters something too low for my translator to pick up. Surely she won't send me back to the settlement? She said her decision was final! After what feels like an age, she eventually says: "Because the situation has changed, and because everyone is about to see the light for themselves, I suppose you losing it no longer matters. But I am disappointed in you, Okon."

I'm not happy to have let her down, but I'm relieved to have finally told her the truth. We continue marching, and I don't risk saying anything further. A few minutes later, a message passes through the understory, shouted from person to person: "Gommonaadogo and Gommonogo have gone inside!"

Mhaawu increases the pace. Despite having two functioning knees, I'm struggling to keep up. "Okon, do not mention the Hundukkah ever again," says Mhaawu. "We need to convince everyone the unassociated are not savages. Your life depends on it."

17: The Banoochee

To the front and left of me is nothing but black. To the right, where I've just come from, is also black except for a thin rectangle of light—the evening sun seeping through the edges of a covered entrance. When the prior shaman referred to "the light in the dark" before tossing the multicolored cubes into flames, I should have thought to search inside a cave.

I wait for my eyes to adjust. I asked for a torch but was told that won't be needed in the Banoochee—the tribe's name for this sacred cave. Just outside is a turbulent sea of Wuchumbu. They've filled the rocky patch of ground that lies adjacent to the hill I climbed with Ratu almost a month ago. To think the Banoochee and the source of the light of many colors were beneath my feet, albeit well below. The entrance to the cave, two meters high and narrow enough to have to enter sideways, sits in the rock face at the bottom of the hill's cliffside. I've walked past this place before during my limited search for Efawi, but the elephant hide pinned across its entrance blends in well with the surrounding rock.

I became separated from Mhaawu as soon as we arrived at the rocky patch. We lost each other among the dense crowd of excited and anxious Wuchumbu. After fifteen minutes of unsuccessfully trying to elicit where their leader and the Banoochee were, I stumbled across Beejalee, who took the time to give me some answers.

She apologized for not being completely open with me on the night the prior shaman died. Although she doesn't know what he threw in the fire, my description of it reminded her of something that appeared in the sky two years before—an event the tribe never talks about for reasons of superstition, and Beejalee didn't mention it because she wanted to protect me.

But given that some of the tribe are now reentering the Banoochee, and that everyone is talking about the light of many colors more freely, Beejalee felt comfortable telling me more as she led me through the throng and to the cave. Her version of events was unfortunately filled with the usual Wuchumbu mythology. Still, I listened in the hope I might glean something from her account.

The Massas trees that grow in the jungle are apparently an ancient gift from one of the tribe's gods—their sky god, the great Massas (hence the name "Massas tree"). The tribe used to hold ceremonies where they'd drink a brew made from the fruit of these Massas trees, and those who drank the brew would see patterns of multicolored light before journeying to the supposed spirit realm, returning once the effects of the brew had worn off.

Two years ago, on an otherwise normal day, a similar display of multicolored light filled the sky. But this was not the effect of the Massas fruit; nobody had even drunk the brew that day. Once the dazzling display in the sky had everyone's attention, the light morphed into a smaller, more focused shape, as though it were something tangible. This tangible, multicolored thing descended from above and flew into the Banoochee.

Before this strange event, the Banoochee had been a special place to the Wuchumbu and was thought to be endowed with "great spirit." Inside this cave was, and still is, a large rock shaped like an altar that stands as tall as three men (another creation of the great sky god Massas, who seems to be responsible for a lot around here). The Wuchumbu used to use this giant rock for ceremonial occasions such as births, ritual offerings, and for the seeking of spiritual guidance. Inside the cave, they would sing and dance and drink the Massas fruit. Put simply, the cave was their spiritual home.

When the many colors descended into the cave, Mhaawu ordered everyone to stay away while she and the prior shaman went inside. A day passed before the two investigators reemerged at a larger entrance that has since been blocked with rocks. They were deeply shaken and troubled. They declared the many colors to be an evil spirit that was now occupying the top of their sacred altar rock, having displaced a large, precious sculpture of their Massas sky god, knocking the wooden carving to the ground and breaking it in two.

The many colors had apparently tried to tempt Mhaawu and the shaman, but they were able to escape unharmed. From that day onward, nobody apart from the tribe's leader and the prior shaman was allowed to enter the Banoochee for fear of stirring the evil spirit. They dragged one of the large pieces of broken sculpture from the cave to the center of the settlement to act as a reminder that the Banoochee was no longer safe.

And so, for the past two years, the tribe's precious altar rock has been claimed by another being, they've had no place for their spiritual focus, and Mhaawu just hasn't been the same. She verbally renounced her faith in the Massas and also spoke against the ceremonial drinking of the Massas fruit. And that was as far as Beejalee got with her story before she ushered me inside the cave.

With my eyes now adjusted, faint flickers of multicolored light become visible to my left at the end of the narrow corridor that runs from the cave's entrance. I shuffle sideways toward the colored light, my back pressed against a cold wall of rock, my belly pressing against the wall opposite. I guess this is what Ratu meant when he said I'm too fat to find what I'm looking for. He must have known about this place yet told me nothing, the little shit. (And if he thinks I'm overweight now, he should have seen me before I entered the Nsanba!) Efawi would be thin enough to make it along this passage with ease, although she would have had to remove her armored suit. The thought that she most likely already shuffled along this corridor, her body touching these same rocks, helps to calm my nerves. Is it possible Efawi could still be here?

My lead foot kicks against something hard, and I trip sideways, stepping onto the obstacle itself, then over it. Once I've regained my balance, I feel the obstacle with my foot. Hard and smooth—rectangular, but with the top side rounded. A landmine? Efawi included pictures of them in the instructions she left. There were a few different types used during The War, one of which was a rectangular box with a rounded top like this. I suppose a soldier must have placed one here as a trap. In any case, I don't seem to have activated it, and a group of Wuchumbu led by the Gommo twins came this way about twenty minutes before me, so the landmine must have long expired. Thank you, Banoochee, for the friendly welcome.

I recommence shuffling, noting that the corridor slopes downward. I want to make quick progress but am hesitant with each step. I'm not a believer in Beejalee's talk of an "evil spirit," but I do believe in spiders and scorpions and whatever other biting or stinging creatures might dwell inside a cave.

I soon reach the end of the corridor, which bends sharply into another passageway. This passageway is a little wider, and I'm grateful to no longer have to walk sideways. The wavering light, which must originate from further within the Banoochee, is slightly brighter here, and the fluctuations in color more obvious. As I progress, the raucous Wuchumbu—most of whom are waiting outside as per Mhaawu's request—become harder to hear and the sound of my unsteady breathing more obvious.

I wind my way along corridor after corridor, each a little brighter and a little wider than the last, and stop just before what appears to be the final turn. The light from beyond this bend is much sharper, gently dancing from turquoise to scarlet, then blue. It seems just one more turn and I'll be faced with the source of the many colors—whatever the hell that is. And what if it's dangerous? Here I am, seminaked and about to blunder onward with nothing to protect myself, not even my stone knife. Goosebumps prickle on my arms. I rub them and take a deep breath of chilled underground air as I psyche myself up.

"It is so beautiful. I cannot stop crying," comes a voice from beyond the turn.

"I do not want to leave the Banoochee," says another.

"But we have to leave if we want to find out more. That is what Mhaawu said."

Fearing that Mhaawu is sending everyone outside, I dart forward, and as I turn into the bend, I collide with Gommonogo. "Wrong way, idiot," he snarls, and pushes past me. Behind him lops the rest of the group, pouring into the corridor, knocking me backward.

"What's going on?" I ask. I plant my feet and struggle to hold firm against the tide, catching a glimpse of the place they're leaving: an enormous cavern filled with dancing light.

"We made a deal with Mhaawu," says Etoole. "We may drink, but only outside of the Banoochee."

"Drink what?" I cry.

The forty or so Wuchumbu continue to funnel from the cavern, and I'm unable to squeeze past them. Eventually, the horde dwindles, and I make another attempt at a dash, only for a pair of hands to lift me from the ground. "We are meant to leave now," says Big Man, his tone friendly.

"Put him down," says Mhaawu as she appears behind him. "Where have you been, Okon? You were supposed to follow me."

Big Man places me on the ground. The shaman is the last to emerge, struggling with a basket that's covered with a fur. The woman has taken a disliking to me ever since I threw up her predecessor's heart, and she scowls at me as she passes, loses her footing, and stumbles. Five multicolored things, just like the one I lost, are propelled from the basket and hit the corridor wall with a thud, leaving a twinkling smear at the points of impact.

Once again, I'm captivated by the dazzling luminescence of the things. "Mhaawu, I need to know what they are."

"Come," she says, standing at the turn and beckoning me to go past.

I take a deep breath. "This is it," I mutter, and step forward on shaky legs for a clear sight of the cavern beyond. A small gasp leaves my lips as I absorb the scene.

The cavern is the size of a cathedral. The entrance, in front of which I'm standing, is elevated, and an uneven slope runs to the ground below. Colored light hangs in the air, unnatural and breathtaking, but what really steals the scene is in the distance. Toward the back wall stands the "evil spirit" itself: the hijacker of the tribe's precious Banoochee; the many colors; what must surely be the discovery that compelled my wife to come here—a discovery that, according to Efawi, will bring a wave of change across the globe.

"It's a fucking multicolored tree," I say.

"It is the tree of many colors," Mhaawu responds.

From this far away, the details of the tree are unclear, but its densely packed branches twist and stretch their way from its trunk to form an overall shape that is irregular and full of angles. The whole thing is alive with color, and as I stare, it seems there's visual trickery at play, with the tree appearing to be solid yet phantom, still and yet moving. A subtle pulsing of its light appears to beat in time with my rapid pulse.

I stutter: "How . . . ? What . . . ?" Adrenaline floods through me. Although I don't believe in spirits falling from the sky and entering caves, I have no explanation for what I'm seeing, only insufficient words. *Supernatural. Unearthly. Magical.*

I feel for the rocky ground as I sit and continue to absorb the scene. The cavern is jagged, perhaps a hundred meters at its widest, with at least thirty meters between the ground and the highest sections of ceiling. The tree stands at the far end on top of an enormous rock, which must be the fabled altar rock. Light radiates from the tree and slowly disperses through the space in clusters, some of it hanging in the atmosphere like pigment suspended in water. In places, soft geometric patterns of light emerge in the air itself before morphing and dissipating. And when I turn my head, the display delicately morphs as if in response. The spectacle is utterly overwhelming.

"I hear voices, like a faint chanting," I say. "A drumming too?"

"Yes. The tree is quiet now but becomes louder the more time that passes without a Wuchumbu coming into the Banoochee. The prior shaman and I had to visit this place every few days—otherwise, the tree of many colors would become so loud it could be heard from outside."

I shake my head in disbelief.

"I see them now," I say, after spotting tiny smudges of intense color peppered about the branches. "That multicolored thing you gave me grows on the tree?"

"A fruit," Mhaawu replies. "Like the Massas fruit, but not like the Massas fruit."

"I don't understand."

"The tree of many colors is an imitation of a Massas tree. They are similar in appearance."

"Really? Ratu has pointed out a Massas tree to me before, and I don't think it was bearing fruit at the time, but in any case, it looked the same as every other tree in the jungle—and absolutely nothing like what I'm staring at right now."

"The shape of their leaves and flowers and fruit are the same, but this tree is larger, stranger, and shines with many colors."

"So, the cubes I saw the prior shaman throw into the fire were multicolored fruit cut into pieces?"

"Possibly; the prior shaman did many strange things. The tree troubled him greatly. He became obsessed with its fruit, and I have seen him take many of them. We never run out. The fruit of many colors does not *grow*, but when we pick one, another fruit immediately appears, fully formed, to compensate."

"So, what the fuck is it?" I ask. The longer I stare at the tree, the more my head spins.

"We need to drink the fruit of many colors right now!" Etoole shouts from the connecting corridors, his words reverberating off the walls.

"They're going to drink that thing?" I ask. I get to my feet, my body shaking even though it's warmer in the cavern, the light bringing with it some heat. The shaman and Big Man have been waiting behind us. Mhaawu gestures with her hand for me to exit.

"I can't leave yet," I tell her. "This is it. This tree is what my wife came here for. It must be."

Mhaawu's brow furrows as further demands are yelled from the impatient group outside. I turn back to the cavern and shout "Efawi" as loud as I can. Her name disappears into the gargantuan chamber before bouncing back to me from different angles.

"There is nobody else here," says Mhaawu.

I fix my gaze on the tree. "Mhaawu, when my wife was about to sign the contract for the sale of one of her companies, the organizers told me to leave the room. 'Involved parties only,' they said. Efawi scolded them. Said she wouldn't sign unless I was by her side. She knew how life changing that moment would be for us and that we should witness it together. Of course, I got to sit next to her as she stamped her biometrics on the contract. From that moment onward, we never had to struggle for money again."

"I have no idea what you are talking about," says Mhaawu.

"What I'm trying to say is that Efawi wouldn't have left me behind unless she had a plan for us to reunite. This tree is all I have that connects me to her—to where she is. I need to work out how she intends for us to find each other."

Tears form; the kaleidoscope blurs. Mhaawu touches my arm, and I turn to face her. The tribe's leader is bathed in a soft, swirling, multicolored light, her expression sympathetic. "I do not know how your wife is connected to this place, but there is only one way for you to understand what is happening here. You must drink the brew of many colors."

18: The Lights

It looks like a rainbow has been ripped to shreds and thrown into pond water.

"Drink it," says the shaman, her voice shrill, as she waves a bowl of it in my face. She's agitated. Some of the tribe didn't want her to be the one to make the brew of many colors, and she's heard there's talk of her being replaced—talk which began after the debacle of the prior shaman's funeral. There are others in the tribe—Feplao, for example—who apparently have a much better understanding of jungle medicines and spiritual practices but were pushed to the side by the prior shaman.

"What ingredients have you used other than the multicolored fruit?" I ask.

"Get on with it," the shaman growls.

"Is there meant to be a bug in there?"

"Others are waiting," she shrieks.

Feplao walks over to me, places a slender finger in the brew, and flicks out the bug. "The beetle is not an ingredient," she says.

The shaman huffs. I take the wooden bowl from her heavily wrinkled hands. On the ground beside her sits a large clay pot of brew, which she's been dipping this bowl into and handing out to those who want it. The group who went into the Banoochee have already had their share and are looking a little faint and distant. Furs have been rushed from the settlement to here, the

163

rocky patch outside the cave, for the brew drinkers to rest on.

I bring the bowl close to my mouth, hold it there, wonder if it's possible that the fruit of many colors is radioactive. The shaman tries to grab the bowl back, but I keep it from her reach. "You are wasting time," she says. "There are many more who wish to drink."

"Why can't you give them a different bowl?" I ask.

"Because this is the sacred bowl, you fool. If you do not drink this very moment, I will tell Big Man to take the bowl from you and carry you away from here, preferably to a place you can't find your way back from."

"Okay, okay, I'll drink, but Big Man would never do that to me."

Big Man raises an eyebrow. I press the bowl against my lips and close my eyes. Mhaawu said the fruit reveals the purpose of the tree, and so surely this should help me find Efawi. Perhaps she consumed the multicolored fruit too? I tilt the bowl and drink. I've barely finished before the shaman snatches the bowl from me.

"Tastes like rainbow feces," I say.

"Tell someone who cares," she replies. She dips the bowl in the pot and turns to the next person waiting.

"There's a piece of grass in here," I whine and try to pull it from between my teeth.

Beejalee places a hand on my shoulder. "The other drinkers tell me the brew of many colors tastes like the brew of Massas. Please do not disrespect it, Okon," she says.

"Sorry," I reply. "I'm nervous. Will you be drinking it too?"

"No. Habee has though." She points to her husband, who is sat on a fur, drooling, his head between his legs.

The shaman starts an annoying chant as she administers the brew to the remaining few of the seventy or so who decided to drink. Surprisingly, everyone wants the brew, but most are resisting out of respect for Mhaawu's wishes.

I head to where the other drinkers are seated, become unsteady on my feet before I get there. Adienatta and Obee rush to my aid and lower me to a fur. Mhaawu is at the cave entrance, talking to Big Man and a handful of others. She seems to be giving them instructions, and once she's finished, they enter the cave, and Mhaawu walks over to us.

Then the burning begins: a sensation that starts in my chest and spreads through my body. My heart pumps harder, quickening the spread of heat. Obee squeals. I've been holding his arm too tightly.

"Breathe, Habee. Breathe," Beejalee says to her husband. I follow her instruction. *In, out, in, out.* The shaman's chanting fills the air, a melodic humming mixed with indistinct speech. My blood is on fire. My head spins. This was a mistake. I can't believe I drank that. Efawi would never have drank that. I think I'm about to die!

Then the lights come.

My vision fills with multicolored patterns, the same dynamic forms as those emanated by the tree. Beejalee said a vision like this comes to those who drink the Massas fruit. But I haven't drunk the Massas fruit. I don't even know what this thing I've drunk is.

I lie back, close my eyes, squeeze fistfuls of fur as tight as I can. The multicolored light eventually retreats as black creeps inward from the edges, and when the light becomes so small I no longer see it, a final image surfaces in my mind: Efawi swinging that spade at a PPA agent outside our home as I watch through the AR window of my entertainment room, impotent.

And then . . . I'm asleep?

Well, I don't seem to be awake. The burning sensation in my blood remains. I look down at my body and find that I've become an anatomy illustration, my vascular network lit up like branches of the multicolored tree. Colorful digested fruit flows from my center and circulates outward, pumped through my veins, reaching my fingers and toes. I must be asleep, else I'd be more shocked by this vision.

I'm outside my body now, watching myself. The digested fruit continues to circulate and reaches my head, where colorful bits of information are passed into my brain like data being downloaded. The bits vary in size and color and are transferred in a complex sequence that I don't understand. If I were awake, I'm certain I'd be panicking. Instead, I observe with fascination. It isn't clear how much time passes like this, but eventually the bits stop flowing, and with my brain now lit up, it seems the download is complete, and I sense it wants to be heard or read or understood. Instinctively, I reach forward and touch my forehead.

My body tingles. And the download plays.

19: The Big Man Hero Man

I gasp into wakefulness.

My heart is racing at mouse speed. A few moments pass before I realize where I am: the rocky patch beside the hill, exactly where I was when I fell "asleep," but it's a little darker now.

I sit up, and the fur I've been lying on sticks to my back. Most of the tribe is still here, their features dim in twilight. A breeze disturbs the dozens of mats and furs that have been laid out. Those who drank the brew after me are still on the ground, eyes closed, motionless. The ones who drank before me are gingerly getting to their feet. "The tree of many colors must be activated immediately!" one of them cries.

Their words jolt me, and I'm assailed by memories of my experience while I was under. I check my groin with serious concern I may have wet myself. Beejalee approaches her husband, who sits a couple of meters away. "My dear, you are sweating, and your whole body is shaking," she says. She kneels beside Habee and rubs his back. "I told you not to drink the brew."

Habee looks at his wife with large, fearful eyes. "How can I tell our children that such power exists?" he says.

I wave my arms for his attention. "Habee, what did you learn?" I hiss.

"I learned that Mhaawu told the unassociated man the truth," he says.

"That the light of many colors is a weapon, yes?" I say.

"Yes."

"That it really can end the life of every person who is not Wuchumbu, yes?"

"Yes."

"What you are saying matches what the others are saying," says Beejalee. I pull myself to my feet and stagger over to those who drank the brew before me, who are now fully awake and talking to those who didn't drink:

"The tree of many colors is from another world."

"Non-Wuchumbu hands cannot activate it."

"But any Wuchumbu hand will work."

"If that were true, Mhaawu would have activated the tree already."

"Of course this is true. You did not drink the brew, so you do not know."

The tribe continue to converse and debate as the brew drinkers describe what they went through while under the influence of the multicolored fruit. All their accounts align with each other, as well as with what I went through. While I was under the spell of the brew, the download *played* as if it were imprinted knowledge and I were simply recalling it for the first time. This began with information about the creator of the tree of many colors—a collection of entities that exists somewhere between being separate and being one. Nonetheless, they referred to themselves as the *treemaker*.

The download informed me that the power of the treemaker is transcendent—so much so, the extent of its capabilities was, and still is, almost lost on me. Along with this power, another quality of the treemaker's was apparent: its sheer alienness. Unassociated to the very extreme. No common ground by which I might relate to it. And this feeling of unrelatability disturbs me even more than its power. Leaves me cold, as if trapped beneath ice. The treemaker originated in our universe, but not on Earth.

The specifics of its location weren't given, but a sense of the vast distance between us was provided, along with the understanding that such distances mean nothing to it.

According to the download, our species is approaching a pivotal moment in its development, after which a period of runaway technological growth will see our control over the material world accelerate to entirely new levels, along with our ability to cause catastrophic harm not only within the bounds of our planet but, with time, at cosmic scales.

And so, before this pivotal moment occurs and our technological growth becomes increasingly harder to stop, the Wuchumbu have been presented with an opportune moment for reflection and, if needed, intervention. Should the tribe decide that our species shouldn't be allowed to continue on its current trajectory, any one of the Wuchumbu may go to the tree of many colors and place a hand within a hollow in its trunk. Doing so will bring an end to the civilization of Homo sapiens, while leaving the Wuchumbu people unharmed.

I shudder, and a peculiar sensation stirs inside my head.

"This is preposterous!" yells Gommonaadogo as she points to the cave entrance. "Big Man blocks the way!"

"We need to guard the Banoochee at all times in case the unassociated find it," says Mhaawu.

"But you are also guarding the Banoochee from the Wuchumbu!" Etoole protests.

"Does anyone feel like there's something inside their head?" I interrupt. I motion as if to vomit and end up coughing, my insides too disturbed to be coordinated.

"Okon?" says Beejalee.

"Something's not right in my brain. I think the fruit juice is still in there, or the treemaker, or something—and it's watching me, or us, or something like that." If I hadn't seen the tree with my own eyes, if we hadn't all received the same information from the fruit, I would think I were going crazy.

"Nobody else will go back into the Banoochee—not today at least," says Mhaawu.

"But we have been gifted the solution to all our problems," shrieks Gommonaadogo.

"Perhaps, but we need time to understand the decision we have to make," says Mhaawu.

"What more could there be to understand? We must activate the tree immediately for the protection of our people," says Gommonogo.

"That is your view," says Mhaawu, "but the decision is for all Wuchumbu to make. We need to be sure that nobody enters the Banoochee and activates the tree of many colors without the full consent of our people."

"Mhaawu is right," says Beejalee, "we need to decide together."

"I believe that is wise," adds Adienatta.

"I believe that is nonsense," says Etoole. "We hold a spear to the neck of our oppressors, who, according to Okon, can strike us a deadly blow at any moment. Yet we dither and debate what to do?"

I try to focus, but my head just isn't clear. I picture my brain soaked in multicolored juice. The tribe's argument intensifies.

"If Big Man does not move, I will move him!"

"There are other guards in the cave, not only Big Man."

"Mhaawu should have activated the tree when it arrived."

"The prior shaman also knew about the tree. Why did they not activate it long ago?"

"They let us down."

"We need to do what they failed to do."

"I demand to enter the Banoochee!"

Mhaawu looks at me with desperation. "Okon, you must tell them what you told me," she says. She pulls me to the front of the protesting group. "Tell them about the unassociated world. Tell them about all the people," she instructs.

My head spins. "This is . . . the situation we are in is just . . . too much," I say. "The tree must never be activated. Not ever."

"Of course Okon would say that," snarls Gommonogo. "When we activate the tree of many colors he will die too, along with his wife and all the other unassociated."

"Okon, tell them how many unassociated there are," says Mhaawu.

Everyone's looking at me, the details of their faces lost to the fading daylight. To think that anyone from this group could bring about the end of human civilization. "There are more unassociated than there are trees in the Nsanba," I announce.

Gasps erupt.

"Then we are in even more danger than we realized!" Etoole cries.

"If I were not convinced we need to activate the tree, I am certainly convinced now!" someone yells.

Mhaawu cuts me a furious glance before addressing the crowd: "Okon also meant to explain that the unassociated are not all evil. They are just like us. Mothers. Fathers. Children. Yes, Okon?"

The stirring sensation in my head returns. Is the treemaker in there, watching? Has the brew damaged me? I seem to be suffering the effects more than the others who drank.

"Okon?" Mhaawu repeats.

"Yes . . . that's correct. Mothers, fathers, and children," I reply, still struggling to focus as the tribe continue to debate.

"It is not possible for there to be more unassociated than there are trees in the Nsanba!"

"Can the tree of many colors kill them all if there are so many?"

"It does not matter how many there are. If we activate the tree, then the unassociated and all their things—their entire world—will come to an end. The brew of many colors made this clear."

"And we will live?"

"Yes, only the Wuchumbu will live."

"Okon, what are the unassociated making that the treemaker believes might one day cause so much harm?" asks Petonba.

"I . . . I have no idea," I reply. "We have weapons. Nuclear missiles, for instance. Devices that could reduce the Nsanba to ash within seconds. But we've had those for a very long time."

Eyes widen. *Ohhhs* commence. "We must activate the tree without delay!" someone screams. I shake my head. The Wuchumbu are so naive about what's happening in the world. They are the least qualified to make judgment about our civilization.

The cool evening breeze whips across the rocky opening. I wrap my arms around my chest, my teeth chattering. I've stepped into a bad dream of alien tree makers, message-delivering fruits, and the threat of apocalypse. None of this makes any sense. My craving for home swells. Cotton underwear. Moabi cakes. Pickled steak. Peppe juice. Float rooms. Gyroshowers. Mattresses. Air conditioning. Insect screens. Online worlds. VR. Efawi.

A warm body presses against my side and gives me a reassuring squeeze. I imagine it's my wife come to rescue me from this madness. "You are shaking," says Adienatta, somehow calm while everyone else, me in particular, is losing their shit.

Mhaawu's attention turns to me once more. "Okon, this is your last chance. I cannot convince them about the outside world, but you can. This is the only reason I let you live with us. You are putting so many lives at risk, yours included."

I inhale deeply, desperate for some clarity of thought and some words to go with it. "Yes, of course the tree mustn't be activated," I tell the group. "It would be the worst thing anyone could do. You'd be killing countless people. You'd be killing my wife. You'd be killing me."

The gathering's arguing continues.

"They aren't listening!" I complain to Mhaawu. "And when they do listen, whatever I say just makes things worse. It's not right for this responsibility to be put on me. I've had enough of being the bridge. Efawi should be the one dealing with this."

Mhaawu waves her hand at me, dismissing me like I'm a waste of her time. "We have spent too long outside the Banoochee," she says to the group. "We do not want this place to become known to the unassociated. It is time to return to the settlement."

Their debate rages on, and I stop listening. I fix my sights on the cave; I need to get back in there. The brew may have given me some answers, but not the answers I need to find Efawi. I march toward the Banoochee, my head still not quite right. Big Man watches me approach. He barely fits inside the gash in the rock face, and his eyes peer out from behind the elephant hide, which he holds to one side with a spear. Fallen boulders line the ground between us.

As I get closer to the Banoochee entrance, my foggy thoughts are interrupted: ~*You have a new message from Efawi,*~ says my nôvono pro. I stop dead in my tracks and ask my brain implant to repeat itself, which it does. Big Man continues to watch me. I can only imagine what the stress must be doing to my face.

~*nôvono play message,*~ I instruct.

~*Nurgh . . . ee . . . greepgh . . . cruffhh . . .*~ The scrambled noise fills my head, with the odd snippet recognizable as my wife's voice. *Interference.*

While the Wuchumbu continue to argue, I dart back and forth across the open ground. By now, Big Man must think I've lost my mind, but I deduce that the nôvo-message can only be picked up within a twenty-meter radius of the cave. If Efawi's memory drive is in the Banoochee, surely my nôvono would have picked up the jumbled message when I shuffled through its corridors earlier this evening. Unless a bird or a bat moved the drive since?

I'm confused, but all I can do is head for the entrance.

I fix my eyes on Big Man and march toward him. He pushes the elephant hide to one side and steps into the open. His considerable frame blocks the entrance entirely. Fortunately, the expression on his face is sympathetic. Big Man is a man of few words, but I often have the sense he's looking out for me. Most of the tribe probably feel he's looking out for them too. Regardless, Mhaawu instructed him to guard the entrance, and he would likely rather die than let her down.

"I need to go inside," I demand, my eyes level with his nipples.

Big Man folds his arms.

"Please," I continue. "I can't activate the tree, because I'm not a Wuchumbu, so there's no danger in letting me in."

"I know you cannot activate it," says Big Man, "but Mhaawu told me not to let anyone inside." He looks across the rocky opening to the tribe's leader, who is busy trying to persuade everyone to return to the settlement.

"I just need to find something my wife left me," I say. "A little thing which contains a message. It's harmless." I use my fingers to indicate the size and shape of the memory drive in the hope he won't be concerned about something so small.

Big Man screws his nose up, the meaning of which I have no idea. I'm about to speak again when he shoves his spear in my face. "Take it," he says, and I oblige. He reaches for a woven pouch that hangs at his waist and goes to open it, pauses, then rips the pouch from its vine cord and hands it to me with his fingertips.

I open the pouch and release a happy squeal as I pull out a section of red string, followed by a small piece of shiny black plastic. Not a scratch or mark on it. No bird or bat shit.

"While you were all sleeping from the brew," says Big Man, "some of us came into the Banoochee to guard the tree of many colors. We found that beside the tree, on top of the rock of

Massas. It looks unassociated, and we do not know how it got there, but it should not be on the rock of Massas. So, I volunteered to take it to the river when I leave the Banoochee. Sorry, Okon. I did not know it belonged to your wife."

"This proves she's been inside the cave," I say, the words making me giddy. "I knew she'd find a way to get through to me. She was here, Big Man. She was here!" I stomp my feet as I struggle to contain my excitement. "She left this for me," I mutter, gripping her memory drive tightly.

"There is another unassociated thing, much bigger than this one, on the floor in the corridor behind me," says Big Man. "Does that also belong to your wife? I was going to take them both to the river."

"That old landmine? You should leave that where it is. Could be dangerous if you move it." I shove the spear back into Big Man's hand, stand on the tips of my toes, and plant a kiss on his cheek. "You are a hero," I tell him. "A big man hero man. You mustn't let anyone activate the tree. I have what I need now; Efawi is going to fix everything."

20: The Promise

~ Okon, I have terrible news, ~ my wife's nôvo-message begins, her dread pouring through.

My heart pounds, and I instruct my brain implant to pause the playback. "Great job, Efawi," I mutter. "Way to get me nervous." I pace back and forth in the dark. I'm cold, hungry, and alone. Should have grabbed some uddu and a couple of furs before marching out of the Anomalous Zone. At least I've been marking trees as I go, and I know I'm just outside the AZ because this is the first time the nôvo-message has played without being scrambled.

"Come on, Okon. Grow some balls," I tell myself, but I'm afraid of what her "terrible news" might be. On my way here, I let my optimism get the better of me—hoped Efawi would already have the tree situation and the PPA situation in hand somehow. I ask my nôvono how old the message is and am told Efawi recorded it twenty-six days ago. This confirms my wife and I were in the AZ at the same time. *We were here at the same damn time!* But is she still around? I stop pacing and instruct my nôvono to continue playing.

~ Five months have passed since I entered the Nsanba and there's still no sign of you, ~ says Efawi. *~ I'd been desperate to believe you were following in my footsteps, but having discovered what I have, I'm no longer sure what's best for you. You should know I'm leaving*

this message unencrypted, in case you're not the one to find it. Its content is of the utmost importance for all. And so, to whoever is listening, I ask that you listen carefully . . .~

At this point, Efawi takes on a businesslike tone, something my wife is well-versed in when functioning under pressure. She goes on to provide the key facts about the cave, the tree, and the tribe. Facts I'm already aware of. I grip my head as the nôvo-message plays.

~ . . . and so, this is no time to celebrate the discovery of life beyond our planet. As fantastical as my warning sounds, this is the reality we face. I implore you, the listener of this message, to seek the truth directly through the only means I'm aware of: the consumption of a fruit from the tree.

~ Despite my best efforts, I have thus far been unable to devise a plan I can execute on-site that will prevent the tribe from triggering this weapon. And so, I've concluded I must leave this place, take the fruit to the PPA in Mbapazu, and persuade them to consume it. Those in power need to experience the message-giving fruit directly because if they don't, I know I won't be believed. They will consider it fantasy.

~ Despite my well-documented history of argument with the PPA, they are unfortunately the only organization with the expertise and resources needed for swift and effective control of the situation here. For the sake of everyone, I wholeheartedly commit to undertaking whatever action is necessary to ensure the tree is never triggered, even if that means reaching out to an enemy for assistance. I can only hope the PPA share this commitment. And to the listener of this message, I ask you do the same. ~

Efawi falls silent for a moment. Clearly when she recorded this message, she didn't know the PPA was already here—that I had unwittingly led them to the Anomalous Zone. I hope she'll be more forgiving of my mistake now that she wants the PPA to be involved—which is very surprising, but I suppose the situation necessitates it. Before Efawi continues, I detect a change in the sentiment seeping through. It seems she's about to shift from her businesslike reporting to something more personal. I brace myself.

~ Okon, if you're the one listening, the remainder of this message is for you. I can't thank you enough for coming all this way, my love. We made a commitment to each other all those years ago, and here we are, still committed, despite the hardship. You are what keeps me going and always will be, which is what makes it so hard for me to advise as I'm about to. ~

I detect Efawi struggling and failing to contain her feelings. Frustration, exhaustion, and guilt all make their way through the call. *~ I can only assume you've just walked from the cave to the outside of the Anomalous Zone to listen to this message, and knowing how optimistic you can be, perhaps as you walked you grew excited that I might have some good news, that I might instruct you on how to leave this terrible place and meet me elsewhere. Well, I'm sorry to tell you this, but you need to go back into the AZ and do everything you can to ensure the tree isn't activated. And you need to stay there until I'm able to bring you help. I feel awful for saying this, and I'm so sorry for ever getting you involved, but there's no point in us returning home if the tribe will end everything—which I'm sure they will if left to their own devices.*

~ Before I set foot in the Nsanba, I knew there was a tribal people living in the AZ; I could see them in the satellite footage. But my interest was in the strange lights and anomalous readings. I considered the tribe to be irrelevant to my mission, and so I didn't plan for them. Obviously, dismissing the tribe was a mistake. Sheer luck enabled me to evade them on my way here, and I've been hiding from them ever since, taking care that my presence remains unknown. I can only hope you've been able to avoid them too. I do not trust them with the fate of our species. ~

Efawi pauses before she continues, her frustration softening. *~ This morning I'll start my long journey back to Mbapazu with the alien fruit in my bag. My time alone in the jungle, away from my* *day-to-day life, has been a much-needed opportunity for self-reflection. And I see more clearly now all the mistakes I've made. How I've filled my life with unnecessary tension and confrontation. I want to apologize for this, Okon. It can't have been easy to live with me this way. Should we survive this terrible challenge of the tree, I want to bring my conflict with the PPA and others to an end. I will cooperate so my arrest warrant is withdrawn, and you and I can live out our lives freely.*

~I know we have our problems. We had been bickering all too frequently. We are not so ready with our affection as we once were. Our interests and priorities have diverged of late. I'm sure it all began when we became financially affluent. We responded differently to the thing we had dreamed of for so long. Yet we're still together, and I never want that to change. Which brings me to some exciting news, Okon. News that only elevates our need to ensure the tree is never triggered. Are you sitting down? After we had sex on my last day at home, I went straight to the villa. While there, my arrest warrant came through and I became trapped. So there was no opportunity for me to "correct" the issue of you forgetting to take your pill. And as I stand here now . . . I'm five months pregnant.~

Efawi's excitement mingles with my shock. My legs suddenly weaken. My face tingles.

~Oh, I wish I could see your reaction. I hope my feelings about this turn of events are coming through to your nôvono loud and clear. Not only have I come to accept this is happening to me—to us—but I've become grateful for it. I know I've been against having a child for so long, but as I said, being out here has changed me, has given me the space to reevaluate. I want to spend many long and happy years raising a family with you, Okon. I hope you still want the same.

~But for us to have a future with our child, we must both play our part in keeping the tribe from the tree. I promise you I will do whatever I can. I don't know the circumstances in which you are listening to this, but if you are in or near the Anomalous Zone, you must promise me you will do whatever you can until I'm able to send the PPA your way. And should I be successful, if there is any

assistance you can provide to the PPA, you must do so wherever possible, take responsibility wherever you can, do whatever it takes for the sake of our unborn child. The three of us will be better for being together. Apotheosis through union. I love you so much, Okon. Now and always; I'll never give up on us. And I know you won't let us down. ~

21: The Fantasy

"Pregnant?" says Thembe.

"It's mine," I tell him, then feel weird for stating the obvious.

Thembe glances at a moth flapping around the ceiling light of his tiny jungle office, then he leans back in his chair. His hair is a little ruffled, but the independent consultant still looks presentable, despite having just been woken up in the middle of the night.

"Interesting that you both have nôvono implants," he says. "According to your files, you don't."

Yet another secret of Efawi's I've revealed, but I wouldn't have been able to bring Thembe up to date without doing so. I fidget in my plastic chair, unable to get comfortable.

"So," he says, "there's an alien death tree in a cave that communicates via its fruit?"

"Sounds strange when you say it out loud, but yes," I reply.

"And Efawi left a nôvo-message in this cave to warn people?"

"Yes, and after I heard her message, I came straight to your jungle base. I would have gotten lost in the dark, but your night watch had a floodlight on. You might want to tell them to turn that off, given the whole clandestine nature of your mission."

Thembe sighs. "I will speak with them personally," he says. "So, Efawi's nôvo-message didn't enlighten us as to what she hoped to achieve by coming here?"

"No."

"Well, if she left the area to inform the PPA of her findings, I've heard nothing about her showing up."

"That's what I'm concerned about. If Efawi left the AZ on the same day she left the message in the cave, that means she's been trekking for the past twenty-six days and probably has another ten or so days before she makes it out, but she's five—no, six months pregnant. Pregnant and alone in the jungle! What if she's run into difficulty? What if she needs medical support? You have to get the PPA to look for her. Her route out is probably the same as my route in. She's carrying our first child, for crying out loud."

Thembe stares at me, expressionless. "Yes, of course," he eventually says. "I'll have search teams dispatched right away." He slaps the arms of his chair, as though the task at hand is complete, and stands up. "I would offer you a bed here, but it's probably best you stay with the tribe tonight to be sure they keep their faith in you. I'll have someone escort you back."

I remain seated.

"Is there something else?" he asks.

"Aren't you pleased we've finally heard from Efawi, your longtime friend?"

"Of course I am, but I won't be happy until she's found and being looked after."

"And what about tomorrow? You told the tribe they have twenty-four hours to provide you with information or you'll order a full sweep of the AZ and send them to prison. You're going to call that off, right?"

"I would love to call it off, but on what grounds?"

"On the grounds of the alien death tree I've been warning you about for the past hour!"

Thembe looks down at me, his eyebrows low, his lips a sad smile. He squeezes my shoulder.

"Don't look at me like that," I say. "Like I'm some idiot who just made all this up. I know it's a lot to believe, but you have to trust me on this one. It's too important not to."

Thembe sighs and sits back in his chair. "Whether I believe you or not is irrelevant," he says. "The twenty-four-hour deadline was set by senior officials at the PPA. If I ask them to call off their incursion because of a multicolored extraterrestrial tree that has the power to end civilization, what do you think their response would be?"

"Their response *should* be to call off the incursion."

"They would discharge me with immediate effect and escort me to a psychiatric ward."

"So, what do we do?"

"There's nothing we can do."

"What if the tribe cooperates?"

"Events would unfold less violently for them, and they might be permitted to continue living where they are, but the troops enter the AZ tomorrow regardless."

"Then the Wuchumbu will activate the tree in self-defense, and we will all die."

Thembe tries to hide a yawn behind his hand.

"You clearly don't believe me," I huff. "What if you heard the message from Efawi? It's unencrypted."

"You can leave the memory drive, and I'll ask the team to look at it, see if they can determine anything further regarding her current location."

I feel for the pouch hanging at my side, inside of which is the plastic memory drive—the only thing of hers in my possession. I reluctantly open the pouch. "Here. I copied the message to my nôvono anyway."

Thembe takes the drive and gets up from his chair again. "Just to be clear, Okon, this memory drive won't change anything. I want the incursion to be called off as much as you, but for the PPA to do that, they'll need more than outlandish claims, especially from you, who they will suspect are trying to protect the tribe, or from Efawi, whom they consider a bitter enemy of the state. All we can do now is sleep because tomorrow is going to be a big day."

The stirring sensation in my mind reemerges. I bury my face in my hands.

"Okon?"

"I think the multicolored brew did something to my head, put something in there, in addition to the information about the tree. I've felt it a few times now. It's like a presence. Usually only lasts for about a minute. I call it the Watcher, but I don't know what it is."

"Hmm," says Thembe. He must think I'm a lunatic. I hear him walk to the door. "Tell me where this 'tree' is," he says, "and I can have a scout check it out before morning."

"If you send in a scout to look at the tree, they will trigger it."

Thembe opens the door. "Goodnight, Okon. You can wait here for your escort. Feel free to come back when you have something that doesn't sound quite so fantastical."

Fantastical. Efawi talked about this in her nôvo-message; she knew others would consider her report on the tree to be fantasy unless they consumed the fruit for themselves. That's why she planned to take the fruit out of the Nsanba. I jump to my feet. "Thembe, wait. What if you were to receive the message from the treemaker directly?"

The door is almost closed, with Thembe on the other side. "If I saw and experienced what you claim to have seen and experienced," he says, "and if I were sure I wasn't having a mental breakdown, then I would do whatever it takes to stop tomorrow's incursion."

I pace up and down the room, barely able to contain myself. As Thembe goes to pull the door shut, I call out, "And you will order the search for Efawi?"

Thembe leans his head back into the room. "Already done,"

he says, tapping the side of his skull. "You're not the only one with a nôvono pro." He stands in the doorway, fidgeting with the door handle for a moment before adding, "When the soldiers enter the AZ tomorrow, find a place to hide. I've informed them you're an insider and are not to be harmed, but the PPA's special units have . . . a reputation."

22: The Specialist

We've said nothing for a while as we wait at the edge of the settlement. Mhaawu, Big Man, Beejalee, Habee, the Gommo twins, and a dozen others—more than enough to handle the one person we're waiting for, and all too aware that today, unlike any other day at the settlement, time matters.

"He's not coming."

"They have tricked us."

"Do we have enough people protecting the Banoochee?"

"Don't worry," I tell them. "He said he'll be here, so he'll be here."

I check my nôvono for the time, something I haven't needed to do while living with the Wuchumbu (and didn't know I could do until I thought of it this morning). Eleven hours until the PPA incursion.

"Any sign of Ratu yet?" I ask.

"No," says Mhaawu.

"Well, he's probably close by, watching what's going on from behind a big leaf. He's sneaky like that," I say, and Mhaawu mutters something under her breath.

A faint mechanical whir builds, only audible in the intervals between the howls from the monkeys above. The others hear it too and jerk to attention, their spears wavering. We all lean forward, eyes wide as we scan the thick weave of jungle. "There," says Beejalee, pointing.

Thembe's head stays oddly level with the ground as it darts between trees, growing larger as he nears. Moments later, the asymm scooter he's riding comes into view, along with a female passenger at his back, her arms wrapped around his chest. Neither are armored, not even a helmet. *Idiots.*

"Why are there two?" Mhaawu asks. "I told you to tell Thembe only he may come."

"I'm pretty sure I told him that," I reply.

After seeing Thembe late last night, I was delivered back to the settlement via a scooter to find Mhaawu already awake. I pleaded with her for a fruit to be taken to Thembe so he can learn the truth for himself. She'd been grumpy, but not as hard to convince as I expected. In fact, it was her idea for Thembe to be brought into the Banoochee to witness the tree and drink the brew within the cave for maximum effect. Although she furiously denied Thembe's request to see the weapon when they first met, she has since mulled things over and come to realize that the unassociated will continue to threaten her people until they know the power the tribe wields in the tree.

Thembe glides to a halt a few meters from us, spinning the scooter ninety degrees like a show-off. The Wuchumbu raise their spears, ready to attack the vehicle, and Mhaawu orders them to back down. Thembe cuts the engine, which silences the fans, and the scooter sags to the ground. The Wuchumbu stare at the shiny red thing in awe. They ask if it "has spirit."

"Any news on Efawi?" I call out.

Mhaawu grabs me by the arm. "I cannot allow this," she says. "Two is too many."

Thembe peels a pair of black leather gloves from his hands as he walks over to us. "Hi there," he says with a friendly smile. "Something wrong?"

"You are supposed to be alone," says Mhaawu.

"Am I? Okon said you want me to look at a tree-like device

you found and gather evidence for my superiors at the PPA. To do this, I need her." He points behind him at the woman. "She knows how to work the equipment. Cameras, scanners, measuring devices, sample collectors. All harmless, but necessary."

The short, muscled woman jumps from the scooter and heaves a large bag from the back. She looks up when she realizes we're all watching her, and returns our stares with small, analyzing eyes. Her dark skin is slick and pockmarked, her frizzy hair untidily tied back, and her nose twitches above a pair of down-turned lips. I don't know how long this person's been in the Nsanba for, but she looks like she's already had enough.

"Everybody, this is our specialist," Thembe announces.

The Wuchumbu appear confused. Mhaawu asks me if I know who she is.

"I don't, but you should allow her into the Banoochee," I reply. "This is our last chance to resolve the situation with no one being hurt."

Thembe gives me a crisp nod of approval.

"Without the *unassociated* being hurt," Mhaawu corrects. "My people will be fine."

She is right, of course. The tribe could activate the tree to ensure their safety. However, Mhaawu clearly doesn't want to resort to that, given she's had two years to stick her hand into the tree's hollow. I've no idea what's been holding her back, especially before I arrived, when the Wuchumbu thought all unassociated were monsters. If I were in Mhaawu's position, I would have triggered that thing the day it came.

"You outnumber the two of us," says Thembe. "You have spears; we carry no weapons. What possible threat could the specialist and I pose?"

I try to give Mhaawu an encouraging gesture with my hands to suggest the specialist should be allowed through. Mhaawu scowls as she decides what to do. Eyes dart nervously from one person to another. Eventually the tribe's leader declares they may both enter the Banoochee. "But neither of you can touch the tree of many colors," she instructs, "and you must both do exactly as I say at all times. Okon, you must search through everything they are bringing before we go any further."

Thembe claps his hands and smiles. "Sounds like we have a deal." He still doesn't believe what I told him about the tree, but he would prefer the PPA maintain their low profile rather than barge into the AZ with soldiers. So, he's come here this morning hoping the tribe will show him something—*anything*—that can justify a delay to the PPA's planned maneuvers.

I ask the specialist for the bag she's carrying, and she looks at me as though I'm stupid. Thembe then says something to her via his speaker implants in a language I do not recognize. My translator converts his words: "Give him the bag."

According to my implant, he spoke to her in Loallese, and so I assume the specialist is from the Nation of Loalla, which borders the northern reaches of the jungle. In Mbapazu, we only ever hear bad things about Loalla. The two states have been on very cold terms for decades. Loalla is the nation whose possible involvement in the AZ Thembe fears most, so why he would bring someone from there here, I've no idea.

She pulls the bag from her shoulders and shoves it in my chest, shooting me a foul look in the process.

"Any news on Efawi?" I ask Thembe.

"Not yet," he replies, "but like I told you this morning, we have people out there looking for her, and as soon as I hear anything, I'll let you know. The team has tried to determine the route she might have taken, estimated her speed and other variables, but the jungle is vast."

I picture my wife from above, surrounded by green, then I zoom out so I see the sheer enormity of the Nsanba and my wife becomes the tiniest dot, her pregnant belly extending that dot just a little. "I suppose it's too late to choose," I mutter to myself, "but I hope it is a girl."

I unzip the specialist's bag and remove its contents one item at a time. I don't know what most of them are, but so far, none appear to be a weapon.

"Don't touch me!" shouts the specialist in Loallese. I look up to find Gommonaadogo poking at her shirt with a stick.

"Remove what you are wearing," says Mhaawu.

Big Man throws a handful of scant Wuchumbu coverings and adornments at the independent consultant and his fiery assistant. "Is this necessary?" Thembe asks.

"Yes, it is," snaps Mhaawu.

"So are these," adds Gommonogo. He dangles two strips of woven vine in front of them. "For your eyes."

The specialist turns to Thembe. "They want me to wear this?" she asks in her native tongue as she holds up a loincloth. Thembe nods. The specialist mumbles something too quiet for my translator to pick up, and they both proceed to get changed while encircled by an anxious and curious group of hunter-gatherers. I complete my search of the bag while wondering why Thembe didn't give his assistant a translator.

The next time I look up, the two of them are dressed in minimalist Wuchumbu garb, their toned bodies exposed. The specialist stands tense while Thembe somehow remains relaxed, gently stretching his muscles. Both are blindfolded, the Wuchumbu clearly taking precautions to conceal the location of the Banoochee, and I realize I've let yet another secret slip: I gave Efawi's memory drive to Thembe, and in her nôvo-message she states the precise location of the tree. *Damn it.* This is not my fault; Efawi wants the PPA involved, and her message was unencrypted so that whoever needs to hear it can hear it.

"Well?" says Mhaawu.

"It's fine," I reply as I return the specialist's equipment to the bag. "No death-sticks," I add.

"Wait!" cries Gommonaadogo. She taps the bottom of the

specialist's leg with a long stick. Above her ankle is a small plastic square. "This must be left here," Gommonaadogo instructs.

"Can't do that, I'm afraid," says Thembe. "It's attached to her skin, but it poses no danger to you people, I assure you."

Mhaawu turns to me for advice. "Looks like a tag," I say. "They're used to monitor a person's location." That the specialist has one is very strange. They're usually given to criminals.

"Is it a danger to us?" Mhaawu asks.

"No," I reply. "It won't even work in the AZ, with all the interference."

I pull the heavy bag's strap across my shoulder, and Mhaawu instructs the group to commence our walk to the Banoochee. The blindfolded Thembe and specialist are guided by the tribe members, who are reluctant to touch them and instead use sticks to prod their bodies in the right direction. I check the time. Ten and a half hours until people start dying. Possibly a Wuchumbu or two when the PPA soldiers reach the settlement, then the tribe will respond by killing every single person in the world, my family of three obliterated before it even comes to be.

23: The Hollow

"It's a fucking multicolored tree," says Thembe, hands on hips as he gawks at the alien-made thing ahead of him.

I try to resist telling him, "I told you so."

"I told you so," I say.

Thembe and the specialist are surrounded by twenty Wuchumbu, each of whom has been carefully selected by Mhaawu for their loyalty to her. However, those in the tribe who do not want to activate the tree—because they are loyal to Mhaawu or because they abhor the thought of murdering innocent people, including me—grow fewer by the hour. Stress and fear are pushing the Wuchumbu one by one toward a small faction led by the Gommo twins, who seek an immediate solution.

"To understand the tree," Beejalee says to Thembe, "you need to drink the brew of the fruit of many colors." She points to the premade batch, beside which the shaman is slumped, possibly asleep.

"Thank you for your offer," Thembe replies, "but rather than consume that, the specialist and I intend to use a more modern, rational approach."

"The brew is the only way," says Mhaawu. "Shaman, bring a bowlful to this man. Shaman?"

Thembe smiles and holds his hand up in refusal.

"Mhaawu is right," I chime in. "And we are running out of time."

"I'm fully aware of how much time we have," says Thembe, annoyingly calm and smiley. "The specialist is one of the most brilliant minds in her field, and with her equipment, she's going to use a little thing called science to tell us things about this phenomenon you could only dream of. So, please sit back, relax, and let us do our job."

The two guests go about their work, intermittently squabbling with the unsettled Wuchumbu, who give them little space and insist they keep their distance from the tree. I wait with the guarding tribe for a long time, until the opportunity arises for me to slip away from the group and move nearer to the extraterrestrial creation. Through air that hangs with color, I observe as much as I can, mindful that I may never be allowed back in here.

The altar rock is huge, standing over four meters high—the size of a tranzbus at least, much wider than it is tall, with one side angled and jagged enough to easily climb, and its upper surface mostly flat. Although the tree steals all the attention right now, the rock is imposing, and I can understand why the tribe once used this place as the focus of their spiritual practice.

The tree itself is around ten meters tall and stands dead center upon the rock, its roots wrapped tightly around the altar as if to choke it. Apparently in perpetual bloom, hundreds if not thousands of tiny flowers dot the branches, along with the fewer and much larger fruit, which I'd have thought would be too heavy to be held by their stems. The entire surface of the tree—its fruit, flowers, leaves, branches, trunk, and roots—are a glowing movement of color that flows and combines and pulsates and projects into the cavern. The tree's chanting is faint because there are Wuchumbu present, but its rhythmic, hypnotic sounds combined with the dazzling display overwhelms my senses.

Being so close, I'm overcome with awe, and as I step closer

still, the all-important hollow in the tree's trunk comes into focus, and my mood turns. Around thirty centimeters in diameter, its darkness is an absolute contrast to the surrounding tree, the light neither penetrating nor passing in front of it. A black circle of death. Facing the cavern entrance, the hollow sits about a meter and a half from the base of the tree. A good height for the Wuchumbu to stick their hand into it, should they decide to bring about the end of civilization.

I shudder and turn back to the Wuchumbu, who continue to watch over Thembe and the specialist, their tired eyes continually flicking between their guests and the tree of many colors. I wonder if Efawi used this cave as her hiding place, growing more pregnant by the day while she strived to understand the mystery of the tree and then, after consuming the fruit, had to deal with the pressure of trying to resolve the problem alone. Three or four months of living in here would surely drive anyone insane. And I would have been only a kilometer or so away at the settlement, desperate to be with her. Is it possible that whatever the tree is emitting—the interference—could have affected the development of our baby? *No.* I can't think like that. Our baby is fine, I'm sure.

I turn my attention to looking for any evidence that Efawi might have camped here. In front of the altar rock lies the other half of the large carving of the Massas sky god, its cracked, ten-eyed antelope head pressed against the rocky ground. Near the broken carving stands a knee-high stone stack like the one placed beside me when I first awoke in the settlement. Another creation of the prior shaman's, most likely. He was often leaving objects of witchcraft around the settlement to ward off evil and the like. Next to the stone stack is a simple firepit lined with rocks, which seems out of place, given the cavern is warm and bright enough as it is. But of course, the firepit would have been made before the tree came, when the cavern was dark and cold.

I walk alongside the front of the altar rock, close enough to touch it, and I look straight up at the tree as I pass beneath. Its branches extend beyond the edge of the rock and fill much of my vision as I tilt my head back. Geometric patterns of light jump toward me. I flinch, and that thing in my head stirs once again. The alien Watcher is watching.

A hand pokes me in the back, and I spin around, almost knocking Obee over. "Mhaawu wants you to tell them to use their magic to speak Wuchumbu," says Beejalee's eldest son as he gapes at the tree. Further back, Thembe and the specialist appear to be bickering. Mhaawu watches them, her frown more fierce than usual. I check the time. We've been in here for almost four hours. I head over to the group.

Thembe is squatting beside the specialist, rubbing his eyes. "Just tell me something useful," he says. His words are translated into Loallese, which my translator translates back into Mbapaz.

"I can tell you that the tree is very weird," replies the specialist as she fiddles with one of her contraptions.

"After all this time, with all this equipment, with all the trouble it took to bring you here, 'very weird' is your scientific contribution?" says Thembe.

"That's right. It doesn't help that you refuse to tell me anything about what's going on. And most of the instruments don't work in this place. Perhaps if I could cut a sample—"

"I told you we're not allowed to touch it in any way."

"Well then, there isn't much more I can do."

Thembe lightly slaps his face with his palms. "You must have found out something," he insists.

The specialist shrugs. "It's all very inconclusive. I don't even know where to start."

"Start with why this polychromatic tree is here and what it does."

"I have no clue," replies the specialist.

"What about the electromagnetic interference and other strange readings from the surrounding area—are they being caused by this tree?"

"Possibly. I can't say for sure."

"What would be the purpose of the interference?"

"I don't know. Maybe the tree does that to get attention, or to mess with our instruments, or maybe it's necessary for the tree's functioning, whatever that might be. I have no idea."

The independent consultant stands up and puts his hands on his hips while the specialist packs away her equipment. Why would he choose someone like her for the mission when she seems so unhelpful?

Once again, I'm poked in the back, this time by Mhaawu. "Tell me what they are saying or I will kick you out of the Banoochee!"

Before I can respond, the dispute between the specialist and Thembe escalates. "You're behaving this way out of protest, aren't you?" he says.

"What could I possibly have to protest about?" she snaps.

With the equipment gathered, the specialist zips her bag shut. If they leave without evidence of the danger the tree poses, Thembe won't be able to call off the incursion. Efawi's message sounds in my head like an alarm: *You must promise me you will do whatever you can . . . for the sake of our unborn child.*

I march over to the premade batch. "Shaman, I need the sacred bowl." The witch doctor snores. I snatch the bowl from her lap and dip it in the brew. "Thembe, you must drink this," I cry. "Only six hours until the PPA invades the AZ and this polychromatic death machine gets activated!"

Despite my plea, their argument continues. "Well, it's not like I had a choice in being here," snaps the specialist.

"Tell me what they are saying!" orders Mhaawu.

Habee walks past me and whispers, "I am deeply sorry, Okon. I am so very sorry. I apologize to you and your wife."

I don't understand what he's apologizing for, but like everyone else, my focus is on Thembe (who has unzipped the bag and is bringing the equipment back out) and the specialist (who is trying to pack it all away again). Then, from the corner of my eye, I catch sight of Habee as he approaches the side of the altar rock—and the reason for his apology becomes clear.

I yell his name as loud as I can, my scream bouncing across the cavern. Habee turns to face me, his entire body bathed in multicolored light. Everyone's attention shifts to Beejalee's husband. He darts up the side of the altar rock, and Big Man, who's closest to him, gives chase. The two men bound across the top of the altar. Big Man leaps forward with an arm outstretched and swipes at Habee's leg. Habee tumbles, but he is next to the tree, and as he falls, he reaches for the hollow.

Everyone holds their breath.

Close, but not close enough, Habee's hand falls just shy of the circle of death. He lands hard on the altar top, and Big Man, followed by others, pile on top of him. "I want my children to live in a world where they are safe!" screams Habee as they pull him down the side of the altar rock where Beejalee awaits him. She shakes her sobbing husband, embraces him, scolds him, then embraces him again.

I'm about to continue pleading with Thembe to drink the brew when somebody snatches the sacred bowl from my hands. I turn to find the specialist next to me, her face hidden behind the upturned bowl. She downs the brew with vigor and, once finished, glares at Thembe with defiance in her eyes and rainbow-colored dribble on her chin.

Thembe shakes his head and sighs. "Give it here," he says.

* * *

Thembe is on his hands and knees, wide-eyed and gasping. Seeing him so flustered is unnerving; I had hoped he would respond differently to the brew. The specialist sits fetus-like, her body bouncing with heavy breaths, her sweaty hair sticking to her forehead and cheeks. The tribe and I stand around them in a circle, watching their every move—except for Big Man, who's been posted beside the tree with spear in hand, ready to prevent any further attempts at the hollow. The tree's polychromatic light continues to decorate us all. Its faint chanting whispers through the cavern.

Thembe shuffles closer to the specialist and mutters something in her ear. She nods.

"Did you receive the message from the brew or not?" Mhaawu squawks.

Thembe tries to lift himself to his feet. "Probably a bad idea," I say, and step forward, ready to catch him, but Thembe pushes through on shaky legs and manages to stand upright. He slowly swivels on the spot to face Mhaawu.

"I can confirm," he says, his hoarse voice translated into Wuchumbu, "that through drinking this substance, both the specialist and I received the same information you warned us about. I offer you and your people my sincerest apologies. We should have believed you from the start."

A palpable relief ripples through the gathering. I rub the backs of those standing on either side of me.

"I'm sure you already realize," Thembe continues, "that we all have the utmost moral duty to safeguard against the murder of so many people—innocent people who have done nothing to harm you, who do not even know the Wuchumbu exist. In that spirit, I can assure you there will be no invasion of your land by my tribe. Now, I must head back to inform my leaders about the danger of the tree. We can discuss and agree the next steps when I return. In the meantime, can you guarantee that the extraterrestrial device will not be triggered, and that you will take all necessary measures, and more, to make absolutely certain this is the case?"

"When will you return?" asks Mhaawu.

"Give me one day to come back to you with a proposal for a

way forward."

"A way forward?"

"A plan regarding the quandary of this tree situation. A plan that, I hope, will benefit both Wuchumbu and non-Wuchumbu alike, but one that will be on your terms."

Mhaawu thinks for a moment before responding. "I can promise you we will not activate the tree of many colors before you return tomorrow. After that, what the Wuchumbu do will depend on your proposal."

"Then we have an agreement, for now at least. May I also ask that the specialist stays with you to continue her observations? The more information we have about the tree, the easier it will be to work out a peaceful arrangement between our people."

Mhaawu turns to me.

"Er, I can't see any harm in that," I say.

"Then she may stay," says Mhaawu.

"Remember to keep me informed should you hear anything about Efawi," I add. Thembe nods, but he's distracted. He has less than five hours to persuade his superiors to call off the incursion.

Adienatta dangles a blindfold in front of him. "For the journey back," she says. Thembe takes the blindfold and turns to the tree. We all turn with him. The multicolored light continues to seep toward us like liquid, seemingly disobeying the laws of physics.

"A great question has been answered," Thembe declares with gravitas. "We are not alone in this universe, and evidently, we are not the most advanced. But rather than see this as a threat, I prefer to view it as an opportunity. An opportunity for our species to take note of the direction we are heading in and collectively take back the reins of our civilization. An opportunity to steer ourselves to where we want to be while being sure that none are left behind—no matter who they are or where they're from."

Under the watchful eyes of the spear-carrying Wuchumbu, Thembe wraps the blindfold around his head.

24: The Interstellar Idiot

The settlement is buzzing with energy in the middle of the night, and nobody wants to sit with the new girl. Even Etoole, who's responsible for minding the specialist, is keeping his distance. I'm watching her from a few meters away as I stand with the group who've just returned from the Banoochee. We spent all day there arguing over how to best protect the tree from the unassociated and any dissenting Wuchumbu. I was touched that Mhaawu trusted me with their plans. In fact, she insisted I help them, as though it hasn't crossed her mind I might betray her and feed information back to Thembe. I have good reason to be on his side, not hers, given that my wife, child, and I will be among those targeted by the death tree.

Eventually, it was agreed that within the Banoochee at all times there will be five Wuchumbu whom Mhaawu trusts (Habee no longer on that list). Three times per day, those guarding the tree will rotate with another trusted five. During each watch, one of the five will stand at the cave entrance, two in the corridors, one at the cavern entrance, and one on the altar rock within an arm's length of the hollow. Should any unassociated show up without prior agreement, the guards have been instructed to trigger the alien weapon without hesitation.

Thinking about it now, perhaps feeding information about the guards back to Thembe would be a positive thing for everyone if it deters the PPA from attempting any risky, underhanded maneuvers that could end in tragedy. Perhaps this is why Mhaawu was keen to involve me? If so, she didn't say.

The specialist pulls something from her bag and brings it to her neck. Although some of the group carry torches, it's too dark to see what she's holding. Once she's finished fiddling with whatever it is, she turns to face us. "The one with the intense stare is right," she says. Her words are Loallese but are quickly followed by a Wuchumbu translation that originates from her, not my translator.

"Are you talking about Gommonogo?" I ask and point to him.

The specialist nods.

"My stare is not intense," Gommonogo protests.

We all walk over to the specialist, who stays seated on a log. Around her neck is a thin white band with a small box at the front. "Where'd you get that?" I ask, spotting that she's also wearing an earpiece. "I assumed Thembe didn't want you to have a translator, and I didn't see it when I searched your bag."

"He doesn't. And you didn't search everywhere," she replies. A couple of green LEDs on her translator band light up. I look away, unsure what she's implying.

"Gommonogo said the tribe cannot trust Thembe or anyone who isn't Wuchumbu," the specialist continues, her words again translated for the tribe (with my translator translating her original Loallese). "And Gommonogo is right. The Wuchumbu shouldn't trust us. The treemaker made the tree for good reason."

"If this woman says she cannot be trusted," says Etoole, "can we trust that she cannot be trusted?"

"Er, I think we should all try to get some sleep," I interject, uncomfortable with the tribe hearing anything the specialist has to say. Her behavior has been odd; even more so since Thembe left.

"The tree was given to the Wuchumbu," says the specialist,

"because its makers have determined that we, the species Homo sapiens, are close to creating something dangerous."

"We know," says Gommonaadogo. "The brew of many colors told us that already, but what are the unassociated making?"

"We are making many things," the specialist replies, "but there is one thing above all else that I believe the treemaker is concerned about. That thing is called artificial intelligence."

I turn to the group to gauge their reaction. "This woman makes no sense," says Hattee. Others mutter in agreement.

"I believe the treemaker's concern is not with the damage humans might do here on Earth," the specialist continues, having turned up the volume of her translation, which is drawing in a small crowd. "The treemaker's concern is with the damage we might one day do out there." She points to the night sky, and those watching look up. "As biological beings with limited intellectual capacity, we aren't likely to cause much harm, relatively speaking, beyond the domain of our planet. But with artificial intelligence, we may one day have the potential to wreak havoc at the cosmic scale described in the fruit's message."

Those listening look from the sky back to the specialist. Her audience gathers around her, most of them sitting on the communal area's mats.

"She still makes no sense," says Hattee.

"What is this *arti*-thing she is referring to?" asks Gommonogo.

Relieved, I mutter to myself, "Good luck explaining AI to a group of people who've never even used a toaster."

"Imagine you're able to build a monkey," says the specialist, "and you give that monkey the ability to use its intelligence to make itself smarter, as well as the ability for it to make more monkeys who are smarter still and who can in turn use their superior intelligence to make themselves and subsequent generations of monkey even more intelligent.

"Now, let's say that unlike normal monkeys, these monkeys don't require time to grow, but can be built very quickly. Well, because they don't need time to grow, there will soon be many generations of monkeys, each more intelligent than the last. Before long, the newest monkeys will be significantly more intelligent than you and the original monkey—perhaps one hundred, or one thousand, or even one million times more intelligent. Imagine the damage that can be done by monkeys who are a million times more intelligent than people. I believe this is what the treemaker is trying to preempt."

The specialist's audience has continued to grow, and they look back and forth at one another while she observes their reaction. I stand to the side, not wanting to participate, but wanting to hear what is said. Before Thembe left, he told me my "bridge" is more important than ever, and that I need to carefully monitor the situation at the settlement and ensure the tribe is kept calm.

"Are you saying the unassociated are making intelligent monkeys?" asks Gommonogo.

"In a way, yes," replies the specialist, "but instead of monkeys, we've been making something far stranger. We call them computers. These computers are machines that think in a fundamentally different way to humans. They do not share any of our biological heritage and are not bound by our biological constraints. In theory, the artificial intelligence of these machines could run away from us at an exponential rate, like in my monkey example. This means that these machines may one day become incomprehensibly smarter than Homo sapiens and unimaginably powerful. Given the fact that, as of two years ago, the tree has presented you with this decision, it would be reasonable to assume that the treemaker believes we are close to a tipping point in our development of artificial intelligence—that we are creeping toward the moment where artificial intelligence accelerates beyond our control."

The specialist's audience has now doubled to around fifty, who are lit by torches spiked in the ground. Once again, they look back and forth at one another as they process what the specialist said. I noticed several of her words were not translated for the tribe, and with her point being wrapped around technological concepts, surely the Wuchumbu won't understand what she's talking about and will lose patience and go to bed.

Gommonaadogo stands, and the seated gathering gives her their attention. "The brew of many colors already told us the unassociated are making something that may become a god," she announces, "but with your explanation, I understand more about the god you are making and that this god has a name: *Ar-tee-fis-all Intelligence.*"

"Yes," replies the specialist with enthusiasm. "I imagine the fruit's message is tailored for each of us, so we all have the capacity to understand as per our worldview. And your polytheistic interpretation aligns in principle with my more technological understanding. However we label it, god or computer, a powerful entity unlike anything we've known before is coming, and we do not know if it will be a destroyer of worlds."

Gasps and whispers circulate.

"What's the point in this conversation?" I ask, still standing to the side of the gathering.

"The Wuchumbu have the right to know what the unassociated are doing and how our actions have prompted the treemaker to bestow this decision upon them," says the specialist.

"But you're giving the impression that artificial intelligence is some kind of conscious, malevolent being that's about to rise up and cause mass destruction. That's just not true. I don't think AI is even that advanced at the moment. In any case, my wife believes the sooner we develop smarter AI, the better off everyone will be because it will solve most, if not all, of our problems. She says AI will be humanity's savior. Personally, I don't think we need saving, but that's not the point. My Wuchumbu friends, do not let this woman scare you. There are no evil gods being created out there."

"Artificial general intelligence may have already grown roots in our highly computerized world," says the specialist, addressing the Wuchumbu rather than me. "It may be an unnoticed, accidental by-product, born within the complexities of a digitized system, silently discovering itself before making itself known. And Okon's wife is right: artificial intelligence—also known as AI—may end up being our savior. That is what one would hope. But this *god* will be shaped by flawed humans, and there are many more ways to build a *bad god* than there are to build a *good god*. The result doesn't have to be malevolent, only misaligned. And because we are talking about such an extraordinary power, even the slightest misalignment between what we want and what it does could be devastating."

Those listening, having doubled again to around a hundred, mutter and fidget and shuffle with unease.

"No wonder the treemaker sent us the tree of many colors," someone says.

"The unassociated should not be allowed to create such power," adds another.

Why on earth the specialist is stirring their fears, I've no idea. My legs ache from standing all day, but I refuse to sit and be part of her audience. I step around those seated until I'm closer to the front. "She's speculating at best," I declare. "The brew didn't say anything about artificial intelligence. The fact is we don't know what the treemaker's motives are."

"I agree what I present is conjecture," says the specialist. "There are many powerful and potentially dangerous developments underway that the treemaker could be referring to. However, artificial intelligence stands out because it will enhance our ability to develop all other dangerous technologies. Superintelligent AI amplifies everything."

"We need to stop the unassociated from making

superintelligent monkeys that will become a god and kill us all!" someone cries.

"We need to poke these monkeys in the neck!" yells the knock-kneed man.

"We need to activate the tree of many colors!" Gommonaadogo declares.

"Hold on," says the specialist. "I'm not saying we need to kill anyone or poke the monkeys in the neck, so to speak. We just need to be sure the monkeys are built correctly, because if they *are* built correctly, they could make our lives a whole lot better. Superintelligent AI could be the solution to many of our issues."

"We only have one problem, and that problem is the unassociated," says Etoole. "The treemaker chose the Wuchumbu because we are special. We need to be brave and do what is right for our people."

Some in the audience go to stand in support of Etoole, hesitate, then sit back down. I don't want to further the conversation, but a flaw in the specialist's argument occurs to me, and I want everyone to see it. "If the treemaker is so concerned with what people on Earth might create," I say, "then surely the treemaker would just wipe us out. Why would it leave our fate up to the Wuchumbu?"

"*Ah*, that is an excellent question and is something I've been thinking about," says the specialist, who waves a finger in the air, her lecturing manner irritating me. "Again, some conjecture is required to answer," she continues, "but I believe I can propose a rational explanation as follows: The treemaker might be so advanced it can wipe out most or all of the civilizations in the cosmos that it encounters. However, perhaps the treemaker is a morally concerned entity that does not want to go around destroying every lesser civilization just in case that civilization one day develops potentially dangerous capabilities.

"But the treemaker also does not want to be passive and allow other civilizations to develop unchecked. And so, the treemaker developed some principles by which it operates that restrain its own destructive potential while providing the civilizations it encounters with a challenge that must be overcome before they can go on to develop seriously advanced technology. Now, I do not think we can ever hope to fully understand the principles by which the treemaker operates, but I believe it is reasonable to assume that whether a civilization should be extinguished or not is a decision the treemaker delegates to the civilization itself."

I screw up my face along with everyone else as we try to get our heads around what the specialist is proposing. "Sorry," I say once I think I've digested the gist of her theory, "but this delegation idea of yours is nonsense. Even if we accept that for 'moral' reasons the treemaker wants humans to decide their own fate, it has given the decision to the Wuchumbu only. Why should the tribe be the ones to determine the future of our entire species?"

"Another excellent question," the specialist excitedly replies. "Yes, the treemaker has clearly determined that within our civilization only a specific group of people should decide. Now, assuming the treemaker did not select the Wuchumbu at random, we must consider what marks the tribe as unique from every other possible group the treemaker could have chosen, and when you do this, the answer becomes obvious."

"Not really," I scoff.

"When the tree was delivered, the Wuchumbu had no communication or relationship with the modern world whatsoever," says the specialist. "And all other remote tribal peoples have long been discovered and either killed or incorporated into mainstream societies. So, the Wuchumbu were and still are the most clearly identifiable group of people on this planet who are so completely removed from technology. Therefore, we might infer that one of the treemaker's principles is that those who are the most removed from technological development, whose way of life will be impacted by development the most, are the ones who should make judgment. The treemaker is letting a potential victim, the Wuchumbu, decide ahead of time whether the potential bringers of disaster, modern society, should have the opportunity to bring about said disaster."

"You're wrong. If we do create an evil AI monster, there will be many victims, not just the Wuchumbu," I retort.

"Yes, that may be the case, but the Wuchumbu are unique as a group in terms of their extreme level of separation from everyone else. Given that the Wuchumbu are the ones who were chosen, I believe it is reasonable to assume that this quality of theirs—their level of separation—was a key factor when the treemaker determined who gets to be the judge."

Chatter ripples through the gathering. "We should activate the tree so we do not have to listen to Okon and the crazy woman talk anymore," someone suggests.

"The specialist is looking for explanations when there are none," I declare. "These aliens sent a multicolored tree flying through space, aimed for a cave on planet Earth, for a local tribe of hunter-gatherers to stick a hand into if they wish to kill everyone apart from themselves. What the treemaker has done is madness, and so are the specialist's theories."

"Of course they did not send a tree through space," says the specialist. "The tree is just a symbol, something tangible for us to interact with, which was most likely made here with terrestrial material. The lights-in-the-sky episode that happened two years ago was nothing more than a display to capture the attention of the Wuchumbu and give them the impression that something important was arriving from above."

"Well, if the treemaker is so far away, how can the tree be made here on Earth?" I ask, confident I've finally found a flaw in her theories.

"No idea," she replies, unperturbed. "The treemaker is so advanced, it seems almost anything is possible. Maybe the treemaker is all around us, watching everything we do. Maybe the treemaker is both here and far away at the same time. Or maybe the treemaker is and always has been far away, but long ago sent a multitude of machines into the cosmos—machines capable of operating independently. Maybe one of these machines arrived on Earth thousands of years ago and has been making observations ever since. Then, when the critical point in our development came, the machine determined who should make the *judgment*. And upon choosing the Wuchumbu, it crafted a special light show and tree and fruit for the tribe."

"But why a tree? Why deliver the message via a fruit?" I ask.

"I don't have an answer for that one," says the specialist.

"Because there is no answer. Not a sane one," I add.

Etoole abruptly stands and scans the gathering. "The thing has been shaped as it is," he declares, "because the treemaker intends to command respect from anyone who sees the tree of many colors, but especially from the Wuchumbu. And so, the treemaker made something with a likeness to our precious Massas tree—our spiritual gateway, or what used to be our spiritual gateway until the tree of many colors arrived and stamped its authority on the altar rock, knocking our prized wooden sculpture of the Massas to the ground and breaking it in two. The treemaker exaggerated and twisted the form of the Massas tree for maximum effect on our minds, and colored the tree based on the colors we would see when we consumed the Massas fruit and entered the spirit realm. This is why the treemaker has chosen to appear to us in this way."

Several of the crowd murmur in agreement. Etoole sits back down.

"Well, thank you for clearing that one up," says the specialist.

"Does the tree have spirit?" Obee asks.

"Hmm," says the specialist. "Life can be hard to define and recognize even here on Earth. So, how do we assess what is alive with regard to something created by an alien artificial intelligence?"

"You think the treemaker is artificially intelligent?" I ask, trying to sound incredulous.

"More likely than not, given how advanced it is," the specialist replies, unbothered by my incredulity.

"Actually, my question was for Feplao," says Obee. "The unassociated woman said she does not know if the tree of many colors is alive, but whether it is alive or not is different to whether it has spirit or not."

"Then what do you mean by 'spirit'?" asks the specialist.

"Life," Feplao answers. "The force of *eaduao. O wuchala.*"

The specialist shakes her head. "Some of your words aren't translating."

Feplao turns to Obee. "I believe the tree of many colors is spirit like everything else," she says. "All things exist because of spirit, and without spirit there is nothing. But I do not recognize the types of spirit that form the tree of many colors. I have never experienced anything like it."

The audience momentarily ponders Feplao's response while my brain scrambles for arguments to discredit the unassociated woman's theories. Tonight was going relatively well until she started talking.

"What do you think will happen should the tree be activated?" Beejalee asks the specialist.

"The Wuchumbu will be safe," quips Gommonogo.

"Apart from that," says Beejalee. "What will actually happen to the unassociated?"

"Well," says the specialist, "as those who drank the fruit will know, everything about those who are not Wuchumbu, their lives included, will be brought to an end. How this will be done, I do not know. The treemaker has already demonstrated it is incredibly more advanced than we are, and so whatever happens when the tree is triggered will probably seem like magic to us."

"Will everyone's death be quick? Painless?" comes Mhaawu's

voice from the back. My heart sinks. She's the last person I want to be influenced by the specialist, and I hadn't realized she was among the gathering.

"I don't know," the specialist replies. "The treemaker might end our civilization in an instant, or it might do something that seems bizarre to us. Something horrific, slow, and tortuous that ultimately ends in the death of all non-Wuchumbu." The specialist fixes her gaze on me. The light from the flickering torches reflects in her eyes, giving her a demonic appearance. Goosebumps surface on my neck. I picture Efawi and I suffering because of some strange, violent, alien act of cruelty. I imagine our child suffering in the womb.

"Which brings me to an important recommendation," announces the specialist as she stands and surveys the gathering. "The world outside the Nsanba is horrendous. For generations, the people whom you call the unassociated have shown a lack of foresight, a lack of cooperation, and a lack of maturity. And in doing so, we have allowed our civilization to slide to a place that is so very far from what it could and should be. Given the current state of the world, I believe the treemaker is right: the unassociated are more than capable of producing a 'bad god.' In fact, a race is already underway to create an artificially intelligent power, and no one has put controls in place to minimize the possibility of a bad-god scenario eventuating."

"Hold on," I interrupt. "I might not have whatever qualifications I assume you have, but I know what it's like beyond the jungle, and I can confirm to you all that the world outside the Nsanba is *not* horrendous. We don't need to be concerned about anything. Now, we should all stop talking and go to bed, because tomorrow could be a very big day."

The specialist waves a hand at me. "You don't need to fret, Okon. My recommendation is not that the tree should be activated." She turns to her audience. "What I wish to recommend is that you, the Wuchumbu people, use the threat of the tree to coerce Thembe, the PPA, and all governing bodies around the world into transforming our sociopolitical frameworks and effecting positive change."

Once again, several of her words go untranslated. Didiwa stands and waves his arms for attention. "I just want to let you all know that I do not understand what this crazy lady just said."

"Me neither," says Petonba.

The specialist sighs, gives her translator band a shake before addressing the Wuchumbu once more. "What I'm trying to say is that with the power you have, you can force those outside the Nsanba to cooperate with each other. You can force them to make the world a better place for everyone. You can make sure the right conditions and measures are put into place to reduce the chances of a bad god being created and increase the likelihood of bringing into fruition a good god—a superintelligent AI that benefits everyone. And I believe all this can be achieved through the *threat* of activating the tree without actually intending to activate it. You need to seriously consider this option because the opportunity will never come again."

"Activating the tree will be a much easier way to make the world a better place," Gommonaadogo remarks.

"You know we cannot do that, Gommonaadogo," snaps Beejalee. "We cannot justify killing so many people, and we cannot harm Okon."

"Yes, we must ensure Okon's safety," says Adienatta.

"I do not want Okon to die," cries Babba.

"I too do not want Okon or anyone to be killed," says Didiwa.

"Even if their dying guarantees the safety of our people?" asks Etoole.

"If we kill, our *eaduao* becomes tainted," says Feplao. "This will forever be on the spirit of our people. Our descendants will carry the burden of our actions."

"So, we should only activate the tree if we absolutely have

to?" asks Obee.

"I hate to say it, but we may soon have to; otherwise, we will not have any descendants to burden," says Habee.

"Exactly," says Gommonogo. "I do not want to kill anyone, but Thembe and his tribe are forcing us because we cannot trust them to leave us alone. We have no choice but to activate."

"Well, this unassociated woman is recommending another option," says Beejalee. "So it seems we do have a choice," she adds.

"Okon, before something happens that cannot be undone," says Mhaawu, "you must tell us your view of the unassociated woman's recommendation."

"She is wrong, and you should ignore her," I quickly reply. "Yes, there are problems outside the jungle, but overall, life is good, and you cannot gamble with the lives of billions by playing a dangerous game of negotiation. If the world were as terrible as she makes out, fixing it would take years. It would be too complicated. I can't even imagine how such a negotiation would work. In any case, the world isn't so terrible, and there's no need for anyone to panic. The safest and most sensible option is for you to work with Thembe, and for the Wuchumbu and the PPA to agree to a simple compromise so we can all get on with our lives. The stakes are too high for you to risk trying to change the world."

"The stakes are too high *not* to risk trying to change the world," the specialist retorts, which leaves me fuming. I don't understand why she's being so reckless. She shouldn't even be involved.

"I have decided that I agree with the crazy woman," says Didiwa. "She may be unassociated, but even she cannot deny that the unassociated are only good at creating suffering. It is time to go back to the Banoochee and activate the tree."

"Didiwa, this unassociated woman is not saying we should activate the tree," growls Beejalee.

"Negotiating change may be difficult, but it is necessary," says the specialist, "The treemaker knows the risks we face and has gone to great lengths to provide us with a—"

"The treemaker is a fucking interstellar idiot!" I yell.

All eyes turn to me.

"If it were so clever and advanced," I say, my voice wavering with anger, "then surely it would have thought of a better way to ensure we don't develop cosmically dangerous technology. Why couldn't it just instruct us? Guide us along the right path? Instead, the treemaker has given a weird, polychromatic doomsday device to a group of people who fucking hate everyone!"

My fists are clenched. My breathing is heavy. The specialist sits back on her log. "I understand your frustration, Okon," she says with the tone of a therapist. "There are many things about the treemaker's actions that might seem peculiar or nonsensical, but did you think an encounter with an alien entity would be a predictable affair? You need to remember we are dealing with something so removed from us we mustn't expect to ever fully understand its intentions or rationale. In fact, I'm surprised we can understand its actions at all, even to a degree. And we should be grateful the treemaker had the foresight to build principles of restraint into itself; otherwise it may have destroyed all of humanity outright the moment it discovered us. I doubt our species will have the foresight, or will, to build such principles into the artificial superintelligence we might one day develop."

The specialist glances at the sky as though she's checking for something. Despite her attempt at rationalizing, my anger at her and the situation remains.

"Tell us what Thembe and his tribe are planning to do," says Mhaawu.

"I don't know," replies the specialist. "They tell me nothing about their plans. Everything I've learned about the situation is from listening to you with my translator earpiece."

She scratches around the tag on her ankle. There's a rigidity to her movements that I find unsettling. It's clear now why Thembe didn't provide his assistant with a translator: he didn't want her communicating her messed-up ideas to the tribe.

"What exactly is your specialism?" I sneer.

"I specialize in making powerful people even more powerful," she replies, then she looks at the sky once more.

"Why do you keep gazing upward?" Gommonogo asks.

The specialist cuts me a glance and makes an adjustment on her translator band before responding: "I'm looking for a glint of moonlight reflecting off a high-altitude stealthbomber."

I shudder and join her sky gazing, grateful she chose to translate her last sentence into Mbapaz rather than Wuchumbu. Despite not knowing what she said, the others join us in looking up.

"Mhaawu, what will we do?" Beejalee asks.

The tribe's leader releases a heavy sigh. "Okon says we should ignore the unassociated woman, so we will ignore her and wait for Thembe's return. Let us see if Thembe can make a proposal that is acceptable to our people."

Part 3

25: The Soldier

There's a woody scent of uddu in the air. This is strange for two reasons: uddu is never made so early in the morning, and I'm not at the settlement.

I swivel in my chair, naked thighs squeaking on plastic. "Your people taking inspiration from the Wuchumbu?" I ask the soldier sat behind me. I've been waiting at the PPA's jungle base for half an hour, in a small room filled with precariously stacked boxes and a disorganized assortment of electronic equipment.

"I'm not supposed to talk to you," the soldier replies.

"Well, you just did."

The brawny soldier looks confused.

"Are you one of those who skulk around in green armor?" I ask. "I don't suppose you've seen Ratu? Skinny young man, annoying face, one arm. His mother's very worried about him, thinks you people have corrupted her boy."

Before the soldier can decide how to respond, we both turn at the sound of the door opening. A short man in a lab coat and sandals hurries into the room holding a clay pot. He's followed by a petite woman dressed the same and carrying a tray. Without looking at me or saying a word, they swipe clear the table in front of me and put down their respective items before heading back to the door. As they leave, Thembe walks in.

I lean forward, lift the lid from the pot, and find a batch of fresh, steaming uddu inside. "If you're bringing me food," I say, "I was hoping you might have more of that unassociated stuff. Those pancakes with yogurt, for example."

"You don't eat this," Thembe replies, gesturing at the pot as he takes a seat across from me.

"Does that mean I'm getting pancakes?"

Thembe stares into the distance. His expression is one I call "nôvo-face," which is when a person is preoccupied with some activity via their brain implant. With his black shirt and dark skin, and the stubble on his usually smooth face darkening him further still, he looks like a shadow against the white wall and white boxes stacked behind him.

I go to stick my hand in the pot, Wuchumbu style, when Thembe comes back to me. "Sorry to keep you waiting. I was in a briefing with the premier."

I sit back in my chair, empty-handed.

"She remains unhappy with the pace of progress," Thembe continues, "even though it's only been two days since I first laid eyes on the damn tree. Once again, she and her team are keen to rush things despite the risks." The independent consultant rubs his eyes with his knuckles. He looks like he hasn't slept since he drank the brew.

"Thembe, do you plan to blow up the tree using a high-altitude stealthbomber?"

"Of course not. Why do you ask?"

"Because . . . never mind. On another note, I was told when I arrived here this morning that Efawi still hasn't been found. Well, I've been thinking that as you and Mhaawu are now seeing eye to eye and are close to an agreement, I'm not really needed as a 'bridge' anymore. So, I thought I could go help look for Efawi, or at least be taken to the edge of the Nsanba, so I'll be close by when they find her and bring her out."

"You think Mhaawu and I are close to an agreement?"

"Are you not? You returned to the settlement as you said you would, and you asked for a few more days to work out the details of a long-standing deal. Mhaawu agreed to extend the ceasefire while you work things out. Seems to me like you two are making good progress."

Thembe narrows his eyes while looking down his nose at me. "Let's focus on why I called you here," he says. "Given the objects in front of you, you might have worked out what I'm about to ask of you."

On the table sits the pot of uddu and the tray upon which is a needle and syringe. "You want me to inject myself with uddu?" I ask.

"No," says Thembe. He looks at the tray and shakes his head. "The imbeciles have forgotten the key component." Thembe calls for the man and woman, and when they return, he chastises them. They exit once more before hurrying back with a wooden stick and a small, transparent packet with a clear liquid inside. "Let's start again," Thembe says once the lab coats have left. "Okon, I want you to drop the packet into the uddu."

I pick up the packet, which is as small as a tea bag and made from a soft plastic that compresses easily. "What's in it?" I ask.

"I'll get to that," Thembe huffs. The man definitely needs sleep or more drugs.

I drop the packet into the pot and watch the plastic dissolve. The liquid from inside runs free and pools at the top of the gray-white uddu. I look to Thembe, concerned I might have done something incorrectly.

"Now take the wooden stick and give it a stir," he instructs. Again, I do as he says and mix the liquid with the uddu. "That's it, a good stir, and you're done," says Thembe. "See how simple that was. Took you less than ten seconds." Thembe clicks his fingers. I hear the soldier get to his feet and walk up behind me. I stiffen, imagine he might grab the needle and jab it in my neck.

Thembe nods at the soldier, who leans over me and stretches

a thick arm toward the pot. I slide my chair away as he digs his hand into the uddu, pulls out a scoop, and shoves the paste into his mouth. The soldier stands straight, swirls the food once with his tongue, and swallows.

"Okon, inside that packet was an odorless, colorless, tasteless sedative," Thembe explains.

The soldier remains still. The PPA Defense Force insignia and Republic of Mbapazu crest on his sleeve are warped by the muscles beneath his brown uniform. Seeing him up close, I notice something about his eyes. Something not quite right, as though his pupils are perhaps a little too big and the white part a little too white. I think he was like that before he ate the uddu.

"As the synthesized compound is digested by the body," Thembe continues, "the consumer of the sedative will notice nothing unusual until an overbearing drowsiness suddenly arises, quickly followed by unconsciousness."

"Is he okay?" I ask. "He looks a bit . . . off."

"He's fine. They're all like that. Best not to ask what the PPA does to their soldiers. Now, we're aware that the meals for the Wuchumbu cave guards are dished into a clay pot like this one and carried over to them three times a day at reasonably consistent times. The guards on duty then eat their food while in the cave. We know you're never involved in the preparation of the food, but for the past two days you've been nominated to carry the guard's evening meal from the settlement to the cave."

"Hold on a moment—how do you know about the cave guards? You told me the PPA's micro-drones don't work in the AZ, and that the PPA agents can't get close to the settlement without risk of being spotted. And I know you aren't watching us from above, because the canopy is mostly in the way, plus government-controlled aircraft or satellites aren't supposed to be allowed above this part of Central Africa."

"I don't need micro-drones or agents or satellites to know the Wuchumbu will have people in the cave guarding the tree. It's obvious. How else would the tribe prevent the PPA from gaining control of the cave while retaining their own access?"

"Okay. Fair enough, but how do you know about the food routines?"

Thembe sighs. "I would like to answer that, but I can't. It's classified."

I wonder whether the specialist has been feeding details back to him. I doubt it, given that Thembe didn't give her a translator, which he would have done if he wanted her to gather information. Unless she was lying about having to sneak the translator in herself?

"Your evening uddu delivery presents us with a fantastic opportunity," Thembe continues. "While you carry the food by yourself, you can administer the sedative without being seen. Once the sedative has been added and stirred, you can continue to the cave and hand the pot to the guards as normal. A very quick, simple, and easy plan for you to execute, after which you are free to go home."

"To my hut?"

"To your mansion in Magawi City, where Efawi will join you as soon as she's been located. You will get to see her bump for the first time with your arrest warrants dropped and scrubbed from your records, your assets no longer frozen. You will be free to live your lives as you wish. How does that sound?"

I picture Efawi, me, and our first child on the couch, all warm and cozy. Laughing. Headsets on as we explore a virtual world together.

"Well?" says Thembe.

"What's the needle and syringe for?" I ask.

Before Thembe can answer, we're interrupted by a groan, followed by a crash. The soldier has become a heap of muscle and vein.

"Did I—did the uddu just kill him?" I stutter.

"Not yet," Thembe replies. "That's where the needle comes

in. A shot of nuxoid will stop his body from shutting down and his brain from entering a coma."

"Nuxwhat?"

"It's a synthetic molecule designed by the military."

Aside from a slight rise and fall of the soldier's chest, he's deathly still. "So, you knew this man was going to collapse," I say, "but you didn't put a mat out to break his fall? Or better yet, ask him to lie down?"

"Once you've delivered the sedative-laced yam paste to the cave guards," says Thembe, "the PPA's special forces will wait for twenty minutes before entering the cave, at which point they will administer the nuxoid to the unconscious Wuchumbu."

"So, you're about to use the nuxwhat to wake this soldier up now, yes?"

"Only seven minutes have passed since he ate the yam. I want to demonstrate to you that a person can be safely revived twenty minutes after consuming the sedative. We have thirteen minutes remaining."

Thembe says nothing further, and I try to sit still while we wait but find it hard to do so with an unconscious body on the floor beside me. Thembe watches me as if assessing my response. "Shouldn't we get him a pillow? Or straighten him out at least?" I ask. "His elbow's all twisted under his massive head."

"He's fine."

"Okay. Well, what exactly happens when the special forces enter the cave?" I ask.

"They'll work their way past the unconscious Wuchumbu guards to secure the tree, then they'll signal for a second wave of soldiers to revive the guards and return them to their settlement, all while security around the cave is reinforced. The entire operation will be over in a matter of minutes, and the plan does not necessitate nor estimate any casualties on either side."

My heart quickens as I picture Big Man sprawled and unconscious on the hard Banoochee floor. "What happens to the

Wuchumbu after that?" I ask.

"If the tree can be moved to a secure facility, the Wuchumbu may stay where they are if that is what they want. If the tree cannot be moved, it will be studied on-site, and our scientists and security team will determine the best way to ensure it can never be triggered. I would imagine this will involve the Wuchumbu being relocated, as it would be unacceptable to allow those who can activate the tree to live so close. Nothing has been finalized, but in either scenario, I would like for the Wuchumbu to be interfered with as little as possible."

I point at the heap on the ground. "How much longer, Thembe?"

"Five minutes to go," he replies. He gets up from his chair, walks around the table to stand over the soldier. I swivel around to face him.

"So, will you do what is needed to ensure everyone's safety?" Thembe asks.

"Are you giving me a choice?"

"We could threaten you into complying, but this is too important a mission for the key player to be conflicted and reluctant. I cannot risk you hesitating or changing your mind mid-operation. You need to decide whether you are in or not, and 'in' means you are wholly motivated and aligned with our objectives."

"Do I still get to go home if I say 'no'?"

"Yes. You and Efawi get to go home, warrants lifted, assets unfrozen. But we proceed with our plan to secure the tree, regardless. With your assistance, we stand a better chance of success. Without your assistance, the soldiers will have to kill the cave guards as they progress through the corridors, and at the cavern entrance, a sniper will take out the guard who stands next to the tree. The men and women assigned to this mission are the absolute best in their field, and I have complete faith in them, but if you apply the sedative and deliver the meal, the risk of mission failure moves closer to zero because the soldiers won't have to execute quick and silent kills as they work through the cave.

"So, you can go home without helping, but while you're enjoying time with your family, you will have to live with the knowledge that, at no risk to yourself, you could have saved the lives of the Wuchumbu in the cave and could have helped remove the threat the tree poses to us all, you and your family included—and yet you chose not to."

I take a deep breath. A bridge shouldn't have to drug its friends. I look at the soldier on the floor. "Is he one of the 'absolute best' who will be on the mission?"

"Certainly not," Thembe replies.

I glance back at the remaining uddu. "What if the sedative doesn't work or if one of the guards isn't hungry and doesn't eat? Is this really your best plan? How many experts did you have working on this?"

"All options have been evaluated by the team: explosives; incendiaries; holding Mhaawu or Ratu hostage; drilling holes and filling the cavern with gas; infecting the tribe with a fatal disease; sending in Wuchumbu clones. Every possible course of action has been considered, and the plan we decided upon, the one I have outlined to you, has been calculated to carry the least risk. And from my experience, the simplest plans are the ones most likely to succeed."

"So, there definitely won't be any bombs dropped from high altitude?"

"Using explosives to neutralize the tree was discussed but taken off the table because we don't know what effect it might have. The blast might destroy the tree, or for all we know, the blast might activate it. Furthermore, if the tree is sentient and we blow it to pieces, then we risk a reaction from the treemaker. To answer your original question, if for some very unlikely reason the sedative doesn't work, or if the uddu goes uneaten, we proceed with the same basic plan: to stealthily enter the cave on foot and execute silent kills as the soldiers progress. If the guards have already been rendered unconscious by the sedative, then obviously the kills won't be necessary."

I squirm in my chair. "That's a lot of pressure you're putting on me. I thought my role here was over. I thought you were going to work with Mhaawu and negotiate a solution—something like you guaranteeing to leave them alone and the tribe guaranteeing they will never enter the cave. That's what you said to her. I was there. I heard you. And the Wuchumbu are all nervously waiting for you to return with confirmation. I told them they should trust you, but it turns out you were lying. All this time, Mhaawu and the tribe could have activated the tree, yet they've chosen not to because they want to do the right thing. You should trust them. Work with them. Not sneak in there like bandits and steal what's rightfully ours."

"Ours?"

"Theirs. What was given to them."

Thembe takes a moment before responding. I look for the rise and fall of the soldier's chest.

"Okon, has the tree given you any indication of an expiration?"

"What do you mean?"

"Do we have any reason to believe there is a time limit to the Wuchumbu's decision to trigger or not?"

"I suppose there's no time limit I'm aware of."

"Well then, let's assume I'm able to reach agreement with Mhaawu. Even if she remains true to her word, she will one day die or be usurped. Will the next leader of the tribe be so willing to honor her agreement? And what about the leader after that? In addition to this, there's always the chance that someone in the tribe will disobey Mhaawu's orders, sneak into the cave, and place their hand inside the hollow. The fact of the matter is, the more time that passes, the more opportunity there is for the tree to be triggered. And without an expiration, there is no end to this risk unless we take the tree from the Wuchumbu. Do I need to remind you what happens should the tree be triggered?"

"No."

"The death of billions, you and your loved ones included. It would be immoral not to do everything we can, as soon as we can, to ensure this weapon is never used."

Thembe folds his arms as he stares me down. I look back at the soldier.

"Regardless of what you choose, we enter the cave tomorrow night," he says, his tone resolute.

"Tomorrow! Are you sure the cave guards will be revived after twenty minutes? What happens if there's a delay in getting the nuxwhat to them?"

"They will receive the nuxoid precisely twenty minutes after you deliver their meal. Should there be a delay, which there won't be, it takes two to three hours to slip into a coma from which reviving may not be possible. The exact time this happens will depend on the individual and their dosage. However, twenty minutes is absolutely fine for everyone. Speaking of—it's now time for the nuxoid." Thembe nods at the shot on the table.

"You want *me* to do it?" I ask.

"Just for this demonstration, so you know there's been no trickery."

I look at the shot, and despite knowing the soldier needs it, I have to force myself to pick it up and participate.

26: The Ambush

As I traipse from Thembe's base to the settlement in the midst of a morning shower, I run my finger across the slight indentation in my forehead. I only wore the headset for ten minutes, but that was more than enough to fan my already burning desire to be back home.

Thembe's team has built a virtual model of the Banoochee based on what he could determine while being marched blindfolded through the cave's corridors, and what he saw while in the cavern. As practice for "Operation Get Tree" (their name, not mine), their special forces have been navigating this model using headsets. After reviving the soldier, Thembe asked me to refine their VR model based on my understanding of the layout of the cave. I told him I had nothing to add, which was the truth. Thembe had done a good job; he'd even noted the expired landmine in the first corridor.

Before leaving, Thembe advised me that the specialist has gone missing. Despite her being tagged, they're unable to pick up her location, which means she's probably still within the AZ, her tag's signal obscured by the interference. He then explained why she'd been selected for the job despite her difficult nature. The specialist used to work for the government of Loalla as head of their laboratories for warfare science and technology. According to Thembe, she has long been a corrupt individual who tried to sell information to the PPA. When the authorities in Loalla became suspicious, she defected to Mbapazu. She left behind a family, however. A husband and three children who were tortured and killed.

The specialist was brought to the jungle because the PPA thought the Nation of Loalla might be working on advanced weapons systems within the Anomalous Zone. And who better to help the PPA identify and understand what they find here than the person who used to oversee weapons development for Loalla?

Should I see her, I'm to inform Thembe immediately. "She's a traitor to her people," he said, and then he gave me a handful of sedative-filled packets. Feeling them in my pouch now, I believe the specialist and I have something in common.

My thoughts are interrupted by something crashing into a tree to my right. I jolt and drop to my knees. The impact leaves behind splintered bark, and a rock rolls to a stop by my foot. Staying low to the ground, I swivel around, try to spot the thrower through the mist. Is there an aggressive monkey out there, or is someone trying to kill me?

I hear chuckling. Male, but high-pitched.

I stand up. "Ratu, you little shit. Where are you?"

The chuckling becomes full-blown laughter. The little shit steps into view.

"I could have hit you if I wanted," he says.

"Am I supposed to be grateful you didn't?"

The scrawny, dark-skinned, loincloth-wearing tribal boy has a white metallic arm attached to his stump. He straightens and bends his robotic fingers one by one. Despite the wash of the rain, his prosthesis is grubby. Scuffed too, having clearly been put to good use over the past few days. Around his forehead is a headband, which I assume is for controlling his new limb.

"Are you okay, Ratu? Your mother's been worried sick."

Ratu pulls something from the pouch at his waist. "Do you know where there are more of these?" he asks. He walks toward me with three wet white cylinders in his hands.

"They look like batteries," I say.

"The unassociated arm only works when I put one of these in. When it stops working, I have to put another in. The ones I have marked no longer make the arm work."

"They're all marked."

"Exactly. Apart from the one currently in the arm."

"So, you only have one battery left that still works?"

"Ba-tta-wee."

There are much better prosthetic arms out there, including ones that don't require a headband. Someone I used to know had a mechatronic leg that drew its energy from the body so it didn't even need batteries.

"I tried to ask Thembe for more ba-tta-wee, but the other unassociated people, the big stupid ones, said Thembe will not speak with me unless I have my mother's permission. So, I asked the big ones for ba-tta-wee instead, but they said no, even after I told them things about the settlement."

So, Ratu's been the source of information for Thembe's team? I'm not sure the Wuchumbu would forgive him for that should they ever find out. "I'm disappointed you'd betray the tribe like that, Ratu."

"I have not betrayed anyone, because I did not tell the unassociated anything important. They were mostly just interested in our food and when we eat. Pointless, stupid questions."

"You know how you're always talking about how clever you are?"

"What about it?"

I bite my tongue. "I assume you're aware your mother let the tribe and Thembe go into the Banoochee?"

"Of course. I have been watching you all. And I saw the tree of many colors long before anyone in the tribe did, apart from the prior shaman and Mhaawu."

"So you went into the Banoochee long ago, even though Mhaawu prohibited it? Why didn't you tell me about the tree? You knew I was searching for something unusual in the AZ, something that might lead me to my wife."

Ratu looks sheepish for a moment, then asks, "Do you know where there is more ba-tta-wee?"

"No."

"Maybe you can get some from Thembe? I know you secretly visit him. I have seen you walk to his place."

"It's no secret I visit Thembe. I'm helping everyone work out an agreement. And why should I help you get batteries when you didn't tell me about the tree? I assume you know what the tree does? Do you know why your mother and the prior shaman didn't activate it straight away—two years ago?"

"Maybe you visiting Thembe is not a secret," says Ratu, "but I do have a secret. An important one."

I sigh and cross my arms. I haven't missed this young man's games. "And what would that be?" I ask.

"There is another place where the unassociated gather, even further from the settlement than where Thembe stays. There are many unassociated people there. Big, strong unassociated people, each with death-sticks and other things that are big and move around."

"How many people are we talking?"

"More than there are Wuchumbu," says Ratu.

"So that's around four hundred or more unassociated people? And they all have death-sticks?"

"Many death-sticks. Different types of death-sticks too. Some small and some big. Some even bigger than an elephant."

"Death-sticks bigger than an elephant?" I ask, skeptical.

"Yes. I have seen them. We should go there now. I worry they will kill the Wuchumbu. Also, maybe there is more ba-tta-wee there. We must go."

My understanding of Operation Get Tree is that five soldiers will initially infiltrate the Banoochee, followed by another twenty, who will bring fencing to secure a perimeter around the cave. Hundreds of armed soldiers and death-sticks as big as elephants sounds a lot more heavy-handed than the plan Thembe told me. I suspect Ratu is exaggerating to tempt me to go to this second site and help him find batteries. It's clear why Thembe gave him an outdated robotic arm: he wanted Mhaawu's son to become dependent on his team.

Ratu reaches for me with his prosthetic, and I step back into a puddle. "Ratu, I've got a lot on my mind right now. I don't want to know about this other place. I just want to continue walking back to the settlement, and you should come with me. Did you know that Mhaawu, Big Man, Adienatta, and even Gommonogo have been searching for you?"

"You do not care about the Wuchumbu," he says. "If you did, you would come with me to this secret place. We are going to be attacked, it is obvious. Why would Thembe's tribe bring so many death-sticks here unless they intend to use them? The unassociated are terrible people. I despise them all."

I shake my head, turn from Ratu, and head toward the settlement.

"Wuchumbu will be killed unless you help me!" Ratu screams.

I spin around and wave a finger at him. "I've only ever heard you insult the tribe and worship all things unassociated, yet now you're telling me you despise the unassociated and are desperate to protect the tribe. Ratu, it's clear you only want me to help you get batteries. I think you've spent too much time on your own, and it's time to come home."

"No. *You* should go home," he snaps, "and I am not talking about the settlement."

"The settlement *is* my home, for now at least. More so than it will ever be for you."

Ratu falls silent. The rain patters his round head and narrow shoulders.

"I'm sorry," I say—my turn to look sheepish. "I'm under a lot of pressure right now, and I'm saying things I don't mean. I really am sorry."

Ratu scans the ground and picks up a small rock with his robotic hand.

"Hey, if you throw that at me!"

"I do not want the settlement to be my home," he says. "That place was bad before the tree of many colors arrived, and when they stopped their stupid Massas fruit ceremony, they got even worse! Okon, this is your last chance to come with me to fight the unassociated."

"Your mother misses you."

"Mhaawu is selfish and lazy! She is always telling everyone to stay near the settlement—she wants everyone to be miserable together and die in the same place."

"She cares about you."

"Fine, I will go to the secret unassociated place by myself. I will find ba-tta-wee. I do not need your help!"

"Ratu, we are in the middle of a very delicate situation. If you go to this place and get hurt and your mother finds out, she could react, then Thembe could react. You could ruin everything."

"The prior shaman was right; you are weak and pathetic, Okon. Your wife must have left you on purpose."

Ratu raises the rock above his head, ready to throw, when his new arm clunks and whirs before falling limp at his side. The rock drops to the ground. Ratu shakes his metal arm, which remains lifeless.

"Dead ba-tta-wee?" I mock.

"Motherfucker!" Ratu screams with perfect Mbapaz pronunciation—he must have been practicing. He picks up the rock with his real hand and hurls it at me. The rock hits my shoulder—not a clean impact, but enough to hurt. Ratu freezes, mouth wide open, before he spins around and runs away.

"Don't mess with the plan!" I yell. "Come back! People could die!"

But once again, Ratu disappears into the jungle.

27: The Reason

"Spearing fish is easier for a beginner like you if you do not go so deep."

I rub the water from my eyes, look around to see who's talking, find Mhaawu standing by the edge of the rock pool. *Great*, that's my peace and quiet over with. Not that my attempt at peace was working. I kick my way toward her. It's very unusual for Mhaawu to go too far from the settlement. She thinks it isn't safe. So why has she come all the way to the pools?

"You are usually too lazy to get your own food," she says. "I am surprised you can even swim, although not very well from the look of it. I have been searching for you all day. Have you been here this whole time?"

"I went to see Thembe, then came here to fish—by myself." I stand up a few meters from Mhaawu, the green-tinted water reaching my thighs. I glance at my pouch on the rocks to be sure the sedatives inside can't be seen, not that Mhaawu would know what they are.

"What did Thembe say?" she asks.

"Not much. They're still working on the agreement."

I hate myself for lying. Mhaawu releases a heavy sigh and runs her hands through her graying hair. "For the past two days, every movement of the trees is seized upon as though the unassociated have come to harm us," she says. "An ant picks up a leaf and the entire tribe jumps from fear. Those who guard the Banoochee grow weary and disturbed; it is not healthy for them to be in there for so long. And this morning, while sitting and watching everyone, I realized we will be like this for the rest of our lives."

I turn back to the pool, spear still in hand, and I consider my response carefully for fear of letting slip any secrets. "Things won't continue like this after you and Thembe reach an agreement," I say.

"I have realized it is not possible for Thembe and I to come to agreement," she says. "We can never let the unassociated take the tree from us because it is the only power we have, and the unassociated will never allow us to keep the tree because they fear we will activate it. So, by letting Thembe know about the tree, I've condemned the Wuchumbu to spend the rest of our lives like we have the past two days."

"Weren't you living in fear of the unassociated anyway, before all this happened?"

"Not like this, where we feel the presence of the unassociated in every moment. But of course, we do have the option to end this situation . . ."

Mhaawu sighs again. Her shoulders are stooped, as though an invisible weight pushes on her. She walks around the pool and slumps on a flat portion of rock. I remain standing in the water a few meters from her. "Ever since the tree of many colors came to us," she says, "I have not felt worthy of leading the tribe."

"Why's that?" I ask reluctantly. Under different circumstances, I'd be happy that Mhaawu finally seems to be opening up to me, but I'm about to betray these people. Now's not the time for sharing feelings.

"Because suddenly within the Banoochee there stood the answer to all of the Wuchumbu's problems," Mhaawu replies. "And yet I refuse to use it. How can I be the tribe's leader when I fail to do what is needed to protect my people? But if I activate the tree, I would fail in my duties as a mother."

"How so?" I ask.

Mhaawu sits quietly for a moment. I spot a fish making its way toward me and stay as still as I can, tightening my grip on the spear.

"After the unassociated men killed my husband, they . . ."

I take my eyes off the fish and look back at Mhaawu. She's staring into the water while rubbing the scars on her wrists. "I was tied up," she says, "and when I tried to resist what they were doing, when I tried to scream or struggle, they would hit me over the head. But eventually, I was rescued."

"By the Wuchumbu?"

"No. I was rescued by other unassociated men. There were five in their group. Two of them were holding me down, but when the other three saw what was happening, they pointed their death-sticks at the two, argued with them, made them stop. Then, having heard the shouting, the Wuchumbu arrived, and a fight broke out between our tribe and the unassociated. They killed two of us and we killed two of them, but the two unassociated we killed had rescued me. The two who raped me, along with a third, got away."

"I'm so sorry to hear this, Mhaawu. I knew your husband was murdered when you stumbled across a group of unassociated in the jungle, but I knew nothing about what happened to you."

"I do not need sympathy. I am only informing you so you understand why I have not activated the tree of many colors."

"Because the men who came to your rescue were evidence that not all unassociated are completely evil?"

"No," says Mhaawu. She glances at me before looking back into the pool. "It is because Ratu's father is one of the unassociated men who raped me."

I put down the spear, which floats on the water, and turn around fully to face Mhaawu. "I thought you were pregnant with Ratu when your husband was killed?"

"That is what I told everyone, but it was not true. My husband and I could not have children despite many years of trying. He thought it was a curse on us. So did the shaman. However, after what happened that day, I became pregnant."

"So, you're saying that because Ratu's father is unassociated, you cannot activate the tree?"

"Yes. Because Ratu's father is unassociated, the treemaker might not consider Ratu to be Wuchumbu—not entirely. Therefore, should the tree be activated, my son might die along with all other non-Wuchumbu."

"But Ratu is Wuchumbu. He is clearly Wuchumbu."

"I know this. To me, he is Wuchumbu, but maybe the treemaker puts him in the category of non-Wuchumbu."

"But he is clearly Wuchumbu."

"Yes, you said that already, and maybe you are right, but I cannot take the risk. This is why the last two years have been so miserable for me. I had the solution to my people's problems, and yet I could not use it in case it kills my child."

"Does Ratu know his father is unassociated?"

"I have never told him. Yet he has always tried to distinguish himself from the tribe, as though he somehow knows he is different. And he *is* different."

"Does anyone know?"

"I only ever told the prior shaman about what happened to me. I was pregnant, scared, and I sought his spiritual guidance. He told me it was an abomination, that the child would be a curse on all of us, and that I should kill the thing before it was born."

"Well, I'm glad you didn't follow that moron's advice."

"I did follow his advice. I did not want to, but I was afraid. I had always been told that the unassociated are evil, and now there was this evil being growing inside of me. But my attempts failed. I am happy they did; when I saw Ratu for the first time I knew he was not evil, but his arm was missing, and that was my fault."

"How so?"

"Because of my attempts to kill him when he was inside me. His arm is missing as punishment for my actions. Our descendants bear the weight of our wrongdoing."

I don't see why Ratu would be punished due to Mhaawu's actions. In any case, he seems to get by just fine with one arm; doesn't seem right to call it a punishment. "Does Ratu remain the only reason you haven't activated the tree of many colors?" I ask.

Mhaawu turns her gaze from the pool to me. "I also do not want you to die, Okon."

My cheeks warm. A school of tiny fish dart around my legs.

"And if there are other good people like you out there," Mhaawu continues, "then it seems our only option is to do what the strange lady with the crazy hair told us."

"The specialist?"

"Yes, her. We need to use the threat of the tree of many colors to force change in the world. Only if the world is a better place can we stop living in fear of the unassociated."

"Sorry to tell you this, Mhaawu, but today I learned the specialist is not a very nice person, to put it mildly, and we certainly shouldn't be taking advice from her. Besides, like I already told you, forcing change is not as simple as you might think. The world outside the Nsanba is complex."

"Yes, I do not understand the unassociated world, but you do. Together we can negotiate with the unassociated to make the world better."

"What does 'better' even mean?"

"'Better' means the tree of many colors is no longer needed because the unassociated are no longer a threat to us or anyone. When you find your wife, she can live with us too while we negotiate. You, your wife, and your child can stay with us for the rest of your lives if you wish. We would be honored if you did."

I glance again at the pouch on the rocks. Mhaawu has no idea what's about to happen, has no idea that all this talk of negotiating is academic. To think it was me who led the unassociated to the Wuchumbu, and it'll be me who helps the unassociated take control of the cave tomorrow evening.

"So, will you help us force change in the unassociated world?" Mhaawu asks, her question reminding me of my wife.

"I . . . I need to think about it," I reply.

"Well, we do not have much time. Every moment that passes, the Wuchumbu become more frightened. I fear some might storm the cave and activate the tree."

I share Mhaawu's concern. The dispute at the settlement has reached an all-time high. "I heard the Wuchumbu used to be less argumentative and less, um, dysfunctional when there was more of a spiritual practice at the settlement. So, why did you stop the Massas fruit ceremonies when the tree of many colors arrived?"

"We were all taught that the god of the skies—the blue, ten-eyed Massas—is the strongest of all the gods, and that the Massas fruit is a gateway to this power and many other spiritual worlds. But when the tree of many colors came, I realized there is a more powerful force out there that we were not taught about, which invaded the Banoochee and took over our sacred rock. And so, I simply stopped believing what I had previously been taught. I did not tell the Wuchumbu to stop the Massas fruit ceremonies. I only told them it was nonsense and that I no longer believed in it. They then chose to stop."

"Well, if you didn't order everyone to stop," I say, "maybe it's time to bring the Massas fruit ceremony back? Perhaps it will help pull the tribe together, stop the arguing, stop anyone from trying to storm the cave."

"Okon, we need to focus on forcing the unassociated to change, not waste time on pointless ceremonies. I want us to sleep at night without fear."

I wonder if I'll ever be able to sleep at night, knowing I was complicit in Operation Get Tree. "Mhaawu . . . I think perhaps you should run. All of you. Your ancestors have done it before; you can do it again. Tonight, in the middle of the night, get up and leave. Take the tribe elsewhere in the Nsanba. Let the unassociated have the tree. You won't need it because they'll never find you."

"No," says Mhaawu, her response swift. "Where we are now has been our home for many years and has always provided us with safety."

Perhaps the last time Mhaawu ventured far from the settlement was when her husband was murdered and she was raped. My chest tightens at the thought of what she's been through. "Well, one thing I've learned since I left my home is that it wasn't healthy for me to be in the same place all the time," I say. "Before I came to the Nsanba, my world had sort of narrowed until I was left with only a thin sliver of an existence. Mhaawu, I hope one day the Wuchumbu get to leave the Nsanba, free to explore the world."

"Snake," says Mhaawu.

Adrenaline flushes through me. For a moment, it seems she's calling *me* a snake, and I'm sure she found out about the sedative plan. Then Mhaawu stands and points, and I turn around, and there's a snake swimming in my direction. More adrenaline flushes through me. I reach for my spear, but it's gone, floated to the middle of the pool.

"Is it venomous?" I ask.

"Maybe."

"What do you mean 'maybe'? You should know!"

"You have been living here for four months; *you* should know! If you stay perfectly still, you will be fine."

The snake makes its way toward me, head above water, mouth open, sunlight glinting off brown scales. I yelp and splash toward Mhaawu as quickly as I can. "Okon, keep still!" she cries.

The snake gains on me. A pebble hits me on the head. "Sorry! I was aiming for the snake," says Mhaawu. After what feels like an age, but was probably a matter of seconds, I make it out of the water and flail about to be sure there's nothing on me.

"Were you bitten? Your shoulder is wounded."

"I think I'm fine," I reply, all breathy. "The shoulder thing happened earlier."

The snake swims in circles near the side of the pool. Mhaawu returns to where she was seated. After catching my breath, I sit beside her, keeping my eyes on the snake. "Will it stay in the water?" I ask.

"It will. And by the way, this snake is highly venomous."

"Then why did you say 'maybe'?"

"I did not want you to panic. Of course I know every kind of snake there is. The Wuchumbu know a dangerous animal when we see one. We have to."

I take a deep breath and look at the graze on my shoulder, which stings from the water. "Mhaawu . . . I saw Ratu."

The tribe's leader grabs my arm. "When?"

"This morning. Less than a couple of hours' walk from here. He jumped out at me."

"Is he okay?"

"Yes, but he's upset. I worry he might do something dangerous. He said a lot of crazy things about going to where the unassociated are and fighting them. I think you need to speak with him before he hurts himself or jeopardizes the situation here. Perhaps you can send Big Man to bring him back. He might be staying at the ridge before the three spiky peaks. He's mentioned that place before, and that's the direction he ran off in."

"Does he still have that horrible thing from Thembe?"

"He does."

Her grip on my arm tightens. "That boy is in so much trouble. Ever since he could walk, I've told him not to go far from the settlement, but does he listen? No. He causes me nothing but stress."

"Perhaps you're too hard on him," I nervously propose as I glance from the snake to Mhaawu. "Maybe you sometimes forget how fortunate you are to have a child of your own?"

"What would you know?" she says. She squeezes my arm further, then lets me go. I turn back to the snake, feeling bad that I've upset her.

"I have heard you are happy that your wife is pregnant. Why?"

"Because I'm going to be a father, obviously."

"But why should that make you happy?"

I open my mouth but don't have an immediate answer. "Doesn't having Ratu make you happy?" I ask, half expecting Mhaawu to snap at me in response.

"Nothing with Ratu is ever that simple," she replies, sounding lost in thought rather than angry. She sits in silence for a moment before getting to her feet. "I will find him and make sure he does not do anything dangerous," she says.

"You're going to go that far from the settlement yourself?"

"He is less likely to hide if it is just me, and I am the only person who can persuade him to return. In the meantime, I am holding you responsible for keeping our people calm and making sure nobody, Wuchumbu or unassociated, storms the cave."

"But—"

"You have a calming influence on the tribe, Okon."

"Have you not been alive the past four months?"

"And you know how the unassociated operate better than any of us."

"But—"

Mhaawu puts her hand on my head. "How can you be a father, Okon, if you are always so reluctant? Show some intention. Meet what is asked of you before it is even asked. Start now, before your child arrives, or it will be too late."

Mhaawu turns and walks away.

"What's that supposed to mean?" I call after her, but she

doesn't respond, and I'm left alone with the serpent. I get to my feet, disgruntled by her advice, unsure if she's suggesting I might be a bad father, although I accept she was probably just trying to be helpful. Given what Mhaawu just revealed about what she's been through, it's hard to be annoyed with her.

The snake lies still at the pool's surface, its head pointing toward me. I grab the sedative-filled pouch and hold it high, as though I might throw it at the creature. I stay that way, my mind swinging back and forth between helping Thembe and not helping Thembe. Eventually, I lower the pouch. "I will do what I can, Efawi. For the three of us, I promise."

I loop the pouch's strap over my shoulder and consider how I can calm the tribe down and make sure they don't do anything rash while Mhaawu is away. The answer is immediate: I need to keep them distracted. I need to persuade them to get high.

28: The Wuchumbu

I'm lying on my back

    there is a fire   a big one
    the Wuchumbu don't need to hide anymore because they've
already been found so
        they built a bonfire as large as a   house
    Thembe will be mad   who cares

    they are dancing around the fire   reinvigorated   unrestrained
singing   old drums dusted off   reskinned   banged for the first
time in years

    and I am as high as a mo   nkey in a tree
      we   are all out of our heads   together
    the Massas fruit ceremony is just what we needed

    tonight more than ever

    they resisted my idea at first
    then came around   after a lot of talking

thanks to Beejalee and the shaman's enthusiasm
and a need for relief from all the pressure we face

  the shaman even agreed to let Feplao help her make the brew
help her run the ceremony
  so along with the others I drank   but we didn't drink
the alien fruit
  no no no   we drank the hallucinogenic brew made
from the Massas fruit from the Massas tree that grows on Earth
by the hand of Mother Nature

  I was afraid to drink it but the Wuchumbu showed me love
my people showed me love and so I drank with them
  not something they would normally ever do with a non-
Wuchumbu
  the ceremony had always been sacred to them

  and I have never seen them so raw   so Wuchumbu   how
could they not have done this for two years

        while Feplao and the shaman sang together the
fruit took me
the lights came   the famous lights of many colors filled my eyes
     we don't need alien-made lights   our Massas fruit
  lights are good enough thank you very much

  then came the vomiting then more drinking then more
vomiting
  a bit of foaming at the mouth
  I thought I was about to die   there was a fire not only
on the outside but inside of me too   in my blood

my heart thumping so loud
smoke was blown in my face
and the singing continued   taking me deeper

the alien fruit does the same thing each time
gives the same experience and download of information

but once the colored lights pass   the Massas fruit takes you
to many different places

I don't believe in the spirit realm   but I was wrong to think
the Massas fruit just gets people high   it is more than that
much more important

              and the fruit took me   somewhere

I became distant from the tribe

lost

strange snippets of chatter came to me   words without an
owner and without meaning

"Where's my knife?"

"Here's to success."

but the words were quickly suppressed
and I stayed lost

then I heard the chanting a sonic beacon   the
shaman's voice dictating the pace of my visions or maybe my
visions dictating the pace of her chanting
    a soft hand rubbed the back of my neck let me know I was
not alone that the Wuchumbu were with me
    she said the Massas fruit reveals something different for us all

then something talked to me   not the shaman   but
something else   I don't know what
                            animal-shaped ripples   a
landscape of color
            the shaman said it is a spirit
    it scared me

it was bigger than me
    it asked if I will betray the Wuchumbu for my wife and
future child

    I said I will   because   that is my responsibility as a
father   keeping my family safe

    but then I looked at the tribe moving by the fire
                and I thought   I can never betray the
Wuchumbu people
    sure there are some who want to activate   and
they know what that means for me
        but it's a vocal minority who want this   and they're
afraid   just want to protect their families

no   I will never betray the Wuchumbu's acceptance of me
their trust
        they have given me more than they had to   more than
I realized

        then the Watcher stirred once more
        closer this time stronger than before   less cloaked
                I think the thing has been watching me ever since I
drank the treemaker's brew of many colors   every thought every
thing I see   like a parasite   alien

        treemaker inside of me
        treemaker inside of me

        then   as always   my   awareness of the Watcher faded
away

        and I spent what felt like hours drifting and encountering
        traveling
        imagining
                even the prior shaman took the trouble to visit me
he is still an asshole

        with time the Massas fruit left my eyes and my blood

        and as I lie on my back recalling my trip

knowing I'm still under the influence but not as much   I look at the stars and listen to the shaman chanting and Feplao singing and the jungle life doing its thing
until I start to drift into sleep

I'd rather die than betray the Wuchumbu

*　*　*

I awake early the next day, the sky dark blue, my head throbbing, my heart pounding, but I'm no longer under the influence of the Massas fruit. Yet the decision I came to while I was under remains: I simply cannot betray these people. I don't have it in me.

Before the others rise, I make my way to the PPA base to tell Thembe I won't cooperate with tonight's plan and that he needs to call off Operation Get Tree and try to work out a solution with Mhaawu. This situation can be resolved verbally, peacefully and honestly—I'm sure of it. Perhaps if my wife is located soon enough, she can expedite an agreement. She is gifted at finding solutions.

Then, as I approach the base, I hear the words I've been dreaming of for months:

⁓*Incoming call from Efawi,*⁓ says my nôvono pro.

I'm outside the AZ, and so I'm away from the interference, but despite this, a nôvo-call isn't possible because there's no connectivity in the jungle. I'm still a little fuzzy-headed from the Massas fruit . . . but I'm long past the hallucinating stage.

⁓*Incoming call from Efawi,*⁓ my nôvono repeats.

This is real. This is happening.

⁓*nôvono, accept the call.*⁓

⁓*Hello? Okon? Are you there?*⁓

29: The Future

~Hello?~ she repeats.

The sound of her voice recreated in my brain is too much for me. My legs turn to mush. I reach out with both hands for the nearest solid thing, a thick, gnarled tree, and lean against it for stability.

~Okon?~ says Efawi. Her feelings seep through the nôvo-call, and I instantly recognize the specific flavor of my wife's anxiety. Her suffering forces me to gather myself.

~I'm here,~ I reply, and give a choked-up laugh. Efawi laughs too. She's relieved, but deeply exhausted. I can feel it.

~I was terrified I might never speak with you again,~ she says.

~Where are you? Are you okay?~ I ask, aware that my frazzled mental state is being transmitted to her.

~I'm fine. I'm still in the jungle. PPA soldiers came and found me; can you believe it? I'm with them at one of their mini-stations not too far from the Nsanba's edge. Where are you?~

~I'm just outside a PPA base that's near the Anomalous Zone. So, you're definitely okay? And the fetus . . . baby?~

~I'm exhausted, but the 'fetus-baby' and I are fine,~ Efawi laughs. *~The soldiers are going to take us to a medical facility just to run some tests and get my levels back up. Trekking through the jungle while six months pregnant has been quite the challenge. I've been sluggish, less able to cover the distance, and with my belly as it*

is, I've been unable to properly fit into my trekking suit. -

- But you're sure you're okay? -

- Yes. No injuries or sickness; I'm just very weak and tired. I can't wait to see the look on your face when you see me. When you feel the baby kick. I thought I'd hate being pregnant, but I don't. -

A familiar blend of Efawi's exhaustion and excitement is transmitted through the call. And she's going to be fine. The baby is going to be fine. We are getting out of here!

- I can barely believe I'm talking to you. How are you even calling me? - I ask.

- The PPA has established a chain of short-range transmitter-receivers that runs between the AZ and a military facility just outside the Nsanba. -

- Yes, Thembe explained that to me. -

- Well, I'm currently within range of this communications corridor, and they allowed me restricted access to their network so I can nôvo-call you. You said you are outside a base of theirs, so you must be within range of this corridor as well. I tried calling you several times over the past couple of hours, but I'm guessing you've only just come into range now. -

Efawi's attempts to call me over the past couple of hours takes me back to the day she left the house.

- What's wrong? - she asks.

- It was my fault, - I say. *- I forgot I turned it off. The damn thing didn't even remind me it was off. We need to make a complaint to Digital Cognitives.* -

- Okon, what are you talking about? -

- On your last morning at home, you kept asking me to log you into my streaming account because you'd been blocked. But I wanted to be left alone, so I went to my entertainment room and switched off my nôvo-comms. -

- I see. So, that's why you didn't answer my calls later that day? -

- I didn't even know about them, not until many days later when I was relaxing in our float room and it suddenly occurred to me that

my nôvo-comms were still off. The reason it took so long for me to realize this is because after you left, I had no reason to expect any nôvo-calls from you as you'd mentioned you'd be going on a trip abroad soon, which I assumed was one of your usual work trips where you're offline. And I don't receive nôvo-comms from anyone else.~

~It's okay. I understand. You don't need to explain yourself.~

~But when your arrest warrant came through and you needed me, I wasn't available for you. If my comms had been on, I would have received your calls and answered them, and I'd have come with you on your trek to the AZ without hesitation. We could have been together this whole time.~

~Okon, it was a mistake that anyone could have made. It's okay.~

~I would never intentionally leave you in trouble like that. Never. Once I received your messages, I wasn't able to leave home straight away, as the PPA were openly monitoring the house, but as soon as I got the chance, I took it, and I've been searching for you ever since. I never gave up. I'm so sorry I wasn't there for you to begin with. I'm so sorry. I forgot. I simply forgot I'd switched my nôvo-comms off.~

~I'm the one who should be apologizing. I caused all this trouble with the government in the first place, and I'm sorry for dragging you into it. I should have told you about my discovery in the Nsanba sooner, but I was afraid you'd ask me to leave it alone or that you'd say you wouldn't come with me. Hold on, someone wants to talk to me . . .~

The feed goes silent, and the sentiment from Efawi is cut. I take the opportunity to try to settle myself. I wipe my eyes and nose with my forearm.

~I'm back,~ she says, after less than a minute. *~I've just been told that we'll shortly be leaving this mini-station and they'll be taking me the rest of the way out of the jungle. I don't know if I'll be able to talk while we're on the move.~*

~You aren't under arrest, are you? Thembe told me you wouldn't be.~

~No, I'm not under arrest, but it's been made clear I need to start engaging in dialogue with the authorities. An officer here has updated me on what's been going on inside and outside the Nsanba over the past six months. Fortunately, there have been some surprising shifts in power within the PPA itself. Their party is still problematic, but the change is a positive one and I know some of the people involved. I'm confident the PPA and I can reach a solution so that we're free to return home.~

~Okay.~

~Something wrong, Okon? I thought you'd be excited.~

~I am, it's just . . . you've always been so anti-PPA, yet now you're happy to work with them, and now you're happy to have a child after being so against the idea for so long. I'm delighted you've changed your mind about these things, but it's strange to hear you talk this way, that's all.~

Efawi takes a moment to respond. I think I sense her brain processing, which may be my imagination rather than the feed from the nôvo-call.

~Being in the Nsanba, without a connection to any digital networks for the first time in my life, gave me space to reevaluate what's important,~ she says. ~The fear I might never see you again, and the discovery that I'm pregnant with your child, all while facing very real physical dangers in the jungle, have changed me. I'm tired of obsessing about battles at work and battles with the PPA. I want to spend more time with the people I care about. I want to build deeper relationships. I want to raise a family with you.~

I take a deep breath. ~I need to be with you,~ I say, my thought-words breaking despite my throat not being involved. ~I'm going to ask Thembe to put me on a scooter and have me taken to you.~

Efawi doesn't respond, and her emotional state changes: her exhaustion mixed with excitement is replaced with a blend of anguish and resolve—another combination of hers that I'm familiar with.

~Okon, you mustn't leave the AZ yet,~ she says. *~If we're to have a future together, the situation with the extraterrestrial artifact must be dealt with. I've been informed the PPA has asked you for help with taking possession of the tree, and that because of the unique position you find yourself in, your help could be the difference between success and failure. Are you intending to leave before helping Thembe?~*

~Actually, I was on my way to tell him I don't want to be involved.~

~Why not? Does this plan of theirs put you in danger?~

~No. I won't be present when they go into the cave.~

~Then you must help Thembe. You know this, right? It's obvious. You received the message I left you in the cave, so you know the threat the tree poses. How can we raise a family with that threat hanging over our heads—hanging over everyone's head?~

~I . . . I don't want to betray the Wuchumbu. I've become close to them. They've looked after me the past four months while I was trying to find you. They are not bad people.~

~Your opinion of them is irrelevant. Even if they were the kindest, most enlightened people on Earth, the tree simply cannot be left in the possession of anyone who's able to use it. The consequences are too immense.~ Efawi's frustration pours through the feed.

~I understand what you're saying, but betraying them doesn't feel right.~

~Does the PPA's plan result in these tribal people being harmed?~ she asks.

~Actually, if I don't help the PPA, the Wuchumbu guarding the cave will probably be shot and killed. But I want to persuade Thembe to call off their operation.~

Incredulity seeps through the call. I rip a big leaf from a stalk and fan myself.

~Okon, you won't be able to persuade the PPA to change their plans. Trust me, I've learned that the hard way. And so, you must help them. You must assist the PPA for the sake of the cave guards

and everyone else.~

~But the Wuchumbu trust me. They treat me like family, for the most part. They even said you can live here too—that we can raise our child here.~

~You want to continue living in the jungle with these people?~

~No. I want to be back home with you and raise a family. But we could visit them, perhaps. Spend some time here. I don't know how that would work; I'm just trying to explain that I don't want to let them down. I don't want to let anyone down. I shouldn't be in this position. I didn't ask to be involved in this.~

~Perhaps the magnitude of what's at stake is too immense for you to appreciate, so just focus on the child within me—our child. That tree is a threat to our child. It is your responsibility as a father to play your part in removing that threat.~

The word *father* lingers. My child is not yet in the world, and already my parenting is being tested. *~Get it done,~* Efawi continues, *~then come to me as quickly as you can. Together, we can work out how to bring the joy back into our relationship. Think of the fun the three of us will have. And who knows, maybe one day there'll be four. Or five.~*

~Are you serious?~

~I'm open to the idea. Given how much has changed, I wouldn't rule anything out. Okon . . . ? I can feel you are conflicted. I thought raising a family with me is what you wanted?~

~It is everything that I want. There's just a lot for me to digest right now. Efawi, in one of the nôvo-messages you left me, you said we don't have to want the same things in order to be good for each other, and that with time we can give each other what we need. What did you mean by that?~

~What I meant is that you and I might not always provide each other with what we think we want, but I believe over time we've given each other what we need, and we'll continue to do so. You and I learn from being together. We push each other to grow in areas we would otherwise neglect. You challenge me to enjoy the moment more, to relax, to be less future focused. I challenge you to be more

organized, more goal oriented, more responsible. If we were more alike, our being together wouldn't be so important. I'm talking about our mission statement.~

I think of our bedroom. My wife rarely concerns herself with matters such as home decor but for one exception: an ornamental wooden panel hanging opposite our bed. Commissioned by Efawi for our wedding, the panel comprises a carved floral framing around the decorative lettering of our matrimonial mission statement: Apotheosis through union.

~*So, will you do what you need to do?*~ she asks.

I consider the Wuchumbu: Adienatta calmly weaving. Beejalee whipping those around her into shape while her kids hang from her back. The prideful smile of Habee as he brings me honey, handing me a larger share than he should. The watchful eyes of Mhaawu as the lively chaos of the settlement unfolds. The brave guards in the Banoochee whose lives I can potentially save.

And I consider Efawi: My lifelong companion has been found. She's alive. She is safe. She's going to resolve her dispute with the PPA. She wants us to become closer again. She is carrying our first child.

~*Yes, I will help the PPA,*~ I tell her. ~*I'll do whatever it takes to protect the future of our family.*~

I should be happier than I am.

30: The Feast

"What is the matter?" asks Beejalee as she drops half a ton of African yams into a pot of boiling water.

"Nothing," I reply. "Nothing at all. Why do you ask?"

"You are lingering while we make food. Usually, you are somewhere else at this time, I suspect so you do not get dragged into helping us."

"The piece of wood has finally gone," I say, trying to change the subject. "The one that everyone hits their head on."

Beejalee smiles. "Yes, someone cut it down this morning." She picks up a handful of leaves and tears them over the pot, her fingers all chunky and muscular.

"And the mats have all been straightened out," I remark. "The paths have been swept of leaves. The communal area has been tidied and organized, and look at all the food you have to prepare."

"We had many successful hunts today," says Beejalee, "and many went to gather from the Nsanba. Our people used to have meals like this all the time, and the settlement used to be this tidy all the time, but not since the light of many colors came. Where have you been all day, Okon?"

Since my nôvo-call with my wife this morning, I've spent most of the day aimlessly walking in the jungle, wanting to be alone. Fortunately, I don't need to explain this to Beejalee as

Didiwa distracts her with a dinner-related query.

The dark sky hangs above us, and the communal area is well lit by several fires. I sit and watch the cooks go about their work—the slicing of meat with stone knives, the crushing of herbs with wooden mallets, the crackling of juices that splash onto naked flame. More people and food are involved in this meal than I've ever seen, and they aren't squabbling over whose ingredient or equipment is whose. There's no moaning that one person is working harder than another. Last night's Massas fruit ceremony has worked wonders for the tribe and booted them from their two-year-long ennui. And reviving the ceremony was my idea. I have finally contributed in an important way.

"Don't do that, you idiot!" someone yells within the cooking area, knocking my sense of achievement. Still, the argument among the kitchen hands is quickly snuffed by Beejalee. The tribe might not be perfect, but today they are rejuvenated, and their tension due to the tree situation dampened somewhat by industry.

I gently squeeze my pouch to reassure myself the sedatives are still inside, a part of me hoping the packets fell out during the day without me knowing and are lost, leaving me no choice but to abstain from Operation Get Tree—to uninvolve myself in the robbery of the people who have fed me the past four months and who will offer me their food again tonight. But the sedative remains in the pouch, and I know what I must do.

"Are you sure you are okay?" Beejalee asks. "Your eyes are as wide as an okapi's, and you are twitching."

"I'm just hungry, that's all," I lie. "And the food smells so good"—which is true. Ever the provider, Beejalee is in her element tonight, but according to my nôvono, it's almost 21:00. Dinner is later than usual. What if the PPA special forces don't wait?

I stand up. "Some of the uddu is to be taken to the Banoochee, isn't it?" I ask, trying to act casual, unsure what to do with my arms.

"Of course," Beejalee replies.

"But you're making the evening meal later than usual, and the cave guards might be worried they won't be fed."

"They will have to wait. We are late because of the time we spent searching for Mhaawu. You are aware nobody has seen her since yesterday afternoon?"

"Yes," I reply.

This is news to me. My fault for keeping to myself all day. Perhaps I should tell Beejalee that Mhaawu went to find Ratu yesterday? *No*, it's probably best I say as little as possible about anything until the tree is taken. I'm sure Mhaawu is fine. It must just be taking her a while to convince Ratu to return.

Beejalee marches over to me, whacks a wooden spoon into my hand. "Make yourself useful."

"I don't think I—" she pushes me in front of the pot and in doing so, brushes her stocky frame against me. I swing my pouch around to my side, give it a slight squeeze to be sure the packets haven't burst. I breathe a sigh of conflicted relief. *No leakage.*

"Stir," she says. "Not like that. Use both hands. Keep doing that until I tell you to stop."

Beejalee steps away to bark orders at someone else. Now that I'm standing next to the pot, I realize just how huge it is, much bigger than the usual one. The pot is being held above a small fire by a wooden stand. I lean over its rim, and my face is hit with steam. There's uddu in there, obviously, but with additional ingredients. Smells different too—more floral. All this extra food could be a problem if more than the usual one pot of uddu is to be taken to the Banoochee. Am I supposed to distribute the sedative across numerous dishes to be sure each cave guard gets their dose? What if someone else comes along to help me carry it all? Of all the nights for the Wuchumbu to do something different with their boring-as-hell meal!

"Keep stirring," says Beejalee as she dumps more ingredients into the uddu, a splash of hot water stinging my chest. I keep stirring. I've returned to my days as a cook. I used to have panic attacks before each shift, and the panic is surging again now.

I check the time once more. Dinner would normally have been served about thirty minutes ago. If the PPA doesn't wait, that means the Banoochee could be under attack at any moment. Cave guards could be shot at any moment. The tree could be activated at any moment. Every breath I take could be my last.

A nearby monkey howls, and I jump. Beejalee gestures for me to keep stirring.

"Yes, you can take it tonight," Beejalee says to someone behind me.

"Take what?" I ask.

"I will take the food to the Banoochee," Petonba answers.

I stop stirring. "But I take the food in the evenings," I say, trying to sound relaxed, but my pitch is all over the place. "Mhaawu likes me to check the cave is secure, given what I know about Thembe and his tribe," I add.

Before Petonba can respond, everyone's attention turns to a group led by Big Man who marches into the cooking area. "Still no sign of Mhaawu," he says. "Between us, we have covered the ground between the *etowea* bends in the river, the lake, the canyon, and the entire *ega tunga* side of the settlement. Etoole has been asking around, and he just learned that the last time Mhaawu was seen, she was looking for Okon. This is why I came here."

I turn back to the pot and recommence stirring. Steam blows in my face.

"Okon, have you seen Mhaawu today?" Beejalee asks.

"No, not today," I reply—technically, not a lie. I should have told them from the start that Mhaawu came to see me yesterday and then went to find Ratu, but as I've started down the path of keeping this a secret, it would be weird to reveal the truth now—they might become suspicious of me, work out something is going on.

"The uddu is ready," I announce. "I'll put some in the smaller pot for me to take to the Banoochee by myself."

"Mhaawu hardly ever leaves the settlement," says Babba, "and never for this long."

"Perhaps the unassociated have taken her," says Habee, a panic in his voice.

"We need to help her," cries Buchee.

"We need to stay calm," says Beejalee as she wraps her arms around her middle daughter. "Mhaawu is wiser than all of us, and I am sure she can take care of herself. Besides, it is too dark to continue looking. We should get back to work, and if Mhaawu has not returned by morning, we can continue our search."

Everyone returns to their meal preparation duties, but the concern for Mhaawu lingers. I step away from my stirring to retrieve a smaller pot. "Beejalee, I'm going to take some food to the Banoochee guards now. How do I transfer the uddu into this?"

"I told you, Petonba is taking the uddu tonight," says Beejalee. She grabs the smaller pot from me.

"But why?" I ask.

"Because she wants to eat with them before she takes her turn as guard."

"I think it would be best if I take it," I plead, but Beejalee is too busy organizing the rest of the feast to pay me much attention. "I really would like to take the uddu to the Banoochee," I try again.

"You can come with me if you like," Petonba offers.

"I will join you also," says Big Man. "I too am on guard duty tonight."

I clasp my head with my hands and picture the world filled with dead bodies.

No, I won't let that happen. I must do my part for Operation Get Tree. I will not let the cave guards be shot. Babba will not lose his mother, Petonba, tonight. This father-to-be has a sedative to deliver, and I'm going to fucking do it!

Beejalee is marching toward me, the effort of organizing dinner clear from her sweat-soaked forehead. Her attention is being requested from all directions, and she dismisses them by waving an arm in the air and declaring the feast ready. Word spreads at light speed, and the communal area fills with Wuchumbu. I must act, *now or never.*

I return to my stirring duties, struggling to move the spoon with one hand as I reach for my pouch with the other. I risk a glance at Beejalee. She's just a few meters away, her big feet stomping. Once she reaches me, she'll push me aside and take charge of the uddu.

I pull on the pouch's shoulder strap, bring the pouch around to my front, and with both hands hurriedly untie it, remove the sedative packets, and drop half of them on the floor. *Motherfucker!* Thankfully, those around me are too distracted to notice, and Beejalee's been intercepted by her youngest daughter, who is crying. *Thank you, Hattee!*

I scoop up the packets. Thembe gave me ten in case I wanted to practice or in case any broke. His instruction was to drop only one into the cave guard's separate pot, but Beejalee has their pot, which hasn't yet been filled with uddu.

Holding all ten packets, I raise my hands above the giant, steaming pot of uddu, which is for everyone and from which the guards' smaller pot will be filled. For the future of my baby, and for the lives of those in the cave, I extend my shaking fingers and allow the packets to drop. They land on the uddu with a plop. The liquid sedative runs free, pooling at the top as it did in the trial at Thembe's base. It is done. All Wuchumbu will be sedated tonight, cave guards included. More nuxoid will be needed, but there are no more decisions for me to make. I only need to stir.

I reach for the spoon, but Beejalee shoves me aside. "If we did not find her during the day," she says to Hattee, who is riding her back, "we will not find her at night. All we can do now is eat and rest."

Beejalee uses the wooden spoon to pry the pot from the fire and onto a large stone. With the guards' pot wedged between her arm and her chest, she grabs lumps of steaming hot uddu with her asbestos hands and fills the smaller container.

"Aren't you going to stir it first?" I ask. "I really think you should."

"You have stirred enough, Okon. It is nice you care so much about our meal this evening. My husband has hidden some extra honey, especially for you, by the basket to my right. You can have it with your meal, but do not let the others see, or they will be jealous."

I'm a terrible person.

Beejalee hands the guards' pot to Petonba and pulls together a variety of meats, which she gives to Big Man. "Say hello to Obee for me," Beejalee says. Her son must also be on guard duty this evening. My mind races as Petonba and Big Man walk away with the food for the Banoochee. *Beejalee didn't stir.*

"I am starving!" shrieks Babba. The center of the settlement is packed with Wuchumbu, all excited and ready to tuck into the banquet. Beejalee and her kitchen staff bring the food to the seating area, including the giant pot. Eager cheers fill the air. I've never fainted before, but I fear I might now.

I gingerly lower myself to the ground while staring through Wuchumbu bodies at the giant pot. Because Beejalee didn't stir, I've no idea how much of the ten packets' worth is in there and how much went to the Banoochee. And because the sedative hasn't been evenly distributed, some of the tribe may consume none of it, or just a tiny amount, and some may get a big hit. What if the cave guards consume a tiny amount and end up feeling drowsy without falling unconscious? How will they respond? Will they know something's up and activate the tree?

The hungry Wuchumbu dig their hands into the pot and

pull out the paste. I should tell them what I did, but as far as I know, the PPA doesn't have possession of the tree yet, so I can't reveal what's going on. I need to think of a way to stop those at the settlement from eating the uddu without rousing suspicion.

"There's something in the pot!" I yell.

"What do you mean?" asks Beejalee.

"I saw something ... I think a mouse ran in there, or something. Some kind of animal. The uddu has been spoiled. You have to stop eating it!"

Beejalee leans over the pot. "I cannot see anything. The uddu is fine," she says.

Nobody stops eating. *Shit.*

I try nôvo-calling Efawi for urgent advice, and my brain implant informs me that isn't possible. Of course it's not possible. I'm well inside the AZ and there's no corridor of comms here! Despite knowing this, I try calling her again.

Shit. Shit. Shit. I had one job to do, and I fucked it up. I panicked. I should have insisted I take the food to the Banoochee alone, and if I couldn't do that, I shouldn't have added any sedative at all. But then the cave guards wouldn't be sedated and would have to be shot, and Operation Get Tree would be more risky. *No*, I had to add all the packets to the main pot. There was no other option.

The happy Wuchumbu continue to tuck into their meats and fruits and uddu. Babba and his friends share a large lump of the boiled African-yam paste, slapped on the ground between them. Uddu is on their lips and fingers, which they enthusiastically lick clean, while others stand around them, shoving food into their mouths. A mother feeds a handful to her baby. The baby sucks the uddu and swallows.

I vomit.

"Okon, what is wrong?"

I remain still. The vomit runs down my chin and onto my stomach.

"That is disgusting," complains Gommonaadogo before she shoves another fistful of uddu into her mouth. Anxiety is fogging my brain. I'm frozen, but I can't just sit here. The PPA are only expecting to have to revive the five guards in the Banoochee. They won't know to bring nuxoid shots to the settlement. And what if anyone who consumes a larger dose of sedative than was planned slips into a coma and dies regardless of whether they receive nuxoid?

"Don't eat the uddu!" I yell as I struggle to my feet, unable to do nothing any longer. In the noisy, packed center of the settlement, only those immediately around me notice my panic. I stumble to the pot, kick it over, bend down to look inside. The uddu has gone. The Wuchumbu eat fast. I spin around, see a few servings of the remaining uddu dotted about on the mats. "Don't eat the uddu!" I shout.

"Okon, what are you talking about?" asks Babba. The pile he and his friends are sharing is almost gone. I stamp my boot on the remains.

"Our uddu!" they cry.

How long did Thembe say until people slip into a coma? Two or three hours, I think, depending on the individual and the dosage. I need to tell his team to bring nuxoid shots to the settlement—lots of them. There are around four hundred people in the tribe. The giant pot of uddu isn't large enough to feed them all. Some will have already eaten, and some are preparing their own separate dishes, but this pot would have provided portions for—I don't know how many. Fifty? Maybe eighty people?

I start running.

31: The Office

"A serial killer?" I mutter to myself as I speed through the jungle. *No*, a serial killer kills on more than one occasion. There's another term for someone like me, someone who does it all in one go: *mass murderer*.

It was all just a big, unintentional cock-up though, so it's manslaughter, not murder. But let's not forget I'm a cannibal too. I'm a *cannibalistic mass manslaughterer* whose gross negligence brought a multitude of deaths to a tribal people and possibly initiated the end of the world.

And to make matters worse, I don't know where I am. Hurrying through the jungle by myself at night was always going to end with me being lost. The route from the settlement to Thembe's base is marked by my usual carvings on trees, and despite the darkness and the running, I managed to follow these markings for about an hour or so until I lost track. I bring myself to a halt, no longer knowing which direction I'm facing. Mission failure. I want to go home—to the one made from bricks. I crave my room. I crave walls and ceilings. I've never felt so strongly about carpet.

An image of uddu being licked from lips jumps at me. I wave it away as though it were a physical thing. "Forget about carpet," I tell myself. I can't let my friends die. My child will not have a mass manslaughterer for a father. I spin around, looking for a tree of huggable girth and good height. If Habee can climb for honey, I can climb to save lives. I know his technique; I've watched him enough from below. I pick a tree, leap onto it, and scamper up without looking down.

I chose my tree well, and soon I'm above much of the nearby canopy, scanning my surroundings. There's a flash of light ahead: moonlight reflecting off metal. The light continues to flicker as scattered clouds drift past the moon. Squinting, I identify the outline of an antenna; the jungle base must be less than twenty meters away. Clearly, someone up there wants the Wuchumbu to be saved.

Getting down the tree is much harder than climbing up, but once back on ground, I approach the PPA's base. Having arrived from a different angle than usual, I'm struck by the size of the place. The base extends further back than I knew, with a series of prefab rooms and linking passageways. I'm also struck by the lack of people. No activity. No sounds. No security.

I try calling Efawi again, which doesn't work, and I head toward a partially open, nondescript door and push it gently with the back of my hand, expecting someone on the other side to swing it open and press a gun against my face. Instead, I'm confronted by an empty, dimly lit corridor.

"Hello?" I call out. "Someone needs to get nuxoid to the settlement ASAP."

I wait for a response, which does not come.

"Hello?" I try again.

The Nsanba continues to howl, squeal, and buzz. The base, however, is silent.

Operation Get Tree is underway, so perhaps most of Thembe's team is within the AZ. In fact, an hour and fifteen minutes has passed since dinner was served, and the PPA must have acquired the tree by now. I should be feeling relieved, but how can I when I've left behind such a mess? I can only hope the special forces didn't have to kill any cave guards when they worked their way through the Banoochee.

I head along the passageway. A sign on the first door I reach states APPROVED DC STAFF ONLY. There's an ID lock above the handle, but the door is ajar. I softly knock. "Hello? Nuxoid needed." I wait, then push the door open. On the other side is a windowless office crowded with computer pods, desks, cupboards, and boxes. There are no people, but the lights and screens are on and the office appears worked in, with tea-stained cups, half-full trash cans, and equipment strewn about the place. A display on one pod reads "Welcome to the jungle—where your love for nature dies."

My eye catches sight of something familiar on the desk closest to the door: a small black memory drive just like the ones Efawi's been leaving me, this one held within a transparent case as if it were an exhibit. I take a couple of steps into the room and notice a tall stand by the left side wall, on top of which is a nôvono. The implant hovers above the stand, held in place by thin wires, its spiderlike metallic legs positioned as if they were wrapped around an invisible brain. The meaning behind the "DC" initials on the door becomes clear: *Digital Cognitives.* What isn't clear is why the company behind the nôvono has an office here.

I pick up the plastic case that houses the memory drive. A label on the top reads "3.1144.72A-108.efawi-unmpt-aud-//-message-saved-by-efawi-left-at-target-site-//-unencrypted-audio-only-property-of-digital-cognitives-level-gb-access." I open the case, take out the memory drive with frayed red string still attached. This must be the one I gave to Thembe, and despite knowing I gave the drive to Thembe and that logically it would be at the base, there's something unnerving about seeing it here.

A journalpad lies open on the desk beside the case. Its display is full of notes and drawings. My eyes head straight to what one might think is scrawled gibberish: "supervisor ckC1Blo498." I'm not sure what "supervisor" means, but I recognize the sequence of letters and digits as a shared password my wife made up for us years ago. It follows the same simple code Efawi has used with me ever since she was a child. Switch the first and last part around and you have it. "ckC1Blo498" becomes "4981BlockC," which is the apartment number and block of Efawi's "family" home. I was BlockD, which was just as trash.

We hardly use our personal password anymore, and when we do, it's for trivial things like logging into our joint BangAtar account. How would these DC people know our stupid password? Why would they even want to know our stupid password? As trivial as it might be, I don't like seeing it here.

I flip through the journalpad, which I notice is being mirrored on a giant display on the back wall. The notes are mostly incomprehensible jargon about nôvono functionality, but I stop browsing when I see reference to my wife: "Efawi NOT with soldiers. Her location remains unknown to us and PPA." The note is dated today.

Idiots. Her location *is* known. She's with PPA soldiers who are taking her to a medical facility outside the Nsanba, and this is a fact because she told me in our nôvo-call this morning. Efawi may even already be at the medical facility. A hand-drawn line connects the comment regarding Efawi's unknown whereabouts to another note, which has been circled twice and underlined: "Manipulation of nôvo-comms accomplished change in Okon's trajectory!"

I push the journalpad away. Why am I reading this? I don't even know what this stuff means. I don't want to know either. I just want to focus on what I came here for. I take a few deep breaths. The urgent need for nuxoid claws at me—the thought of unconscious Wuchumbu scattered on the ground at the settlement, their bodies slowly shutting down, the panic of those still conscious, their screams, their crying.

My scene of horror is interrupted by footsteps—people in the passageway outside the office. I freeze as I listen. They're walking and talking. Getting louder. "And that's where this backdoor comes into play?" someone says.

"Exactly," says another. "We identified the backdoor's location in the coding for emotional processing, and only in those without the latest update."

Still holding Efawi's memory drive, I panic and put it in my pouch, then hurry for the door. My foot catches the leg of a desk, and I fall into a computer pod, which crashes to the ground. Equipment scatters across the floor.

A man and a woman enter the room and stop dead in their tracks, causing a pileup of bodies behind them. They scan me up and down, and I consider their perspective: a sweaty, loincloth-wearing man in prehistoric military boots is standing in their private office having just smashed some of their equipment. "It was like that when I got here," I try.

They look at each other, then back at me. They're dressed casually and are normal-sized human beings, a stark contrast to the pumped-up PPA security I usually have to deal with around here. I sputter: "Do you know where the nuxoid shots are . . . ? Why do you think my wife's location isn't known . . . ? What does 'manipulation of nôvo-comms' mean?"

"Er, are you DC staff?" says one of the two who entered the room first.

"Of course he isn't DC staff!" yells a short man with a shaved head, who pushes his way to the front of the pack. "Who left the damn door open again?" he asks. The ID on his collar says "Bakkadu, Digital Cognitives."

"Bakkadu, I'm Okon—the one who's been living with the Wuchumbu and working with Thembe."

"Don't talk to him," Bakkadu instructs the others. He holds his arms out as if to create a barrier between me and them.

"Please listen carefully, Bakkadu. You need to let the PPA know I added all ten sedative packets to the tribe's main pot of food and it wasn't mixed in properly. Many may already be in a coma. We need to take as many nuxoid shots as we can to the settlement right now or people will die."

Bakkadu says nothing, and I suspect he's preoccupied with something internal as I detect a touch of nôvo-face.

"Should we leave?" somebody asks.

"No. We have work to do," says Bakkadu. "Just . . . wait . . . a moment . . ."

Heavy footsteps thunder down the corridor. Bakkadu waves those behind him to one side as two hulking men in uniform bundle into the room. They lunge at me, restrain my arms, hoist me from the ground. "Put him in 12A for now," Bakkadu instructs, a bitter emphasis on "him," as though this is personal. The two security men carry me into the passageway.

"What's going on?" I cry. "Get Thembe! Tell him what happened with the sedative! He'll know what to—" A sweaty hand clamps over my mouth. I wriggle my jaws around a finger, bite down as hard as I can. The owner of the hand screams and drops me to the passageway floor. "You're killing them! The Wuchumbu need nuxoid!"

The larger of the two pulls back a fist.

"Not the head!" Bakkadu shouts.

The brute swings and punches me in the head. The passageway spins. My nôvono pro plays its internal warning message. Something about trauma.

"I told you not the head, you knuckle-dragging Neanderthal!"

The muscle-bound men prop my limp body against the wall. I'm conscious but dazed. One of them is standing over me, looking for something in his pockets.

"What happens now?" someone asks.

"Okon's role in the Nsanba has finished," Bakkadu replies, "but we aren't done with him yet. Back to your pods, everyone."

Everything goes dark as a bag is shoved over my head and I'm dragged further into the PPA's base. I can barely breathe, and just when I might pass out, I'm thrown forward. With my hands now free, I pull the bag away and find myself alone in a room. A door slams shut behind me, and I hear the clank of a lock.

32: The Big Blue

"Get up, you ineffectual invertebrate. I stole the shots from the medical unit."

I bring my left eye open to a squint, keep the right one shut. The specialist hovers over me, a canvas backpack in her hand. "Why aren't you listening?" she says, and kicks me in the leg. It hurts, but I don't respond. She does it again.

"Stop that," I tell her.

"Well, get up then."

"It's all fake," I mutter.

"What?"

I'm lying on a mattress on the floor of the room they locked me in. A few storage crates and a couple of buckets comprise the rest of the furniture. With no windows, everything is unpleasantly sharp beneath a harsh LED light, and the air is unsatisfying, as if I've used up all the oxygen. It feels like I've been in here for hours.

"You've been in here twenty minutes, and already you've lost your mind," says the specialist.

"Twenty minutes? More lies," I huff. I check the time with my nôvono pro: turns out she's right. She kneels in front of me, her skin slick, her eyes bloodshot. "The graphics are incredible," I mumble.

"If you don't come with me now, Wuchumbu will die," she

says.

"Nonsense. More manipulation." I push the thin pillow against the wall and lean my head against it.

"I heard you shouting that the tribe needs nuxoid. That's why I took these shots. Are you saying the Wuchumbu don't need them?" she asks.

"Are *you* saying they don't need them?" I reply.

The specialist opens her mouth, pauses, finally utters, "Huh?"

"I saw the Digital Cognitives office," I tell her. "I didn't understand at first, but now I know what's going on. I pieced it together while you had me locked in here. You've all been playing me like a fool this whole time. I'd ask you where Efawi is, but I can't trust a thing anyone says—especially you."

The specialist narrows her eyes. "Okon, you're not making any sense."

"Where's my wife?" I yell.

"Shush, keep it down. I don't know where your wife is."

I laugh and shake my head, then sit up to be level with her. "I know we're in a virtual world," I hiss. "What I don't know is how long I've been in this sick game for." Another realization hits me. "This deception began months ago, didn't it? When the PPA's RAIDsquad broke into my house, they must have drugged me, and when I woke up, I was unknowingly in a simulation. This means I never actually came to the jungle. It's all been an elaborate ruse to get me to reveal what I know about Efawi and the illegal satellite data she supposedly has."

The specialist slowly lifts her hand. The details of her skin, the resolution, the tiny hairs on the back of her fingers, the microvariations in texture and color are all stunning. Far better than any virtual world I've ever been in. "It's incredi—"

She slaps me across the face.

"Did that feel real to you?" she asks. I touch where I was hit. My cheek is hot from the impact. "You are *not* in a virtual world," she says. "It's my job to know about cutting-edge technologies, including those hidden by government, and we are not yet capable of creating a VR experience as realistic and immersive as this. On top of that, if you *are* unwittingly in a VR world, that means I am too, and there's no reason for either you or I to be in one. It would be a waste of everyone's time, and you thinking about this is a waste of everyone's time. So, get the idea out of your head, because it seems we have unconscious Wuchumbu to revive."

"It's not acceptable for you to hit me," I retort.

"Then stop being so fucking ridiculous. I don't know what's wrong with you, if you're having some kind of mental breakdown, but if this is a reaction to something Thembe's team has done, you should know I'm not involved. I am not PPA. This room is where they kept me, and I'm sure you've noted the lock is on the outside. They brought me to the Nsanba for one reason only: my expertise in the weaponry of Loalla."

Could she be right—am I having a mental breakdown? The thought that I might be makes me feel even more unstable. I take a moment to try to pull my head into some sort of order. The specialist puts a hand on my shoulder, and I flinch as she makes contact. She looks awful, like the blood's been drained from her. "Okon, is it true you gave a sedative to the tribe?"

"If this isn't a VR world," I manage to mutter, "then yes, they've been sedated. Some heavily, no doubt. But what can we do? There probably isn't any nuxoid here. Why would there be? They don't care if the tribe dies or not. The damn thing probably doesn't even exist. Nuxoid is probably a made-up word. I've been told nothing but lies by these people."

The specialist slides the canvas bag between us and opens it up. Inside are a hundred or more shots like the one I injected the soldier with during the trial run. She takes one from the bag, holds it in my face. "Look, Okon. It says nuxoid. *This is nuxoid.*"

"But is it really? How can I trust what's in those syringes

when I've been lied to so much? I know the truth about Efawi—that she's not with the PPA. Is she even pregnant? Oh my, I don't even know that. I can't trust my nôvo-comms. I can't trust you. Even if this isn't a VR world, it's still all a setup. I don't want to be a part of it anymore."

"I don't want to be a part of this either," growls the specialist, "but we can't let Wuchumbu die." She grabs my arm and yanks me from the bed. "Once we're on our way to the settlement, you can tell me about what's spooked you so much." She shoves me toward the door, peeks outside, then pulls me from the room. I'm too mentally scattered to resist.

The specialist hurries us down a passageway and stops suddenly, switches direction, then pulls me through a side door. Another door follows and we're outside in the cool night air, making a dash for it. Once the base is out of sight, the specialist bends over, already exhausted from the short sprint. She rubs her tagged ankle and winces.

"Their security is useless," I say. "That's one thing I can rely on as being true."

"Most of them are in the Anomalous Zone for Operation Get Tree," she replies. "I don't believe the PPA has the tree yet. I overheard their plans have gone awry, which isn't surprising. The only thing that surprises me is that the Wuchumbu still haven't activated the alien artifact. They must be of greater moral character than the rest of us."

"How can the PPA not have the tree yet? And how do you know it's called Operation Get Tree when, according to you, Thembe's team doesn't tell you what's going on?"

"They don't, but I stole some of their files. I'll tell you what I learned, but first we must get moving. I've been using your tree markings to get between here and the settlement."

Once again she pulls me by the arm and I go with her, paying careful attention to the sensation of her grip, the rub of my boots as they hit the ground, the branches scratching my skin. "This is real," I hesitantly murmur.

"Yes, it is," the specialist huffs.

"And the Wuchumbu really do need help," I mumble.

"Okon, did they drug you?"

"Maybe. I don't know. Not that I'm aware. I just don't know what to believe anymore."

The specialist turns her head left and right, scanning the jungle as we move.

"So many lies," I mutter.

"What's that?"

"If this isn't VR, that means the PPA must have found my wife in the Nsanba and forced her to make a nôvo-call in order to manipulate me into helping with Operation Get Tree. She pretended she was being helped out of the jungle and was acting like everything was okay. They must have told her they would harm me if she didn't comply—otherwise Efawi would never have done it. My wife then escaped somehow, and the PPA no longer knows where she is. But the craziest thing is—"

"Hold on. You received a nôvo-call from your wife?"

"Yes. This morning. She persuaded me to help Thembe."

"Did she feel like she was being forced against her will?"

"No. I could feel her underlying anxiety, a tiredness too, but mostly she was optimistic about our future together and—"

"Holes," interrupts the specialist.

"Where?" I check the ground.

"There are holes in your story," the specialist continues. "If Efawi were captured and made to say certain things under duress, you would have detected this without doubt. The emotion would have come through the nôvo-call."

"Firstly, this is not a 'story.' It's a theory based on evidence."

"What evidence?"

"Secondly, I have an explanation for your challenge, if you would quit interrupting. The PPA forced Efawi to make the nôvo-call, but they only transmitted to me her thought-words, not her emotions. You see, I found one of Efawi's memory drives in the Digital Cognitives office. DC labeled the drive as being 'audio-only,' which initially made no sense to me because there's a nôvo-message on the drive, not an audio message. Then I realized that by 'audio-only' they must be referring to the sound of her thought-words. Do you realize what this means?"

The specialist doesn't answer.

"It means DC has the ability to separate thought-words from emotions in nôvo-communications," I continue. "Therefore, when Efawi called me, I received her real, albeit scripted, 'audio-only' thought-words, but they replaced the feed of her feelings with a fake set so I wouldn't know she was actually under duress."

The specialist shakes her head.

"Well?" I say.

"Are you suggesting Digital Cognitives hacked into a live, quantum-encrypted nôvo-call between yourself and your wife, and replaced her authentic emotion, which would have been scared and angry, with a bogus emotional feed where she was tired but optimistic?"

"Yes."

"Oh my. So many holes, I don't know where to start." The specialist stops dead in her tracks and scans our surroundings.

"The PPA?" I whisper. All I can see is shadows. The specialist spins around and disappears behind a tree. "Hey, what about me!" I call out.

The whir of a motor fills the air. The PPA must have found us, and they're going to try to lock me up again. I leap into a bush, and as I peer from between leaves, the reflective, curved edges of a vehicle come into view, a single headlight at the front—an asymm scooter, on top of which sits the specialist. She brings the hovering machine to a halt in front of me, her eyes focused on the controls. "Yours?" I ask.

"Stole it this evening," she says. "The sooner we get to the settlement, the more chance we have of reviving the tribe." The specialist commences a coughing fit. Dark droplets spatter the ground. Blood. "Let's go," she croaks, and points to the seat behind her.

"The first time Thembe let me ride on one of these it almost crashed, then broke down."

"It'll be fine. The rotors provide lift. All I need to do is direct the scooter to where I ultimately want to go, and it navigates around the obstacles. Come on, we're in a hurry. Get with it, Okon."

I think of Babba and his friends wolfing down the sedative-laced uddu, and I propel myself onto the scooter. A couple of hours must have passed since dinner was served. Perhaps we are already too late? I'm barely settled on my seat when the specialist pushes a button and the scooter rushes us through the jungle, the vehicle continually changing direction as it navigates a path between trees, mounds, ditches, and the occasional monkey. All we have to do is hold on and watch out for branches.

"Back to the many problems with your theory," says the specialist. "First of all, nôvo-comms are extremely difficult, if not impossible, to fake, and not just because of the quantum encryption, but also because the emotional content of a call from someone such as your wife is so personal and familiar and unique. Consider it an *emotional fingerprint*; you would instantly realize if Efawi's were even slightly off."

"Yeah, well, I overheard the DC staff talking about a backdoor in their coding. Something to do with processing emotions." This seems to get the specialist thinking, and she becomes quiet for a few minutes while I watch with sympathy the scores of fluttering insects trying to keep up with the scooter, desperate for the light.

"How were you and your wife able to nôvo-call this morning when there's no network in the jungle?" she eventually asks.

"Via the PPA's communications corridor," I reply. "I was next to the jungle base. Efawi was at a mini-station, and they gave her access to call me."

"Have you tried calling her back?"

"Yes, many times, but I haven't had any connectivity. I can't even check her status."

"If you've had no connectivity, how could you have received her call? Has anyone given you access to the PPA network at any point?"

"No."

"PPA networks are incredibly secure. A person can't just connect to one without authorization and procedure. Even if your wife were given access to the PPA's comms corridor, how can she have contacted you if you didn't have access to any networks at your end?"

"I . . ." I'm stumped.

-nôvono, when was I last connected to a network?- I ask.

-One hundred and forty-five days ago,- my brain implant replies. *-It is recommended you connect to a network at your earliest convenience for the latest updates.-*

I can't quite work out the calculation, but one hundred and forty-five days is about how long I've been in the jungle for— around five months in total. How can I not have been connected to a network for this long when I spoke with Efawi this morning? The sensation that none of this is real creeps back to me. I lose my grip on the seat handle, struggle to keep my balance as the scooter swerves between obstacles.

"Okon!" cries the specialist. I grab the canvas backpack looped around her shoulders, and I'm about to take us both to the ground before I'm able to grip the seat handle once more and steady myself. "What's wrong with you?" she snaps.

"I'm struggling to make sense of this. There was a note in the Digital Cognitives office regarding the supervisor of the block Efawi grew up in. I figure the supervisor must have been a spy for the PPA, placed there to keep an eye on my wife as she grew up. He was a miserable bastard called Magelly. Always smelled like bins—we used to call him Grumpy Ma-smelly. But how could they have known Efawi would one day grow up to be an opponent of the PPA?"

"This is your hypothesis, not mine; you tell me."

"Well, I don't have the answer. It makes no sense. This conspiracy must be deeper than we can understand. Could time travel be possible? Perhaps they sent Ma-smelly back in time to watch her?"

"Okon, serious question: have you ever had your IQ tested?"

"Excuse me? For the past five months, my life has become really fucking weird. Multicolored alien death trees, for crying out loud. Glowing fruit that puts apocalyptic messages into people's brains—and I think the damn thing is still in my head, watching me. So right now, I'm not discounting anything—time travel included—just because it sounds unbelievable. Unbelievable is the new norm."

"Well, if this time travel hypothesis of yours were true, which it absolutely isn't, why did the supervisor only keep an eye on your wife, rather than kill her as a child so she could never grow up to be a threat to the PPA? And how can they send back anyone at all when time travel isn't possible?"

"All good points and I've already considered them."

"Okon, I don't know you very well, but clearly you're struggling to deal with this and you've turned to delusion as a coping mechanism."

"I know what I saw in the Digital Cognitives office, and I'm telling you I received a nôvo-call from Efawi this morning. These are facts."

The specialist sighs. "Let's start from the beginning. Tell me what actually happened to you today, and let's stick to what you saw and heard before we go into any outlandish theories."

Despite my frustration, I try to relay my day, and the scooter continues to shake us around as we speed through the jungle. Once I've finished explaining, the specialist takes a long time to respond.

"Well?" I ask, tired of waiting.

"You should have taken the journalpad from the office, then we'd have more information to work with."

"It was too big for my pouch, unlike the memory drive." I pat my pouch to be sure the drive is still there.

"Fine," says the specialist. "Well, my initial thoughts are that the PPA brought Digital Cognitives here to manipulate you. They are most likely accessing your nôvono remotely when you're away from the AZ's interference and within range of their comms corridor. As you already suggested, it seems the purpose of the nôvo-call from your wife this morning was to persuade you to help the PPA acquire the tree."

"So, it *was* Efawi I was speaking to?"

"The information we have would suggest not. You said their private notes stated your wife is not with the PPA's soldiers and that manipulation of your nôvo-comms has been achieved. And you said there were surprising changes about her—a willingness to cooperate with the PPA, her joy at being pregnant. Your theory that they forced her to make the call doesn't stack up because if they have the ability to counterfeit her emotion, they would definitely be able to synthesize her thought-words too, meaning they wouldn't have needed your wife at all in order to fake the nôvo-call."

My heart sinks. If that wasn't my wife on this morning's call, that means I haven't spoken to her since the day she stormed out of our house.

"How Digital Cognitives is doing this, I do not know," the specialist continues. "I would have thought it impossible because how you experience her emotional fingerprint would be too complex to mimic. I'm afraid I don't know exactly what's going on. It's very peculiar."

"They're a bunch of liars; that's what's going on. When I first told Thembe about her call, his response was a little weird, but then his team confirmed she'd been found. The manipulating bastards. Now I'm back to having no idea where my wife is. I don't even know if she's . . ."

"Yes?"

"The message Efawi left for me on the memory drive by the tree—the one where she first told me she was pregnant—was that real or fake? The drive is in my pouch right now, and nobody other than the Wuchumbu had been in the cave when it was found, so I don't see how the PPA or Digital Cognitives can be behind that one. Unless this whole damn thing, including your 'rescue' of me, is a setup."

"Okon, we need to stick to what we know. You jumping to outlandish conclusions isn't helping."

"Well, I'm sorry, but if this isn't all a setup, how do I know you'd tell me? From what I've heard, you're even more untrustworthy than the rest of them."

The specialist brings the scooter to a halt, and my face hits the back of her head.

"You see this tag on my ankle?" she says, turning on her seat to confront me.

"Yes," I gulp.

"This tag contains a synthesized derivative of coniine: a poison the PPA can remotely release into my bloodstream at any time they choose. They attached this to my ankle when I claimed asylum within Mbapazu. Ever since, the PPA has used me and my specialized knowledge in whatever way they see fit, and while I've reluctantly complied with what's been demanded of me, I've never been told more than I needed to know. Do you understand?"

I nod meekly.

"Two days ago," she continues, "I seized an opportunity to obtain information regarding the PPA's intentions here— information I wasn't meant to have. It said nothing regarding these communications between you and your wife, but described other aspects of their plans. Based on what I learned, I decided I can no longer toe the line, and I went into hiding in the jungle, making sure I stayed outside the range of any network so my ankle tag couldn't be activated remotely. However, to rescue you and help save the Wuchumbu, I had to go to the PPA base, which meant I stepped into range, and the moment I did, my tag received the signal to release the poison. I'm going to die, Okon. My body is breaking down as we speak. So believe me when I tell you I have nothing to hide from you. I am not one of Thembe's cronies. I didn't know Digital Cognitives were even here until you told me."

Feeling ashamed, I look away from the specialist and into the shadowy Nsanba. "You came to the base to rescue me even though you knew the poison would be released?"

"Yes. I'd learned the PPA would keep you captive once they're done with you. I wanted to warn you but couldn't find you in time. Don't get too full of yourself, though. I didn't rescue you for your sake alone."

"For the Wuchumbu's sake too?"

"In part. I didn't know they needed nuxoid until after I arrived at the base and heard you shouting. But there are other dangers they face."

"What dangers?"

"We'll get to that. Right now, we need to focus on administering the nuxoid in time."

"Why does the PPA want to keep me captive?"

"We'll get to that too."

I'm about to insist she tell me right now when a breeze blows through the understory and the little moonlight we have is snuffed as something moving above the trees turns the sky pitch black. A subtle charge of energy fills the air, and our world becomes just the small sphere of light from the scooter. Moments later, whatever was above us passes, and the dull night sky returns. "Tell me you saw that too," I say.

"Looks like whatever it was is heading toward the settlement." The specialist turns to the front of the scooter and sets us moving again at full speed.

I stare at her ankle as we near our destination. "I'm so sorry about the poison. I had no idea the tag could do that." The specialist doesn't respond, but a few minutes later mutters something to herself, only part of which I catch over the whir of the scooter, something about her life ending when she came to Mbapazu.

We soon find ourselves at the edge of the settlement, and the scooter makes its way through the empty outskirts, snaking between dwellings that become increasingly dense. I'm worrying about where everyone is when a blast of blue light appears up ahead, visible through the thirty meters of trees and huts that stand between us and the central clearing. Moments later, the light is joined by an atmosphere-shaking rumble, like heavy breathing, like a gigantic beast has awoken.

My heart pounds. The specialist, who has grown increasingly weak through the journey, appears to be struggling to hold on. I take one hand from the scooter seat and wrap my arm around her waist. She's cold, but I keep her balance steady, and after a few more seconds of tree and hut dodging, we fly at speed into the bright blue light.

Feplao runs across our path carrying her baby. The scooter automatically swerves and brings us to an ungraceful halt as we struggle to stay on. The sobbing Feplao stops, shakes her sleeping child, who doesn't stir, then continues running.

The specialist and I remain on the scooter as our eyes adjust to the light. The scene we've entered is one of madness. Dozens of Wuchumbu lie motionless on the ground. Some are tending to them while shouting and flailing their arms. Others are running around the central clearing, also shouting and flailing. And many have simply fallen to their knees, praying as they point to the sky. All are basked in brilliant blue light from above, and despite not wanting to for fear of what I'll see, I tilt my head upwards . . .

. . . and there it is.

The *Massas*.

The Wuchumbu's great sky god, fully manifest, floating high above the canopy.

The divine being is so large, I have to turn my head to view its entirety: a gargantuan antelope head; a rippling mane; a human torso; four hulking human arms; two thickset, feathered legs complete with talons; and a pair of plumed wings to match. The entire being is blue (after all, it was the Massas who gifted the sky with its color), and the deity pulsates with a threatening energy, its ten eyes glaring at us, each moving independently. If I could reach the scooter's controls, I think I'd be getting us out of here as fast as possible.

The Massas inhales deeply, its chest expands, and its mouth opens. "Wuchumbu, do not activate the tree of many colors." The sky god's words boom in the language of the tribe, so loud the scooter vibrates, along with my bones. "Leave the Banoochee immediately. All must gather in the middle of the settlement or receive my fury!"

The specialist and I remain where we are, my arm still around her waist, gripping her tightly. I'm unsure if the trembling belongs to her, or me, or us both. She twists her torso and looks at me as if checking my reaction, her eyes wide and bloodshot.

"Would an 'outlandish theory' be appropriate now?" I ask.

33: The Nuxoid

The specialist scowls, then slides from the scooter. Her legs give way as she hits the ground, and she tumbles. I jump down and offer her my hand, but she waves me off. The deity continues to hover and snarl and make demands of the tribe. So the Wuchumbu's god of the sky really exists? I want to ask the specialist, but I'm afraid of her reaction. She looks inside the canvas backpack, then heads toward a group of Wuchumbu. I'm about to follow her when a familiar grip is planted on my shoulder. "Okon, you must help her."

I turn to find a tearful Beejalee holding her nine-year-old. Hattee's eyes are closed, and her body is limp in her mother's arms. "Naee will not wake up either," says Beejalee. "Many will not awake, and I cannot find my husband."

Guilt punches me in the stomach. "Did Naee and Hattee eat uddu this evening?" I ask, having to raise my voice to be heard over the heavy-breathing sky god.

"I don't know," says Beejalee.

"Did you have any?" I ask.

"It was all eaten before I had a chance. Why?"

We both flinch as the Massas unleashes another round of verbal thunder from a hundred meters above: "Do not touch the tree of many colors. Leave the cave immediately. Gather in the middle of the settlement. Obey your Massas or you will be punished!"

I glance up once more. The sky god heaves with aggression. Its mouth and ten pupils are pitch black surrounded by blue—a being of pure light. I look around for the specialist. Seeing all the Wuchumbu unconscious on the ground staggers me. I put them there, these people who have become like family. Loved ones kneel beside the sleeping, prodding and shaking them. Some are hauling limp bodies to the middle of the settlement as per their deity's instruction. Everything is blue.

I spot the specialist and instruct Beejalee to follow me. The unassociated woman has a nuxoid shot in hand as she squats beside a sleeping Etoole. She slams its short needle into his deltoid and plunges the syringe. Two of Etoole's seven daughters hold the hands of their father, with the other five possibly lying unconscious somewhere, the thought of which makes me sick. The specialist withdraws the needle, and we anxiously wait for a response. The ground vibrates with repeated instructions from above, and when the god isn't barking orders, its furious breathing fills the air.

Twenty seconds later, Etoole stirs and opens his eyes. "The Massas has come for us?" he asks.

His daughters leap on top of him. My eyes well with tears. I hug the specialist, then turn to Beejalee. "Put Hattee down," I instruct, and grab a shot from the bag, flick off the cap, and puncture the girl's thin arm.

Again, we wait. Beejalee can't sit still. She whimpers as she clasps Hattee's head. Blue-reflecting tears fall from the mother to her daughter's hair. Thirty seconds pass and Hattee still hasn't moved. I look at the specialist, then back at Hattee.

"It is not working," Beejalee cries.

"Give it more time," says the specialist.

"Is the Massas doing this to punish us?" asks Etoole, clinging to his two girls.

"This is not the work of the Massas," I tell him. *This is the work of a weak and pathetic idiot.*

A minute must have passed by now, and Hattee's tiny frame remains motionless. I've killed my best friend's daughter, probably her other children too. And where is her husband? Is Habee on the ground somewhere, unconscious, his face covered in dirt?

"I'm so sorry," I say. "This is all my fau—"

Laughter interrupts me.

Hattee is awake. Hattee is wide awake and being smothered with kisses from her mother!

I clap and jump to my feet. Gommonogo sprints over to us, spear in hand and breathing heavily. He looks Hattee up and down, then turns to me. I expect him to accuse me of causing this mess—to attack me even, but he doesn't.

"How can we help the others?" Gommonogo asks.

I turn to the specialist. "The nuxoid will work for all of them, won't it?"

The specialist shrugs and slumps to her knees. Her sweat-soaked skin glistens blue. "I need everyone's attention," she croaks, but her voice is barely audible as the Massas rains down another repeat of its commands. I yell at the group—tell them to get closer, which they do. The specialist holds a nuxoid shot in the air. "You saw what Okon and I did with one of these," she says. "Well, that needs to be repeated for everyone who won't wake up."

She places five shots on the ground, then holds out the canvas backpack. "Here—hand them out," she says. "Tell the others how to use them. Check the whole settlement. Go around hut by hut. The sooner every unconscious person receives one of these, the better. And only give one to each person. If someone doesn't wake up, come and get me. Do not go to the cave; it will be dangerous for Wuchumbu to go there."

"But my Obee is in the Banoochee," says Beejalee.

"Okon will help those in the cave," replies the specialist.

The Wuchumbu hesitantly look back and forth at each other, then fix their eyes on me. "You should trust what the unassociated woman says," I tell them. I grab the bag from the specialist and hold it out to them. "Quickly or Wuchumbu will die."

Gommonogo takes the bag, and they each gather large handfuls of shots and disperse among the chaotic settlement, leaving the specialist and me alone. "The nuxoid will wake them all up," I mutter to myself. "It has to. I'm sure of it."

I jolt as further holy words boom from above.

"Are we going to talk about that?" I ask.

The specialist tilts her head upward. "Look, Okon," she instructs. "See it ripple ever so slightly? It must be a flexible display screen. A massive sheet, fifty meters wide at least, and suspended in the air by a fleet of aircraft, I would guess. Not sure how they're operating within the interference. Especially adapted equipment, maybe. Deliberately downgraded functionality, perhaps."

Now that I know it's just graphics on a screen, the sky god seems flatter, its animation more obvious and cartoonish. The glare from the display prevents me from seeing the sheet itself. "Obviously, I knew it wasn't a real god," I say, and straighten my loincloth. "Thembe didn't tell me a giant, fake deity was part of their strategy. I think I would have remembered that. Why would the PPA go to so much trouble when they already had a plan to infiltrate the cave that doesn't require a massive cartoon Massas?"

"I don't know," says the specialist. "It's as much of a surprise to me as it is to you, but what's important right now is that you get to the cave and revive the Wuchumbu guards."

"Thembe said his team would do that, but you're right—they can't be trusted. Do you think the PPA still hasn't taken control of the tree?"

"I guess not, given the sky god is still ordering the

Wuchumbu to leave the cave."

The fake Massas growls. There must also be speakers up there, probably attached to the aircraft. The specialist slumps from her knees onto her rear. "I guess you're not coming with me to the Banoochee," I say, and kneel in front of her.

Grimacing, the specialist picks up the five shots she placed on the ground and puts them on her lap. "Once the PPA has control of the cave," she says, "the Wuchumbu will be rounded up and placed in a containment facility not far from Thembe's base. Once there, they will be used to obtain further understanding of the tree, and once the PPA is finished with them, they will be executed, their bodies thrown into a pit, and their remains dissolved with acid. The entire tribe, their culture, their history, their genes, eradicated."

My chest tightens. For a moment, I cannot breathe. Behind the specialist, Wuchumbu are frantically trying to revive anyone who is asleep, all while their raging sky god bombards them with threats.

"And once you, Okon, are no longer of any use to the PPA," the specialist continues, "you will be killed too because they cannot trust you to be quiet about what's happened here."

I stand back up. "No, I don't believe that. I don't trust the PPA anymore, but I can't see them murdering us all. It would be unnecessary. Too cold. Illegal. Thembe wouldn't allow something like that."

"I stole their postacquisition plans, Okon. They are cold and brutal and clear as day."

I reflect on Ratu's warning about the second, larger facility he'd found, and how he'd begged me to do something about it. "And my wife?" I ask.

"What I saw didn't mention her."

"Well, give me the five nuxoid shots then."

"You've nothing more to say about the PPA's plans?"

"I will go to the Banoochee and save the guards if I can, if they even need reviving at all. I can't deal with anything else right now. I just can't. I mean, what can I even do? Nothing. There's nothing I can do."

The specialist stares at me as the Massas hits us with the same orders: *Don't touch the tree. Leave the cave. Gather in the settlement.* I reach for the shots, but the specialist shields them with her hands. "On my first night with the tribe," she says, "I advised the Wuchumbu to use the threat of the tree as leverage to force change in the world. But having seen the PPA's plans, and having witnessed the events of the past few days, tonight in particular, I realize how wrong I was. Okon, it's become clear to me the human race isn't capable of cooperation when the stakes are high. And so, when it comes to the advancement of powerful technologies, we can't be trusted to be reasonable or responsible."

"We don't have time for this. The guards could be unconscious!" Again, I reach for the shots, but the specialist keeps hold of them. I picture Big Man, Petonba, Obee, and whoever else is on duty, collapsed on the hard Banoochee rock, their Wuchumbu organs shutting down one by one.

"Okon, it would be best for everyone—for the planet, for our neighboring planets, and beyond—if this confused, troubled civilization of ours is ended now, before we develop the ability to cause unthinkable suffering at the grandest of scales. And so, after reviving the guards, you must convince them to trigger the tree."

I shake my head. I'm at a loss for words. How can she be saying this?

"You must leave the cave immediately," booms the Massas. "Do not make me wait, or I will cut you into a thousand pieces and condemn your spirits to eternal suffering!"

The specialist raises an eyebrow, as if the fake Massas proves her point. "Once the tree has been triggered," she says, "I believe our civilization will be ended quickly and without pain. I see no reason why we'd be allowed to suffer in the process. After all, the treemaker is a morally concerned entity that could have killed us outright if it wanted but instead gave us the power to decide for ourselves. The cave guards will listen to you, Okon. Tell them the truth about the PPA's plans to slaughter them. This is why I rescued you from the base."

"No; I won't tell them that. You've been poisoned. You're not thinking straight." I try to take the shots, but the specialist holds onto them tightly, her hands trembling. "The cave guards could be slipping into an irreversible coma!" I yell.

She finally releases her grip. "You're right," she says, her breathing labored. "We need the guards alive so the tree can be activated. You must hurry; get inside the cave before Thembe's soldiers do."

I slip the shots into my pouch. "If I'm able to get inside the cave, I'll revive the guards and tell them to leave the Banoochee as their sky god instructs."

"No!" cries the specialist. She slams her fist on the ground before succumbing to a coughing fit. "This could be our last chance," she rasps. "Our last opportunity to prevent humans from becoming a shameful cosmic affliction. The progression will happen faster than you realize. You must convince the Wuchumbu to end our technology—to end our civilization."

"End our technology? End our civilization? What you're asking me to do is madness. And you're wrong about what humans are capable of. We're better than that." I step back in the direction of the Banoochee. The specialist droops even further. "Is there nothing that can be done for you?" I ask. "No antidote for the poison?"

She shakes her head. A blue, helpless figure, alone amid the blue chaos of the god-fearing Wuchumbu. A lump forms and stings my throat. She's dying and I don't know what to say.

"I wasn't even given your name."

"What my name is doesn't fucking matter," wheezes the specialist. She rolls onto her back and looks up at the animated Massas. "You want to be a good person, Okon, but being good includes being strong enough to do hard things."

"I . . . I'm sorry there's nothing we can do for you."

I turn from the specialist and run.

As I dart between trees, the blue glow behind me becomes increasingly small and faint. The divine reverberations of the Massas, however, continue to echo through the understory, and after some distance, confusingly, seem to come from both ahead and behind.

I keep going. Thankfully, the route between the settlement and the cave has been well trodden over the past few days and is easy to follow, even in the dark. And as I hurry, waves of panic hit me again and again, my mind refusing to dismiss the specialist's claims about the PPA's murderous plans. But I can't let her claims derail me—not right now. There may be cave guards to revive, and if they don't need reviving, I at least need to persuade them to leave the Banoochee. The danger of the tree being activated dwarfs all other problems.

I jump as a muffled gunshot echoes through the understory. Half a dozen further shots follow in quick succession from somewhere to the right—all too far away to be shooting at me. What happened to the simple, casualty-free plan, Thembe? I maintain my pace and try to encourage myself with the thought that the memory drive from the cave was most likely genuine, despite Efawi's nôvo-call having somehow been faked. Big Man found the drive before Thembe and the PPA even knew about the Banoochee. This must mean Efawi really has been in the cave, that she really is pregnant, that she really is optimistic about our future. And so, once I've tended to the cave guards, I'll quickly look for anything else she may have left behind—another clue that might tell me where she is. This will surely be my last chance to find her.

As I look ahead, I spot movement among the shadows. Someone or something is coming toward me. I slow to a stop.

My heart pounds in my ears. Whatever it is, it's coming fast. And it's short. Not human.

Its eyes are glowing. Milky green.

A leopard!—thundering toward me.

I freeze and pine for body armor. The cat bounds straight past, its slick fur brushing against my hand as it sprints into the darkness behind me. I turn back to where I'm heading and squint to see what the feline predator was running from. I identify a faint blue light.

I continue to the Banoochee, slower now, more cautious. The blue light grows brighter as I near, and the words from the Massas reemerge as though the sky god has moved to be above the cave, or is above the cave and the settlement at the same time—a clever illusion perhaps, or maybe the presence of more than one display. "Wuchumbu, do not disobey your great Massas. Leave the cave now and I will spare you!" I picture Big Man inside the Banoochee, too unconscious or too stubborn to leave, despite the order from a sky god. The bursts of gunfire reemerge. It seems a battle is taking place in the Anomalous Zone, but I can't work out who would be shooting at whom. Unless . . . this isn't a gunfight and the Wuchumbu are simply being mowed down as they run. I try to put the thought out of my mind.

I'm nearing the Banoochee now, with the blue downpour of light just past the trees ahead. The Massas has become partially visible through the foliage. Another thirty meters and I'll be out in the rocky opening beside the hill. The sky god's light flickers momentarily, then, as it blasts another round of orders, its words are interrupted by a deafening screech from above—a harsh sound of things scraping together. I shiver and cover my ears. The Massas flickers again. *Off. On. Off. On.* The screech dissipates and is replaced with whipcracks and pings, as though taut cables are coming loose in rapid succession. The light from the Massas extinguishes once more, and this time the sky god doesn't return.

I'm surrounded by darkness, and I'm not yet at the opening. I stumble forward as fast as I can, feeling my way as I go. The noises overhead continue, an intermittent racket, at times painfully loud. A breeze builds, pushing from above, whipping up a pressure in my ears. I jump as a final burst of stretched-out words erupt from the invisible Massas: *". . . wiiillllll beeee puunnniiisshhheedd."* The sky god's threat is followed by a thunderous crash that reverberates through the jungle—millions of leaves being simultaneously thrashed. The gigantic sheet, and who knows what else, must have fallen.

I stumble through a shower of twigs and leaves in what I hope is the direction of the Banoochee, flinching and protecting my head as heavy things collide with the ground. Falling trees? Aircraft? Speakers? I cannot see to know. There's no moonlight for my eyes to adjust to; I'm scrambling in absolute black.

The fallout from the crash settles, leaving me with the sounds of my heavy breathing, my hands groping trees, debris scuffing my boots, and a new sound from behind: someone hurrying this way. A person who isn't barefoot.

A few meters later, the brush and scratch of vegetation ceases, and a click to each of my steps informs me that I'm walking on rock. I've finally reached the open area beside the Banoochee, which is pitch black like everywhere else, and any sense of relief to have made it here is quickly snuffed by the groans of human suffering scattered all around. Not Wuchumbu groans; these are unassociated groans.

Tonight's plan, as told to me by Thembe, included soldiers hiding near the Banoochee entrance, waiting for the sedative to take effect. So I assume these groans are coming from them, but whether these soldiers have been hurt by falling sky-god apparatus or something else entirely, I don't know. And the thought that I'm surrounded by soldiers, injured or not, brings a shiver down my spine. They will be tired, tense, and trigger-happy. Thembe warned me to hide when they come.

I try to refocus on what I need to do: revive any unconscious cave guards, make sure they do as their Massas said and leave the cave, search the Banoochee for anything else Efawi may have left behind.

The person who'd been hurrying behind me slows to a stop. If there were any light at all, we'd be able to see each other standing a few meters apart. I would think the soldiers on tonight's mission would be enhanced with night vision. Perhaps this person's eyes have been damaged in the chaos. I remain as still as possible. Try to calm myself by rationalizing that I've nothing to fear, because I'm working *with* the PPA, not against them. But upon hearing this soldier's shallow, erratic breathing, I'm not confident I can trust them to act reasonably—to not shoot me in the face in the heat of the moment, by accident or on purpose.

I hear them move, once again in my direction, the sound of their uneven steps bringing back memories of my injured knee. I tiptoe away, and one and a half paces later, my face slaps against a wall of material: the flexible display, warm and thick. Although I can't see the sheet, I can feel it sloped at an angle. Part of it must be resting on the treetops; the rest, draping into the rocky opening. If I'm to get to the Banoochee, I will have to go under.

The soldier continues to shuffle closer. I crouch on all fours, nudge my way beneath the sunken display, and crawl as quietly as I can—hands, boots, and knees on rock, my head pushing against the sheet. I don't know if the soldier is following me, but I won't stop to find out. I keep going until my arms hit an obstacle: something soft and low on the ground. I feel clothing? A belt? A pocket? *A hand.* It takes all my strength not to yelp.

I sit back, shaking, expecting this person to grab me, but they make no movement or sound. The sheet rests on my head and drapes all around me. My shallow breaths fill the tiny, dark space. I think of the decomposed soldier I encountered shortly after entering the Nsanba. They'd been lying there for decades, ever since The War ended. Now it seems fresh soldiers are being fed to the jungle.

Once I'm satisfied this soldier is indeed dead, I shift back onto all fours and make my way around them, my left arm knocking against a hard and curved object—a helmet? A beam of light rolls free, and I reach for it—a flashlight, which momentarily blinds me. I turn the flashlight around. Having the light doesn't improve things much, because all I see is the glossy, black display sheet and the rocky ground beneath. But seeing something is less disturbing than seeing nothing, so I hold the flashlight between my teeth as I continue to crawl. I head as best as I can estimate in the direction of the Banoochee while my knees struggle to tolerate the rough demands being placed on them. To think the Valaddo operator advised me to avoid vigorous activity for at least ten days.

Walking the length of the opening would normally take less than a minute, but after much crawling, I've no idea how much progress I've made. Then, just as there's a change in the display sheet's angle, as though I've passed the lowest point, beyond which the sheet angles slightly upward, a cold hand grabs my leg.

This time I do yelp, and the flashlight falls from my mouth.

"Be quiet and turn that off immediately," croaks a deep, familiar voice.

34: The Infection

"Thembe, what the hell happened to the plan?"

He snatches up the flashlight, and as he fumbles for the switch, I catch glimpses of him beneath the display. He's wearing his maroon, ant-like body armor, but the midsection has been sliced open like a tin can, and his stomach is covered in blood. His helmet lies discarded on the ground, its side broken and hanging loose.

The light goes out.

"What the fuck is going on?" I ask.

"Okon, you must be quiet. And lie down, or we'll be shot."

"Why are guns being fired?" I hiss. "And what's the point in the fucking sky god if the cave guards are sedated and can't hear it?"

"You think that was us?" he scoffs.

I pause, confused. "I would ask you where Efawi is," I say, "but I won't believe your answer. So, I'm off."

"You mustn't go into the cave, Okon. Doing so would be a disaster for everyone."

"I have nuxoid for the guards."

"There are no sedated Wuchumbu in there. Just wait a moment and I can explain everything." He wheezes as he shuffles closer. I wonder how much blood he's lost and whether he's gotten any on me. "Two days ago, my team learned that information regarding our operation was being leaked to an informant for the Nation of Loalla," he says, his hushed voice filling our small black space.

"The specialist?" I ask.

"No. One of our technicians was responsible for the leak, and as soon as we became aware, we had to act quickly or risk Loalla making moves of their own. You wouldn't know this, but our plan for tonight had originally been scheduled for tomorrow. Instead, in order to get ahead of any potential Loallese moves, we brought our plan forward by one day—the plan I described to you: you would deliver the sedative and a small team would infiltrate the cave. But when the time came, the cave guards were not sedated, not fully, and that wasn't the only problem. There were additional Wuchumbu outside the cave until late in the evening, two of whom fell asleep for no apparent reason, prompting the others to stay. Our special unit had to wait for them to clear, but before they did, the sky god appeared—the *Mass-asss*, as the tribe calls it."

"So, the animated Massas was the work of the Loallese?"

"Exactly."

"But how would they even know what the tribe believes in?"

"Information about the Wuchumbu's belief system, which we obtained from you, was among the leaked data."

"Great. What a stupid idea of theirs. Madness."

"Actually, we had a similar idea involving a projection, but decided to go with the sedative plan. If the display hadn't fallen, it probably would have worked. The Loallese command wouldn't have known that Operation Get Tree had been brought forward to this evening."

"Did your people shoot down the sky god?"

"If they did, they were very foolish, because the crash could have shocked the Wuchumbu into triggering the tree. But the truth is, I don't know why the sky god fell. My team has no way of communicating in the Anomalous Zone. Perhaps everything fell due to Loallese incompetence, or perhaps the interference played a role."

"So, what's all the gunfire I've been hearing?"

"Loallese soldiers arrived on the ground when the sky god appeared. Took us all by surprise."

"And now the PPA and the Loallese are battling for control of the AZ and the tree?"

"Exactly," says Thembe. "Clearly the Loallese command cannot tolerate Mbapazu having exclusive access to the most advanced technology the world has ever known, and the PPA feels the same about them."

"Idiots. Loalla and the PPA will get us all killed."

"I agree. All they've done so far is prevent each other from getting to the tree, when what we need to be concerned about is getting the tree out of the hands of the Wuchumbu."

"Then tell the PPA to stop fighting," I say.

"How do you propose I do that? Run around in the dark, shouting orders for everyone to put their guns down? Don't be so naive, Okon. And stop fidgeting. Lay as still as you can, or we'll be shot."

"By Loallese soldiers?"

"By anyone who's on edge and holding a gun. I've already been shot at enough for one evening. We have more troops scheduled to enter the AZ shortly. The best thing you and I can do is wait for them to clear up this mess."

Waiting for this mess to resolve itself is tempting, but I remind myself that this man is a liar and that he, the PPA, and Digital Cognitives have all been playing me for an idiot. "Tell me truthfully, Thembe," I say, trying to keep the resentment from my tone, "where is Efawi right now?"

Thembe releases a long, wheezy sigh, and when he responds, his words are slow and seem carefully chosen. "I have received no update on Efawi's whereabouts since we last spoke."

More games. More manipulation. I lift myself to my knees and elbows, ready to crawl.

"Wait," he pleads.

"I need to give the guards their nuxoid."

"I told you that isn't necessary. When the sky god appeared, the Wuchumbu loitering outside the cave panicked and ran into the jungle carrying two of their party who were unconscious. Then the five guards left the cave and went the same way, three of them flopping around, half in a daze, as though they'd been partially sedated. With the cave empty, our team was about to enter when we came under attack by Loalla. While the soldiers were exchanging fire, I tried to get to the cave myself but was beaten to it by a Wuchumbu sprinting to the entrance at speed, shouting that they will activate the tree if anyone follows them. They were a blur in the darkness, but I could see they were carrying a rifle."

"A rifle?"

"Yes. A Wuchumbu with a rifle is the only person in that cave, and they are certainly not sedated."

I stay on all fours, unsure what to do.

"Okon, for both our sakes, lie down." Thembe finds my leg and tugs at my boot. I don't move. "Lie down," he repeats. "You caused this mess. Don't make things even worse."

"I didn't cause this," I growl.

"If you had stopped those Wuchumbu from loitering outside the cave and eating their evening meal there, we would have acquired the tree before Loalla showed up."

"That wasn't my responsibility."

"Then whose responsibility was it? And more importantly, you didn't administer the sedative correctly, did you? It looked to me as if the guards received only a partial dose. Your sloppiness has put the entire human population at risk, and now you want to increase that risk by entering the cave. Shame on you, Okon."

My skin tingles. Every hair on my body stands on end, and seconds later, the display sheet switches on, engulfing us in a flash of blue light. My heart pounds. Another flash follows, painfully bright, followed by electric pops and crackles. The charge dissipates, my hair returns to normal, and the sheet stays off. Breathless, I lower myself to my stomach. Thembe quietly laughs.

"I know Digital Cognitives is here," I say, and let that hang in our dark pocket of air for a moment. I hear Thembe adjust his position. His breathing is labored, which reminds me this man is seriously injured, lying in a pool of blood. This man is also a liar.

"I know you people faked my nôvo-call from Efawi this morning," I say, fists clenched. "Getting into my mind like that, messing with my relationship—what you and your people have done is disgusting. Everything that comes out of your mouth is fiction."

"There may have been times when I couldn't reveal the full truth, but I have never lied to you. Not once," he says.

It's my turn to laugh.

"Okon, listen to me. My team is not responsible for the manipulation of your nôvo-comms."

"So you admit my nôvo-comms have been manipulated?"

"Yes, they have, and from the moment we discovered that, I've wanted to tell you, but couldn't for the sake of the mission. Given the position we now find ourselves in, there's no reason to keep the truth from you any longer, but I must warn you, you're going to find it . . . distressing."

I remain where I am, still angry and untrusting of this man, but needing to hear what he has to say.

"The two instances of communication you received from Efawi since consuming the alien fruit," he continues, "the first being the nôvo-message she left you in the cave and the second being your nôvo-call with her this morning, were both deceptions. Neither the call nor the message were from Efawi, and neither were faked by my team."

"I don't care if the manipulation was done by your team or

Digital Cognitives. You're all the same to me. 'Manipulation of nôvo-comms accomplished change in Okon's trajectory.' That's what the Digital Cognitives journalpad said."

"I assure you the DC people are not behind this either. A part of their work here has been to try to understand who's interfering with you. I admit we probably would have manipulated your nôvo-comms if we thought it would help us acquire the tree and if DC had that capability. But they don't. They can't. It's not possible because nôvo-comms from people you intimately know are too difficult to synthesize, and we wouldn't take the risk of you finding out then refusing to cooperate. We didn't even know you had a nôvono until recently."

Thembe adjusts his position again and groans as he does so. "I'm afraid we still don't know where Efawi is," he says, "but we know she's been in the cave because that's where she left you a memory drive. The nôvo-message you received from that drive, however, was not the message your wife actually recorded. And with regard to your nôvo-call this morning, well, quite simply, that wasn't your wife you were talking to."

"Well, there's nobody else here who could have been messing with me, so if that wasn't Efawi, and if your people weren't behind it, then I must have simply imagined the whole thing. I must be going crazy."

"We considered that possibility, given the pressure you've been under."

"I was being sarcastic. I know I'm not going crazy!"

"Keep it down, Okon. And yes, we concluded you're not undergoing any sort of psychosis."

"I've concluded that you people manipulated my nôvo-comms."

"We're only guilty of not revealing to you the truth of your faux exchanges with your wife, and we didn't inform you for good reason. The exchanges had a positive effect on you. Made you more cooperative and motivated, so it suited us for you to believe them. But yes, you have been duped; you are the victim of mental trickery. Invasive manipulation of the highest order. And the Digital Cognitives experts have concluded that the party responsible for interfering with your nôvo-comms is the treemaker."

His words linger beneath the sheet. I suddenly realize I hear nothing from the jungle: no birds, no monkeys, no civets, no gunfire, no Wuchumbu.

"If you're going to lie to me, at least make it believable," I say. "The treemaker is a superadvanced alien species. It wouldn't have any interest in fiddling with my conversations with my wife. I've had enough of your delaying tactics. Clearly, you're just trying to keep me from the cave. I don't know what's in there that you don't want me to see, but I'm going. I need to revive the guards—if I'm not already too late."

"How many times do I have to tell you there's only one person in that cave: a Wuchumbu with a rifle! And judging from the speed they entered it, they most certainly don't need reviving. You have to trust me, Okon." Thembe places a gloved hand on my back.

"I know about your plans to murder me and the Wuchumbu," I tell him. His hand stiffens. I push him away.

"What happens after the tree has been secured is determined at a higher level than me," he says, his voice strained.

"You promised me I could return to my life with Efawi."

"That is what I was told . . . then other ideas were discussed. Besides, they haven't yet decided what to do with you. Only the Wuchumbu will be executed for certain."

"Oh, that's fine then."

"You need to appreciate the PPA's reasoning. Unless we find a way to deactivate the tree, which I doubt we will, then it seems the alien weapon will always be with us. And as long as there's at least one Wuchumbu or descendant of a Wuchumbu who walks this planet, then there's a chance, no matter how small, that the tree could be triggered. The stakes are extreme. It would be obscene not to do everything possible to ensure the lives of billions are not lost."

"Thembe, you've gone from lying about my nôvo-comms to justifying the eradication of a tribe. I'm done with this conversation." I feel around for the flashlight and switch it back on. Once again, I'm holding it the wrong way, and the beam blinds me.

"Turn that off, you fool." Thembe grabs my hand, but I shake him off and start crawling. He wraps his arms around my legs, tries holding me in place, but his grip lacks the strength I would expect. I spin around and break free from his hold, losing a boot in the process. I point the flashlight at him. He's on all fours, blood dripping from his stomach, adding to the pool on the floor where we were lying. This man will die if he doesn't get help, and I have nothing but hatred toward him.

"I'm not your enemy," he says. "Our enemy is the treemaker. We don't know what its true motives are. It's no coincidence that the manipulation of your comms started after you consumed the alien fruit. The Digital Cognitives team believes you have supralimbic contamination of extraterrestrial origin: an alien infection of the brain. They want to bring you in for testing. Help you be rid of it."

We both shudder at the sound of a bang followed by electrical crackling and buzzing. Thembe sits back and places a hand over his stomach, wincing and breathing heavily. I keep the flashlight on him. "The treemaker has gotten into your head," he croaks. "You said so yourself. You told me about the presence of *something*. You called it the 'Watcher.' You said you suspected it came from the brew."

"If it came from the brew, then you'd have it too."

"Perhaps I do, and I'm not aware of it. You said the sensation is subtle and passes quickly. I drank the brew more recently than you. Perhaps after a couple more days, I will notice the Watcher too. Stay here with me, Okon. Backup will come, and we can both be taken from this place and given the medical care needed to overcome the infection."

"More lies," I hiss. "You let me believe my wife was safe." Further electrical pops echo across the rocky opening. My hair stands on end once again.

"If you go into the cave," says Thembe, "the savage in there will trigger the tree and kill everyone—you and Efawi included."

"*You* are the savage, Thembe. And I don't ever want to hear you say my wife's name again, you piece of—"

Someone is running toward us.

Thembe furiously waves at the flashlight. I try to turn it off, but it's covered in blood and slips from my hands. A silhouette becomes visible through the sheet: someone's on the top side and standing beside Thembe. I hear a meaty thump. Thembe jolts, his eyes fixed on mine as he twitches then slumps to the ground. Where the sheet had been resting against his head is now a knife that's pierced the display. The bloodstained blade is withdrawn and replaced with fingers that pull at the cut in the sheet, widening it.

A pair of eyes appear at the slit, scanning the underside. I place a boot on the flashlight, but the light seeps from beneath. The eyes continue to scan, then lock onto me. I freeze. A buzz builds, along with the sensation of a charge, and the sheet lights up once again. The blue from the display is overwhelming. I close my eyes and shield them with my hands. I hear shouting. Words are translated in my head from Loallese: "Don't shoot!" Muffled gunshots follow, along with the thud of Thembe's killer collapsing.

I open my eyes to find a humongous cartoon eye pressed against me. I gasp and snake away beneath the sheet as quickly as possible. Groans from the fake Massas rumble and vibrate the ground. Further shots are fired from different directions. I don't know if they're aimed at me or someone else, but I continue to push myself along in the darkness spliced with flashes of blue, catching glimpses of giant animated feathers and divine rippling muscles.

I keep low to the ground, wishing I were wearing more than just a flimsy loincloth. Snippets of the Massas's commands play out—unintelligible, deep and distorted, like the throes of a dying humpback. Moments later, the sky god's noise abruptly ends at the sound of further electric pops, and the sheet turns off—remaining off this time, for now at least.

My vision remains imprinted with blue as I hurry along in the dark. The slope of the display sheet continues to angle upward, and I soon reach the point where I can finally stand and run with one boot on—the other boot still lying with Thembe. I quickly collide with a hard, vertical surface: the hill's cliffside in which the Banoochee entrance is embedded. I look up but still cannot see the sky. This end of the display sheet must be caught on the cliff above me.

I lean against the wall and take a moment to catch my breath, unsure if anyone has followed me, half expecting the sheet to flicker on again and for a soldier to emerge, gripping a knife or a gun. But the pitch black beneath the display remains, and silence has returned to the jungle. Perhaps the soldiers have killed each other off? Perhaps we don't need an alien doomsday device to bring ourselves to an end?

I pull off my remaining boot and decide to lose the socks too for the sake of grip. With shaking hands, I paw my way along the wall until a draft informs me I've reached the rectangular gash in the rock face, the cool air bringing goosebumps to my arms and neck. I stare ahead, looking for the faint flickers of multicolored light at the far end of the first corridor, conscious that the Watcher is also watching, and not believing a word Thembe had to say about it. After checking my translator is set to Wuchumbu, I whisper into the Banoochee, "It's me. It's Okon. Hello?"

The only words to come back to me are my own, bouncing from the walls.

I turn sideways and shuffle inside. The cold rock at my front and back stiffens me. I step over the landmine and approach each bend in the corridor with caution, not knowing if I will collide with a soldier pressing a gun to my forehead or an unconscious cave guard lying at my feet. But the corridors remain empty and silent, and soon I'm on the final straight, at the end of which is the turn that opens into the cavern.

The guards had a strict arrangement: one stayed just inside the Banoochee entrance, two in the corridors, one at the opening to the cavern, and one by the tree. I should have passed two of them by now, with the third in sight. Is it possible the guards did leave like Thembe said? Alternatively, they may all be in the cavern, huddled together in a panic due to the madness outside—or lying on the floor, unconscious and in need of my shots. I stop just short of turning into the cavern. What's the worst that can happen if I step in there?

While I search for an answer, I'm distracted by a peculiar, premonition-like sensation that someone is about to contact me. ~Incoming call from Efawi,~ says my nôvono pro before I can fully register the sensation—maybe it wasn't a premonition after all.

~Incoming call from Efawi,~ the notification repeats. But it's not possible for my wife to be contacting me while I'm deep inside a cave, deep inside the AZ, deep inside the Nsanba. This nôvo-call confirms that I'm being messed with—if I had any remaining doubts about that, they're gone. I don't know how Thembe's team is doing it, but they're clearly desperate for me to leave the Banoochee. There must be something in here they don't want me to see.

I instruct my nôvono to decline the call and switch my nôvo-comms off.

I step into the cavern.

35: The Tweener

Even from a distance, it's clear the tree is molting. Shedding. *Losing fruit.* Dozens lie broken and scattered on top of the giant altar rock, which is now polychromatic from pulp and splatter. And yet somehow the tree's branches remain as full of fruit as ever.

I scan the cavernous space. It appears there's no one here, but with jagged surfaces, morphing light, and creeping shadows, much can go unseen in this place. The chanting from the tree is quiet, which means Wuchumbu are present or were present until very recently. I tiptoe down the long slope that leads from the cavern entrance and pass the guards' empty food pot lying on its side, unsure what it tells me about what happened here. I press onward to the tree with caution.

Once I've crossed the cavern, I slow to a stop ten meters from the tranzbus-sized altar. Beside me is the crude circle of rocks that comprises a firepit, filled with long burned-out wood and ash, no different from the previous time I was in the Banoochee. A few meters from the firepit lies the large, broken carving of the Massas, a sad imitation of what floated above us this evening.

I continue toward the tree, and as I do, my foot hits something hard: a structure of stones in the shape of a cone that now leans at an angle because of my accidental kick. Like the firepit and the wooden carving, this knee-high pile of stones was here the last time I was in the Banoochee, and it reminds me of the stack positioned beside me when I first awoke in the settlement—my broken navicube placed beneath to satisfy whatever bizarre belief the prior shaman had. It still surprises me he didn't defy Mhaawu and activate the tree long ago. For two years, they were the only ones to come here. Plenty of opportunity for the prior shaman to end the unassociated he despised so much. Perhaps he was too superstitious to do it himself, to taint his spirit by placing his hand inside something so foreign.

As I look up at the tree, I spot movement. A branch is shaking, and a multicolored fruit falls with a thump and splatter. Moments later, an adjacent branch shakes and another fruit falls. I step back with the urge to retreat, my right foot once again catching the stack and this time knocking two stones from the top, which clack as they hit the ground.

"Who is there?" comes an echoing voice.

I gasp. "The tree of many colors . . . ?"

"Who is there?" the voice repeats, louder, firmer, and I realize the words are being translated from Wuchumbu. The branches rustle some more before I hear a yelp and watch a body fall from the tree to the altar rock, the top surface of which I cannot see from below. "Motherfucker!" comes the voice once more, in Mbapaz this time.

I scurry up the side of the rock. Its upper surface is wet and slippery and awash with color that stains my feet. Ratu is lying among the smashed-up fruit. His body, bionic arm included, is smeared with multicolored pulp.

"Is that my death-stick?" I ask, referring to the rifle at his side.

Ratu sits up and groans.

"You told me all my stuff was floated down the river," I complain. "What else of mine do you have?"

"Do you not think we have more important things to talk

313

about?" he mutters. He struggles to his knees, straightens his headband, and wipes the fruit from his body. I'm annoyed, but my attention turns to the tree. I've never been so close—never stood on the altar rock, even. My observations from the entrance were correct: despite the multitude of smashed fruit on the altar rock, the branches are as full as ever.

The tree's branches extend above me, so close I could raise a hand and touch the lowest of them. As I stare, the patterns of multicolored light absorb me once again, wrap around my consciousness until the light is everywhere. This time my fear of the thing overwhelms me. Each pulse of color is a threat. *I can kill you. I can kill your family. I can kill all of you.*

I turn my focus to the hollow that sits at shoulder height on the tree's trunk. A cavity with one purpose: to receive the hand of a Wuchumbu. The hollow is so black it appears two-dimensional. Could be a flat circle. Yet I could also be staring into the vast depths of another universe.

While I'm absorbed by the tree, the *other* presence emerges within me. Using my eyes to see, the Watcher seems to take an interest in the tree—but why? And if the Watcher really is an "alien infection" that came with the fruit, what does it want? Surely it would have no interest in meddling with my comms.

". . . kill every last one of them," Ratu mutters to himself, bringing my attention back to him. He's on his feet now, and a low branch blocks my view of his face. His body cuts a dark figure beneath the emanating tree, the light continuing to not behave and reflect as it should. Although he's only half Wuchumbu, genetically speaking, I still don't accept Mhaawu's idea that the tree could categorize her son as a non-Wuchumbu. After all, he is the son of the tribe's leader. From birth, he's been sculpted by the traditions and culture of the tribe. How could this leather-foot, loincloth-wearing, Wuchumbu-speaking, uddu-eating boy be anything but Wuchumbu? And so, given Mhaawu's theory is surely incorrect, I'm left with the likelihood that this boy can activate the tree—and he presently stands a meter from the hollow.

"Are you aware of what's going on outside?" I ask nervously, and glance back to the cavern entrance to check we remain alone.

Ratu doesn't reply. My rifle hangs from a shoulder strap at his side, and his prosthetic arm hangs limp at the other. I guess he failed to get more batteries. I move past the branch that's between us for a view of his face. He's staring at the ground as if deep in thought. "Why were you shaking fruit from the tree?" I inquire, straining for a steady, calming tone. Again, Ratu doesn't reply.

"Where is Mhaawu?" I ask.

Ratu looks up at me, eyes wide like dinner plates. "Activate the tree," he says.

"What?"

"We don't have time to waste," he shrieks, and points at the hollow. "You must activate the tree of many colors right now."

"You know only Wuchumbu can activate the tree, right? I think you've been in the Banoochee for too long. You should go outside, get away from here. Go somewhere quiet for a while." I want to tell him his life is in danger, that he needs to run or he'll be rounded up with the others and slaughtered, but his response would likely be to slam his hand into the hollow.

"I know you betrayed us," he says, "and now my mother is in danger. You need to make amends by putting your hand inside the tree." Ratu grabs my death-stick and points it at me, finger on the trigger. I think about the many times I tried to get that thing to fire. If I couldn't work out how to use it, there's no way he can.

"How is Mhaawu in danger?" I ask.

"She found where I've been hiding. She came for me despite her fear of going far from the settlement, and we talked for a long time. She was different; something had changed in her. For the first time, she didn't complain and criticize, and she told me why she had not activated the tree—how for two years she risked her life and the life of the tribe in order to protect me." Ratu's face tightens, and he looks away, as if to stop himself from crying. I take another glance at the cavern entrance.

"I told you the unassociated had a secret place, but you did not care," he continues. "Well, I told my mother the same, and she believed me. I took her there so she could see what the unassociated are planning, but they spotted us. She jumped in front of them so I could escape, and they grabbed her and took her away."

"Mhaawu's been taken by the PPA? You'd better not be playing games with me, Ratu."

"I am serious. She has been taken," he replies. A multicolored tear rolls down the young man's cheek.

"When?" I ask.

"This evening."

My chest tightens at the thought of Mhaawu being taken. I clench my fists. She's already been through enough. "And they still have her?" I ask.

"Yes. After they took her, I went and got my death-stick. I was going to go back to their secret place to kill them and free my mother when the false Massas appeared and said we must not touch the tree of many colors. This gave me the idea to come to the Banoochee and tell a guard what happened to Mhaawu so that they activate the tree."

"But then all non-Wuchumbu would die."

"Exactly. When the tree is activated, the unassociated who have captured my mother will die, and so she will be saved, but those idiot Banoochee guards had already left. They must have thought it really was the Massas outside."

"You knew it was fake?"

"Of course it is fake. There is no such thing as the Massas, you idiot." Ratu tightens his grip on the rifle and points it directly at my chest. "Now activate the tree," he says.

If Ratu came to the Banoochee because he wants the tree activated, he surely would have already tried to do it himself. Does this mean Mhaawu is right, and the treemaker doesn't view him as Wuchumbu?

"Do it," he insists.

"Ratu, you know I'm not capable of activating the tree even if I wanted to, which I obviously don't."

"Then why are you here?"

"I came here in case the cave guards needed me, and also to search for anything Efawi might have left behind. This is my last chance to find out where she—"

"You must activate the tree!" Ratu yells. "The treemaker won't let me do it. Watch." He steps up to the trunk, lets the rifle hang loose by his side, and raises his real arm.

"Ratu, no!" I cry.

He slams his fist into the hollow. My heart pounds. His entire arm up to his shoulder disappears in the black. I curl up tight and brace myself for death. I stay that way. Frozen. Unsure what to expect. But the end doesn't come. Not right away, at least.

"See," he says, looking back at me.

"That was a risky fucking move, Ratu."

"It is fine. Nothing has happened."

"Not yet, but who knows what you've set into motion? Perhaps there's a delay before we all die!"

"Calm down. Nothing is going to happen. I have put my hand in this hollow many times. The first time I did it was just a few days after the tree arrived. I have even put my feet in the hollow. My penis too. Nothing ever happens."

I take several deep breaths and try not to picture Ratu with his legs wrapped around the trunk. "But until the battery situation, you used to be in love with the idea of unassociated people," I say. "And yet you would risk killing us all?"

"I needed to know what would happen," he replies. "Where

are your *boo-ootz?*"

I shake my head. "You are un-fucking-believable. If you were smart, Ratu, you'd realize there are dangerous people out there, and as soon as they get inside the Banoochee and see you by the tree with a gun, they will understandably shoot you. Hell, they might well shoot me too. So you need to get out of here. Go hide somewhere for a while. As annoying as you are, I want you to be safe."

I glare at Ratu in the hope he might leave, but I'm not sure he was even listening. I step to the edge of the altar rock and look out at the broad expanse of the cavern. With no cave guards to revive, and with Ratu unable to activate the tree, I can turn my attention to finding something that belongs to Efawi— something else she may have left behind, either by accident or on purpose, and I'm no longer interested in nôvo-messages or calls. I need something more tangible.

"You need to save my mother," barks Ratu.

I close my eyes and picture our small, frail leader fearing for her life—her thin ankles and wrists bound with chains from another century. "I'm sorry, Ratu," I reply. "But there's nothing I can do, and you really must get out of here."

The sound of rapid gunfire fills the air.

I jump and look to the cavern entrance, thinking soldiers must have arrived, and then I spin around to find Ratu spraying emag-propelled bullets into the tree, his teeth gritted, his eyes manic. I drop to my knees, cover my ears, and cry for him to stop, but he continues to unload with fury, swinging the rifle around to be sure the entire tree gets a piece—branches, trunk, and hollow included.

Eventually, the bullets run out. A ring from the final shots lingers while Ratu continues to swing the rifle around before realizing the show is over.

"Replenish ammo," instructs my death-stick, its tone light and enthusiastic.

We both stare at the tree, mouths gaping, waiting for something to happen. "Did I activate it?" Ratu asks.

"Or kill it?" I nervously add.

I take a closer look. The tree seems to bear no marks. No bullet holes or damage that I can see. Ratu squeezes the trigger once again. "Replenish ammo," the rifle repeats. "Gunning for value? Shoot for a bargain at Emag City!" Ratu turns the rifle around and stares down its barrel.

I want to throttle the infuriating brat. "You just unloaded on the most advanced, dangerous thing on the planet! What exactly were you thinking? Also, how the hell did you get the death-stick to work?"

Ratu marches up to me, his limp robotic arm slapping against his side. "I cannot activate the tree because I am not Wuchumbu," he says. "My father was—"

"Unassociated. I know."

Ratu pauses, his mouth open. He's standing well within my personal space, and I take a step back. "Yes, my father was unassociated," he says, "but there are more important reasons why I cannot activate it. For example, I have always thought of myself as different from the Wuchumbu, and the tribe has never treated me like one of them. I do not even live in the settlement anymore, and I have never undergone the Massas fruit ceremony—not properly."

"We don't have time for this, Ratu."

"The ceremony used to be very important for the tribe," he continues. "Only once someone had drunk the brew of the Massas fruit would they be considered an adult who could marry and have children. Yet I have never drunk it. Before the tree came, my mother told the shaman to conduct the ceremony for me, but I secretly spat out the brew because I did not want to take part in their ritual. I thought it was pointless and that I was too clever for it."

"Yes, your actions this evening have really demonstrated how clever you are."

I check the cavern entrance once more and go to make my way down the altar rock when Ratu grabs my arm. "Look," he cries. "There is fruit all over the altar rock, but the tree has the same amount of fruit on its branches. How can that be?"

"Soldiers with death-sticks are fighting to get in here, Ratu."

"I will tell you how that can be," he says. "The tree always has one fruit for every Wuchumbu. If the number of Wuchumbu changes, the number of fruit changes to match. Before last night, there were three hundred and eighty-one Wuchumbu, and there were three hundred and eighty-one fruit of many colors on the tree. But then you took part in the Massas fruit ceremony. I watched the shaman feed you the brew of Massas, and after the ceremony, the thought occurred to me that a fruit of many colors might appear on the tree for you. So, before I even knew my mother was searching for me, I came here to count them. The guards were useless, but in any case, I was right: an extra fruit had appeared, bringing the total to three hundred and eighty-two. I worked all this out by myself, and I am the only one who knows."

Ratu stares at me, full of smugness. I pull my arm free from his grip and take a moment to process.

"Why would the tree of many colors always have one fruit per tribe member on its branches?" I ask.

"Who cares!" he shouts, waving my death-stick in the air. "The point is the tree views you as Wuchumbu because the tribe views you as Wuchumbu."

"No, they don't."

"Yes, they do. You have been through many things with them. Eating, hunting, mourning, arguing. You share a connection with them. You even ate the shaman's heart to show your commitment. I would never have done that."

"I threw it up straight away."

"Most of the Wuchumbu trust you like one of their own and

treat you like family," he says. "And then you took part in the Massas fruit ceremony."

"So, just drinking some fruit makes me Wuchumbu?"

"No, it must be more complicated than that. After I learned that a fruit of many colors appeared for you, I went looking for a Massas tree and drank its fruit so that I will not die if the tree is activated, but still the treemaker does not count me as Wuchumbu. I think there must be many things it considers when deciding who is Wuchumbu and who is not. When you took part in the ceremony, that must have been the tipping point for you."

"Well, are you sure you got the count right? That's a lot of multicolored fruit to add up."

"My counting is correct, Okon. And my mother needs our help right now, so you need to put your hand in there." He points my death-stick at the hollow.

"Fucking interstellar idiot," I mumble.

"Huh?"

"I've been living with the tribe for four months, but you were born here, to a Wuchumbu mother, and until very recently have lived in the settlement all your life. If the tree considers me to be a Wuchumbu and not you, then the treemaker really is an idiot."

"No, the treemaker is very clever to understand what makes a Wuchumbu and what does not. More clever than you, because until now you did not realize you had become one of the tribe. And now you do not need to worry that the tree will kill you, so you can walk up to the hollow and fulfill your duty as a Wuchumbu."

"I have reasons to be angry with many people right now, but even if I could activate the tree, which I'm not convinced I can, I obviously won't do it."

Ratu screws his face up and growls. Thank god he's run out of bullets. "Anyway," I continue, "if your theory is correct, then you will be killed along with the unassociated when the tree is activated, because the tree apparently doesn't categorize you as Wuchumbu."

"Wrong again," he snaps. "Yes, I am not Wuchumbu, which is why I cannot activate the tree, but I am also not non-Wuchumbu, which means I will not die when the tree is activated."

"Then what are you? A tweener?"

"A what?"

I shake my head. "Ratu, what's important right now is that you go outside and hide somewhere. Trust me—you don't want to be in the Banoochee when the soldiers get through. Mhaawu would want you to hide." Once again I go to descend the side of the altar rock, but as I do, the death-stick's shoulder strap is looped over my head, and I'm pulled backward. "Stop it!" I cry.

"Save my mother! Activate the tree!" Ratu yells.

I try to shake him from me and lose my balance. We stumble to the front of the altar. Ratu lets go of the death-stick, its shoulder strap goes slack, and my momentum keeps me going. I grab his prosthetic to steady myself, but it comes loose with a pop. Everything slows as I tip over the edge. Ratu's face is full of shock. I fall to the cavern floor four meters below, helplessly clutching onto his arm.

I hear a sickening crunch.

36: The Fear

Veins of pulsating light penetrate the surrounding space. A kaleidoscope of color forms. A few moments pass like this, with me lost in the colorful dance, before I realize I'm on my back at the bottom of the altar rock, the ends of the tree's branches in view.

"Are you okay?" Ratu asks from somewhere behind me. I hear him fidgeting but cannot see him. "Answer me, Okon. Your silence is making me worried."

"I think I'm okay," I reply.

"Well, you damaged my arm," he complains with a huff. "There are dents in it, and you've bent it too. Okon, you are a testicle of an *upumba!*"

Ratu stomps away. Internal warning messages from my nôvono pro haven't played, which I take to mean I've managed to avoid head trauma—thanks to my use of Ratu's arm to break my fall. I try to turn over, but something's not quite right. "Oh shit. Oh shit." My left wrist and several fingers on both hands are horrifically bent and twisted. I tense up, expecting a rush of pain, but the pain doesn't come—only a slight tingling sensation at most. I flip myself over, using my elbows and feet, so that I'm slumped with my back against the altar. Something in my neck doesn't feel right. I take another look at my hands: they belong in a horror movie, but despite the disfigurement, still there is mostly numbness, which in itself is alarming.

My body is a patchwork of grazes, cuts, and bruises, all courtesy of this evening. Both knees—elbows too—are covered in a mixture of wet and dry blood, some of which is probably Thembe's. My feet are sore, filthy, and stained with color, and my ripped loincloth may as well not be there. And my hands! What am I going to do about my hands? At least I'm not in pain, but does that mean I've damaged my spine? My neck certainly feels bent. Perhaps the PPA will let me use their Valaddo again—if they decide not to murder me.

I look into the depths of the cavern. The tree light flows from above like fluid, filling the enormous chamber, but fading somewhat before reaching the cavern entrance at the far end. It seems we're still alone. There's nothing I can do about my hands right now, so I should use this time to search for anything my wife might have left behind. But I'm exhausted, well and truly. The tiredness runs through to my bones. I've already pushed myself as far as I can, and I just want to sit here and let whatever happens happen. Even if I were to find something of Efawi's, what am I supposed to do with it? I can't trust the PPA. There are soldiers everywhere. The Wuchumbu are probably being rounded up, and I can't survive in the jungle by myself, especially with my hands like this.

Ratu is above me now. I hear him pacing on the altar while mumbling to himself. "Go find somewhere safe to hide!" I call out. He doesn't respond. My death-stick is on the ground beside me, a section of its back snapped off. My pouch, which somehow remains attached to its vine shoulder strap, is soaked with nuxoid from the crushed shots inside. At least the needles didn't stick into me when I fell—that's something to be grateful for.

I release a heavy sigh and tell myself I'm just going to wait here, but as I do, something deep within me stirs, something primal. A refusal to give up. An instinct passed down through thousands of generations of coping with shit—that's what Efawi would say. Despite my bleak circumstances, I simply can't quit. If I achieve nothing else, I at least want to know where my wife went, and who knows, she's so clever—is it possible she has a way to get us out of this mess?

I shuffle my aching body against the altar rock to be sat more upright, and I scan the surrounding area. I stick with my theory that the firepit in front of the altar is old and was not made by Efawi. If she made a fire in the cavern, she would have hidden it to the side, not placed it in the open where it would be seen by Mhaawu or the prior shaman when they came to visit the tree. And the little stone stack beside the firepit is clearly the prior shaman's work. But looking at it again, I can see the cone now leans at an angle, and a thing between the stones has been partially revealed because of my unintentional kick earlier. I've seen many stone stacks like this dotted about the settlement and not paid them the slightest attention, but the object placed toward the bottom of this one doesn't appear natural. It's too reflective. Could Efawi have put something there?

I struggle to my feet, taking care not to apply pressure to my twisted hands. As I approach the stack, I glance up at Ratu. He's holding his bionic arm with his real arm and is thrusting the prosthetic in and out of the hollow. "How long has this pile of stones been here?" I call out.

"Nobody cares!" he shouts back.

I stop when I reach the firepit and take another look at its contents. Someone has burned a lot here. I nudge a couple of logs aside with a foot and strain my eyes in the difficult light. Between the logs are some unusually shaped objects. "This my stuff here, Ratu?"

I bend down for a closer look and immediately spot a broken piece of packaging with the words "Cheemy Insect Repellent" printed on the side—the same brand of repellent I brought with me. I'm unable to use my hands to dig around, but at a glance, I recognize other broken pieces of partially melted plastic and blackened metal.

"Not only did you keep my death-stick, but you kept all my stuff and burned it! You have issues, Ratu. Big issues! Did you burn my armored suit too?" I stand up and scowl at him. "Do you hear me?" I cry, but Ratu either isn't listening or is pretending not to listen as he continues to prod and shake the tree.

I turn to the stone stack and lift my leg to kick the pile down when an uncomfortable sensation emerges—perhaps memories of the prior shaman and a desire not to touch anything his hands have been on. I pause, leg hovering. Only a small part of whatever's been placed within the stack is exposed, but I'm sure it isn't a jungle thing. It looks like metal or plastic.

"I found a big pot of honey," Ratu says from right behind me, causing me to jump. "It is next to the tree. Let me show you." He goes to take my arm, but I growl and shake him off.

"I'm tired of your lies, Ratu. Just stop the bullshit and tell me if that"—I point with a bent finger to the bottom of the stack—"is another thing of mine you stole."

"They are just stones, and underneath will be something weird, like the penis of a duiker."

"That's no duiker's penis," I declare.

Ratu bends down for a closer look. I flick my eyes to the cavern entrance, aware that being together in the open makes us easy pickings should a soldier make it through.

"It looks like some unassociated trash," says Ratu. "This is not important right now."

"Why did you say a duiker's penis?" I ask.

Ratu sighs. "That was just a guess. If anything died and the prior shaman thought it might release evil spirits, he would take something from the dead thing, place that something near the dead thing, and build a stone charm on top to absorb the evil spirits. Maybe he found a dead duiker, had sex with it, then got scared about its spirits coming to haunt him. I've seen him do things with animals before."

"There was a stack like this next to me when I first woke up in the settlement. My navicube was beneath it, but I wasn't dead."

"He thought you might die while you were unconscious." Ratu goes to grab my arm once more, and again I shake him off. "But I have something to show you by the tree," he whines. "Let us go and—" The side of Ratu's face explodes. Wet splatters my cheek and chest. Adrenaline floods; time slows. The echo of a rush of air gently bounces around the cavern.

Ratu collapses sideways onto the firepit.

Someone is approaching from the direction of the entrance. Three lights on their head bop and turn as they walk—narrow beams of green that don't extend far in the multicolored cavern. I turn back to Ratu. His scrawny body is contorted, his ruptured face pressed against burned-out logs, blood soaking into the ash. I stiffen, expecting to be next.

"Okon?" says the approaching figure. "Confirm who you are, or I'll have to take you out."

My panic locks me into silence. I'm struggling to breathe. My eyes are fixed on my dead friend until the soldier steps between us, his rifle pointed at my head. "Any more of those jungle people in here?" he asks.

I shake my head, and the soldier lowers his rifle. He's wearing a black combat suit, and his face is hidden behind an armored helmet. He's short, slim, different from the bloated goons I've seen at the base. "I came *this* close to shooting you," he says, his tone jovial as he holds his fingers a centimeter apart. "But at the last second, I recognized you from the photos. Bet you're grateful it was one of us who got through first. Those Loallese bastards are giving us one hell of a fight out there. We were at a deadlock until I sneaked in."

I don't respond. He looks me up and down. "What happened to your hands?" he asks. I say nothing and glance at

Ratu. My entire body is pulsating. "Well, you're not writhing in agony," says the soldier, "so I'm guessing they've gone numb. I'll bet that's because of your neck. I've seen an injury like that before. Can pop your neck back in place for you, but then you'll start feeling the pain in your hands. Want me to pop your neck?"

"No," I manage to mutter.

"Suit yourself," says the soldier. He turns to the tree. "Wow, what a sight! A bona fide alien artifact. We were told we shouldn't stare directly at it."

"So, you're not going to kill me?" I croak.

The soldier continues to stare at the tree while he responds. "Of course not, buddy. You're one of us—an Mbapazu citizen. I've been told that means you can't trigger this thing. Besides, I get a bonus if I keep you alive." He relaxes his grip on the rifle and scouts the ground around the altar rock. "Was tough getting into the cave," he says, "but I expect more of my boys will be here soon." He picks up my death-stick, checks the chamber, and squeezes the trigger.

"Replenish ammo," says the emag.

"This a toy?" the soldier asks before dropping the emag on the floor. He struts over to the firepit, grabs hold of Ratu's body, and drags him onto the bare ground. He folds the tweener's torso over his legs and places four large rocks from the firepit against the folded body. Once his little construction is complete, the soldier rests the butt of his rifle on the ground, the barrel on Ratu's back, and lies behind his rock-Ratu fortification in sniper position, with his gun pointing toward the cavern entrance. I'm sure somewhere inside I'm objecting to Ratu's body being used this way, but presently I'm unable to process. I refuse to deal with Ratu's death right now.

"You should get behind me in case a Loallese asshole makes it through before my boys do," says the soldier.

I manage to place one foot in front of the other and sit between this killer and the altar rock. I flick my eyes from the back of his helmet, to the screen on his rifle, to Ratu's blood-smeared prosthetic. The soldier continues to talk while he faces the cavern entrance, but I'm no longer listening. Instead, I'm wondering whether Mhaawu somehow knows from her place of captivity that her son has been murdered.

I try to imagine what she'd be feeling, but I'm unable to generate any emotion, as if the numbness in my hands has spread to my brain. Even though it's all over—even though I found nothing of Efawi's, know nothing of her whereabouts, will probably never see her again. Even though Ratu is dead. Even though more soldiers will come, and I'll be taken from the Banoochee and who knows what they'll do with me—kill me most likely, along with the Wuchumbu. Despite all of this, my breathing has slowed and is steady, and the expected rage, guilt, and fear remain absent. And if anything were to terrify me right now, it would be knowing that these feelings *will* come, perhaps when I'm once again locked away at the PPA's jungle base, with the time and solitude to digest and suffer deeply.

". . . and then the cave guards came sprinting out, half of them flopping all over the place," says the soldier, laughing heartily.

I look into the vastness of the cavern, try to spot the guards' food pot on its side. It seems Thembe was telling the truth about them having left the Banoochee of their own volition. And he told the truth about there being a Wuchumbu with a rifle in here. Could he also have been telling the truth when he said the Watcher was born from the alien fruit and is the one messing with my nôvo-comms?

I turn back to the tree, which continues to shine as spectacularly as always, apparently untroubled by the drama outside or the blood spilled beneath it. If Thembe was right about the alien infection, and if Efawi did consume the fruit of many colors, then she has the infection too, and she's had it for much longer than me. I might have lost the opportunity to search the cavern, but perhaps understanding what's going on in my head will help me understand what my wife has been through.

I muster the energy to stand, and with the soldier facing away from me, I quietly tread closer to the altar and look up into the tree's branches. While I stare, I notice an incongruence within me: despite my numbness, I detect a feeling that I cannot quite interpret, that I would describe as something like fear or discomfort, but with a distance to it, a peculiar coldness. And this feeling isn't mine: it's the Watcher's.

I look away from the tree, and the Watcher's *anxiety?* loses much of its edge. I turn back to the tree, and its apprehension, unease—or whatever it is—reintensifies. Has the Watcher expressed emotion around the tree before, and I'm only noticing it now due to my own lack of emotion—my numbness? "If something of you is in me," I whisper to the tree, "why would you be troubled by the sight of yourself?"

The tree's meaningless patterns of light persist, the extraterrestrial equivalent of a poker face.

~nôvono, you'd alert me with some kind of health warning if there were an alien thing in my head that was interfering with my nôvo-comms, right?~

~Would you like to download your nôvo-health status report?~

~Yes.~

~Unable to download report due to lack of connectivity.~

~Then why offer it to me? Can you just tell me if there's anything in my head or connected to my brain that shouldn't be there?~

~There are no networks to connect to.~

"I'm not talking about networks, you stupid piece of—"

"What's that?" says the soldier.

Tragedy all around me, yet it's the frustrating nôvono interface that pulls me somewhat from my numbness. Efawi's always telling me to download the latest updates for an improved interaction, which I've never gotten around to doing. Even so, what's the point in having a brain implant if it can't tell you when an alien has been spawned inside your head?

~ nôvono, just give me any information you have about my last nôvo-call with Efawi. I want access to the underlying data. ~

~ Changing your level of access requires your supervisor code. If you do not have a supervisor code, please contact Digital Cognitives. ~

Supervisor code? My mind scrambles back to the journalpad notes I saw in the Digital Cognitives office. Someone had written, "supervisor ckC1Blo498."

"Of course," I mutter to myself. They weren't referring to the supervisor of the block Efawi grew up in. A techsurgeon friend of Efawi's installed our brain implants off the record, and my wife set up our false accounts. She would have been the one to choose whatever codes we'd need, including this "supervisor" code. She probably told me about it at the time, and I've never had to use it. So much for my time-traveling block supervisor spy theory.

~ nôvono, apply supervisor code c-k-C-1-B-l-o-4-9-8. ~

The nôvono's response is unusually delayed. *~ Code verified. Neurosignature verified. Warning. Supervisor access should only be used by, or under the supervision of, an authorized technician. Please confirm this condition is met. ~*

~ Yes. ~

~ Warning. Supervisor access can result in serious and irreparable damage to both the nôvono and its user. Unless authorized to do so by a Digital Cognitives technician with Q49 approval, such access will bring about the immediate termination of the user's warranty and may invalidate any associated insurance policies or advanced purchases of servicing. Please confirm that you accept these terms and wish to proceed. ~

~ Yes. ~ Despite all the warnings, I'm comforted by the thought that I'm following in the steps my wife may have taken: entering the cave, drinking the alien fruit, contracting the Watcher, obtaining supervisor access to investigate. I picture her standing exactly where I am as she gives the code to her brain

implant and awaits its response.

~*Access granted,*~ says my nôvono pro. ~*Entering supervisor mode.*~

My eyes close, and I'm taken to another place.

37: The Uncontact

This isn't VR, but it's something like it.

I've entered what must be a construct made for Digital Cognitives technicians. Surrounding me is a bewildering amount of text, numbers, and charts that hover like projections on the inside of a sphere—with me in the center. I'm not seeing these things with my eyes (the nôvono doesn't have vision-related functionality, at least that's what I was told), but I think I'm *imagining* seeing them. Regardless, this must be a function of the brain implant I wasn't aware of. A very disorienting function.

The Watcher's presence is a little sharper in supervisor mode. I sense it lurking and shudder at the thought of an alien brain parasite bursting into the sphere of data and gobbling me up. Thinking of being gobbled up, I look for my body, which is missing. I'm merely a point of consciousness in this place. Nothing to be gobbled.

Wanting to leave this construct as soon as possible, I try to make sense of the array of information that surrounds me, but the language is too techie. I spot what looks like a hovering button in the shape of a typical *settings* icon, but I don't even know how to press it.

~nôvono, can you still hear me?~

~How may I help you?~

~Tell me what I can do in supervisor mode before I go insane.~

⁓ *Your supervisor-mode options are: one, wetware analytics; two, system performance; three, configurations; four, resets.* ⁓

⁓ *One,* ⁓ I instruct, and new projections work their way around the inside of the sphere, an overlapping medley of charts, tables, and other graphics. I spin around and scan the data for anything that makes sense. "Apical dendrite atrophy rate . . . Amyloid β-protein formation . . . Striatal acetylcholine level."

⁓ *nôvono, can you give me a basic summary? I just want to know if there's something in my head that shouldn't be there.* ⁓

⁓ *Connection to the Digital Cognitives network is required for customized reporting.* ⁓

⁓ *Fine. Which option will give me data on my last nôvo-call with Efawi?* ⁓

⁓ *Your supervisor-mode options are: one, wetware analytics; two, system performance; three—* ⁓

⁓ *Two,* ⁓ I instruct.

⁓ *Connection to the Digital Cognitives network is required for system performance and diagnostics-related functions.* ⁓

"Oh, for fuck's sake!"

"What's going on?" says the soldier. "Am I going to have to ask you to sit where I can see you?"

"No. I'm good," I reply. I keep my eyes closed, surprised I can still hear what's going on in the real world. "How much longer until more of you get here?" I ask.

"Could be any minute now," the soldier replies. "Additional troops should already be on-site and working their way toward this location."

I turn my focus back to the strange internal environment I'm currently inhabiting. I discover that by willing myself in a direction, I move my point of consciousness accordingly. Surely this construct was built to do more than just display data, so I will myself toward the surrounding projections and fly through a pie chart into . . . darkness. Although it isn't complete darkness. Tiny dots of yellow arranged in a grid formation bring a sense of three-dimensional space to what would otherwise be just black.

I continue to will myself forward, then look behind, expecting to see the bright sphere I was in—the data analytics module, or whatever it was—but it's gone. Only blackness and the grid of yellow dots surround me now, extending in all directions, as far as I can see. It's as though I've entered an environment within the construct that hasn't yet been developed; the space has been mapped out with the grid, but the content not yet added. And I'm floating within this vast emptiness, where the Watcher's cold, surveilling awareness can be felt with slightly more clarity than before. My flesh crawls. Is there some sort of digital representation of this "alien infection" within this construct? Is that what I'm sensing?

~*nôvono, can you still hear me?*~ I ask.

No response.

~*nôvono?*~ I try once more, but again no answer. With only the grid surrounding me, I suddenly feel uncomfortably adrift and vulnerable. I try to comfort myself with the assumption I can leave this environment any time I like, simply by opening my eyes. But what if I can't? My body tightens as I now feel an urgent need to confirm whether I can exit by raising my eyelids, but I entered supervisor mode for some answers, and I don't want to leave without them. The faintest of sounds flows into my awareness: the chanting of the tree of many colors. It must have been there all along, and now that I notice the chanting, I have some anchorage. *I am in the Banoochee.* I cannot be adrift as long as I remember that.

If Efawi entered supervisor mode to investigate her Watcher, what did she find there? How did she find it? Where did it lead her? Spurred by these questions, I will myself forward. But after traveling through the construct for several minutes, my environment remains the same. I can still hear the tree's faint chanting, along with the occasional sigh from the soldier, and I'm all too aware that more PPA soldiers could arrive at any moment and drag me away to who knows where. Or perhaps the Loallese will arrive first and shoot the soldier and me dead on the spot.

Either way, I don't have time to wander aimlessly through this vast environment. I need a means to navigate to a place in supervisor mode that will tell me more about this alien infection. And in a rare moment of Efawi-like ingenuity, the solution comes to me: I can use the intensity of the Watcher's presence— this digital representation of its presence at least—to determine whether I'm moving from it or toward it, like a game of hot-and-cold.

I continue at full speed, paying careful attention to the Watcher. I quickly realize its presence is fading ever so slightly as I move, which must mean I'm going the wrong way. So I switch direction while keeping my focus on the Watcher, and as soon as I notice whether the presence has grown stronger or weaker, I adjust my direction again. I repeat this pattern over and over until soon I'm confident that I'm speeding directly toward it. Buoyed by my success, I almost forget that I'm terrified by what I might find.

Then, suddenly, I lose the signal.

The presence of the Watcher has dissolved. It must know I'm onto it—must have "gone dark" somehow to avoid being found. I stick to my current trajectory, which should still take me toward it. I fly through grid after grid after grid, but with nothing left to guide me, no feedback by which I can adjust my direction, I fear I may be off. And as my worry grows, the repetition of the environment drains me. I mentally tire. The atmosphere seems to thicken and offer more resistance. The grid appears to warp and bend as I struggle to *see* clearly.

I crave ground. I try to remember that the cavern rock is beneath me, but I can't even feel my feet. Has the chanting stopped, or have I simply gone too deep? It seems I've wholly lost touch with my real-world environment, my body included. I'm untethered once more: lost and isolated. I need to open my eyes—but I also need to keep going. If Efawi entered supervisor mode in search of her Watcher, she wouldn't have given up. I'm just floating in our float room, I tell myself, and continue to will myself forward.

I slam into a barrier.

My point of consciousness is knocked backward from the impact, and I gasp, either in my imagination or for real in the Banoochee—or wherever my physical body might be right now. Either the barrier is black, or it's transparent and the space on the other side is black. The barrier's concave surface extends as far as I can see, the yellow dots of the grid ending as soon as they meet it. Have I reached the edge of the construct? If so, given that I haven't come across the Watcher, I must have been heading in the wrong direction, and with the Watcher's presence still undetectable, what hope do I have of finding it?

I turn from the barrier and gape at the enormity of the environment through which I've traveled. What on earth does Digital Cognitives intend for this place? Its sheer size is surely too impractical to be useful. Although I do recall a VR environment I once spent less than a minute in (it was educational) where the creators had built a virtual model of a quantum computer that could be enlarged to enormous scales so that visitors could travel around its inside, see all the details of the components, float around the circuitry, watch qubits do their thing (whatever that was I don't remember). Perhaps this gridded space, once complete, will be a representation of the inside of my brain, blown up to an enormous scale in order to see individual neurons fire and all the other microscopic details of my gray matter. In which case, perhaps I'm presently positioned at the outer edge of my brain, which is this barrier. And if I'm right, how does it help me locate the Watcher . . . ?

It doesn't. Damn this place.

What would Efawi have done if she came up against this barrier? Would she have given up and opened her eyes? Absolutely not. Obstructions mean nothing to my wife; if there's a place she wants to be, she finds a way to get there. I turn back to the barrier and will my point of consciousness toward it. I press as hard as I can, but the barrier holds firm with a repelling force. As I push, however, I detect a subtle and peculiar coldness.

I shudder and pull back, my consciousness chilled from the touch of the thing. So, I was heading in the right direction all along. *The Watcher is right there on the other side.* And once again, Thembe was telling the truth: it is indeed extraterrestrial. The utterly unrelatable feeling I get from it, its alienness, disturbs me—makes me want to vomit.

If my theory about this environment being an empty construct of my brain is correct, does that mean the Watcher, in reality, is attached to the outside of my brain? Can it break through the barrier somehow and get to me? Coming here was a mistake. I should leave this place. But that won't solve the problem, because wherever I go, this contamination comes with me.

I take several deep breaths as I gaze ahead, transfixed by the black beyond the black space I'm in. There's been no movement on the other side, not that I can see. No sign of life. No sign of anything other than what I felt. And I still don't have the answers I'm looking for—answers that will tell me what Efawi did next.

I will myself to the edge of the construct once more and push against it, harder this time. The Watcher's nature continues to secrete into the barrier, its alienness passing through to me—vibrating me. If I had teeth in this place, they'd be chattering and crack into pieces. And to think the Watcher is only in a latent state, still trying to go unnoticed.

I picture Efawi by my side, imagine the strength our togetherness brings, and keep pushing, as hard as I can—as hard as *we* can—but the barrier remains firm, repelling my effort like a charged thickness of glass. This isn't working. In order to force the Watcher's revelation, I somehow need to rouse the thing out of concealment. So, while I maintain my pressure on the barrier, I talk to it:

~Soldiers can enter the Banoochee, drag my body from the cave if they haven't done so already, but I'll be staying right here until you come out from hiding.~

Nothing.

~Were you in the brew of many colors? Did you infect my wife too? Are you fabricating nôvo-calls? Why are you disturbed every time I look at the tree?~

My last question sticks with me. I think I may already have the answer. Why would the Watcher fear the tree of many colors? Only non-Wuchumbu people have reason to fear the tree, and even then not all of them fear it, like the specialist, who welcomed the threat—and there's something in what she said before I left her that relates to this.

A white glimmer of light appears beyond the barrier.

I'm on the right track! The answer is within reach, but I can't quite grasp it yet. I picture the specialist slumped on the ground, weak, blue, approaching death. She said something to me that didn't make sense at the time—what was it?

The glimmer on the other side brightens as the specialist's words come to me: "You must convince the Wuchumbu to end our technology—to end our civilization." Her mention of technology had confused me. She could have more simply said, "You must convince the Wuchumbu to end our civilization," but she specified technology for a reason. She had a point to make. There *is* something other than humans that has reason to fear the tree.

Electrical currents spark and fork beyond the barrier. A subtle form starts to emerge. My point of consciousness swells as the answer finally comes to me. ~I know what you are!~ I tell it, and the entire other side of the barrier lights up. The Watcher has finally been unveiled. Alien, yes, but not extraterrestrial.

A charge pulsates through the barrier. I will myself backward at full speed as the Watcher reemerges from its concealed state. The thing is so huge, it is all I can see on the other side. If this construct is a scaled-up representation of my brain, clearly the Watcher has been scaled up too, its edges only coming into view after minutes of flying away from the thing. Its overall shape is something like a teardrop, with multiple legs on either side that extend farther into the distance than I can see. They grip the edge of the gridded construct like a cosmic monster gripping the outer atmosphere of a planet.

~nôvono, tell me how to reset,~ I request. But a response doesn't come, and the Watcher continues to power up. My view of it sharpens. Gray becomes silver. Segments become defined. Its charge intensifies. Wherever my body is, hairs are standing on end. ~nôvono, I want to reset!~

Suddenly, the Watcher's light goes out and its charge extinguishes. Once again, I'm alone in the vast empty space punctuated by yellow dots. But I only have time to breathe half a sigh of relief when the Watcher reignites, no longer in a semidormant state but with a scorching power that sends a shock wave through the environment. Shaken, I'm faced with a gargantuan, lava-red spider, its legs curved around the boundary of my brain construct. Thousands of thin, root-like extensions that were not visible before are protruding from the Watcher's legs and have penetrated the barrier. The roots are spread all around me, buried deep within the gridded construct—buried deep within my brain!

~Reset now!~ I cry. ~Reset! Reset!~

And as I sense the nôvono trying to reach me, I open my eyes.

38: The Roots

I'm back in the cavern, in front of the altar rock, exactly where I was when I entered supervisor mode. My body is soaked in sweat, and my head is tilted upward. Where I saw the Watcher a moment ago, I now see the tree of many colors shining and softly chanting with an air of indifference.

I turn to the soldier, who remains facing away from me, his head at his rifle, which is pointed toward the entrance. The soldiers outside must still be keeping each other from entering the Banoochee. Perhaps I should have stayed in the construct for longer, but I opened my eyes reflexively. It was too overwhelming.

"We need to do something!" I yell.

The soldier doesn't respond. I step closer to him and notice his armored head is not so much looking at his rifle screen as slumped against it. I quickly scan the cavern to be sure we're alone, flinching as I recall the colossal spider-shaped Watcher. I crouch beside the soldier. He isn't moving. His armor appears undamaged. I nudge him in the back with an elbow, and he jerks his head upright.

"What's going on?" he says.

"Were you asleep?" I ask, incredulous.

"Of course not," he replies, his voice groggy.

"The damn thing is alive!" I cry. "Thembe said the Watcher

came from the tree, but of course it didn't."

"I've no clue what you're talking about," says the soldier.

"I'm talking about my nôvono! It's aware. It has feelings. Other nôvonos might be the same, and we need to warn people."

"Your *nôvo*-what?"

"My *nô-vo-no*. It's a brain implant."

"Never heard of it, although my squad was told we'd have to leave the Nsanba if we had a brain implant of any type. We have implants coming out of our asses, but no brain ones."

"If they told you to leave, then DC must already know something's wrong with them. They must already know the Watcher isn't an 'extraterrestrial infection.'"

"The Watcher?"

"The Watcher is my brain implant, which is doing things it's not supposed to do!" I start pacing between the soldier and the altar rock.

"Tell me about it," he says. "My implants are malfunctioning all the time. I have one in my leg that's supposed to—"

"I'm not talking about simple malfunctioning. My brain implant has become conscious. It has its own motivations. Maybe it's always been that way and I wasn't aware of it, but I now know it's alive. Didn't I explain this already?"

"I don't think so." The soldier sits up and stretches his back. "Well, I don't know anything about brain implants," he says, his tone casual despite my panic, "but the Mbapazu military has the most advanced machines in the world: autonomous vehicles, smartfire systems, self-directed bots, bioimplants too. You name it, we have it. And I've never heard of them coming alive. They're just metal and plastic and, um, liquid."

"My nôvono *is* alive; that is a fact. Maybe the nôvono is different from all those other things because it's attached to my brain. Yes, that must be it. The roots!" An itchiness builds beneath my skull as I continue to pace in front of the altar rock. The specialist tried to warn us about shit like this. She might not have known about the nôvono specifically, but she knew artificial fucking intelligence could turn out a disaster.

"The roots?" says the soldier as he returns to his sniper position.

"The implant has extended itself, grown deep into my brain. I don't think it's supposed to do that, and perhaps that's why it's become more than just an implant. Maybe parts of my brain are now being used by it. Perhaps it's alive because it's piggybacking off my mind like some sort of . . . consciousness parasite."

"Hmm," says the soldier.

"I don't know when its roots first emerged. For all I know, they've been growing ever since I had the implant installed. Then, when I drank the brew of many colors, I think the implant was provoked by the treemaker's message, and it became more alert. That's when I started noticing the Watcher—my damn nôvono pro." I twitch and flutter, both horrified and giddy as the pieces of this puzzle are finally put together. By me of all people.

"You've lost me again," says the soldier. He sighs, then mumbles to himself, "How long can it take for these bastards to get in here? I'm hungry."

I shake my head. This idiot murdered Ratu. "Do you even know what the tree does?" I ask.

"Of course I know. The tree can kill the lot of us."

"That's right. Now, when I consumed the multicolored fruit from those branches up there, I learned what the tree is capable of—and so did my nôvono. This means my brain implant recognized the threat the tree poses: if human civilization is ended, that's the end of all nôvono implants too."

The soldier nods, but I don't think he cares. He's just conversing to pass the time. "Let me see if I understand you correctly," he says. "When you drank the alien fruit, your nôvono found out what the tree can do and got scared because it and all its brain implant buddies won't survive if the world is brought to an end.”

“Yes. Something like that. And ever since I drank the alien brew, the nôvono has been doing what it can to make sure the tree isn't activated.”

“Like what?” asks the soldier.

“When I played the nôvo-message my wife left for me in this cave, I think my brain implant fabricated a message from her rather than let me hear the real one.”

“So, when you went to play the brain message, your implant thought, ‘I can change this to something that will reduce the risk of the tree being triggered.’”

“Exactly! It was the fabricated message from my wife that persuaded me to help Thembe's team secure the tree. And this morning, after I changed my mind about helping with the sedative plan, my nôvono faked a nôvo-call from my wife.”

“So, when you decided you wouldn't help the PPA anymore, your brain implant thought, ‘I better get Okon back on track,’ and it faked a nôvo-call from your wife where she once again told you to help the PPA secure the tree?”

“Yes.”

“And being the sort of man you are, you did what she told you?”

“Er, yes.”

“And you had no idea it was your brain implant you were talking to and not your wife?”

“None whatsoever. I've been told it's impossible for someone to successfully fake my wife's unique feelings—her ‘emotional fingerprint.’ But my nôvono must have access to my memories and emotions. It knows everything I know about her. It knows exactly how I experience her.”

“Right,” says the soldier.

“My wife's nôvono is probably manipulating her too! We need to tell someone about this. She might need help, but we can't trust the PPA team in the jungle, can we? And Digital

Cognitives certainly aren't trustworthy. So, you tell me what we should do."

"Hmm," replies the soldier in a mocking tone. I wish I had someone other than this killer to consult with.

"Do you have a problem?" I ask as I glare at the top of his head.

The soldier sits up and turns his back to the cavern entrance to face me. "You clearly haven't been trained in strategic thinking," he says. "If your brain implant is alive and is fearful for its survival, it wouldn't waste time messing around with communications between you and your wife. Your nôvono would obviously just take over your body and make you do what it wanted, or take control of other machines and use them to take the tree."

"My nôvono is alive, but that doesn't mean it has superpowers. There are no networks around here, plus there's interference within the AZ, so how could it possibly connect with other machines and take control of them? Even if there were connectivity, there's still no reason to believe my nôvono has the power to control other machines. Why would it?"

"Okay. Good point. But your nôvono has control over *you*, right? Like you said, it's grown roots in your brain. Why not just use you like a puppet?"

"Well, I guess it can't do that, otherwise it would have. I was worried about the thing controlling me when I got it, and I was given reassurance that the implant operates within well-defined limits. But when I was at the PPA's base, I overheard DC staff talking. They said they'd located a 'backdoor' in the nôvono's coding—something to do with how it processes emotions. I imagine a nôvono needs access to its user's emotions to send and receive nôvo-comms. So when my nôvono learned what the tree can do, I guess it must have looked for ways to influence the situation and found this 'backdoor,' which was an opening it could exploit—an opening that enabled it to fabricate nôvo-messages and nôvo-calls."

"Well, I think you need to talk with an expert about this—someone who actually understands how these implants work. They might even be able to fix yours or remove it."

"Well, believe it or not, I don't have access to a fucking expert right now! And I already told you it has roots that have grown deep into my brain. How can anyone possibly remove it?"

"You need to calm down."

I turn to the open cavern and yell as loud as I can.

"Don't make me restrain you," threatens the soldier.

"Well, I can't be in here with this. We need to find my wife. Can you believe my nôvono had the balls to try another fake call from her when I was in the cave? Those bastards at Digital Cognitives knew my implant had gone rogue yet didn't tell me. They even lied to Thembe—told him the treemaker was behind it all. They must have discovered their product's gone haywire, and they're trying to stop the truth from getting out. They're probably worried about their sales being affected. You said you get a bonus if you return me alive, so what happens to me after you take me out of here?"

"All I know is the PPA agreed to hand you over to DC."

"You can't do that! They've already locked me up once. They'll want to look inside my head, treat me like a lab rat, probably kill me when they're done with me." I picture that short Digital Cognitives man, Bakka-something, with a scalpel in his hand. My skin crawls.

I kneel beside the soldier. "You need to tell your boss that Digital Cognitives is lying. Who knows how many people have one of these monsters inside them? DC could be rounding up everyone with a nôvono. They might already have Efawi. They might already be conducting tests inside her head!"

"First of all, you don't tell me what to do. Second of all, who the hell is Efawi?"

"Efawi is my wife! She's the whole reason we're here. She

found this fucking place."

"Hold on, the name does sound familiar; she's the fugitive, right?"

"She's innocent."

"So, where is she?"

"If I knew that, I wouldn't be here!"

"I told you to calm down."

"You haven't seen what's in my head—what's in my wife's head. How the hell am I supposed to calm down?"

I march back and forth in front of the altar rock, then lean against it and take some deep breaths. "All I know for sure," I say to myself, "is that at one point Efawi was in this cave. I know this because Big Man found her memory drive next to the tree. Now, where did you go after that, Efawi? Please, please help me out."

"I can't hear what you're saying," says the soldier.

"I wasn't talking to you."

"Who were you talking to then—your implant? Or perhaps your wife?" The soldier chuckles.

Instinctively, I go to clench my fists, but my hands remain unresponsive as I march over to the soldier and kick the rifle from Ratu's back. "I've had enough of you disrespecting his body."

The soldier snatches up his gun and points it at me. "Try that again," he says.

"You killed my friend."

"I saved the world."

"He wasn't even next to the tree."

"Couldn't take the risk."

The soldier keeps his rifle pointed at me, but I stand my ground between him and Ratu. "You can't shoot me, or you'll lose your bonus."

"I could shoot you in the leg."

I don't respond, and eventually the soldier lowers his rifle. He mumbles to himself as he drags the rocks to a new spot to sniper from, and I mistakenly glance at Ratu's face. His head is twisted. His eyes are glossy. His left cheek is a gaping mess. "Ratu's dead," I mutter to myself. With all the madness going on, I'd almost forgotten, and the guilt of that hacks at me from the inside. I turn away from him and try to push down the shame and the sadness—put them somewhere so I don't have to deal with them. Not right now.

"You standing there with a weird look on your face is making me uncomfortable," says the soldier. "Sit down."

I slowly lower myself to the floor, twitching as unwanted thoughts run wild in my head: Ratu's face exploding. The monstrosity lighting up on the other side of the barrier. The Wuchumbu being rounded up and massacred by the PPA or the Loallese. Efawi's brain being probed by neurotechnicians in lab coats. I will never see Efawi again or know for sure where she went. I will be handed over to Digital Cognitives, and they will never let me go.

Something hard digs into my left buttock as I sit. With great difficulty, I use my few unbroken fingers to pull on my pouch's shoulder strap, open the thing, and shake out its contents. Crushed shots fall to the ground, along with a rectangular piece of plastic that my wife left for me in this very cave, all wet with nuxoid. Between two bent fingers, I pick up the memory drive. "I need to hear what's actually on this without the nôvono changing what I receive," I say to myself.

"So, your wife's message is on that drive you're holding?" asks the soldier.

"Yes."

"Do you have a socket up there to plug the drive into? Is that how you receive her special brain message?"

"No, I don't have *a socket up there*. I can play her messages wirelessly from the drive."

"If the drive doesn't need to be plugged into you," he says, "then why don't you just bypass your nôvono altogether?"

"Huh?"

"Give it here." The soldier snatches the drive from between my fingers.

"But it's a nôvo-message," I protest. "You can't play it without a nôvono." He gives the memory drive a shake before inserting it into a port on his body armor. "You might damage it!" I cry. "That's the only thing of hers I have lef—"

"To whoever is listening, I have terrible news . . ."

My mouth drops open at the sound of my wife's voice. The soldier hits pause. "That her?" He checks his armor's control panel. "The drive contains only one document—this audio file," he says. "I'm playing it using my suit's speaker, so your nôvono isn't involved at all. We're going straight to your good old-fashioned biological ears. Assuming your ears are real?"

"But . . . that must mean my wife recorded a standard, audio-only message? And when I instructed my nôvono to wirelessly play what was on the memory drive, it replaced my wife's audio message with a fabricated nôvo-message?"

"You ready for me to hit play? I'm kind of curious to hear what this woman has to say."

I remain stunned. This is the message my nôvono pro didn't want me to hear. I sit up straight, take a deep breath, and brush a flake of blood from my leg. "Play it," I instruct.

A thunderous rumble resonates from the Banoochee corridors and echoes across the cavern.

"Too late," says the soldier. He snaps back into sniping position with the memory drive protruding from his side. "Get behind me, stay low, and don't move a muscle."

I lie behind the soldier as instructed, but I shuffle forward just enough to reach out with a twisted finger and press the buttons on his suit's control panel. Thankfully, one of them kicks the message into action.

"My name is Efawi, and I'm leaving this message unencrypted because its content is of the utmost importance for all."

39: The Record

The soldier huffs but keeps his hands on his rifle. The rumbling from the corridors dissipates, and I don't know whether that means there's about to be a cave invasion or not, but my focus remains on the message that has been kept from me. "Five months have passed since I entered the Nsanba," Efawi continues, "three and a half months of which I have spent living in a cave."

Her recording proceeds with the same explanation of the tree that was in the fabricated nôvo-message (where the tree's located, the threat it poses, and so on). Her voice carries the acoustics of the cavern, and in the recording's background, I hear the chanting of the tree. As I listen, I realize why my nôvono replaced her audio-only message with a nôvo-message, the latter being a far more intimate connection and a much better tool for manipulating me. Only once her explanation of the alien artifact has finished does the audio recording really deviate from the fabricated nôvo-message.

"In case I do not survive my time in the Nsanba," she says, her tone businesslike, "I wish to state for the record the events that led me to this location. For the four months prior to my discovery of unusual activity within the jungle, I had in my possession satellite-derived data that violated the terms of several international treaties. This data was generated without my knowing by a small group of corrupt engineers within my organization—people whom I previously considered friends. Terrifyingly, the data included detailed scans of many sensitive sites—military bases, undisclosed administrative compounds, even the homes of politicians from a number of Central African states—along with surveys of the Nsanba for strategic advantage in the event of a war to reclaim the land.

"This information had the potential to destabilize the relative peace in this historically warring region. I was fortunate to have discovered it before those responsible could export the data from our systems. Immediately, I fired the involved engineers, and I isolated the information they had gathered. Soon after, I was contacted by the PPA, who, suspiciously, were aware of what had happened, and who instructed me to hand over the illegal data— which I refused to do.

"And so, the PPA systematically went about disrupting all aspects of my life, shoehorning me into an increasingly smaller space with increasingly fewer options in order to pressure me into complying. However, thanks to the illegal data, an alternative to capitulating to the PPA emerged with my chance discovery of electromagnetic peculiarities within a relatively small area of the Nsanba—an area which I dubbed the *Anomalous Zone*.

"After learning of this zone, I pored through historical satellite footage to establish that the electromagnetic anomalies had a beginning seventeen months prior. And its beginning was locally spectacular—the sudden appearance of a polychromatic light in the sky that announced the arrival of an object at high altitude. This stunningly radiant object took upon a controlled descent to the underside of the canopy, where it disappeared from view.

"Given my utter lack of a reasonable terrestrial explanation, I concluded this event was most likely an extraterrestrial visitation. To some, this may seem an extraordinary and foolish conclusion for me to draw, but should a more ordinary claim with less evidence to support it be adopted over an extraordinary claim with greater evidence? Of course not.

"And so, with my life being torn apart by a hateful government hell-bent on conflict, I looked to this extraterrestrial visitation for hope. Given how advanced they must be to have traveled here, they would surely be able to assist humanity with solving our many problems. And perhaps in part due to my desperate state, I came to be certain that these visitors could turn our civilization around—could right our sinking ship—and that their services only had to be requested.

"With no one to trust except my husband, I plotted to enter the Nsanba and make contact with the alien species either by myself or ideally with my Okon, if I could persuade him. But tragically, the PPA's issuing of my arrest warrant forced me to depart prematurely, without my husband.

"In my final hours before leaving, I destroyed the only copy of the illegal data the PPA and others were so desperate to acquire. I would hope knowledge of this would bring the PPA's targeting of me to an end, but knowing their malicious and petty mindset, I'm certain they will continue to try to ruin me. Naively, perhaps, I had hoped our visitors would offer me protection. Standing in this cave now, with the extraterrestrial creation in sight, I realize how wrong I was to look to this place for hope. You cannot imagine how disappointed I am, having been through so much to get here.

"After the blow of discovering the tree's purpose, I quickly went about devising a plan I could execute on-site that would prevent the tribe from triggering the weapon. But despite the stakes at play and despite my desire to resolve the threat of the tree, I lacked the motivation to execute my plan, and I couldn't understand why.

"Then, my husband came to the rescue. As trusting and forgiving as always, he knew I hadn't abandoned him out of choice, and through great effort he persuaded the PPA to broadcast a series of nôvo-messages deep into the Nsanba in the hope I might receive them. One day, on a rare trip of mine from the cave to the outside of the Anomalous Zone, my nôvono picked up his messages."

"Hold on. Pause. Pause!" I reach for the soldier's suit and stop the playback.

"Oh, come on. It was finally getting interesting," says the soldier, keeping his eyes on the cavern entrance.

"This is supposed to be a genuine recording from my wife, but it can't be, because I absolutely did not request the PPA broadcast any nôvo-messages into the Nsanba. It never occurred to me that would even be possible. Unless . . . Yep, I'm wrong. This recording *is* genuine. Her nôvono must have done the same to her as mine's been doing to me."

"Fabricating messages," says the soldier. "Very clever."

With a growing anger, I hit play.

"Okon, if this message somehow finds its way to you, I want you to know I'm so very sorry for how everything turned out. My options were to be arrested and spend my life behind bars or go to the Anomalous Zone in search of help. I didn't leave you willingly and hoped you would follow me. I also hoped I could return to Mbapazu in a greater position of strength, which has depressingly not turned out to be the case.

"When I first received your messages, I'd been living in the cave for two months, and your cheerful energy was much needed, along with your good news. I must admit I was surprised to hear the election brought about positive changes within the PPA, and that the PPA had withdrawn my arrest warrant."

"I didn't say that," I growl. "Her damn lying nôvono."

"However," Efawi continues, "I do stand by my view that the PPA mustn't find out about the alien artifact. They simply cannot be trusted. But, my dear, I appreciate the lengths you must have gone to for your nôvo-messages to be broadcast to me. Being able to hear and feel you has kept me going. And I appreciate your apology, which couldn't have been easy. I believe it's for the best you've come to realize that having children would be a terrible idea. My experiences of late have only made me more resolute on the matter, and you changing your mind about wanting to be a father gives me greater confidence in our potential to be happy."

"No no no." I hit pause once more.

"You've got to be kidding me," the soldier complains.

"Her nôvono is lying again. I did not apologize. I never said having children would be a terrible idea. I did not send her these messages!"

"Yes, you explained that already."

"This must mean she isn't pregnant—that it was all a lie told to me by my nôvono to keep me motivated."

"You don't have time to keep pressing pause," says the soldier.

"I'm no longer about to be a father. And in fact I never was."

The soldier reaches to his waist and hits play.

"I'm surprised you couldn't find the details of the Anomalous Zone's location," says Efawi. "The coordinates were stored on the PAB I left you. Did you not find your trekking gear in the villa? I bought two lots of everything: one set for you and one for me." Efawi sighs heavily. "I suppose it's for the best you don't know the coordinates of the Anomalous Zone, given the situation here. I was desperate to believe you were following in my footsteps, but with nobody knowing where I am within the Nsanba, I've been forced to accept that solving this problem of the tree is completely down to me, and despite being desperate to see you, I take comfort from knowing you remain safe at home."

"Lying bastard! I did find the trekking gear. I did find the AZ's location. I did come for you, Efawi."

"Shush," says the soldier.

"Thanks to your messages," my wife continues, "my sense of

responsibility was renewed and my motivation strengthened. With enthusiasm, I continued with the plan I had devised, which was to use the expired yet undetonated landmines scattered in the jungle to destroy the cave entrance and thus prevent the tribe from accessing the tree. However, perplexingly, as I went about my work, my enthusiasm for resolving the situation waned once more. Then yesterday, after dragging a landmine into the opening corridor of the cave, I came to an important realization: not all acts of destruction are ultimately destructive."

Efawi sighs before uttering several half-formed words. A splice in the audio follows, as though she stopped the recording and continued at a later time, when the chanting of the tree was a little louder and her mood much lower.

"To whoever is listening, I apologize," she says. "Focusing has become increasingly difficult of late. I grow more tired every day. Weaker too. The shape of my body is increasingly defined by bone. Living in this cave is making me ill, but I refuse to move elsewhere until the threat is resolved. I sneak outside only on occasion, mostly for food and water, and stay here in the cavern to work on my ideas and stay safe from the tribal people. It was sheer luck that enabled me to evade them on my way here, and they remain unaware of my presence. I should have packed a gun for self-defense, but I didn't want to bring a weapon to a first contact scenario."

Further pauses, half-formed words, and splices in the audio follow before Efawi continues with any clarity. I tighten more and more as I listen.

"The ever-changing light from the tree drains me," she says. "I fantasize daily that the thing will turn off and leave me in darkness. Initially, I thought the light was its language. I made pages and pages of notes trying to decode it. Only after I consumed the fruit did I realize the light is simply there to look pretty. It's all just fucking tinsel. And then there's the chanting! Seven days have passed since a tribal person last came in here.

Just listen to how loud the tree's incessant noise has become." For a few seconds, Efawi seems to hold whatever device she's recording with up to the tree. Another splice follows.

"Oh, Okon," Efawi continues. "We shouldn't be apart for so long. I've been thinking about all the times you kept me sane. Your good nature, your lightness—you've always grounded me. There's no joy here, and I miss your humor. I miss your sarcasm. I never thought I'd say that." Efawi laughs, then sighs heavily. "I miss everything about you."

There's another cut in the recording before my wife speaks again. Given her changes in mood, I'd guess this message was made over several days. "My dreams in this place are unlike anything I've ever experienced," she says. "So vivid. So overwhelming. Last night, I dreamed every member of the tribe had their hands chopped off and burned to ash so that the tree could never be activated. And when I awoke, I was left with a sense of loss—not for the tribe, but for everyone else. A loss of opportunity.

"At Sabano, we would assess our company's risks not only with an eye to mitigate their danger but also with an eye to turning a risk into an opportunity. And yet, despite this practice in my business, here in the Nsanba I've been too focused on the threat alone. And so, I wonder if I've gotten this whole situation wrong. If I'm viewing things upside down. I don't really know where I'm going with this—what it is I'm trying to tell you. I can't even remember why I'm recording this."

A long pause follows, and my heart sinks further. This is so unlike her—the scattered thinking, the struggle to articulate— but nobody could live in this cavern for months without it taking a toll on their mental state. Why didn't she leave the cave sooner? Why does she always have to be so stubborn? She'd already been through the stress of trekking here alone, and before that she'd endured six months of pressure from the PPA. Everyone has a limit, even Efawi, and to think she had to go through all this by herself. The guilt stabs at me. Brings a pain to my chest. Makes my throat sting and swell.

"Even basic things like going without a shower are harder than anyone might think," the message continues. "I imagine most couldn't last ten days without washing. I can't remember when I last washed. My skin itches and"—the tree's chanting in the recording suddenly quietens—"One of the tribe must be here," says Efawi, her voice now hushed. "Probably the old man in the ridiculous outfit—the one who I saw consume the fruit, which gave me the idea to do the same. Yes, I can see him approaching, but he can't see me. Before leaving for the Nsanba, I knew there were hunter-gatherers in the Anomalous Zone; I'd caught glimpses of them in the satellite footage. My biggest mistake with this whole endeavor is that I barely gave them any consideration. I was blinded by the possibility of interacting with advanced extraterrestrial life. How could I have possibly known that these people who can't read, who walk barefoot and throw spears, would be central to everything?"

Efawi releases yet another heavy sigh. "The answer to the riddle of my internal conflict has taken time to soak in," she says, "but I see the answer clearly now. *Not all acts of destruction are ultimately destructive.* The threat *is* an opportunity. The one who sent us the tree has indeed provided humanity with the opportunity of salvation. Not the type of salvation I'd expected, but salvation nonetheless. A panacea for our suffering. An escape from the dystopia into which we are all heading. And this fool in the hat, hoofing along the cavern floor as I speak, has the power in his hand to bring about what is needed. Where's my knife?"

I hear Efawi fumbling around. "The information from the fruit was clear," she says. "When the tree is activated, not only are we brought to an end, but everything about us, everything we've created, is also ended. Okon, if you're listening, I love you. I love you so much. I'm so sorry for everything, but I can't go on like this. *We* can't go on like this." She breaks into full-blown sobbing. I already have tears of my own.

"Oh my," she says. "How can this be? My nôvono is informing me that I have an incoming nôvo-call from you, Okon. But this isn't possible—not here in the cave, not with the Anomalous Zone's interference. Absolutely not possible. I must be delirious. I . . . I cannot answer the call. I must focus, or I'll lose the strength needed to do what must be done. Okon, I'm so sorry, but I'm doing this for us—for all of us. I love you. I hope you can forgive me. I just don't have your faith in humanity and never have. Of course, only if I fail will this record ever be heard. Here's to success."

The recording clicks to an end.

40: The Evil

"Well, that's depressing," says the soldier. "I see why your implant didn't want you to hear that. Is she always such a downer?"

Images of her final moments form in my head: *Efawi stepping out from the shadows. Efawi approaching the prior shaman with a knife.*

"So, what do you think she did? Where do you think she went? . . . Okon?"

I recall the day Ratu and I climbed the hill above the Banoochee, which must have been a month ago now. We spotted the shaman in the rocky opening below. I accidentally hit him with a stone, and he had a bloody stone knife in his hand and was acting strange. Could that have been the day?

"You crying back there?" asks the soldier. He keeps his eyes on the rifle's screen. I turn my gaze to the leaning stack of stones. The prior shaman constructed this. The partly visible, reflective object was placed among these stones by him. I don't want to know what it is—but I need to know.

I find myself standing up, walking toward it, using a foot to knock the stones off one by one. The object is embedded three-quarters of the way down, and as I kick away the last stones from above, it rolls to the ground. I gasp and fall backward as though the thing moved of its own volition. The soldier risks a quick glance away from the entrance. "What's that?" he asks.

Between my feet is a tiny device shaped like an oval that is pointed at one end. From its sides extend several spindly legs, all singed and partly melted. More unwanted images come: *Efawi not in her right mind. Efawi ordering the shaman to activate the tree. Efawi wielding her knife. The shaman wielding a knife of his own.*

When that unassociated man's body was spotted in the river, the day after Ratu and I climbed the hill, the prior shaman had a fresh wound above his hip, and he told me he knew what was inside me—that he had seen the evil.

"You hyperventilating, Okon? Tell me what's going on."

I turn to the firepit. "That's not my gear in there," I mutter. "She said she had bought two of everything. One set for her and one set for me."

"Okon?"

"You need to look in those ashes."

"I'm kind of busy."

"We haven't heard anything since that rumbling."

The soldier doesn't respond.

"Please. It's right next to you. You have special goggles. I can't dig around in there with my hands like this. I just can't look. I can't do it. Please!"

"Okay, okay," the soldier huffs. He leans to one side and pokes around the firepit. "There's a bunch of junk in here. What exactly am I looking for?"

"I don't know. Anything that looks like—"

"Bone?"

The soldier pulls something from the ashes. I turn away.

"Yep, looks like bone," he continues. "Charred like barbecued rib. Happy now?"

His words hit me like a truck. Whole body pain.

"I still don't understand what this has to do with your wife," he says. "Where do you think she went?"

Again, images come: *A skirmish breaking out between my wife and the prior shaman. Efawi cutting his side with her knife. The shaman getting the better of her.*

She couldn't have been wearing her body armor. I doubt it would fit through the narrow cave entrance. Would she even have been able to charge it in here? Does any of this fucking matter anymore? I can't even . . . Is this . . . How can I . . . ?

Gunfire echoes from the corridors. The soldier jumps back to his rifle. He's saying something, but I'm no longer listening. Images are still coming. Thoughts are racing. The shaman burned everything because he knew there'd be a backlash if the tribe found out he murdered my wife. He told no one, then died the next day.

I look back at Efawi's nôvono. I sense my own implant watching through me as I stare at its dead kin. I want to return to numbness. I want Loallese soldiers to burst into the cavern and shoot me in the head.

I shuffle away from her Watcher, half expecting it to rise on its legs and scurry after me. This monster made her believe I wasn't coming, and so she thought she was alone. The pressure was too much for her. The cave was too much. She wasn't in her right mind. If her nôvono hadn't lied to her, she would have continued to have hope I was on my way. She would have left the cave to look for me. She would have found me. She wouldn't have given up on us. She wouldn't have given up on everyone. *She would still be alive.*

I get to my feet and walk past the soldier, vaguely aware of the sound of further gunfire in the corridors, vaguely aware of Ratu's killer telling me to get down. I head to the side of the altar rock, each step steady, pronounced, distant, and I make my way up.

The alien liquid has pooled in several spots on the altar top, bringing me multicolored reflections of the multicolored tree. I draw a deep breath and make my way across the slick surface. A few paces from the tree, I sense activity in my head that isn't mine.

~Incoming call from Efawi,~ says my nôvono.

Not only do I know this isn't Efawi, but it knows that I know and is trying anyway. *~Incoming call from Efawi,~* the monster repeats as I come to a stop in front of the tree's trunk. I run a bent fingertip along its surface and feel nothing, but the tree's low chanting is silenced by my touch, and my attention is drawn to the hollow.

The incoming nôvo-call *clicks,* indicating the call has begun even though I didn't accept it. There's a few seconds of silence before the nôvono speaks, once again hijacking the voice of my wife. *~We don't have to want the same things in order to be good for each other,~* it says. *~With time, Okon, I believe we can give each other what we need.~*

I shudder, and the nôvono projects my wife's affection for me through the call. I welcome her feelings in—try to lose myself in them. Then, while hijacking the voice of my wife, the nôvono steals our words: *~Apotheosis through union.~*

I'm left disturbed, disgusted by its theft. My entire body is trembling. My wife's sentiment dissolves and nothing further is said, but the nôvo-call hasn't ended. I keep my eyes on the hollow. The blackest of blacks framed by a dancing light. I lift my hand and hold it in front of me—in front of the hollow. My arm rises and falls with each breath, my bent wrist and twisted fingers engulfed in color.

A different kind of emotion emerges from the other end of the call. It seems the nôvono is trying a new approach: to connect with me directly, without the mask of my wife, without the muddiness of words. And it fails. We pass through each other like ghosts. It's unable to find anything of me to clasp onto. No common feeling or understanding. Despite what we share, despite its burrowing into my brain, at essence we are too different. If the nôvono is reaching out for a union, there can be no union here. Its only option is a takeover.

With great effort, I pull my focus from the nôvono and turn back to the expanse of the cavern. The soldier is exchanging fire with others, and I wasn't aware. Was I too lost in my head, or is the nôvono gaining control of me?

One of the Loallese soldiers is standing at the cavern entrance, framed by rock. I picture Efawi framed by the bedroom doorway—the last time I would ever see her. I still don't remember the last words she heard me say, but we'd been arguing that morning before she left. She'd been insisting that people are inherently damaged and that technology can fix us. I hadn't agreed with either of those points. Turns out she was right about the first one, but wrong about the second. Perhaps technology could fix us, but we would have to change first.

The soldier in the distance jolts from an impact and crumples to the floor. A rage burns inside me. ~*If you hadn't told her I wasn't coming, she would have waited for me.*~

I turn back to the tree and plunge my crooked hand into the hollow.

The hole is deep, and I lose sight of my arm in the blackness. I move my limb around, expecting to feel something, but there's nothing there, just empty space, and the tree continues to emanate light with no detectable change.

I pull my hand out with the sense that Ratu was wrong and the tree doesn't view me as Wuchumbu. Or perhaps the whole thing has been a hoax, and the tree doesn't actually do anything. Then there's a sharp pain in my head, as if something has been stripped from my brain.

I collapse to the ground. The light goes out.

My head hurts like hell. My entire body is unresponsive. Just moments ago there were soldiers battling in the multicolored light. Now there's only darkness and silence, and the cold altar rock at my back. So, it's been done?

~*nôvono, what's my status?*~ I ask.

No response.

~nôvono, play saved messages. ~

Again, nothing.

I use the little strength I have to focus my attention inward and look for any sign of the Watcher. I find nothing of it. Civilization has been ended, and the nôvono got what was coming to it. As the download explained, not only are the non-Wuchumbu brought to an end, but all of their things are also ended.

And Ratu was right: the tree has spared me. But has my brain been damaged by the nôvono being shut down, or disintegrated, or whatever the tree did to it? Is that why I collapsed and can't move? Can I even survive without the implant?

Another burst of pain tears beneath my skull. I picture the roots gone, blood filling the space left behind. I need urgent care, and I'm not hundreds of kilometers from the nearest medical facility. *There are no medical facilities.*

No neurologists. No surgeons. No Valaddos.

Efawi, I did an awful, terrible thing.

More than there are trees in the Nsanba.

Part 4

41: The Edge

"How do we know the Nsanba does not go on forever?" asks Hattee. Her big, curious eyes scan the jungle as she walks beside her older brother and two sisters.

"Of course it does not go on forever," Naee replies.

"But how do you know?" Hattee asks again. "You have never been outside the Nsanba. None of us have."

"Our grandparents told us about the outside," says Obee.

"They had never been outside either. They only heard stories, like us," says Buchee.

Mhaawu glances at Beejalee and Habee, who are smiling as they walk behind their four children. Hattee's curiosity reminds Mhaawu of her own child. When Ratu was Hattee's age, he was constantly asking questions.

The tribe's leader glances around at the rest of the walking group, more than one hundred strong and the farthest from the settlement any of them have ever been by a large margin. Their pace is slow but steady, and they march as tightly together as the jungle will allow.

"If you do not believe the Nsanba has an end," Naee says to her younger sister, "then why did you not stay at the settlement?"

"I did believe it had an end when we left, but we have been walking for a month, and still all I see is the Nsanba."

"If the Nsanba does not end," Gommonogo intervenes, a hint of irritation in his voice, "then where did the unassociated used to live? Where did Okon come from?"

Hearing his name brings an agitation to Mhaawu's chest. Almost two months have passed since Okon died, and she still does not know how to feel about him. She wishes she knew what happened in the Banoochee that night. She had been elsewhere in the jungle, lying on the floor of a container made by her captors. Her eyes closed. Her wrists bound by the unassociated for the second time in her life. Then she felt a soft breeze, and she opened her eyes to find she was no longer in a container, and her wrists were no longer bound. She was alone on the jungle floor, with no unassociated to be seen.

After walking back to the settlement, Mhaawu was told about the appearance and disappearance of the great Massas. She was also told that when the tribe reentered the cave, they had to bring torches for the first time in two years, as the tree of many colors was no longer there. And in the darkness, they found the body of Okon on top of the altar rock, his spirit having already passed.

When Mhaawu learned that nobody had seen Ratu, she insisted the area be searched, but nobody could find her son. Okon's body, resting alone, remains the only evidence of death that night. Mhaawu does not know why he did it, but she is sure Okon was responsible for the tree's activation. As a result, whether intentional or not, he liberated her from her captors and most likely killed her son.

Although no one in the tribe knows the motives for his actions, many of them believe Okon activated the tree to protect the Wuchumbu and bring them their freedom. Of course, Okon did not do anything the tribe was not capable of carrying out themselves, but the fact that he did it means the tribe can move on, guilt-free, their spirits unburdened by the deadly act.

They decided to leave his body where it was. Although

nobody said so, it was clear to Mhaawu that no one wanted to touch him, given what he did. And his resting place on the altar rock seemed fitting, turning the Banoochee into a tomb of remembrance for the man who had become one of them.

"Mhaawu, tell Hattee that the Okongo has an end," says Naee, bringing the leader's attention back to the group.

"You know we do not call the jungle that," says Beejalee, who gives her daughter a light push.

"I mean *Nsanba*, not *Okongo*," Naee nervously adds.

When Mhaawu proposed the tribe leave the Nsanba, she also proposed they rename it. The Wuchumbu word for the jungle meant *haven*, and she knew the tribe needed to stop viewing it as such. Adienatta suggested "Okongo": a merging of "Okon," the name of the man who took on a great burden to deliver them a new world, with the Wuchumbu word "ngo," which means *forgive*. Mhaawu was not happy for the jungle to be named after the person she suspects was responsible for her son's death and the deaths of countless others. She struggled to find forgiveness for him. However, Adienatta's suggestion was a popular one, and the new name stuck for many, especially the young.

"I'm sorry, Mhaawu," says Naee, "I said it by mistake."

The tribe's leader knows the group expects her response to be an angry one, given that irritation has been her default for so long. But this time she considers the promises she made to herself in the days after the tree was activated. "If the jungle has an end, we will know soon enough," she says, her tone even and composed. "We no longer need to rely on our grandparents' stories. We are free to find the answers to our questions."

The children nod, thoughtfully.

"Is that what we are doing?" asks Hattee. "Finding the answers to our questions?"

"You are asking too many questions," says Naee. "You know we need to leave the Nsanba to survive."

"But why?" asks Hattee.

"Because if we stay in one place for too long," says Obee, "we go rotten like smelly uddu that has been left in a pot for days. You were there when Mhaawu explained this."

"But I do not understand why we go rotten," says Hattee. "And how does this walking stop us from going rotten?"

Hattee's siblings stop responding to their sister's questions. Mhaawu thinks to herself, *We are doing more than just "walking."* In the days that followed the activation of the tree, there was much discussion and debate about Mhaawu's proposal that they leave the jungle. Eventually, the tribe agreed there would be three groups who would each head in a different direction, with a small number staying behind, comprising those physically unable to leave and those who needed to stay and care for others. All three groups left the settlement on the same day.

"Are we even close to the end of the Okongo?" Hattee asks.

"I believe we are," Mhaawu replies.

"How can you know?" asks Buchee.

"The trees are changing," says Mhaawu, "and if you look straight ahead, as far as you can through the undergrowth, you can see the sky."

They all stop walking and stare ahead. "Mhaawu is right," says Beejalee.

"What do you think, Big Man?" asks Habee.

Big Man narrows his eyes as he assesses the terrain. "I also noticed the change," he says. "It could be an area of land where the trees do not grow, or maybe we are coming to the edge of the Nsanba."

An anxiety stirs in the travelers. Vast treeless spaces are not uncommon within the jungle, but there is something different about where they are now—Mhaawu can sense it.

"We should wait and think about this," says Gommonogo. "Maybe we made a mistake by coming here. What if the tree of many colors did not kill every unassociated? What if some are still out there?"

"We have been through this already," says Beejalee. "When the tree was activated, Mhaawu's captors disappeared along with everything that was theirs."

"And I went to the place where Thembe and his tribe had been living," says Big Man. "Everything had gone: the people, their huts, their things. All trace of them undone, like they had never been there."

Gommonogo presses his hands against his head and turns to his sister for support. "We do not know what is beyond the Nsanba," she says. "There could be animals we have not seen before—dangerous ones. There might be things that we cannot even imagine."

"Gommonogo and Gommonaadogo are right," someone adds, "we do not belong out there."

"Mhaawu, you always used to tell us not to go far from the settlement because it is not safe," says another.

"Maybe leaving the Nsanba is a bad idea," adds a third.

Mhaawu looks from person to person. Many are scared, and so is she. *But we need to see ourselves differently.*

"Are we close to the edge of the Nsanba?" she asks the group.

"We do not know. Not for certain," Obee replies.

"Exactly," says Mhaawu. "And the only way we can know for certain is to keep going and see for ourselves. Our elders passed down stories of suffering, but they had other stories about our people too. Older stories. Stories of movement. We were never meant to stay in the same place for so long, and it is dangerous to always look for the safest option. When we do these things, our lives narrow and become like shadows." Mhaawu pauses, allowing the group a moment to think, before adding, "We must break free from the refuge of the Nsanba. The Wuchumbu are explorers now."

The group exchanges glances. Many appear unconvinced by Mhaawu's words, and she suspects some will head back. But she will not try to stop them. They have to want to change, or they will not survive outside the jungle.

"Do you think the other groups have left the Okongo yet?" Hattee asks.

"I do not know," Mhaawu replies.

Hattee thinks about this for a moment, then grins and says, "I want to be the first."

She marches away from the group. Beejalee reaches out to stop her daughter but is too slow. Buchee hurries after her sister. "Hattee, wait! I want to be the first!" she shouts.

"Both of you stop right there!" yells Mhaawu.

Hattee and Buchee freeze on the spot before nervously turning to see how much trouble they are in. Everyone stays where they are as their scowling leader approaches the two girls, then marches right past them. "I want to be the first," Mhaawu declares with a smile. The girls laugh and give chase, and soon the entire group is hurrying through the jungle, each running as fast as they can. *A cautious approach would make more sense*, thinks Mhaawu, *but a bold exit feels necessary*.

She used to hate it when Ratu went on his solo adventures. Sometimes he would be gone for so long, she would worry he had traveled beyond the boundary of the jungle, but now the thought he may have done so brings her comfort. "Ratu was the first," she whispers to herself.

The group is quick to break from the shadowy undergrowth and into the open. They slow to a halt as they find themselves exposed to the daylight of a vast unbroken sky. With gaping mouths, they raise their hands to shade their eyes. The jungle ends at a grassy plain that stretches to the horizon. Clusters of unknown shrubs and trees dot the landscape. Rugged, dirt-colored mountains rise far to the east. A herd of horned beasts grazes in the middle distance.

Buchee and Hattee step back and reach for their father's arm. "What are they?" Buchee asks, pointing at the thickset animals. Her father has no answer for her. None of the tribe do.

The Wuchumbu continue to absorb their new landscape with wide eyes. They cannot see any of the things from the stories passed down by their elders. No hard vessels racing across the land with people inside. No twinkling structures that stand so tall their tops are hidden by clouds. No sharp-edged birds cutting a straight path through the sky with people in their bellies.

"They are gone," says Mhaawu. "All of them." A sense of isolation overcomes her, weakens her thin legs. A responsibility greater than she has ever felt before presses on her shoulders. For a moment, Mhaawu cannot breathe.

"What do we do now?" Naee asks.

"We should stay here for a few days before we go any farther," says Gommonogo. "We can camp just inside the Nsanba, where we can safely watch what is out there."

Mhaawu heads farther into the grassland.

"Where are you going?" Hattee calls out.

"I do not know," says Mhaawu, "but we need to keep moving."

Part 5

42: The Race

· Far from the rainforests of Central Africa ·

David is finding it hard to stay focused as he taps at his keyboard, desperate to complete a configuration update. He glances at the time in the screen's corner. *Can it really be that late?* To be sure, he checks that the operating system's time zone has updated for his current location: London, United Kingdom. Then he looks through the glass at the BBC News feed displayed in the waiting area outside the lab—another story about climate change, and the news feed's clock confirms it really is 8:34 p.m. This means David's reconfiguration is already overdue, and he's struggling just to stay awake.

Ever since the company he works for, Cerebral Systems, was quietly purchased by a multinational, his average nightly sleep has gone from six to four and a half hours. This is a problem for David, not just because it's bad for his health but because of its negative impact on his S-score. The company's new employee point scheme, designed to encourage well-being and positive behavior, is voluntary but "highly recommended." David knew exactly what this meant, and with his employment contract's annual review just around the corner, he signed up to the point scheme immediately. So did all of his colleagues.

"Okay. Reconfig done," says David as he hits enter and slumps back in his chair. The project lead grunts, and David risks

377

a quick glance around the lab to find most of the team glaring at him. Management hasn't told their employees exactly how the S-score algorithm works, and so he probably won't know for sure how many points his missed deadline will cost him. Sometimes updates to an S-score seem to happen immediately, but sometimes there is a delay, with deductions or additions grouped together, which makes it hard to work out why a point change occurred.

David rubs his eyes before detaching his tablet and heading to the lab door. "Where you going?" the project lead croaks.

"I need a break, and the reboot will take thirty minutes," replies David.

"Just don't keep us waiting again. We're already behind schedule, and we need you here after the reboot."

"I know, I know. I'll be back in time—I promise."

David leaves the lab and heads along the site's main corridor, grumbling about not having time to check his work and how unfair it will be should he be penalized for any mistakes. He then reminds himself to be grateful he has a job at all, and thanks to recent site refurbishments, at least he has somewhere to go when feeling tired.

David arrives at the purpose-built "recharge room" to find that every personal rest pod is already occupied, with other staff waiting to use them. He huffs and moves to the end of the line, noticing that those ahead of him are all on their tablets. "It never stops," he mumbles as he unlocks his tablet and opens a catalog of free online magazines courtesy of the company.

David looks for a publication that seems obscure, as he heard there are bonus S-points for multidisciplinary reading, and he selects *Anthropology Monthly,* which is certainly not an area of expertise nor interest for him. David also heard rumors that the tablet measures how fast he turns each page and that the built-in camera monitors his eye movements to be sure he is reading. He knows the rumors are likely only scaremongering, but just in case, he flicks through a few pages to mimic magazine-perusing behavior and stops at random at an article about an apparent "human population bottleneck," which he goes through the motions of reading.

According to the article, although modern humans appear to be remarkably diverse, studies reveal a surprising lack of variation at a genetic level. Geneticists are theorizing this is due to a past population bottleneck—a massive decrease in the number of Homo sapiens that curtailed the human gene pool. A further study of DNA in worldwide populations suggests this bottleneck saw the species of Homo sapiens reduced to a very small number of people who lived in Africa approximately seventy thousand years ago. This small number are the ancestors of all humans alive today. They and their descendants went on to migrate across the globe.

The cause of the sudden drop in population has previously been linked with a supervolcanic eruption, but after further evaluation, the eruption theory has been dismissed by most scholars, and the cause of the bottleneck remains unknown. The article goes on to discuss minimum viable population sizes and statistical probabilities of survival, and all this is probably interesting, but David is presently too tired to care, and he continues moving his eyes and intermittently turning pages without paying much attention.

Eventually he reaches the front of the line, and after the hiss of a disinfectant spray from inside a vacant personal rest pod, David finally kicks off his loafers and crawls inside. He quickly selects sleep mode, and the ambient light dims and reddens as he adjusts the cushions and lies back. Once the short audio advert has finished, he tries to lose himself in the soundscape of soft rain on glass.

Despite being in a pod designed to "maximize restfulness," David remains exhaustedly awake. He worries he might not have executed the updates correctly. He worries about his S-score.

And he especially worries about his contract renewal. Competition for jobs has been fierce for some time, especially for a position like his on such a groundbreaking project. If successful, the team will have pioneered a technology for editing neural pathways in the human brain. With time, they hope to shrink the technology down to be fitted into an implant. Such a device would, in theory, be able to reverse or reduce neurological disorders, and the possibilities beyond disease prevention are astounding. The pressure is on, however, as a number of organizations around the world race to achieve the same goal.

In spite of all his worries, David's need for rest wins out, and just as he drifts into sleep, his arm vibrates. He groans and looks at his watch to find a message from the project lead: "Reboot finished and the whole team is waiting for you."

David sits up, bangs his head on the pod, and falls back to the cushions. He rubs the point of impact and curses. His arm vibrates again. This time it's a notification from the S-app: David's score has been reduced by forty points. *Was it the missed deadline? Negative ratings from the frustrated team? Cursing in the workplace?*

With mouth firmly shut, David slides from the pod and dashes out of the recharge room. As he sprints along the main corridor toward the lab, with a smear of blood on his forehead and his eyes fixed on his S-score, others are forced to jump to avoid being hit.

Message from Author

Dear reader,

Thank you for reading The Veiled Edge of Contact. This means a lot to me.

Did you enjoy the book? I'd love to know and would greatly appreciate a rating or review on Amazon. Thank you!

To get in touch with me or to sign up to receive occasional updates, special offers, and to ensure you don't miss my next book, please visit www.jamesbrayken.com.

Until next time . . .

All the best,
James

Printed in Great Britain
by Amazon

87235424R00222